VANISHING TRAIL

THE TAKING OF JONATHAN BISHOP

VANISHING TRAIL

THE TAKING OF JONATHAN BISHOP

STEPHEN KOSA

LANGDON STREET PRESS, MINNEAPOLIS MN

Langdon Street Press
212 3rd Avenue North, Suite 290
Minneapolis, MN 55401
612.455.2293
www.langdonstreetpress.com

ISBN-13: 978-1-62652-245-9
LCCN: 2013942952

Distributed by Itasca Books

Cover Design by Steve Porter
Typeset by Jenni Wheeler

Printed in the United States of America

My sincere gratitude to my wife, Diane, for her patience, friendship, and encouragement. A special thank you to my son, Gabe, for his support and inspiration. And thanks to my parents for the experiences that shaped my youth. Lastly, many thanks to our dear friends, Richard and Rossi, for enriching our lives with their experiences from South America, and to Rossi for assisting with the language translation for this novel.

PROLOGUE

The frost was settling in, a friendly reminder of the winter that would soon come to visit the small town of Maple Creek. Even the tiny creatures of the night were too numb to disturb the silence.

As the young boy slept soundly in his upstairs bedroom, his father sat alone on the porch swing, nursing what remained of the lukewarm coffee in his mug, wishing it were three fingers of scotch instead. It was the end of another long day in yet another bitter custody trial. There were some days even a hot shower couldn't wash away.

So many unhappy marriages, so much hardship—it was a bittersweet combination of recurrent heartburn and job security for the young attorney. *What happens to people?* He thought to himself. *They meet that perfect someone, fall madly in love, have two and a half kids, and before they know it they're growing apart. All of life's little stressors filter into their days. They become indifferent, discontented, even hostile. Then come the games, the indiscretions, the affairs. And worse yet, the Kobs trial—a child born as the result of a drunken, torrid one-night stand. Another innocent pawn now victim to a lifetime of his parents' resentment and dysfunction.*

As he tried to purge the day's drama from his mind, the counselor pulled a worn photograph from his shirt pocket and gazed at the image in the glow of the porch light. She had been gone for three years now, but he still missed her desperately. Not a day could pass without taking a moment to memorialize her. He had been one of the lucky ones, that fraction of a percent of the population who stumble through the universe and collide with their perfect companion. Not even the angels could compete with Blanca Vasquez. She was a creature of remarkable beauty. Pure, kind, intelligent—a woman of genuine character.

His rocking slowed slightly as his mind drifted. He could still see her, running vigorously along the sandy beach, just paces ahead of her pursuer. Her feet churned heavily in the thick sand as she struggled to pull ahead. She gasped for breath while her heart pounded fiercely—her freedom just strides away. She was young and athletic, but ultimately no match for the swift moves of the former wide receiver from Wisconsin. With a burst of power he closed the gap between them. It was inevitable. He reached for her and with one fluid motion cradled her in his arms as they spilled gently to the ground.

"You run pretty fast for an attorney," she said with a thick Spanish accent, giggling and gasping for breath.

"You're not so bad yourself for a stodgy old museum curator."

"Jacob Bishop! Who are you calling old?" she asked, giving him a playful slap on the cheek. "I seem to remember staying several paces ahead of you on our hike today."

"You were amazing today. I love to watch you work."

"Did you have a good time?"

"How could I not? It's not every day a man gets the

opportunity to hike miles into the forest to witness his wife working on the excavation of an ancient Sican tomb. That was the most extraordinary thing I've ever witnessed."

"You *were* paying attention. I'm very impressed, Jacob."

A slight smile appeared on his face as he lost himself in her large brown eyes. He knew he was the luckiest man on earth. "Tell me it will always be like this. Tell me it will always be the two of us, together, exploring ancient civilizations, walking hand in hand on the beach."

"Well, my love, I can tell you that it will always be the two of us…plus one."

He stared at her inquisitively, attempting to process her announcement. "What are you saying? Are you…?"

"Pregnant? Yes, Jake. I took the test twice. I wanted to be sure before I told you."

Instantly, he beamed with approval. It was the perfect end to a perfect day. The gods had smiled upon him once again—a wonderful life, a beautiful wife, a successful career with the most prestigious firm in Chicago, and now, a child. What could he possibly have done to deserve such blessings?

"Say something, Jacob."

He embraced her tenderly and they rocked in each other's arms. "We're going to have such a handsome son," he replied.

"Or a beautiful daughter."

"We're going to need a bigger place."

"That shouldn't be a problem for a senior associate,"

she said proudly.

"Will you be able to keep your position at the Field Museum?"

"My career is very important to me. I can manage both."

"I know you can," he agreed. "If anyone can do it, you can. My god, I wish my father was alive. He'd go crazy over a grandchild."

She smiled tenderly. "I can't wait to tell my parents."

A contented silence ensued as they watched the sun slide into the ocean like a giant orange ball melting into a mirror. He would never forget that day in Peru. It was a magical day—a day of life, a day of hope, a day of promise. It was the beginning of their life together, the life they had both dreamed about. But like so many dreams, reality was certain to trickle in.

He slipped the photograph back into his shirt pocket and headed inside to bed. Tomorrow would bring another long day in court—another act in the seemingly endless theatrical production.

CHAPTER 1

THE GUARDIAN

The judge's eyes were closed and his chin was propped upon his folded hands, his elbows resting soundly on the bench. There had been little movement from him in nearly an hour. He resembled a weathered statue cast into a meditative pose, pondering the thoughts of the day. An inexperienced lawyer may have feared the old judge had expired, or that he was inattentive to the vital evidence being presented to the court. But the judge was very much alive, and very much awake.

After twenty-seven years on the bench, Judge Miles Montpetit could effortlessly detect and discard the lies and the fluff, and categorically store the credible evidence that was germane to a case. Determining the value of evidence was second nature to the judge, and he could usually forecast where the case would lead well before the attorneys could. And unlike the younger judges who relied on their computers behind the bench, Montpetit recorded the information in his mind and on his yellow legal tablet. He despised technology and longed for the days when there were no smartphones, PowerPoint presentations, or video conferences complicating his courtroom.

The judge's superior ability to retain detailed information was perplexing, as was his profound knowledge of the law. When His Honor put his decision on the record at the close of every case, he always tied the facts and the law together in such a way that rarely left grounds for appeal.

Currently, Judge Montpetit was hearing a child custody proceeding. The trial was nearing the end of its third day, and the weary participants were determined to make this day the last. The case appeared on the court's docket as *In Re the Paternity of S.K.*, as the law required the child's initials be used to protect his identity. But everyone in the courtroom knew *S.K.* to be little Sammy Kobs.

More than two years had passed since the initial paternity hearing that established Daniel Norby to be the biological father of Samuel Kobs. Eager to learn the truth about his suspected offspring, Norby had requested genetic testing to confirm the boy was in fact his son. Such requests often come from the mother seeking to establish paternity to obtain child support. Not so with Sam's mother. Katherine Kobs never asked for a dime from Daniel Norby. When she discovered she was pregnant with Sam, she made every effort to disaffirm Norby as the father of her child. Her actions were initially fueled by her state of denial, as well as her desire to salvage what remained of her failing marriage to Kenny Kobs.

But the science could not be refuted. The probability of Mr. Norby's parentage was found to be 99.67%, and there were no other candidates, aside from Katherine's husband Kenny, whose DNA took a very distant second. This proved to be the fatal blow to Katherine's marriage.

In the years that followed, Daniel Norby and Katherine Kobs battled over the finer points of joint custody and physical placement. As the judicial field of combat was bloodied by motion after motion, hearing after hearing, and witness after witness, Katherine Kobs developed a fierce disdain for her former lover.

Today's trial was different than the previous squabbles, and the stakes were higher than ever. Katherine's poor decisions and carefree lifestyle had finally caught up with her, and she now stood a genuine chance of losing custody of her son.

Katherine was an attractive woman who was well known around town. For eight years she had been waitressing at the Rusty Bucket, a downtown bar and grill known for its broasted chicken and one-dollar taps. She often bragged to customers that it was a temporary job, as she was only fifteen credits short of completing her associate's degree in dental hygiene. Somehow she always failed to mention that she hadn't seen the inside of a classroom for over a decade.

Katherine came to know Daniel Norby from his regular visits to the Bucket. Norby ran the insurance agency around the corner and enjoyed stopping by the bar two or three nights each week after work. There he would meet his good friend, local mortgage banker Max Lehman, to discuss the day's events—a conversation that would inevitably end with some thoughtful banter about the good old days.

Katherine often flirted with her customers as she

delivered their drinks, but Norby always found her advances harmless. While he was attracted to her shapely body and the depth of her blue eyes, he never gave serious thought to betraying his wife. Besides, Katherine had a wild reputation, and Norby always joked that he had never met a woman he trusted enough to keep her mouth shut about an affair. But truth be told, Daniel Norby was very much in love with his wife.

The irony was almost tragic when Norby learned that his own wife was being "serviced" by the owner of a local car dealership. His discovery of the affair was abrupt and painful. There had been no warning signs that his wife was straying, and Norby was ill-prepared to cope with the end of what seemed to be an ideal marriage. The same night he learned of the affair, shortly after closing time, Katherine comforted the intoxicated Norby, resulting in the conception of little Sam.

Young Samuel Kobs, now three years old, was the only person absent from Judge Montpetit's courtroom. He was the only member of his dysfunctional family allowed to avoid the theatrics. He would never be questioned by his father's attorney, nor cross-examined by opposing counsel. He wouldn't have to listen to days of grueling testimony from the numerous witnesses and experts appearing before the court to determine his future.

Instead, Samuel was represented by his court-appointed *guardian ad litem* (Latin for "guardian for the lawsuit"). As with most cases involving a minor, a guardian was necessary to represent Sam's best interest throughout the litigation. It was the guardian's job to investigate, participate in discovery, present evidence, cross-examine witnesses and experts, and ultimately recommend custody and placement arrangements for young Samuel.

Like many judges, Montpetit despised involving young children in their parents' often ludicrous legal battles, and he relied heavily upon the guardian ad litem to present a clear and unbiased version of the facts.

Although he was fairly compassionate and tolerant, Montpetit was easily frustrated by people who brought children into the world only to selfishly tangle them up in their irresponsible lives. Throughout his years of service on the bench, the judge had seen it all. He'd seen children's lives derailed by their parents' addictions to alcohol, drugs, gambling, or pornography. He'd seen children who suffered from neglect, and those trapped in homes infected by domestic violence. He'd seen families destroyed by mental illness and physical afflictions. But the cases that frustrated him the most were those in which the children were intentionally exposed to their parents' constant obstinacy and poor judgment.

Jennifer Bass had served as Sam's guardian ad litem during previous proceedings, but due to her relocation to Madison it became necessary for Montpetit to appoint a replacement to investigate the latest round of disputes. There was a very short list of attorneys in Crescent County willing to accept such an appointment, and that list was comprised mostly of younger, hungrier attorneys who were desperate to pay off their student loans. Most veterans were no longer willing to perform such onerous work in exchange for the mandated minimal hourly fee.

Jacob Patrick Bishop was the attorney who drew the short straw for the job. Although his name was not among the regular appointees maintained on the list, it wasn't uncommon for the court to recruit outside counsel if the need arose. Jake had plenty of work, and his initial inclination was to respectfully decline the appointment. But he was eventually persuaded by Marlene—the judge's snippy judicial assistant—that it would be in his best interest to accept the invitation to serve. Jake had dodged this bullet in the past, and knew he was running out of viable excuses and would soon risk offending the judge.

Bishop was a respected young attorney and well liked among his colleagues. He grew up in the quiet little town of Maple Creek, Wisconsin, the seat of Crescent County, where his father had practiced law for nearly forty years. The late Henry Bishop was a prominent man with a generous heart, revered by nearly all who knew him. Every noon hour on his way to the diner, Henry would stroll about town in a handsome suit, acknowledging everyone by name, smoking the sweet aromatic pipe tobacco that had become known as his trademark blend. Although he had been gone for several years, he frequently received honorable mention among the locals.

Jake's initial reluctance to accept the Kobs appointment

was entirely self-serving. His caseload was manageable, and he had no interest in refereeing parents too pigheaded to work out their custody disputes. And although he worked closely with guardians on the divorce cases he handled, he had no experience actually serving as one. But after meeting little Samuel and working on the file, he actually came to enjoy the role. He even contemplated adding his name to Judge Montpetit's list of guardian ad litem appointees.

After a lengthy investigation, Jake had submitted a preliminary report and recommendation to Sam's parents and their attorneys. His report was thorough and unbiased, and his recommendation for custody and placement was squarely in Sam's best interest. He had hoped the recommendation would help broker a settlement, but it was hastily rejected by Sam's mother, against the advice of her attorney.

No recommendation would have been acceptable to Katherine Kobs, short of obtaining full custody of her son, along with an order calling for Norby's execution. To her, the litigation had become all about punishing Sam's father, which was no surprise to Jake. He knew from his family law practice that most custody cases were nothing more than legalized combat.

And so, there sat the weary warriors, monopolizing Judge Montpetit's courtroom, attempting to wrap up yet another day of grueling testimony. Jake tried to conceal his yawn into his cupped hand as he struggled to stay awake through the tail end of Daniel Norby's testimony.

But Norby's predictable narrative suddenly took an unpredictable turn, and this caught Jake's attention.

"I tried to reason with her. Very calmly I told her it wasn't healthy for our son to see her and her new boyfriend wandering around the house naked. But she started yelling. She told me to mind my own f-ing business. She told me that she was sorry she ever met me, that I was a worthless piece of shit. Then, right in front of little Sammy, she said that she was sorry she ever laid eyes on me, sorry she screwed me in the bar that night. She said she never wanted to see me again and that she wished I would just drive my car off an f-ing cliff."

Jake was instantly flush with emotion. Sadness, disgust, anger, frustration—it was all there. Sometimes people's hatred and selfishness was more than he could process. But deep beneath the surface, it was Kathryn's alleged death wish that struck a nerve with Jake.

Jake's mind was suddenly back at O'Hare International Airport. He and Blanca were wrapped in each other's arms, their young son sandwiched snugly between them. It was a long embrace, neither of them willing to be the first to let go. Blanca had taken other trips back to Peru alone, but the goodbyes were never easy.

"Are you sure you don't want me to come with you?" he asked.

"I would love for you to come, Jacob. But there will be no time for us to play. I'll be meeting with the Minister of Culture, then the Director at the museum, then I'll be in the field for at least three days, and then..."

"Okay, okay. I get it. All work and no play this time. I understand," he replied, smiling. He gently brushed the hair away from her face. "I'm so proud of you, you know."

"I'm proud of you too, counselor. I'll miss you boys so much." Another hug was inevitable.

"Please travel safely; we need you home in one piece," he whispered in her ear.

"I'll be home before you know it. We'll go to Navy Pier when I get back."

A soft kiss on the lips and he watched her walk away, her shapely body swaying confidently down the terminal corridor. She disappeared into the crowd like a beautiful mirage. It was the last time he saw her alive. He could still picture the twisted wreckage of her rental car at the bottom of the canyon.

Jake jumped slightly as the gavel hit the bench, drawing his attention back to the courtroom. "We're adjourned for today. We'll reconvene at 8:30 tomorrow morning," Montpetit announced. "Don't be late, counselors; it's gonna be a short morning."

Jake slowly packed up his briefcase as the participants cleared out of the courtroom. It had been another exhausting day. He couldn't help but think about how Katherine Kobs had needlessly engaged the litigation, turning it into a colossal consumption of resources. But he reminded himself that justice was rarely efficient, and sometimes never achieved. He had long since accepted the fact that divorce and custody matters were the most inglorious of cases—the least rewarding work in the legal food chain. It was just another day at the office for Jake. Every file helped pay the bills. He would close one and open the next, rarely hearing from the parties again. But this file would most certainly come back to haunt him.

CHAPTER 2

COURT IS ADJOURNED

Despite the exhaustive efforts of counsel to complete the trial in the allotted three days, the Kobs case once again appeared on the court's morning docket. Montpetit had reluctantly cleared three hours of his calendar to conclude the matter, with a stern warning to counsel that they best wrap things up by noon.

As day four of the trial commenced, Katherine Kobs and her weary adversary, Daniel Norby, sat quietly in Branch II of the historic old courthouse listening to the testimony of the last witness, Dr. Francis McCabe. McCabe was the psychologist who conducted Katherine's psychological evaluation. Montpetit had ordered the evaluation upon the motion of Jake Bishop. Jake had initially debated the need for a psychological evaluation, but ultimately concluded that he had no choice given Katherine's history.

Dr. McCabe was poised and professional as he sat in the witness chair and fielded the questions of Daniel Norby's attorney, Oscar King. King was a high-priced barracuda from Chicago who was well known in his jurisdiction as a relentless and unyielding adversary in the arena of family law. But King's shiny black Lexus and two-thousand-dollar suits appeared somewhat misplaced in Crescent County. Although King was licensed in Wisconsin, he rarely made an appearance as the money was simply too easy in his neighboring Illinois. But Norby had scraped together enough money to pay King's enormous retainer and convinced him that he would enjoy his time in the tranquil town of Maple Creek.

King's examination of Dr. McCabe lasted for nearly two hours, and as expected, the testimony was quite damaging to Katherine Kobs. King methodically dissected every aspect of McCabe's report as Montpetit's practically inanimate court reporter quietly typed the record. McCabe's testimony revealed Katherine's long and disheartening struggle with mental illness. The earliest evidence of psychological trouble was her hospitalization as a teenager back in Michigan after swallowing an entire bottle of her father's pain medication. There were two subsequent hospitalizations involving psychiatric holds, the most recent stemming from a traffic accident after which Katherine was arrested for driving while intoxicated. Her ER records revealed that the doctors nearly lost their struggle to revive Katherine after pumping the vile mixture of vodka and antidepressants from her stomach.

McCabe believed that Katherine suffered not only from anxiety and major depression, but that her profile was consistent with the diagnosis of a personality disorder. Her psychological evaluation was brimming with traits such as "manipulative," "deceptive," "evasive," "unstable," and "impulsive." McCabe further described Katherine as being immature and self-centered, and opined that she was in constant need of attention.

But the evidence that Jake found most concerning was Katherine's history of suicidal ideation. She couldn't deny the references to suicide that had been memorialized in her medical records over the years. Jake may have dismissed the failed teenage suicide attempt as an aberration, had that been the only time Katherine embraced the thought of ending her life. But it seemed Katherine frequently questioned the value of living, which had become a common topic of discussion between her and her doctors. While Katherine had never admitted to it, McCabe speculated that her last intoxicated vehicular mishap was likely another failed attempt to end her life.

Attorney King finally took his seat after his long dance with the doctor, having aired Katherine's mental illness to everyone in the courtroom—including Judge Montpetit. Katherine's attorney would finally have his chance to tear into the good doctor—to discredit him as the quack she knew he really was.

Attorney David Emerson was a scrappy middle-aged man with a rough exterior and thick, seasoned skin. He reminded Jake of an old pit bull he once saw saunter down the street after being hit by a large Buick. Emerson's clothing was usually disheveled, and he often grumbled to himself while questioning a witness he didn't care for. But despite Emerson's raw appearance, he was an intelligent man and a skillful litigator. Katherine was lucky to have him in her corner, especially since he had been patiently accepting her meager monthly installments to reduce the extensive legal fees she had amassed over three years.

Emerson had served Katherine well during her past legal clashes with Norby, and she had high hopes that today would be no different. But as she sat at the counsel table trying to discreetly wipe her sweaty hands onto her wrinkled navy slacks, Jake detected a look of desperation in her tired eyes.

Her expectations appeared to fade as she watched how well Dr. McCabe handled her attorney's cross-examination. Despite Emerson's aggressive attempt to outwit the doctor with questions about the psychological testing protocol and his possible misinterpretation of the test results, the doctor handled the pit bull with ease. Emerson was ultimately unable to leave the judge with a positive impression of his client.

It was just after 11:30 a.m. when Judge Montpetit settled into his fatigued leather chair after returning from a short recess.

"All right, folks. We're back on the record in the matter of the paternity of S.K., case number 05PA23. The attorneys for the petitioner and respondent have each informed the Court that they have no further witnesses. Mr. Bishop, do you have any witnesses you wish to call?"

"No, Your Honor. Nothing beyond the testimony that's been presented, but I'm prepared to offer my recommendation to the Court when Your Honor would like to hear it."

Montpetit glanced at the clock as he contemplated how best to allocate what little time remained of the morning. "Counsel, at this time I'd like to hear Mr. Bishop's recommendation. Since we're not going to have time for closing arguments, I'm going to ask each of you to submit those to me in writing." King and Emerson gave an approving nod, each realizing they were already on borrowed time with the judge.

"Mr. Bishop, please proceed."

"Thank you, Judge. Your Honor, I feel I've performed a thorough investigation of this matter. I've met individually with each parent, and I've observed each with the child. I've reviewed the medical and police records, and I've interviewed various family members and collateral references. I have also given careful consideration to the evidence that has been presented to the Court during the past few days.

"It's clear to me that both parents love this child very much. Each has a special relationship with Samuel, and each is convinced that he or she is looking out for Sam's best interest. But several things trouble me as I consider the evidence in light of the applicable statutory factors. First off, it's clear to me that the communication and cooperation between these parents has disintegrated. The evidence has shown that Mr. Norby has made his best effort to be civil and cooperative with Ms. Kobs, and that she has made no attempt to reciprocate. In fact, it's clear that she frequently speaks poorly about Mr. Norby in Sam's presence, and takes advantage of every opportunity to sabotage Sam's relationship with his father. Under the circumstances, I don't believe that Ms. Kobs is able to support Mr. Norby's relationship with this child, and I fear that she will likely continue to interfere with that relationship in the future. As the Court knows, this makes a joint custody arrangement very problematic."

As Jake continued, he remained focused on Montpetit's thoughtful gaze, trying to ignore the condemning stare from Katherine Kobs.

"Furthermore, there's been little predictability or stability for this child during the past three years. The evidence has established the shady assortment of babysitters who have cared for Sam late at night while his mother was working at the bar. We've heard testimony about one of those care providers being caught in a drug-induced stupor by Mr. Norby when he stopped by the Kobs residence to drop off a birthday present for his son.

"And then there are the boyfriends. There seems to be plenty of credible evidence to establish that Ms. Kobs's promiscuity has increased dramatically since her divorce and that she has exposed this child to things no three-year-old should be privy to. Even her own roommate could not deny that Ms. Kobs has frequently engaged in audible sexual relations with her guests while Sam was awake in the next room.

"We also have evidence of criminal activity—two arrests in three years for driving under the influence, one of those with the child in the car, and the most recent of which a serious motor vehicle accident. One shoplifting charge last February, and the misdemeanor drug possession two months ago when Ms. Kobs was also cited for disorderly conduct.

"But perhaps the most concerning evidence, Your Honor, is Ms. Kobs's history of mental illness. Despite her best efforts and intentions, I don't believe Ms. Kobs is able to recognize the harm she is causing herself and her son. She has a history of depression and suicidal ideation. She has a history of mismanaging the medications prescribed to help minimize her symptoms. She has a history of abusing alcohol and illicit drugs. And according to the professional opinion of Dr. McCabe, Ms. Kobs has a personality disorder that manifests itself through several unpleasant traits, many of which we have witnessed in this courtroom during the past three days.

"None of us is perfect, Your Honor. We all have a skeleton or two in our closet; we've all done things we're not proud of. We all know people who have driven while impaired or have smoked a little weed. And people get caught shoplifting every day. Any one of these incidents, as an isolated occurrence, could look fairly innocuous. Had it just been the one suicide attempt, the one drug charge, the one DUI, the one shoplifting arrest, or the one sexual encounter in the presence of the child, we probably wouldn't be wasting the Court's time here today. But, Your Honor, I urge the Court to focus on the totality of the circumstances. Together, these conditions and events prove that Katherine Kobs has been engaging in a pattern of self destruction.

"I sincerely hope that Ms. Kobs can get the help she needs to put her life back in order. However, in the meantime, I strongly recommend that sole custody and primary physical placement be awarded to Samuel's father, Daniel Norby. I recommend that any placement with Ms. Kobs be supervised."

Jake gave a soft nod to the judge and took his seat, still afraid to make eye contact with Katherine.

"Thank you, Mr. Bishop. The Court greatly appreciates your hard work on this case. Counsel, I want closing arguments on my desk by no later than close of business on Tuesday. Keep them brief. You each get five pages; I won't read a sixth. We'll convene here on Thursday the 2nd at 10:00 a.m., at which time I'll issue my decision. We're adjourned."

CHAPTER 3

DRINKS WITH THE PROFESSOR

The engine rumbled effortlessly as the old Buick wound its way along Tamarack Trail, a route it had traveled hundreds of times before. Henry Bishop knew how much Jake had admired the old Riviera as a child. His last will and testament contained a clause specifically directing the car go to his only son.

Henry had owned many cars before the Riviera and many cars after. But there was something about the boat-tailed Sandalwood coupe that was impossible for Henry to part with. Jake's mother often hounded Henry to sell the old relic, hoping to free up space in the garage. But Henry was content to park his treasure in its designated shrine, liberating it only on fair-weather days. Jake diligently honored the tradition out of respect for his father.

Jake smiled slightly as he drew in a deep breath of air. He could still detect the smell of Henry's tobacco seeping from the pores of the leather seats. Despite countless lectures from his doctor over the years, old Henry refused to give up the pleasure of his heavenly tobacco. The pipe was still warm the day Jake discovered his father's lifeless body in the study. Even a man as great as Henry Bishop was no match for the cancer that eventually devoured his lungs.

Although Jake had been devastated by the loss of his father, his family and friends were able to convince him that Henry would have wanted him to head off to college and move on with his life. And so he did.

Jake was a small-town boy at heart, but everyone knew he was destined for greatness. Everything came easy for him. He was a diligent student, but the grades came effortlessly. He was blessed with good looks but had the common sense not to flaunt them. He had a silver tongue but knew not to overuse it. And he was a sincere and genuine person, qualities that made him easy to admire.

As the years passed, Jake's dreams were realized right on schedule. Four years on the honor roll at Northwestern University, graduation with honors at Northwestern Law School, a successful clerkship with Bingham & Stein in Chicago, and a high-paying associate position in their litigation department upon graduation. By the time he had completed his first year at the firm, Jake was settled into the American Dream, and he was enjoying the perks worthy of a brilliant young lawyer. He had a lavish apartment, a luxury car, an intelligent and stunning wife, and a newborn son.

Chicago was the perfect fit for the young couple. Jake was making a name for himself as a skillful civil litigator, and Blanca's archaeological background made her the perfect fit for the assistant curator position at the Field Museum.

Blanca Vasquez was a Peruvian beauty whom Jake met during law school. She was pursuing her Ph.D. in archaeology at the University of Chicago when the two were introduced through a mutual friend, Professor Jonathan Albright.

Albright, or "Prof," to those who knew him well, had been a lifelong friend and colleague of Jake's father. Prof and Henry Bishop grew up together, served time in the army, and attended law school together. After law school, Henry settled into his small practice in Maple Creek, while Prof headed off to Chicago in search of the big money.

But Prof never neglected his roots back in Wisconsin and remained very close to Henry and his family. After Henry passed away, Prof became like a surrogate father to Jake, and over time the two men became the best of friends. It was Prof who steered Jake into pre-law and later encouraged him to remain in Chicago to attend law school at Northwestern where Prof proudly served as an adjunct professor. He also helped Jake secure the clerkship at Bingham & Stein, where Prof was a well-respected senior partner. This eventually led to an associate position at the firm upon Jake's admission to the bar. Jake and Blanca greatly admired Professor Jonathan Albright, and when it came time to name their newborn son, no discussion was necessary. Jonathan it was. Jonathan Patrick Bishop.

Jake had always been willing to accept Prof's advice when it came to important decisions, and the advice always proved sound. When Jake's fairytale life ended abruptly the day Blanca was killed in a fiery car wreck during a visit to her native Peru, Prof made no effort to persuade him to stay in Chicago. He watched Jake spiral into a deep depression, losing interest in the things that had previously motivated him. He saw him struggle to hold himself together, dealing with the harsh realities of surviving as a single parent. Prof understood that Jake's best opportunity for happiness and fulfillment existed back in the sleepy little town of Maple Creek, close to friends and family, away from the pressures of the city.

Jake and Jonathan comfortably settled into small-town life in Maple Creek, and as each day passed, Jake grieved a little less.

His family law and estate planning practice now afforded him a comfortable living, and he operated with very modest overhead. This was thanks to the nominal office rent he paid his uncle, the majority shareholder of the bank located just below Jake's practice. It was also a consequence of Jake's simple lifestyle, compared to that of most attorneys in the valley. He had lost his desire to drive the latest foreign luxury car. He didn't own lavish toys, nor did he partake in expensive vices.

He still loved the law, but it was no longer his passion. He was still a hard worker, but no longer a workaholic. And Jake still had a desire to make money, but only enough to be comfortable. He now strived to focus on the big picture, and he pitied professionals who let their egos drive their actions only to lose sight of the realities of the world around them.

Blanca's death made him realize how short and fragile

life could be, and Jake was determined not to waste another minute of it. He refused to let his career interfere with the life he had made with young Jonathan.

Jake drove at a leisurely pace, admiring the brilliant fall colors. The air felt crisp and exhilarating as the season seemed to magically change before his eyes. It had been over two weeks since the conclusion of the Kobs trial, and he was still trying to put the debacle behind him and dig out from the backlog of files that had accumulated on his desk.

Prof's invitation to join him at the cabin came at the perfect time. Jake received a card in the office mail mid-week, and his face lit up as he read the handwritten message.

You are cordially invited to join me this Saturday at noon for cocktails on the porch.
Your Friend,
Professor Jonathan Albright.
P.S. Bring the Scotch.

Prof's cabin was in a neighboring county nearly an hour's drive from Maple Creek. Jake loved the drive up through the valley. The breathtaking landscape of forested ridges and bluffs, surrounded by the gently rolling farmland, made him think about the glaciers that had inched their way through the region thousands of years before.

There was a scattering of small towns along the route, each possessing its own unique charm. The trail was popular with fall sightseers who took in the colors and visited the little mom-and-pop boutiques along the way. Each town had something to offer. Westbrook was known for its apple orchard, bakery, and delicious little confectionary called Sweeties; Brinkley was popular for its antique stores; Murdock for its Amish furniture and textiles; Birchcliff for its cafes and winery; and Mayville was known for its assortment of handmade-crafts stores.

As Jake drove, his mind wandered back to an autumn day six years earlier when he and Blanca had taken the same journey, stopping to stroll about the same towns with the other tourists. It had been Blanca's first trip to the country since moving to Chicago from Peru. She was taken by the charm of the towns and the warmth of the people. Jake remembered how much she savored the fresh apple turnover and the hot cider while they sat on the outdoor patio at the Orchard Café. He remembered her smile as she affectionately petted the calf at the roadside farm. He remembered the quilt she insisted on buying at the Amish store, the one Jake still tucked Jonathan into each night. And he remembered the hand-carved Christmas ornament he secretly bought for Blanca after seeing her admire it.

The journey to Prof's cabin always conjured memories of Blanca. Prof had been like an American father to her. He met her at the Field Museum during the opening of an exhibit of ancient Peruvian artifacts from the tombs of

Sipan. Blanca was serving as an assistant to the curator of the museum at the time and was intimately involved with its operations.

Prof was a frequent visitor of the museum, especially when a new exhibit came to town. He had always been fascinated with the "Ancients," a term he enthusiastically applied to whatever past civilization he was interested in at the time. His dream as a child was to be a great archaeologist, traveling the far reaches of the earth in search of the next significant discovery, a discovery as worthy as Machu Picchu, Tutankhamen's tomb, or the ancient city of Pompeii. But he yielded to the wishes of his father and joined the distinguished list of lawyers and judges in his family's ancestry. It seemed his passion for the ancients and his search for the lost city of El Dorado would remain nothing more than a dream.

From the instant he met her, Prof was captivated by Blanca and inspired by her vast knowledge of archaeology and art history. Although Blanca grew up in an impoverished country, she had been fortunate to come from a moderately privileged family. Her parents were humble, middle-class people of Spanish descent. Her father was an engineer for a large firm in Lima, and her mother was a respected teacher at a private primary school near the edge of the city.

Blanca received her undergraduate degree in archaeology from Pontificia Universidad Catolica Del Peru, the country's oldest and most prestigious private university. She graduated at the top of her class and was highly respected by her professors and fellow students.

Although she did not come from great wealth, Blanca had always been somewhat uncomfortable with her family's prestige. She never overlooked the plight of Peru's native people. She would often tell Jake stories about the highland Indians who occupied various regions of the Andean mountains, many who desperately struggled to eke out a living by raising llamas and working small plots of land.

Blanca embraced the rich culture of her country, and as a child she loved visiting the cities and villages throughout the highlands. By the time she was in college, she was spending her summers in Cusco, guiding tourists up the Inca Trail to explore Machu Picchu, the lost city of the Incas.

Near the end of her college career Blanca met an entrepreneur from Arequipa by the name of Arturo Arroyo Lopez. Lopez was the only child of a powerful mining mogul, and the sole prospective heir to his family's vast fortune. He, too, shared a passion for ancient history and had spearheaded many significant archaeological expeditions. A number of his findings were legendary among the scientific community, but rumors circulated of his questionable practices and his playboy lifestyle.

Blanca began working for Arturo Lopez almost immediately after college. Lopez asked her to supervise the delicate excavation of several tombs his team had recently discovered near the Peruvian coast just north of Trujillo. Blanca's expertise in the field proved to be a major asset to Lopez, and they formed a promising professional alliance, an alliance that, over time, became more than just professional.

When Blanca began working for Lopez, she had little knowledge of his reputation. She was enamored with his charm and good looks, his love for archaeology, and his family's status. Her life at that time was everything she had dreamed it could be.

Eventually, however, even she became suspicious of Arturo's methods, and as their professional relationship evolved, there were too many warning signs to ignore—the mysterious omission of various pieces from the team's internal artifacts registry; the missing footage and documentation from their digs, reportedly looted from their camp; and the restriction of personnel from certain sites to which only Lopez and his close entourage were granted access.

Blanca reluctantly suspected that Lopez was involved in the global black market for illegal antiquities. He held many private meetings with businessmen from America, Switzerland, Germany, and Italy, none of whom appeared to have any legitimate business in Peru. Her suspicions were realized when authorities found the wreckage of one of Lopez's private planes on the rim of the Amazon Basin. Amid the wreckage were pre-Columbian artifacts including a burial shroud, two gold facemasks, and a priceless copper scepter. The wreckage also contained several pounds of coca leaves, likely on their way to a Colombian refinery.

Lopez's father and his team of lawyers were able to convince the authorities that the pilot was a rogue employee, running a black market antiquity ring and trafficking drugs. Blanca, however, had seen all she needed to see and immediately terminated her relationship with Arturo Lopez and his team.

After Blanca's academic migration to America and subsequent marriage to Jake, the couple made several trips back to Peru to visit Blanca's family. Prof accompanied them on three of the trips, during which he ventured off to play Indiana Jones with expeditions Blanca arranged through her connections at the university. Blanca also made an occasional business trip back to her home country for the Field Museum, sometimes bringing Jonathan with her to visit family. But Blanca's last visit to Peru was made solo, and was one from which she would never return.

Jake's mind continued to drift as he navigated down Cove Road, the narrow passageway that led to Prof's wooded hideout. He thought of the phone call he had received three years earlier from Cecilia, Blanca's oldest sister. She was barely able to speak, but every word hit Jake with a striking blow.

"Jake, we have lost our dear Blanca. It was an accident—down the mountain. They don't think she suffered. I am so sorry, Jake. I am so sorry."

Jake was numb from alcohol for most of the flight to Lima for the funeral.

The accident occurred on a remote mountain pass that Blanca had traveled countless times before. There were no skid marks. No witnesses.

Authorities concluded that Blanca had fallen asleep at the wheel, or perhaps suffered from a medical emergency. Her documents and belongings were strewn about the ravine, and little remained of her rental car but a heap of charred steel and melted plastic.

The casket remained closed—Blanca's body burned beyond recognition. Jake tried to speak at the ceremony, but was unable to maintain his composure long enough to form the words. Never in his entire life had he felt so helpless, so alone.

Jake blinked the tears from his eyes as the Riviera approached Prof's long, meandering driveway. A dense canopy of tree limbs sheltered the length of it like an eerie tunnel. He carefully steered through clutches of restless branches to avoid defiling the car's virgin finish.

He let out a heavy sigh as the cabin appeared through the foliage. He knew his remaining trips to visit Prof were numbered. Prof had returned to the cabin six months earlier when his doctors convinced him that further efforts to battle his cancer would be futile. The killer that had taken Jake's father thirteen years earlier would soon claim the surrogate father Jake had come to love so dearly.

As he tucked the Riviera into its shaded grassy parking spot, Jake noticed Prof on the front porch. He was tightly wrapped in a red plaid blanket, gently rocking in his weathered wooden rocking chair. Jake recognized the tattered old blanket from the many Wildcat games he and Prof attended at Ryan Field back in Chicago.

"You've still got that ratty old blanket, I see," Jake said as he cautiously climbed the rickety porch steps.

"And you're still driving that old relic," Prof replied as he pulled the blanket tighter around his neck.

Jake situated himself in a rocker next to Prof's. The two rocked for a while without speaking as they watched the leaves slowly dance toward the ground. It was familiar and calming.

"Did you bring my scotch, Junior, or is that your lunch in that bag?"

Jake smiled and shook his head in a disapproving manner as he handed the paper bag to Prof.

"That stuff will kill ya, you know."

"With any luck it will. How was your trip?"

"It was good. It's a beautiful drive this time of year. Where are you keeping Adele?"

"She's inside baking me some apple crisp. God that woman can bake—for a city girl."

"You're a lucky man," Jake said with an affirming nod.

Prof met Adele twenty years earlier when his firm was representing her father on a products liability case. Addie was clever and quick-witted, but had a very attentive and caring demeanor. She had worked for a large public relations firm back in Chicago for many years, but insisted on retiring when they learned about Prof's prognosis.

Prof interrupted his rocking as he slowly leaned over to pour a shot of scotch into his empty coffee cup.

"What's new at the office?"

"It's the same old stuff. Grudge matches and pissing contests. No matter how well I do, the clients are never satisfied with the outcome."

"That's the nature of the beast, Jake. Do you remember Skip Satterfield from the firm?"

"Yeah, I remember him. Wasn't he the associate who kissed a woman cop on the lips when she was administering his field sobriety test?"

"That's right, and he passed that test I'll have you know," he said as he raised his cup for a sip. "Anyway, about the time I started with the firm, Skip had just won one of the biggest maintenance awards in Cook County history. It was a nasty divorce, and Skip had a nasty client. This gal had a doctorate degree, hadn't worked in seven years, and had been burning through hubby's money by the truckload. Most judges would have thrown her out on her ass and denied the claim. But Skip put on a hell of a case and caught the judge on the right day. His client was set for life. Her last words to Skip as she left the courtroom: 'I can't believe we didn't get that goddamn Persian rug.' Trust me; they're never satisfied, Jake."

Jake laughed softly as he gazed up toward the treetops.

"Yeah, I guess I didn't get into this line of work for the praise and the gratitude, did I?"

"Speaking of thankless jobs, how did Montpetit rule on that custody case that you served on as guardian ad litem?"

Jake's smile slowly disappeared. "He went with my recommendation—gave sole custody to the father. He really didn't have much choice under the circumstances."

"How'd the mother take it?"

"Not well. Not well at all. She came unglued when Montpetit issued the ruling. It was gut-wrenching. She cried and howled like a wild animal caught in a trap. When her attorney tried to calm her down, she started throwing his files and exhibits all over the room. Then, she starts running toward me! The bailiff finally got her under control—but she looked right at me with these crazy eyes, called me a bastard, then screamed that she would get even with me no matter how long it took. Montpetit admonished her for it, but I'll tell you, she got her point across. I've never seen anything like it in all my years of practice."

"Do you think she's crazy enough to worry about?"

"Oh, she's plenty crazy. I've been keeping my distance since the trial. I haven't been down to the Rusty Bucket for two weeks. She doesn't have a history of serious violence, but you never know what someone's capable of when you take their child away. And for some reason, she was more pissed off at me than she was the judge."

"Maybe you should bring all of this to Chief Coleman's attention, just in case."

"I've already called him. He told me he'd have his men keep an eye on her. I can now sleep soundly at night knowing Maple Creek's finest are on the job."

"You don't sound so assured."

"I've tucked my 9mm into my bed beneath the mattress, and I've got Henry's old .38 in my desk drawer. That's as assuring as it's gonna get," Jake said as he glanced over in Prof's direction.

"Be careful, Jake. You and Jonathan have suffered through enough tragedy."

"Oh, don't worry yourself. I'm probably overthinking it."

"Overthinking it? Do you remember Judge Simmons in Chicago?"

"The one in the wheelchair?"

"That's right. He's in that wheelchair because some disgruntled asshole shot him in the back when he didn't like his custody ruling. Stay alert, Jake."

"I can't bear to think about what would happen to Jonathan if I weren't around. He's such a great kid. He asks about his mother all the time. I show him pictures, but he has no memory of her."

It was rare for them to broach the topic of Blanca. They hadn't spoken of her since the day Prof gave the harsh and unyielding intervention when Jake was spiraling out of control. He made Jake realize exactly what was at stake—Jonathan, his only remaining connection to Blanca. Jake's love for his son proved to be his light in that dark time. He became obsessed with being the best father he could be—one who would make Blanca proud. Eventually the days became more manageable, the nights more forgiving, and Jake learned to coexist with the haunting memories of his past life.

"We all miss her, Jake," Prof said with a gentle smile. "Some of the best memories of my life were the trips I took with you to Peru. She had such a love for her homeland—such a hunger for knowledge. Nobody knew more about the ancients than she did."

"I can't help but think that it was her hunger for knowledge that got her killed."

"Her death was an accident, Jake. It could have happened out on Interstate 94 just as easily as it did on that mountain pass. There was nothing you could have done to prevent it."

"I know that, but something has haunted me ever since I lost her. She was hiding something."

"What makes you think so?" Prof asked. This was the first Jake had ever spoken of his concern.

"During our last few trips to Lima she acted differently. She seemed more cautious, almost covert. She had little interest in journeying out. She used to be so excited to show me the countryside, but during those later visits she wanted to spend most of our time in the city, or at her parent's place."

"I think you're reading too much into it, Jake. I'm sure the novelty of acting as your tour guide had simply worn off and she was eager to spend time with her family."

"I don't know," Jake said. "I can't quite explain it, but something was troubling her. And there's something else." Jake paused as if conjuring an image from the past. "The day of the funeral, there was a man there. He was standing alone in the distance, almost obscured from view. I was so numb that day that it didn't register until later. But I'm almost certain it was Lopez, the man she used to work for."

"Really?" Prof asked, intrigued. "Did you approach him?"

"No, he disappeared before I could get a better look at him. But I remember feeling as if there was something suspicious about him, something misplaced."

"That was a difficult time for you, Jake. You weren't yourself. But that's all in the past now. Don't ponder over every little detail, or all the ghosts will come back to haunt you. It's okay to let her go. Blanca would want you to move on, create a new life for yourself—find a new soul mate."

"It's not in the cards, Prof. There could never be another Blanca."

"She was indeed a treasure," Prof conceded. "But never say never, Junior. One thing I've learned during my journeys is that you sometimes find treasure where you least expect it. Don't give up hope." Prof's tone was sincere as he imparted his wisdom on his surrogate son.

"Thanks. You've been good to me. I owe you so much."

"Nonsense, it's my job to keep you in line. Henry left me strict instructions."

Jake smiled at the mention of his father. "Well, I should hit the road so I'm back in time to pick up Jonathan. But I suppose I better step inside and say hello to Addie first or one of us will be in the doghouse."

As Jake rose from his rocker, Prof placed his hand on Jake's knee. Jake sat back in his chair and looked into Prof's tired eyes. He realized there was more to discuss.

"Jake, when I'm gone I want you to handle my affairs and take care of Addie."

Jake nodded.

"All of my papers are in a safe deposit box in your uncle's bank. Addie will give you the key. It's all self-explanatory, nothing you can't handle, as long as you follow my instructions carefully."

Jake was trying to be strong, knowing how difficult it was for Prof to confront his destiny. "I'll take care of everything. Don't give it another thought." Jake paused as he looked down at the ground, trying his best to choke back the tears. "I'm gonna miss you so much, old man."

"I'll miss you too, son. More than you'll ever know. Now go inside and eat some apple crisp or I'll never hear the end of it."

CHAPTER 4

THE VISITORS ARRIVE

The wheels of the Hawker 4000 chirped as they hit the runway at Miami International Airport. It had been a long flight, over 2,600 miles. But the lavish interior of the luxury jet made the journey more than tolerable for the pilot and his two passengers.

Entering the United States was a routine procedure for the pilot. He had flown the same route for his employer more times than he could remember. As always, he taxied the jet toward the executive terminal to meet his agent at Royal Air, Inc.

Royal Air was one of several fixed base operators, or FBOs, that provided amenities to weary pilots and passengers. Unlike other operators, however, Royal catered only to the wealthiest of travelers, those who would pay for the comforts of home: plush sleeping quarters, elaborate lounges, executive conference rooms, spotless locker and shower facilities, and even finely catered meals.

As the pilot taxied, he noticed his handler from Royal Air approaching by foot on the tarmac. It was mandatory that all business with Royal be conducted through one particular agent, and no other. The man was a trusted business partner, known for discreet handling of his clients' delicate issues while on U.S. soil.

A customs official was trailing just steps behind the Royal agent, who politely greeted the pilot and his two passengers when they stepped out of the aircraft. There was a friendly exchange about the long journey, the beautiful weather, and the pending business the travelers would attend to in the United States. But the discussion was soon interrupted by the customs officer who was eager to complete his inspection and move on to his next aircraft.

The pilot casually produced his license and medical certification, and the certificate of registration from his country of origin. The passengers were screened for their passports and visas, and produced their multiple-entry B-1 business visas.

They were traveling light and had little to declare, so the search of their luggage was brief. The officer passed through the aircraft and found everything to be in order. The requisite customs forms had been completed, so he processed the aircraft and its passengers quickly. No long lines, no hurrying and waiting. There were perks to being an elite traveler at an executive terminal.

After ensuring that the jet was towed to its hangar and safely stowed away, the Royal agent returned to his office where his clients were sipping cocktails and relaxing in his overstuffed leather furniture.

Even after several hours of flight, the travelers still appeared fresh and rested. The woman and her gentleman companion were both attractive, dressed in finely tailored suits, appearing to be in their late twenties to early thirties.

The woman had a magnetic quality about her, an exotic, captivating beauty.

The pilot was a tall middle-aged man with silver hair and dark, cratered skin. He seldom spoke, but when he did it was in broken English and with a thick Spanish accent. He, too, was nicely dressed, but not to the level of his esteemed passengers.

The agent had worked with the trio several times before, but knew very little about them. He was aware of their dealings in precious metals and stones, but suspected there was more to their activities in the United States than custom jewelry.

For a time, he suspected they might be affiliated with a terrorist organization, but their country of origin was not typically affiliated with such activity, and the clients simply didn't fit the profile.

Drug trafficking could not be ruled out, but they had passed countless customs searches during their previous trips, including the scrutiny of drug-sniffing canine units.

The most likely scenario, he suspected, was that his clients were laundering money. Precious metals and fine jewels are highly concentrated forms of wealth—easily transportable and quickly converted to cash with little difficulty. Although the U.S. Department of the Treasury subjects precious metal and jewelry dealers to the same anti-money-laundering requirements as financial institutions, the agent knew it was not impossible for quasi-legitimate businesses to circumvent these rules by following the minimum requisite protocol.

What he knew best, however, was that these particular clients always paid well for his additional services, and they always paid in cash. His superiors at corporate would certainly not condone it, but they were hundreds of miles away and concerned with other business.

The items his clients requested for this visit were a bit unusual and highly illegal. He had pushed himself to the edge of his morals in the past, but for the first time he knew he was being asked to cross a very dangerous line. Just a month earlier, he had respectfully told his client that he would not be able to procure the items they requested. He did, however, know of a person who he thought could help them. But the client was persistent, and the agent's initial reluctance served only to invite a counteroffer that was simply too tempting to pass up.

They reached an agreement, and once again the agent lived up to his reputation. He managed to compile everything on the list. The sport utility had been completely reinvented and re-titled. The registration was clean and would pass the scrutiny of any state trooper. The new driver's licenses were impeccably forged, right down to the holograms. Even the agent was astonished by their quality. His clients were now documented U.S. citizens... so to speak.

Most of the requested supplies were new and untraceable: one satellite phone, three cellular phones, a GPS device, telephonic surveillance equipment, computer spyware, and other items that would quickly arouse the suspicion of customs.

The hunting supplies were well concealed within the vehicle—high-caliber rifles, 9mm pistols, several boxes of ammunition, along with road maps and satellite images of their destination. The agent had no idea what they were hunting, and he had every intention of keeping it that way.

After briefing his clients on their new identities and accounting for each item on their checklist, he escorted the travelers to their new vehicle. He feared that somehow this transaction could return to haunt him. His clients complimented him on his efficiency and instructed him to give the inside of the jet a thorough cleaning while they were gone. He understood the request.

The agent discreetly nodded to his clients as they drove away from the terminal. He then proceeded to the hangar and entered the Hawker. It was a beautiful aircraft. He was used to working around luxury jets, but this plane was second to none.

He folded down one of the plush chairs located near the aft of the aircraft and hinged open the carpeted door of the storage compartment below. He pulled the electronic key from his pocket, pointed it toward the compartment, and gently pressed the key's thumb pad. There was a muffled popping sound as the false bottom to the compartment sprung open.

Deep within the hidden compartment was a steel-plated briefcase. He removed it and dialed in the combination to the lock. He opened the lid and examined the contents: a thick layer of U.S. currency, neatly bound and arranged. He would count it later, but knew there was no need to do so.

CHAPTER 5

THE BISHOP BOYS

Children poured from Evergreen Elementary at the end of the school day. As he sat in the Riviera, Jake carefully watched for his little student in the sea of bobbing backpacks. Jonathan typically rode the bus to Grandma Margaret's house after school, where Jake would pick him up just before supper. But at least once each week Jake tried to clear his calendar so he and Jonathan could spend an afternoon together.

Jake was hoping Jonathan would remember his instructions from earlier that day to watch for him in the pick-up zone. Jake knew Jonathan was forgetful, so he tried to find a parking spot that offered a good view of the buses. But Jake soon saw Jonathan racing toward the Riviera with an enormous grin on his face.

Jonathan loved riding in the "oldie car," as he called it. He never knew his Grandpa Henry, and the old car was a treasure filled with clues to the legend who everyone admired. The sweet, smoky smell of Henry's pipe still filled the car's interior, and his old hat, now faded and dusty, was still perched in the car's back window. In the glove box was a stash of old Dean Martin tapes, and Jonathan loved to listen to the warped sound of old Dino on the barely functioning eight-track tape player. And everywhere they went, people would tell Jonathan how they remembered when his Grandpa used to drive that old car around town.

Jonathan settled into the passenger seat and proudly held up the project he had completed in kindergarten.

"What did you make for me?" Jake asked enthusiastically.

"This is Henry, our Thanksgiving turkey," Jonathan answered with an introductory tone. "The teacher told us we had to give our turkeys a name. Lots of kids named their turkeys Tom, but I named mine Henry," Jonathan said as he stretched to reach his inherited hat from the back window.

"Well, I'm sure Grandpa would have been honored to have such a fine turkey named after him," Jake said as he motioned toward Jonathan's seatbelt with an instructive nod.

The old Buick began to roll, and Jake carefully navigated through the adolescent chaos and the crossing guards.

"What else did you learn in school today?"

"Not much. We watched a movie about the pilgrims. It was boring. Elizabeth Baler hit Danny Fitzpatrick right in the face on the playground today! She hadda go to the principal's office."

"Why in world would she hit that boy in the face?" Jake asked as he chuckled quietly to himself.

"Danny called her a slut."

Jake waited for the impending question.

"What is a slut, anyway?"

"Well, let's just say it's not a nice word. Just make sure

you don't ever use it, okay?"

"I won't. Hey, are we going for ice cream?"

"It's a little chilly for ice cream, buddy. How about we stop by the Cottage for hot chocolate?"

"Alright." Jonathan adjusted the oversized hat on his tiny head.

The Cottage was a quaint little coffeehouse in a charming old converted bungalow on the edge of town, which over time had been united with the expanding business district. Although the calendar had not yet rolled past Thanksgiving, the exterior was already adorned with evergreen garland and Christmas lights. The owner, Maggie Cooper, loved the change of seasons and was always eager to decorate. From the street, the Cottage resembled a Norman Rockwell painting, the perfect picture. An enchanting landmark. Inside, the hardwood floors had a beautiful luster. The handsome maple wainscoting complemented the warm tones of the textured walls, which were boldly accented by the white cove molding and dark tin ceiling tiles. Maggie Cooper had the right touch.

She was always pleased to see Jake whenever he stopped in. She and Jake dated for a year in high school, but Maggie ended the relationship when the football quarterback asked her to the prom. He turned out to be a buffoon, but Maggie didn't acknowledge this shortcoming until the end of her five-year marriage to the man.

Maggie's face lit up as the boys entered the shop. She adored little Jonathan. She had no children of her own, but her goal to be a mother one day was often on her mind.

"Do you like my turkey, Maggie? His name is Henry!"

"That's a fine turkey, Jonathan Bishop," Maggie said earnestly. "Such a turkey is certainly deserving of a pumpkin bar." She slid open the glass door of her bakery case.

"What do you say to Maggie, Jonathan?" Jake prompted.

"Thank you for the pumpkin bar, Maggie."

"You're welcome, sir. Would you care for some hot chocolate?"

"Yes please, with whipped cream."

"Are you and your dad hanging out today?" Maggie asked as she steamed the milk for Jonathan's order. Jonathan delivered an affirmative nod, his mouth full of pumpkin bar.

"Yes, I have important errands to run, and I've requested the company of my valued associate," Jake said proudly.

"Well you couldn't have picked a better man for the job!" Maggie said loudly over the sound of the steam purging from the latte machine.

"Yes, he's my hardest worker," Jake replied, patting Jonathan on the top of his head.

Maggie dialed down the steamer. "Say, Jake, I've been meaning to ask you how Prof is holding up."

"As well as can be expected," Jake said with a despairing shake of his head, one he carefully kept above Jonathan's radar. Maggie nodded with regret. Prof and Addie Albright were regulars at the Cottage whenever they were in town, and Maggie was always entertained by Prof's colorful stories.

"Here's your hot chocolate, Mr. Bishop. Be careful not to burn yourself," she said as she gently handed the large mug to Jonathan.

"Thank you, Maggie."

As he slowly walked toward the back of the shop, he loudly slurped the sweet chocolate elixir through the heaping mound of whipped cream. Maggie kept a supply of children's books and puzzles in a small room adjacent to the seating area, and being a regular patron, Jonathan had a designated stool. Jake stood at the counter while Maggie prepared his usual latte.

"So, how long do you think he has? Prof, I mean."

"It's hard to say. It could be weeks now, even days. He tries to hide it, but I can tell he's in a great deal of pain."

"How's Addie taking it?"

"You know Addie, she's a strong soul. I think she's accepted the fact that he's near the end, but she lives every day like it's their first. It's gotta be hard for her."

"They've had such a wonderful life," Maggie said with a smile. "Such a wonderful marriage. It's not fair that it should end this way."

There was a temporary lull in the conversation as Jake's mind seemed to drift.

"No, it's never really fair, is it?" His tone was sad.

Maggie realized she had unintentionally opened an old wound. She had met Blanca once. Jake brought her by the Cottage during one of their visits back to Maple Creek. She was enchanted by Blanca's beauty and enjoyed listing to the confident English spoken through her thick Spanish accent. Maggie also took great pleasure in sharing stories from Jake's past.

"What are you guys doing for Thanksgiving?" Maggie asked, trying to change the subject.

"I guess we're going over to my mom's house for the traditional feast. My sister is planning to come home for a few days."

"Well, that'll be nice. If I remember correctly, Margaret is quite a cook."

"That she is. But she's getting older now. I suppose I'll have to put on the apron and lend a hand this year."

"Oh, I'd really like to see that!"

Maggie was an only child and her parents now lived in Arizona. She was probably planning to spend another Thanksgiving alone, Jake thought.

"Why don't you join us for Thanksgiving, Maggie? We'll have plenty of food and I know everyone would love to see you again."

"Oh thanks, Jake, but I couldn't impose. Besides, I have a turkey pot pie and a can of cranberries that would simply go to waste if I didn't eat them!"

Jake knew Maggie was not one to eat Thanksgiving dinner out of a box and a can. Even a single place setting at her Thanksgiving table would be a meal to make the pilgrims proud.

"Nonsense, it's no imposition. If you don't join us I'm going to recruit Jonathan to persuade you."

"No, no. Don't do that. You know I can't resist those dark eyes and that sad face. I'd love to join you."

"Marvelous. We'll probably eat around two, but why don't you show up at about noon so we can all catch up."

"Thanks, Jake. I'm looking forward to it. Can I bring anything?"

"Well, if it's not too much trouble, maybe you could bring a batch of those award-winning pumpkin bars."

"My pleasure!" she said with a smile, unable to contain her enthusiasm.

Jake gathered up his young associate as he prepared to leave for the next stop on their journey. After they said goodbye, Jake couldn't help but question himself. He had come in for a latte and left with a date. A *Thanksgiving* date. What the hell was he thinking? How could he have let his guard down?

As he stepped outside into the cool November air, Jake took a deep, cleansing breath. "Now don't get carried away. It's not a date; it's just dinner," Jake mumbled to himself.

"What, Dad?" Jonathan asked.

"Oh, I was just saying that we'd better stop by the office to check on things."

Jake lucked into a parking spot in front of his office. Having a practice above a busy bank on Main Street often made parking scarce. Being on the second floor was also a detriment, especially for his elderly clients who sometimes found it difficult to scale the narrow flight of stairs.

But the arrangement had its benefits. The leasehold

offered him a separate entrance to this historic old building. It was well preserved with a handsome profile. He had full use of nearly 900 square feet, all of which the bank had authentically restored four years earlier. If not for the presence of the modern office equipment and water cooler, Jake's clients would have surely felt as if they'd stepped into a beautiful turn-of-the-century law office. And thanks to his uncle Benjamin, Jake paid only $750.00 per month, a fraction of what he would pay elsewhere in town. The benefits were reciprocal, however, as Jake often provided legal services to the bank at a reduced rate.

Jonathan sprinted up the stairwell to Jake's office, slowing down at the top of the stairs.

"Hello Gertie," he said softly as he opened the door to the reception area.

"Hello, half-pint," Gertie barked as her fingers pounded the keyboard. Gertrude Liddle, Jake's loyal but cantankerous assistant, ran the office with military precision, and she wasn't much for chitchat. Some thought her to be rude, but those who feared her described her as direct. Jonathan wasn't afraid of her, but he always approached her with caution.

Despite her last name, Gertie had a very generous physique. Jake wouldn't describe her as fat, but the words "brick" and "house" certainly came to mind. When Jake returned to Maple Creek in need of a secretary, Prof stressed that the proper candidate should possess certain qualities: loyalty, discretion, and intelligence. "Brains before beauty!" Prof declared. "Hire someone who won't distract you. There's no room for romping and romance in the workplace."

Gertie had no formal education beyond high school. Her skills had all been acquired on the job. She worked as a legal secretary for an old classmate of Prof's named Kerman Krattley—right up to the day Krattley expired behind his desk from a massive heart attack. She tried early retirement, but after sitting at home for a year with her husband Lyle, a retired Army lieutenant, Gertie decided that it was either time to get divorced or go back to work. And as fate would have it, she met all of Prof's criteria.

Gertie rattled off the day's messages without missing a beat. "Jake, Sandy called from the Register in Probate's office—she's pressuring me for the inventory on the Stevens Estate. You'd better polish that up and file it; I can't stall her any longer. You got a ton of discovery in the mail today on the Jacobson divorce; I've already sent copies of the interrogatories to Mrs. Jacobson with an instruction letter. I finished making the revisions on your brief for the Negard file; it's sitting on your desk waiting for your signature. You also got some B.S. motion on Wilson that you'll probably want to take a look at. Oh, and I received a call from that little squirt, Roland Fuller—he said he's not going to sign the consent form you sent him for his mom's estate. He thinks the house should sell for twice that price, and he thinks his brother, the executor, is trying to put the screws to him."

"Anything else?" Jake asked with a grin.

"Nothing that needs immediate attention. It's all on your desk," Gertie said as she leaned down toward Jonathan and peered over the top of her reading glasses. "Whatta ya have there, sprout? Is that a turkey?"

"This is Henry. He's our Thanksgiving turkey."

"That's a great turkey, son. Did you take him for a ride in the oldie car?"

"Yeah, we went to Maggie's for a hot chocolate."

"Oh, you went to Maggie's, did you?" Gertie delivered a grin and an elevated eyebrow in Jake's direction. "How's little Maggie doing nowadays?"

"She's great. She gave me a pumpkin bar."

"I've tried those pumpkin bars. Those are some tasty bars," Gertie said. "Did your dad find any treats at Maggie's place?"

"No. He never eats much. He's too busy talking to Maggie."

Gertie chuckled with approval as she could see she was embarrassing her boss. She often told Jake that he should try to stir things up with the Cooper girl.

"Well, I've got everything I need," Jake said as he quickly tucked the last file into his tattered briefcase, hoping to take his leave of Gertie before she started planning his wedding. "We'd better head home and figure out what we're having for dinner, buddy."

"You boys behave. And, Jake, don't forget you've got the Bakke depositions at nine tomorrow," Gertie said as she resumed her thrashing of the keyboard.

"Goodnight, Gertrude," Jake shouted sarcastically as he and Jonathan disappeared down the stairwell, the mahogany door closing slowly behind them.

Gertie shook her head and smirked. "Smart ass," she mumbled to herself. Gertie hated being addressed as Gertrude and tolerated it only from Jake.

CHAPTER 6

MAJOR PROBLEMS

The headlights washed across the front of the Bishop house as the Riviera turned into the driveway. It was a dark evening, the moonlight nearly obscured by a thick blanket of clouds stretching across the November sky. The streetlight on the corner had been burned out for a month, and Jake silently scolded himself for neglecting to call the utility company.

The old Cape Cod-style home was nestled in a cluster of mature oak trees that formed a dense canopy. The trees provided excellent shade during the summer, but the twisted and leafless limbs were eerie during the cold winter months when the darkness set in early.

As the car came to a stop, Jake was startled by a large dog that appeared suddenly at his window. The massive front paws of the beast were perched firmly on the ledge of Jake's door, and the stern expression of the animal clearly announced that there was business to address.

"What's Major doing outside?" Jonathan asked.

"I'm not sure, Pal. Sit here for a minute while I check things out—and keep the doors locked."

An uneasy feeling came over Jake as he walked toward the side door of the house. He was certain he had locked Major inside when he left earlier that day. He remembered issuing the routine instruction just before closing the door behind him, "Now you be good today, boy. We'll go for a walk when I get home." Although Major was a fairly intelligent Labrador, Jake was certain the dog had neither the brains nor the ambition to unlock and open a door.

The inside of the house was pitch dark. As he peered through the door's window pane, Jake cautiously turned the knob. Still locked. *If Major had left through that door, he would have locked it behind him*, Jake speculated, trying to lighten his uneasiness. As he walked toward the front door, Jake glanced over at the Riviera. Jonathan was craning his neck to secure a better view through the car window.

Jake worked his way around the house, inspecting each door and window for a breach, but all entries appeared to be soundly locked and there were no signs of tampering.

He took a deep breath. *Don't jump to conclusions,* he thought. *There must be a logical explanation. Just unlock the door and inspect the inside of the house. It's no time to be a coward.*

Think like an attorney. What would I tell a client to do if one called me under these circumstances? Jake took another deep breath. *I would say there was a little boy in the car and that it was no time to be a hero. Be smart. Call the police.*

As he flipped open his cell phone, Jake decided against dialing 911. He didn't want his conversation recorded for a replay on the evening news or quoted in the newspaper. Instead, he scrolled through his cell phone until he came to STONE HOME. Eric Stone was a good friend—a friendship that dated all the way back to grade school. Stone was now Maple Creek's one and only police detective.

"Stone here," the detective answered authoritatively.

"Stone here," Jake mimicked. "Christ, you sound like a Dragnet Detective."

"Are you calling to report a homicide, sir?"

"No, but my cat's stuck in a tree and I understand that's your specialty."

"You're a riot, Bishop. What's up?"

"Sorry to bother you at home, but I'm outside my house and I'm a little concerned. Jonathan and I just got home and we discovered Major running around outside. I'm certain he was inside the house when I left earlier, and all of the doors are still locked up tight."

"Who else has a key to the house?"

"My sister has one, but she hasn't been home for a few years now."

"Any signs of a break in?"

"None that I saw, but it's awful dark out here and I haven't been inside yet."

"Maybe the dog just went out for pizza."

"Nah, I've ruled that out—he's been cutting back on the carbs."

"And you're sure he was locked inside when you left?"

"Positive."

"Well, better safe than sorry. I'll be right over. Don't touch anything until I get there. I'll call dispatch and ask them to have a cruiser meet us."

"Thanks, Eric. I owe you one."

"I'll add it to the list. See ya in a few minutes."

Major and the boys sat in the Riviera with the motor running as they waited for the cavalry. Jake rubbed his chilled hands near the heater as the hot air blew in.

"Why aren't we going inside, Dad?" Jonathan asked.

"Well, buddy, Eric and I are going to check the house out to make sure nobody's been inside, but I'm sure everything is fine."

"Why do you want Eric to help you?"

"Because there's safety in numbers, my boy."

Jake caught the puzzled look on Jonathan's face as the five-year-old attempted to process the day's lesson.

"It means that the more people you have with you, the safer you are. Safety in numbers," Jake explained.

"Oh, I get it. Who do you think was in our house?"

"Probably nobody. But it doesn't seem right that Major is outside by himself with all of the doors locked behind him. And when something doesn't seem right to you, it's best to call for help. So, Eric and I will check the house out to be certain everything's okay, and we'll all be able to sleep tight tonight," Jake said.

Soon a pair of headlights pulled in behind the Riviera, and Jake carefully investigated them through his rear view mirror. It didn't appear to be a squad car. *Probably Eric*, he thought. As he left the car, he told Jonathan to stay put.

"Did you just get home, dear?" Margaret asked as she walked toward Jake with her casserole dish in hand.

"Mom, what are you doing here?"

"Well, that's a fine greeting. Am I interrupting something?"

"I'm sorry; it's been a long day. What do you have there?"

"I made some hot dish for you boys. Have you eaten yet?"

"No, not yet. You shouldn't be out making dinner deliveries on such a cold night, Mom. You should be home curled up under a blanket," Jake said. His mother was only seventy-two, but within the last three years she had been diagnosed with rheumatoid arthritis and macular degeneration, had undergone knee-replacement surgery, and was recently showing signs of Alzheimer's. Jake once confronted her about retiring her driver's license, but the conversation was not well received. They compromised that she would drive only during the day, and only within the city limits. But given the circumstances, Jake wasn't in the mood to address her violation of their agreement.

"Well I stopped by earlier to drop this off, but nobody was home," Margaret said, ignoring Jake's attempt to discipline her.

"What time did you stop by?"

"Oh, I don't know. It was just starting to get dark, so it must have been around 4:30. Why?"

"Did you notice if anyone else was around?"

"No, I didn't see anyone."

"What about Major, did you happen to notice if he was outside?" Jake asked as calmly as possible.

"No, what's going on, Jake? Is Jonathan alright?" She may have been getting older, but Jake knew she could always tell when he was hiding something.

"Everyone's fine, Mom. It's just that Major was running loose when we got home, and I'm a little concerned that someone may have been in the house. Eric Stone is coming over and we're going to check it out just to be sure."

Margaret's jaw dropped, conjuring up the worried motherly expression Jake was trying to avoid.

Just then Detective Stone pulled up with a squad car trailing closely behind. Stone was alone, but the squad was occupied by two officers, one male and one female. As they got out, the troops were careful not to do anything that could alarm the neighbors or scare off potential intruders. There were no flashing lights or wailing sirens, only dim parking lights, the dull thuds of car doors, and the monotone dispatch woman rattling off the evening calls over the radio.

"We've had a complaint from the neighbors that you've been peeping into windows, Mr. Bishop," Stone said as he approached, magnum flashlight in hand.

"Hi, Eric. Thanks again for coming over. You remember my mother, Margaret?"

"Of course. Good evening, Ma'am."

"Hello, Eric," Margaret said, still holding her casserole dish and appearing somewhat dazed.

"Mom, why don't you sit in the car with Jonathan and Major while we check things out. You'll be warm there, and we'll make sure you get home safely once we're done," Jake said in a gentle tone as he escorted her to the car.

Jake ordered Major into the backseat and helped his mother settle in. Detective Stone huddled with officers Griffin and Jensen to devise a plan.

"How would you like to do this, Eric?" Jake asked as he approached the huddle, excited by the opportunity to join the team.

"You have a key, right?" Stone asked as he extended his hand.

Jake gave him the key and waited for his assignment.

"Alright, Jake. Wait here for a minute while we get situated, and make sure you stay away from the windows."

As Stone and the officers walked toward the side of the home, they tested their radios. Stone quietly unlocked the side door, but didn't open it. Officer Griffin would cover that location, while Jensen secured the back door.

After Stone unlocked the doors and got his officers into position, he circled the home and met with Jake by the front porch. "Jake, I have an officer posted at each door; they're going to remain outside for now just in case I flush anyone out. I'd like you to wait here while I make sure things are secure."

"Do you really think that's necessary, Eric? I'm sure this is all for nothing."

"Does Major usually wear a collar?"

"What?"

"A collar—does your dog usually wear one?"

"Yes, why?" Jake hesitated.

"Did you notice he's not wearing one tonight?"

"God, you're right. With all of the excitement, I didn't even notice it was missing. Why would someone take the collar and not the dog?"

"Maybe it slipped off when that someone was trying to get the dog back in the house. Why don't you wait out here with your family? I won't be long."

Jake nodded and returned to the Riviera. Since the car was full of family, hot dish, and hound, Jake leaned against the outside where he could give them a play-by-play through the window.

Stone unsnapped the safety strap on the holster of his service revolver as he approached the house. "I'm entering the front door, folks. Stay alert," he said softly over the radio.

The front door creaked open. Stone took one step into the living room and stood motionless, listening to his surroundings. The home was silent. He felt three light switches on the wall and flipped the one closest to the door. He was startled by the ceiling fan as it began to spin. After a deep breath, Stone flipped the other two switches, illuminating the living room and the front porch.

Stone carefully scanned the room, looking for anything that seemed out of place. Jake and Jonathan kept a relatively neat home for a couple of bachelors. Nothing appeared to be disrupted, the television and electronics appeared untouched, and there were no signs that the doors or windows had been tampered with.

He canvassed the main level, lighting up each room as he progressed. He inspected the inside of every closet, beneath every desk and table, behind every door and drape. Nothing.

"Grif, Jensen, the main level looks clear. Come on in and we'll check out the rest of the house," Stone announced over the radio.

"What's happening, Dad?" Jonathan asked as Officer Griffin entered their home.

"It looks like everything's fine, pal. It shouldn't be long now."

They watched the second floor of the home light up, one room at a time.

"You boys are staying at my house tonight," Margaret declared, attempting to preempt any negotiation.

"That won't be necessary, Mother. We'll be just fine," Jake answered confidently.

Jake usually afforded his mother the requisite dose of respect, but Margaret had an annoying way of taking charge. She had learned from the best. But she always overlooked the fact that Jake had also inherited a trait or two from the great Henry Bishop.

After they exited the house, the female officer, Dana Jensen, approached the Riviera. "Everything checks out okay, folks. Detective Stone is going to take a few photographs and make some notes. He'll be out in just a few minutes."

"Thank you, officer. I can't tell you how much we

appreciate you coming out tonight," Jake said.

"All part of the job, Mr. Bishop. Don't hesitate to call me…I mean, to call us…that is, if you have any more problems tonight, or anytime. That is, you can call me, um…us, anytime," Jensen said, her face flushed.

"I will. Perhaps I could impose upon you to follow my mother home? She doesn't drive much at night anymore, and she just lives a few miles down the road."

Margaret rolled her eyes.

"We'd be glad to make sure she gets home safely."

As Margaret fired up her Park Avenue, Jake leaned in and kissed her on the cheek. "Thanks for making dinner, Mom. It'll come in handy tonight."

"You're welcome, dear. They're not going to turn those darn police lights on are they?" Margaret said, gesturing toward the squad car behind her.

"No, Mother. They're just going to follow you home so we don't have something else to worry about tonight."

"Alright. You make sure you call me before you go to bed," she said, attempting to issue the last instruction of the evening.

"I will, Mother. Now you drive carefully, you hear?" Jake said with a smile.

Margaret backed out of the driveway, pretending not to hear.

"Is it okay to come in?" Jake yelled as he and Jonathan stuck their heads in the front door.

"Yes, come on in, boys," Stone said as he finished

scribbling in his notepad.

"Well, what did you find?"

"Everything's just fine; nobody's been in the house. You boys can sleep sound tonight," Stone said as he patted Jonathan on the head. "Could I have a minute with you to go over some paperwork, Jake?"

"Sure. Jonathan, why don't you go watch TV in the kitchen while I finish up with Detective Stone? We'll eat some hot dish in a minute."

Jonathan trudged into the kitchen dragging his backpack and winter coat on the floor, Major lumbering happily behind him. Stone waited until he heard the television before continuing.

"Jake, I want you to go through the house tonight to see if anything is missing or out of place."

"I thought you said nobody was in the house?"

"That was for Jonathan's benefit. But I am a little concerned."

"About what?"

"Well, a few things. You have caller I.D. on your upstairs phone?"

"Right."

"There's a call on there that came in just after 2:30 p.m. today. I called in a trace, and Audrey tells me it came from the payphone outside that old diner on the edge of town."

"I don't follow. Why should we be worried about a stray payphone call?"

"Because intruders sometimes call right before they hit

a place, just to make sure no one is home."

"But why didn't they toss the place? Everything looks okay."

"Things do appear to be in order. I found your 9mm tucked under the mattress; thank God they didn't take that. You'd better be careful with that damn thing, Bishop," Stone warned with a look of concern.

"I will. It's just part of my homeowner's insurance," Jake replied.

"Just make sure Jonathan doesn't find out where you keep the clip. That reminds me. Speaking of clips, I did notice some stray paperclips on the floor next to your desk over there. Do you remember dropping them?"

Jake examined his desk in the alcove just off the living room. "No, no I don't. In fact, Jonathan and I just vacuumed in here on Sunday. And that cup of paperclips seems out of place. I usually keep it over here closer to the computer monitor."

"Maybe these guys got startled and knocked something over; it's hard to say."

"Maybe Margaret spooked them when she was here earlier to make her hot dish delivery. She said she stopped by around 4:30."

"Did she see anything?" Stone asked.

"No, just rang the doorbell, peeked in the garage to check for my car, and then left for the store to pick up a few things."

"I'll stop by and talk with her tomorrow. Maybe she'll

remember something else."

"Go easy with her. I'm sure she's already organizing the neighborhood watch."

"I will."

"Eric, how do you think these guys got in? I'm fanatical about locking the doors."

"I don't see any damage at the points of entry. Could be they found a window partially unlocked—jimmied it open. Could be they're experienced and knew how to manipulate the lock. Could be they got a duplicate key somehow. I'll take a closer look around the outside tomorrow, but I don't think we'll find much. This looks like a pretty clean entry, and whoever it was didn't want you to know they were here."

"Have there been any other break-ins around the neighborhood lately?"

"A couple of juvenile garage hits, nothing major."

"Do you think we're in danger?"

"Probably not. If they wanted to harm you, they would have stuck around. I wouldn't lose any sleep tonight."

"That's easy for you to say, Detective," Jake said as he set his briefcase next to his desk.

"Do you keep any important files on that computer?" Stone asked.

"Just miscellaneous documents I'm working on from time to time, nothing juicy."

"Any client data?"

"No. All of our client files are kept at the office. When I work on a stray document here I usually save it to a memory stick and bring it to work. Why?"

"What else do you use the computer for?"

"Well, Jonathan and I get personal e-mail here, family photos, I do my personal bookkeeping on that system, and I have software that synchronizes my work calendar with our calendar at the office. Do you think they were after something in the computer?"

"Probably not, but it might be wise for you to have it checked out by a computer guru. They can track every keystroke nowadays."

"Can you guys do that for me?"

"I would, but the chief isn't going to authorize me to spend any tax dollars on it. We've really been getting the shitty end of the budget cuts. But you could certainly bring it in and have it looked at."

"Alright. What else?"

"Do an inventory of the house. See what else may look out of place. Make a list of anyone who may have a grudge against you, or who might want to do you harm. Think about any disgruntled clients. I'll talk with the neighbors tonight to ask whether they saw anything, and I'll check out that diner where the call came from. Let's talk tomorrow and compare notes."

"Fair enough. Say, Eric, it's probably a coincidence, but I did have a threatening episode in court a few weeks ago."

"Katherine Kobs?"

"You heard?"

"Yeah, the chief briefed us on it. He asked us to keep

an eye on her. I plan to question her about her whereabouts tonight, but honestly I think this is a little sophisticated for Katherine. She's more of a slash your tires kind of a gal."

"Thanks for everything tonight, Eric. You're a good man."

"Tell that to my wife," Stone said with a laugh as he stepped outside. "Listen, Jake. It wouldn't be a bad idea to install some beefier locks on these doors, with a new set of keys."

"I'll call on it tomorrow."

"And you might consider sending that dog of yours off to burglar school—or maybe trading him in for a Rottweiler," Stone joked.

"I'll give that some thought. Good night, Eric."

Jake switched off the porch light as he stood in the doorway and watched the detective's sedan disappear into the darkness. On any other night he could have disregarded the ominous clouds and the haunting limbs of the twisted oaks swaying in the wind—but not tonight.

"I've got to call on that damn street light," he muttered.

CHAPTER 7

THE THANKSGIVING LIST

A vintage machine from the days of the carburetor, Henry's old Riviera was somewhat temperamental on cold mornings—a lengthy warm-up was always necessary. As they sat in the car with the motor running, the boys patiently watched for Jonathan's school bus to appear. Without fail, old Edna would wheel the big yellow machine around the corner at precisely 7:22 a.m. If Jonathan wasn't at the end of the driveway ready to board, Edna would linger for only 30 seconds before departing for the next stop. She ran a tight ship.

Jake used his glove to wipe the light coating of frost from the inside of the driver's window then took a sip of strong instant coffee from his travel mug. Jonathan was well rested, scarcely affected by the previous evening. Jake, however, had slept with one eye open—his mind racing all night about their intruder.

He turned up the fan motor on the heater and adjusted the dial on the old A.M. radio. The weatherman was predicting the season's first snowfall on the tail end of the seven-day forecast, possibly as much as four to six inches. Jake sighed as he glanced at the latest blanket of leaves that had accumulated since he last raked two weeks earlier.

After watching Jonathan board the school bus, Jake

began his routine drive to the office. But the journey didn't feel so routine today. Everything appeared to him in a different light. Maple Creek was a small town with a population of fewer than ten thousand people, and Jake personally knew a good share of them. But as he passed each cordial motorist, every friendly store clerk, each congenial neighbor, Jake couldn't help but think to himself, *Could that be my intruder?*

When he arrived at the office, Jake exchanged a quick greeting with Gertie, but headed straight for his desk to prepare for his nine o'clock depositions. He wasn't sure if news of the break-in had circulated back to Gertie yet, but given the morning's tight schedule, he chose to wait until later to discuss the details.

The last swallow of bitter coffee went down harshly. He would have traded his kingdom for a refill, but he knew better than to summon Gertie to prepare a fresh pot. There were only a few things she considered to be outside of her job description, and making coffee was among them.

She had placed a pile of messages squarely in the center of his desk to guarantee his attention. After flipping through the stack of pink slips, he was pleased there were no fresh disasters to tend to. Detective Stone had already called requesting that they meet for a cup of coffee at 2:00 p.m., and of course there was a message from his mother that he should call her as soon as he arrived at the office. Jake was certain she too had slept poorly the night before, and he decided to call her before diving into his morning project.

Their conversation took another twenty-minute bite out of his morning. Margaret had developed several theories during the night as to who might have broken into Jake's home. Jake's head bobbed as he struggled to stay awake through her conspiracy theories.

The Bakke deposition was fruitful, but draining—another three-hour fishing expedition for divorce assets hidden deep in Dr. Gerald R. Bakke's Sea of Deception.

Like many witnesses, Dr. Bakke's answers were evasive and ambiguous. Jake found himself asking five separate questions to obtain one complete answer. But Jake was patient and well-prepared. He calmly interrogated Dr. Bakke, peeling away the layers, one half-truth at a time. Jake knew that a smart witness like Dr. Bakke would avoid being impeached under oath and would be cautious not to offer an answer that was altogether false. It was a matter of extracting each valuable seed of information from the several pounds of worthless chaff.

A careless witness, on the other hand, would compound the lies until no resemblance of the truth remained. Jake usually gave these witnesses several miles of rope that he would later hang them with at the trial.

Even though he was only half awake, Jake cruised through the deposition on autopilot. When it was over, the parties and counsel exchanged their frigid goodbyes and quickly left the building. Jake returned to his office, closed his door, placed his head on his desk, and released a heavy sigh. He was exhausted.

It wasn't just the lack of sleep. He hated the divorce work. It was drenched in malice, each spouse constantly undermining the other. Each playing a never-ending game of hide the assets and manipulate the kids. And the bitterness was mind-boggling. These were people who had once fallen madly in love, had taken a vow to love and cherish each other for eternity, had dreamed of a better life, together.

But once the divorce petition was filed, they looked to the law to fix problems that it was not designed to solve. And the Bakkes were no exception, making no eye contact and exchanging no words other than the occasional profanity spitefully mumbled off the record.

Jake's catnap was cut short by Gertie's voice blasting over the intercom. "Jake, I need to talk with you about a few files when you have a minute."

Jake slowly lifted his head from his desk and squinted to focus on his watch. Almost noon. If he were going to grab lunch before his meeting with Stone, he had to catch his second wind. "Let's do it now, Gertie. I'll be right out," Jake answered through the speaker.

Jake took a few minutes to brief Gertie on the events of the previous evening with the instruction that she and Lyle be on alert for the next few weeks. He then helped

Gertie triage the stack of files and projects that covered her desk and advised her that he was leaving for the afternoon.

Jake had just enough time to grab lunch at home before meeting with Stone at the Cottage. As he pulled into his driveway, he was angered by the uneasiness that overcame him. Never before had he questioned his safety upon returning to his own home.

He was relieved to see Major sitting at attention in the kitchen, calmly peeking through the small window panes of the side door, his tail wagging with anticipation. *At least the dog is on the right side of the door this time*, Jake thought.

He opened the door and patted Major on the head. He would normally turn on the television and assemble his lunch, but he felt another home inspection was required. The locksmith wouldn't arrive until the next day, so whoever had been there the night before could easily have returned for another mystery visit.

Jake had moved the 9mm earlier that morning to an upper kitchen cabinet far above Jonathan's reach. He had considered tucking it into the pocket of his wool overcoat, but decided against carrying it since he didn't have a permit.

After walking through the house, loaded pistol in hand and Labrador by his side, Jake discovered his mother's leftover hot dish on the bottom shelf of the refrigerator. "We have a winner," Jake declared to Major, who was waiting patiently for any morsels that might come his way.

He warmed the concoction in the microwave, lightly buttered a piece of whole wheat bread, and steamed a few stalks of broccoli to give it the appearance of a healthy meal.

Jake didn't exactly classify himself as a health nut, but he did try to eat well. No fried foods, no white flour, very little sodium, no soda, and no bad fats, with the exception of Margaret's all-fat hot dish. After losing his father so young, Jake had a strong desire to stay healthy. And now that Blanca was gone, he was determined to make certain that Jonathan had family in his life for as long as possible. So he ate right, exercised, got plenty of rest, and tried to keep his stress low. He never smoked, but knew he had inhaled his fair share of Henry's second-hand pipe tobacco. And he rarely drank alcohol, with the exception of the six-month bender following Blanca's death.

Jake sat at the kitchen table enjoying his lunch and scribbling his Thanksgiving shopping list. He confirmed each item with Major, who offered very little feedback. This was the first year Margaret had agreed to let Jake handle the shopping and prepare the meal, and he was nervous about living up to her expectations. Jake was relieved that she had agreed to sit on the sidelines this Thanksgiving. Her arthritis and her knee replacement had made it difficult for her to be on her feet for long stretches of time. Although Jake would never admit it, Margaret's cooking wasn't what it used to be. Even her hot dish tasted like it was missing an ingredient or two.

Jake's mind drifted back to the Thanksgiving of his childhood. His mother and his sister Sarah working in the kitchen, talking and laughing for hours as they prepared the feast: roast turkey, homemade stuffing, green bean hot dish, mashed potatoes and gravy, and pumpkin pie.

Margaret always played classical music softly on the phonograph while Henry watched football in the next room, but even he did his fair share. Between yelling at the television, he would prepare and baste the turkey, clean the fresh shrimp, arrange the hors d'oeuvres, pour the wine, and stoke the fire. It was a dirty job, but Henry always soldiered on.

Jake recalled the delightful aromas of savory buttered turkey, hot apple cider, spicy pumpkin pie, pipe tobacco, and burning oak all blending into an unforgettable fragrance.

Jake missed Henry. When he was a boy he thought his parents would live forever. But Jake's losses made him realize that life has its own agenda.

His daydream was interrupted by the vibration of an incoming text on his cell phone. *I'm at the Cottage. You're late, Bishop.*

CHAPTER 8

CRIME & COFFEE

Jake made good time to Maggie's place. He found a parking spot out front, two spaces behind Stone's black sedan. It was difficult to negotiate his large Buick into the compact space, one that was obviously not designed to accommodate a car from the seventies.

He plugged a nickel into the old mechanical parking meter, enough for an hour. Two hours for a dime, 8 hours for a quarter, and a parking ticket was still only two dollars. This always amused Jake after paying the large parking fines in Chicago.

As Jake passed the storefront, he saw Maggie behind the counter talking with an elderly woman. He paused for a moment, watching her through the snowflake decals and Christmas garland partially obscuring his view.

She was smiling a genuine smile, and she hung on the woman's every word, gently nodding in affirmation. She listened more than she spoke, but when she spoke it was soothing. It was a mystery to Jake why she was still single. Perhaps she was just gun shy from her failed marriage, or perhaps Maple Creek simply didn't offer an eligible bachelor worthy of her company.

As the old woman slowly shuffled to her table to join her clan, Jake resumed his stride and made his entrance.

"Good afternoon, Ms. Cooper. Lovely day isn't it?" Jake said. He hadn't seen Maggie since inviting her to Thanksgiving dinner, and he was still struggling to convince himself it was nothing more than an innocent gesture from one friend to another.

"Good afternoon, Mr. Bishop. It *is* a lovely day," Maggie replied. "I understand you had a little excitement at your house last evening?"

"News sure travels fast. Has Detective Stone been interrogating all of the fine citizens of Maple Creek?"

"No, actually I heard about the incident from Delmar Speltz, who ran into Tom Sanders at the hardware store this morning. Tom heard about it from his wife, Mabel. I'm not sure where she picked it up, probably at the beauty parlor. If it helps any, I haven't mentioned it to anyone," Maggie said raising her eyebrows.

"Oh, to live in a small town," Jake said with a grin. "These people haven't had this much excitement since the mayor got picked up for drunk driving last month."

"Well, there was the incident a few weeks ago when Mrs. Johansson got caught with Mr. Frank in the dressing room over at Davidson's Department Store. That blew over—so to speak. You'll be yesterday's news soon enough."

"I suppose you're right. Would you be kind enough to steam me up one of those fabulous skim lattes of yours?"

"My pleasure. Do you have a busy day in court today?"

"Not today. Depositions this morning, off for the afternoon. I left Gertie buried in a pile of paper, so it's probably a good day for me to be out of the office."

"How's my little buddy Jonathan?"

"He's fine. He's under the impression that the break-in was a false alarm, so I hope he doesn't hear otherwise at school today. I didn't think our little incident would make the headlines. I guess it's been a slow news day."

"Did the intruder do any damage?"

"None we're aware of. It's pretty mysterious actually."

"Well I'm sure glad you and Jonathan weren't home; I'd hate for anything to happen to my favorite boys," Maggie said, flashing her large brown eyes as she handed Jake his coffee.

"We'd sure put up a hell of a fight. That burglar would be sorry he ever messed with the Bishop boys."

"I have no doubt about that. You just be careful, Jake."

"I will. Are we still on for Thanksgiving?" Jake asked, trying to change the subject.

"Absolutely, I'm looking forward to it."

"Great. Jonathan is really excited that you're coming."

"Are you sure I won't be imposing?"

"Not a chance. Just make sure you bring those pumpkin bars," Jake said as he drifted away from the counter to join Stone at his isolated table tucked into the little nook near the front door.

Jake could tell by Stone's cagey grin that he had been eavesdropping. "What are you smiling about, Detective? Did you incarcerate another felon today?"

"Thanksgiving dinner, Counselor? When did this happen?"

"Nothing *happened*, it's just dinner. Maggie didn't have anyone to spend the holiday with, and Jonathan and I just thought it would be nice to invite her to join our family," Jake said in a hushed tone.

"I think it's a great idea, Jake. Maggie's a wonderful woman. And you'd be wise to grab her up quick, because once Sonya divorces me, Maggie is next on my list."

"There's not going to be any grabbing, it's just dinner—one casual family dinner. And the only way Sonya is divorcing your ass is if she wins the lottery."

"You know you two are perfect for each other?"

"Who, Sonya and me?"

"Very funny. Maggie is a great catch. Everyone knows she's crazy about you," Stone said, nodding in Maggie's direction.

"So, what did you find out about my home invasion?"

"Alright, changing the subject," Stone said as he reached into the overcoat draped over his chair. "We found this in the bushes not far from your backdoor," he said, handing Jake a large blue nylon dog collar. "I gather it belongs to Major based on the tags."

"That's quite a piece of detective work, Columbo," Jake joked as he examined the collar. "Yeah, this belongs to the guard dog alright," Jake said, sliding the collar back across the table toward Stone.

"You can keep it. We checked it for prints—it's clean. There also appeared to be a lot of foot traffic coming in through the woods behind your home. We didn't get any good footprints, but judging by the trail, I'd guess there had to be at least two of them."

"Do you think they could have been kids?"

"No, not likely. I also found this in the woods." Stone discreetly showed him a clear plastic evidence bag.

"What the hell is that, a hairnet?"

"Close, it's a surgical slipper. The kind surgeons pull over their shoes to keep things sterile. The kind intruders wear when they don't want to leave evidence. It must have fallen out of someone's pocket on the way back through the woods."

Jake sighed as he slowly shook his head. "Did you find anything else?"

"No, we went over everything pretty well. It might have been better if we'd had some snow on the ground. It's hard to get a good footprint with all of the leaves blowing around this time of year, especially in that thicket behind your house."

"What about the neighbors? Were you able to talk with any of them?"

"Mrs. Ellefson heard a dog barking around 4:00 p.m., which may have been when they were trying to get Major back inside the house. I bet they came pretty close to crossing paths with Margaret when she tried to drop off her hot dish the first time."

"Oh, man, don't mention that to her. She's already coming unglued. What about that payphone call; did you check that out?"

"I spoke with the staff at the Roadhouse. The payphone is out in the parking lot. Everyone tells me that it doesn't get much use anymore—most people carry a cell phone these days. But there's a good view from the cash register, and one of the waitresses remembers a light-colored SUV parked by the phone yesterday afternoon sometime after 2:30."

"Did she get a look at the driver?"

"Not a good look. She didn't really have a reason to take notes. All she remembers is that the man on the phone was cute and had black hair. She's also pretty sure there was a female passenger."

"That doesn't narrow it down much, does it?"

"No, but it's better than nothing. I've got a bulletin out on the vehicle, but there are probably dozens in the vicinity that fit that description. It's too bad we don't have part of the plate."

"What about Katherine Kobs? Did anyone talk to her?"

"Yeah, I spoke with her this morning. She's got an alibi with that new mutt of a boyfriend of hers. I wouldn't call it a watertight alibi, especially given this guy's priors. But I seriously doubt she's got the moxie to pull this off, Jake. And if she somehow managed to gain entry into *your* house, she'd probably destroy everything in sight."

"I don't doubt that. I'm sure she took me off her Christmas card list shortly after the trial. So what should I make of all this, Eric? Are we in danger?"

"I don't think so. It's probably just a fluke. Maybe they were looking for something in particular, something of value. You have a pretty nice home for this area, perhaps they thought they might score some fine jewelry, art, cash, who knows? Maybe they've been in ten other houses this week, entirely undetected. It wouldn't surprise me if we get some other home invasion reports in the next few days. Sometimes these guys sweep through a small town like this in a couple of days and move on. My advice is to get the new locks installed. Stay on your toes. Be extra alert for the next couple of weeks. Be mindful of anything that seems out of place. I'll have a cruiser pass by every few hours at night to check things out. Don't be alarmed if you see a spotlight shining around the perimeter of the house."

"Thanks, Eric. I appreciate your hard work on this. I know you're taking good care of us."

"No problem, compadre. You'd do the same for me," Stone said as he stood up and slipped on his heavy coat. "Just one more piece of advice, Jake," Stone said in a serious tone.

"What's that?"

"Whenever someone's concerned about safety, I always recommend the buddy system. I suggest you recruit Maggie to stay with you for a few nights until this thing blows over," Stone said grinning.

"Stick to the detective work, Sherlock," Jake said loudly.

Stone gave a casual wave, his back toward Jake as he

exited the shop.

Jake sat alone, warming his hands on what remained of his latte. His mind drifted from thought to thought, from place to place. He thought about the intruders creeping through his house. He thought about the files piled on Gertie's desk, each one ultimately requiring his attention. He thought about Prof sitting on his front porch, rocking in his chair and sipping scotch from a coffee mug. He thought about the leaves in his yard that needed raking. He thought about the Thanksgiving dinner he had to prepare. And he thought about Blanca and the visits they had made to Maple Creek. He could almost see her sitting across from him—her beautiful black hair flowing gently over her dark shoulders, her bright smile, the depth of her thoughtful brown eyes, the gentle curves of her body. And suddenly he realized something. He was sitting at the very table where he and Blanca had sat. A feeling came over Jake that was eerie yet comforting.

"Can I get you a refill, Jake? Maybe a muffin or a scone?" Maggie asked as she wandered by on her way back from checking on the coffee clutchers in the back room.

"No thanks, Maggie. I'm just going to finish my drink and hit the road. Jonathan and I have Thanksgiving shopping to do."

"Please let me know if you need any help with that," Maggie said as she worked her way back to the front counter where a couple was waiting to order.

"I will, Maggie. Thanks."

Jake watched Maggie work behind the counter as she chatted with her new customers. He wondered what Blanca would think about his Thanksgiving guest list.

CHAPTER 9

WINTER DREAMS

The shrill alarm clock interrupted a most peculiar dream. Jake fumbled for the snooze button after making the groggy decision for another five minutes—a futile attempt to recapture the images.

Although the dream had been vivid, the images that remained were in fragments. As he drifted back to sleep, he remembered being somewhere in the jungle—perhaps the rainforest. He was following Henry and Prof down a pristine and open pathway that wound through dense walls of vegetation. The weather was perfect. The dream was missing the stifling humidity and gigantic insects he had experienced during his conscious visits to the Amazon. He walked briskly, but had a difficult time keeping pace with Henry and Prof, despite their slow and casual gait. He made numerous inquiries of their destination, but Henry only responded with a motion for him to follow.

Every once in a while, a native would step out from the thickness of the jungle, offering him a handful of trinkets. Each trinket appeared old and frail. Not knowing what to make of the artifacts, he gently tucked each one into the weathered leather satchel he carried over his shoulder.

The men came to a fork in the trail. Henry and Prof chose the left fork without hesitation, paying no mind to the alternate route. As he peered down the other path, he noticed a woman in the distance standing quietly in the middle of the pathway. She was wearing a long white gown, a white flower in her hair, her face partially obscured by the dove perched within her hands.

He stared at her, but she appeared not to notice him. There was something haunting and familiar about her—her size, her shape, her stance, the way she tilted her head. When she finally lowered the dove he saw her face. It was Maggie Cooper. He called out to her, and then he called again. She smiled softly but offered no reply. She turned slowly to walk away, still holding the white dove settled comfortably in her hands.

He tried to follow her but was unable to move, as if his feet were in quicksand. He heard a loud whistle and saw Henry directing him to follow the route they had chosen. *Just one last look at Maggie*, he thought. But as he turned, the jungle consumed the pathway, leaving no route but the one Henry and Prof were now advancing.

He walked briskly, trying to catch up, his stride breaking into a run. There were several more natives along the way, several more trinkets. He no longer wasted time examining each article that was handed to him; he simply slid them into his satchel as he struggled to reach his elders.

As the journey progressed, the gap between them grew considerably, and he noticed only one figure in the distance. He could tell by the safari hat that it was Prof who was still blazing the trail, and it was Henry who had disappeared. He looked up and down the trail frantically, but didn't catch sight of Henry in either direction. It was as if he too had been consumed by the jungle.

As the darkness set in, the silhouette of Prof's figure slowly began to fade into the trail. Jake ran as fast as he could, trying to catch up with his remaining guide. When he finally realized he was making no progress, he reduced his pace and came to rest in the pathway. His eyes strained to catch one last glimpse of his leader. Just then, Prof stopped walking, turned back toward him, and raised his canteen in a toast as if preparing to take his last sip of scotch. As he did so, his silhouette slowly vanished, leaving no trace of the great man.

Jake stood in the path catching his breath while the last remaining light of the day disappeared into the jungle. Standing alone in the darkness a feeling of helplessness overcame him. What was the purpose of this journey? Why was he allowed to get so close to his father only to have him stripped away?

Then a sliver of light appeared at the end of the trail, first faint, then growing wider, brighter. It was as if a door were opening into another universe, revealing an intense light to show the way for weary travelers. As he ran toward the light, he realized its source was a doorway to a massive stone structure—a structure that seemed to extend so far into the sky that the jungle stalled at its mighty walls.

As he neared the doorway he slowed his pace, questioning whether he should enter into the brightness.

Then, she appeared—a beautiful figure standing in the doorway, the light spilling around her, illuminating her silhouette. Although he could not see her face, there was no question it was Blanca.

He stood motionless, unable to breath, unable to speak, entirely bewildered. How could it be her? How could Henry and Prof possibly have known where to find her?

He was within steps of the doorway, but as he approached, the door began to close, slowly drawing the light back in. Blanca seemed helpless, standing still, her hands folded gently over her chest. He fought his way toward the fading light, but his body responded slowly, as if walking through the suspended time of another dimension.

The alarm clock wailed once again. He glanced at the bright green numbers—4:05 a.m. His five-minute reprieve was over. *How does Stone talk me into this nonsense every year? A smart man would be sleeping in on a Saturday morning,* he thought.

As he sat on the edge of his bed gathering the strength to drag himself to the shower, the phone rang.

"Hello," his voice cracked.

"Bishop, it's Stone. You up?"

"Unfortunately."

"I'm just making sure you didn't hit that snooze button. That big buck's waitin' for ya!"

"Maybe you should call him to reschedule."

"Come on now, Sunshine. Get yourself together and I'll pick you up in a half hour."

"Alright, Rambo. See you then," Jake said. As he hung up the phone, he peeked through the blinds on his bedroom window. As predicted, the snow had arrived just in time for the deer hunting opener. White flakes were blowing furiously across the yard, mixing in with the fallen leaves. "Marvelous," Jake said. "I don't even like venison."

Stone arrived at 4:30 on the nose. He took his deer hunting seriously. He and Jake had been hunting together since they were in junior high. As a young man, Jake had always looked forward to deer season. It was once a cherished tradition he associated with Thanksgiving. But since Henry passed away, it had become less appealing.

And after Blanca's death, he couldn't see the purpose of taking the life of another creature for sport. But each year, he stocked up on ammunition and supplies, cleaned his rifle, wrapped himself in several layers of blaze orange, and hopped into Stone's old red pickup truck to make the twenty-minute journey to their sacred hunting spot. It was, after all, a tradition.

By the time Jake lugged all of his gear out to his front porch, Stone had already dropped the snowplow on the old four-wheel-drive and made three passes up and down Jake's driveway.

"You gonna shovel my sidewalk, too?" Jake asked as he slid his rifle into the truck behind the passenger seat.

"Not today, pal. Load your ass in here and let's make sure you didn't forget anything."

Being an ex-military man, Stone was meticulous about

his preparation for the hunt. The regimen amused Jake, but he played along.

"Got your license, Jake?"

"Check."

"Ammo?"

"Check."

"Compass?"

"Check."

Stone rattled off his inventory list: knife, license tag, rope, matches, hand warmer, dried fruit, candy bars, rubber gloves, thermos, toilet paper, towels, flashlight, whistle, etc., each item receiving the *obligatory* "Check" from Jake.

One last pass with the snowplow and the great hunters were on their way. Jake chuckled at the irony of exploring an uncharted tropical jungle with Henry and Prof less than an hour ago, and now riding shotgun in a drafty '72 Chevy pickup with a bad defroster, barely able to see the road ahead through the darkness and blowing snow. For a moment Jake contemplated sharing his dream with Stone, but decided to spare himself the analysis that would inevitably follow.

"Where's little Jonathan this morning?" Stone asked, talking loudly over the chorus of sounds emanating from the rickety old truck.

"I dropped him off at Margaret's last night. He loves it over there. She spoils him rotten."

"Well I guess that's what grandmas are for," Stone replied, straining to keep the road in sight. "I was thinking about Henry when I was loading the truck this morning. Remember the huge breakfast he used to cook us before we would hit the trail to go hunting? He must have gotten up at 3:00 a.m. to put that mess together."

"Yea, Henry sure liked his breakfast."

"It's too bad Jonathan won't ever have the chance to hunt with him. He was a real character."

"I don't think Jonathan's going to be much of a hunter. I thought I was going to have to put him through therapy a few months back when I ran over a squirrel with the Buick."

"Well, hunting with a Buick isn't for everyone. He's a great kid. He'll grow up to do great things just like his old man."

"Remind me again about all of the great things I've done?" Jake said with a hint of sarcasm.

"Oh, don't be such a pessimist, Bishop. If Jonathan accomplishes half the things you have, he'll be twice the man I'll ever be," Stone proclaimed.

"Boy, are you full of shit this morning!" Jake laughed. "What is it that I've accomplished?"

"Are you kidding? Traveler of the world, earner of degrees, divorce attorney to the masses, probator of estates, father of Jonathan the Great, hunter of deer, your life is full of accomplishments!"

"You forgot slayer of dragons."

"Oh yea, and slayer of dragons."

"Just keep your eyes on the road, Aristotle," Jake said, shaking his head.

CHAPTER 10

THE HUNT

Daylight was beginning to break as they turned onto the trail that led to the hunting shack, but the heavy snow made it difficult to see. Stone preferred to be in the woods perched on his hunting stand well before the sun came up, but the treacherous drive had slowed their progress. If it were up to Jake, they would have cancelled the trip, but he knew better than to suggest this to the diehard.

Anticipating the rough terrain ahead, Stone stopped the truck and locked in the front axel for the long fire lane to the cabin. Jake could tell that Stone was in a hurry. There were things to do before they could journey into the isolation of the forest. They needed to haul supplies into the cabin, fire up the generator to provide electricity for the lights and portable television, start a fire in the potbellied stove, and take one final inventory of ammunition and supplies while they tucked everything into the numerous pockets and compartments of their hunting gear. Jake knew the drill a little too well.

He enjoyed the ride to the cabin from the main road. The surrounding forest was thick and rugged. There were mostly bluffs and rolling hills blanketed with old hardwood trees and dense patches of evergreen. Since the region was too difficult to develop, it had remained undisturbed for centuries. It was the perfect habitat for wildlife.

Stone bought the hunting rights and access to the cabin from an old-timer who had purchased the property back in the '50s. The old man rarely visited the cabin due to health, and outsiders were strictly prohibited from hunting there. But Stone had special privileges. He had revived the man's only daughter after a car accident off Route 47 and was later bestowed with lifetime hunting rights. Given the diminishing presence of public hunting lands in Crescent County, this was indeed a privilege.

Stone squinted at the blinding white path ahead as he carefully navigated the old truck to keep it on course.

"Jake, doesn't it look like someone's been driving in here recently?"

"I was just about to say the same thing; probably some road hunters who wandered through."

"I suppose. I hope they had four-wheel-drive or I doubt they were able to wander back out." Stone dropped the Chevy down into second gear to make the hill ahead. "Maybe you should load your rifle in case we stir up some deer."

"A loaded rifle in a moving vehicle during deer hunting season? Isn't that a no-no, Detective?" Jake asked, reaching behind the seat to search for his rifle.

"Just don't crack open any beer cans. One moving violation at a time," Stone replied with a grin.

Stone's large hunting boot slammed the brake pedal and the truck came to an abrupt stop, causing the engine in the old beast to stall out. Jake flew into the dashboard before he was able to grab his rifle.

"What happened?" Jake asked, turning around and gathering his senses.

"Look!" Stone pointed to three deer leaping into the woods on the opposite side of the road. "We almost bagged our limit without getting out of the truck."

"Well, at least we could have spent the rest of the day in the cabin watching football," Jake said as he refastened his seatbelt.

"No such luck, pal." Stone replied, firing up the truck. Once again his boot was on the accelerator, the engine roaring.

The truck crested the final hill when the men noticed a steady plume of gray smoke rising from the distant treetops. As they traveled closer, they saw that the smoke was billowing from the chimney of the cabin, *their cabin*, and a white Ford Explorer was parked in the deep snow near the entrance.

"Who do you suppose could be staying at our little abode?" Stone asked, slowly bringing the truck to a stop some 400 yards from the cabin.

"This is a first," Jake said. "Do you think old Eisner is up here hunting?"

"I doubt it. Last time I saw him he was stuck in a wheelchair."

"Maybe he's letting someone else hunt up here this year."

"Maybe, but I think he would've called me."

They watched the smoke roll from the chimney, trying to figure out what to do next.

"I'm going to call the station and get the old man's phone number." Stone pulled his cell phone from his orange hunting vest.

"We didn't get any service up here last year, remember?"

"And we aren't gettin' any this year either," Stone said as he panned the phone around the interior of the truck in search of a signal.

"Well, whatta ya want to do, Detective?"

"Let's go down and introduce ourselves. Maybe they've got breakfast ready for us."

As the old truck rolled closer to the cabin, Jake noticed some movement from behind one of the windows. The tattered curtains were drawn closed, but they could see someone discreetly peering at them through a thin opening near the edge of the window pane.

"Someone's home," Jake said softly.

"I see that."

As the truck came to rest, Stone reached inside his hunting vest and slid the safety strap off of his revolver.

"You're not expecting any trouble, are you?" Jake asked.

"No, just force of habit," Stone replied as he opened his door.

Stone politely knocked on the door as the two men stood on the front porch. Thirty seconds passed with no response, and Stone presented another rhythmic series of knocks on the old fir door.

A dull thud came from inside the cabin, as if someone had stumbled into a piece of furniture.

"Anybody home?" Stone asked loudly with another rap on the door.

"We just stopped by to introduce ourselves," Jake added.

"Who is it? Who's there?" came a female voice from behind the door.

"It's Detective Eric Stone and Jake Bishop—from Maple Creek—we're friends of the owner," Stone answered.

They heard the distinct sound of a hammer cocking back on a firearm. Stone reached into his vest placing his hand on the butt of his revolver while pushing Jake away from the front of the door. "We're not looking for any trouble, Ma'am. We just wanted to talk with you for a minute."

The door creaked open slightly as the woman peered out from the narrow opening. "My husband's not here, but I have a gun. Please leave."

"It's okay, Ma'am. We're not here to harm you. My name is Eric Stone. I'm a police detective," Stone said as he held his credentials in front of the crack in the doorway.

"Why are you here?"

"We're friends of the owner, Eisner Platt. He lets us stay here each year during the deer hunting season."

There was a long pause as the woman processed the information. "I'm sorry, what was your name again?" the woman asked as if stalling for time.

"Stone. Eric Stone and Jake Bishop. We're from Maple Creek. We come here every year. We have permission from old Eisner."

Another long pause. "You're friends of old Eisner? Uncle Eisner?"

"Yes, we're friends of old Uncle Eisner," Stone said as he shrugged his shoulders for Jake's benefit.

"My God, I'm so sorry. I got scared when my husband took off hunting and left me all alone in this old shack," the woman said as she opened the door slightly wider.

"We understand, Ma'am. Did I hear a gun in there?" Stone asked.

"Yes, I'm sorry. I was frightened."

"Would you mind placing the safety on and setting it down? We wouldn't want any accidents."

"Certainly," the woman replied as she leaned the rifle up against a table near the door.

"Do you mind if we come in for a minute?" Stone asked as he glanced through the opening of the door.

"I guess that would be alright," the woman said in a more inviting tone, opening the door enough for them to walk inside.

Jake extended his hand. "Jake Bishop, Ma'am."

"Danielle. Nice to meet you, Mr. Bishop."

"And this is my hunting partner, Detective Stone."

"Nice to meet you, Mr. Stone. How do you men know Uncle Eisner?"

"Uncle Eisner?" Stone asked.

"Yes, he's actually my husband's great uncle on his mom's side," the woman answered casually.

"Your husband is out hunting this morning?"

"Yes. We're actually from Chicago; my husband is going through some mid-life crisis—got some wild idea to take up deer hunting this year. He said Uncle Eisner had the perfect place for it. I'm so sorry if we interfered with your plans; Eisner must have forgotten to contact you."

"That's alright. We live close by. We can change our plans a bit," Stone said in a forgiving tone. "When did you folks get in?"

"Just two nights ago. My husband wanted to come in early to scout out the area. He doesn't have much hunting experience; I hope he doesn't shoot himself out there."

"I'm sure he'll be fine. The area is heavily posted, so we don't get many hunters. And he'll hit a road if he travels a few miles in any direction, so it's hard to get real lost in here," Stone said as he glanced about the room.

"That makes me feel better, Detective. Thank you. Can I offer you gentleman some coffee? I have a pot on the stove."

"No, thank you. We don't want to impose. We really need to get into the woods ourselves. We just wanted to make sure everything was okay here. We're not used to seeing any visitors at the cabin."

Jake could tell Stone was processing the room as he questioned the woman. He had an exceptional ability to interrogate a person without them even being aware of it.

He had a gentle, calming smile, and presented himself with a soothing yet authoritative tone.

"Oh, we're all fine here. Just waiting for the storm to blow over and for my husband to get back from playing in the woods."

"May I ask what your husband's name is in case we run into him in the woods?"

"Jason. His name is Jason." This was the second time the woman neglected to offer a last name.

"How long has he been gone this morning?" Stone asked.

"Probably about an hour now, I suppose."

"Are you folks planning on staying long?"

"I think we're just playing it by ear. I'm hoping Jason will come to his senses so we can head back to Chicago."

"What part of Chicago are you from?"

"We live in a suburb on the north side. We've only been there for a few months. Jason moves around a bit with his job."

"North side, you must live near Tinley Park?"

"Yes, very close."

"What type of work does your husband do?"

"He's a consultant, one of those computer geeks."

"Well, he must find plenty of work in Chicago."

"Yes, he seems to keep very busy."

"I notice you have a sport utility outside. Have you been able to get around alright with all of this snow?"

"Well, we haven't been out much since the storm. I

hope we don't get snowed in here. I think that thing has four-wheel drive, so we should be okay."

"And I see you got the generator running alright?"

"Yes, we were able to start it up just fine. I'm not used to having to start a motor just to get the lights working. We really take things for granted back in the city."

"Yes, I suppose we do. Do you folks need anything else to help you get settled in?"

"No, thank you, gentlemen. I think we've got all the amenities we can handle."

"Well, if you have any trouble, please don't hesitate to track us down. We'll be hunting up the road for the day. Just look for the old red truck," Stone said as he opened the door to leave.

"We will. Thank you, Detective. Mr. Bishop, it was a pleasure meeting you. Happy hunting, gentlemen."

They loaded themselves back into the truck and travelled farther down the fire lane to park.

"So, what do you make of all that?" Jake asked.

"I don't know what to make of that. It doesn't feel right."

"How so?"

"Well, for starters, how does a city girl know how to operate a 30-30 Winchester? And did you notice any hunting gear anywhere in the cabin? I didn't see any, but they seemed to have enough food and water to hold them over for a month."

"Maybe her husband was wearing all of his gear. And

maybe they overestimated their supplies."

"Maybe. Did you notice the black leather coat draped over the coat rack? Looked like a pistol holster sticking out from beneath it. Not the weapon of choice for a computer geek. And the equipment over in the corner behind the rocking chair, I'm almost positive that was a satellite phone. And she mentioned that they hadn't been out much since the storm came in, yet those tire tracks can't be more than an hour old." Stone paused as his mind continued to process the contents of the cabin. "The coffee cups—why were there three coffee cups on the table? And, Jake, you lived in Chicago. What side of Chicago is Tinley Park located?"

"South side."

"Right, the south side. It's no northern suburb, Counselor."

"God, you're paranoid. You've been a gumshoe too long; you should really think about retiring."

"You may be right. But I'm still going to give old Uncle Eisner a call when we get back."

The old Chevy found its way to their landmark clearing. From there the men would go on foot, catching the trail that would lead them deep into the woods. Stone's hunting stand was located half a mile to the northeast of the cabin. He would settle into his secluded stand, a haphazard wooden fortress situated ten feet above ground, constructed mostly of lumber he'd hauled to the site over several years. It was framed by three large trees, with a rickety ladder that provided access from the ground.

Once perched in his stand, sitting comfortably on his portable orange cushion, sipping hot coffee from his thermos and nibbling on snacks, Stone would sit quietly for hours, watching the deer prance through the run below, waiting for his trophy buck. To Stone, it was paradise.

Jake, on the other hand, was not one for sitting motionless for hours, waiting for the perfect buck to saunter by. He preferred to keep moving—walking slowly, quietly through the woods, exploring fresh tracks and droppings in the snow, scanning his surroundings for activity. Stone frequently reminded him how difficult it was to sneak up on a deer in the woods, but to Jake it was more about enjoying the wilderness than it was about dragging a deer home.

Once they entered the woods, the environment seemed more inviting. It was still snowing, but the cover of the forest sheltered the men from the howling wind. The flakes of snow filtered playfully through the dense canopy of trees, looking for a place to land. A good ten inches of snow had already fallen, creating a soft white blanket over the greens and grays of the forest.

The men reached the fork in the trail where they usually parted—Stone heading northeast toward his deer stand, and Jake venturing west for his three-mile circle through the forest, a route that ultimately returned him to the truck.

"Good luck, Jake. And remember, fire off three quick shots if you get into any trouble," Stone said.

"Yeah, I'll throw a few rounds over your head just to

make sure you're still awake over there," Jake said as he checked the bearing on his compass.

"If I don't see you sooner, why don't we meet back at the truck around noon and we can head in for some lunch."

"It's a deal," Jake said as he tucked his compass back into his pocket. "Be careful out here, Eric; visibility is still pretty rough."

"Are you afraid I'm going to shoot you, Bishop?

"No, just don't shoot any Bambis."

"Not today. Today I bring home the trophy," Stone said as he began trudging through the snow.

As the blaze orange figures journeyed in opposite directions, it wasn't long before they drifted from each other's sight, drowned out by the snow that continued to fall.

Jake stepped stealthily as he worked his way through the forest, stopping periodically to check his compass and to scan the landscape for any signs of movement.

Nearly an hour of hunting produced no signs of the elusive whitetail. A fresh snow was usually helpful to reveal any recent signs of deer in the area, but it was snowing so heavily that tracks were quickly covered.

In need of a rest, Jake found a fallen tree and brushed off an area of snow just wide enough to sit on. He propped his rifle against a sturdy branch and released a big sigh as he sat squarely on the oak. *Surely Stone is settled on his stand by now,* Jake thought. He was probably on his second cup of coffee and munching on his candy bar or dried fruit.

Jake never understood how Stone was able to bag a deer every year considering the noises and smells that emanated from his tree stand.

As Jake sat against the tree gazing into the ravine just below him, he noticed the snow tapering off. His visibility was improving and the wind was noticeably calmer. The change in the weather brought a sense of serenity to the woods. A peaceful feeling came over Jake as he focused on the silence. No phones, no clients, no family, no worries. Just silence. This was what Jake searched for each year. This was his prey—the pure absence of chaos.

Jake's tranquility was interrupted by a rustling sound echoing from a nearby grove of poplars. At first he thought it might be a squirrel stirring in the fallen leaves, but realized the fresh blanket of snow was too thick. The noise became louder and noticeably closer, and Jake's heart began to pound as he tried to identify it.

Perhaps Stone became restless on his tree stand and decided to go for a stroll, Jake thought. Or maybe it was the new tenant from the cabin out wandering about. But the sound was unlike that of a person hiking through the woods. It was more erratic and untamed. Jake had heard this sound before; it was the sound of a large animal thrashing through dense branches.

As the beast approached, Jake could hear the muffled pounding of its hoofs cutting through the snow and connecting with the ground. It was close now, so close that he could see the branches moving on the edge of the thicket. Then suddenly the thrashing stopped and the animal emerged into the clearing.

It was a magnificent sight. The enormity of the animal was astonishing. The massive buck stood motionless, cautiously searching for obstacles that might impede his safe passage across the clearing. He held his head high and proud, using little effort to buttress the large multi-tined rack he wore like a barbaric crown. Jake could see breath billow from its snout as it purged warm air from its lungs.

Jake was not sure whether the buck had spotted him yet and debated whether he should risk reaching for his rifle. It appeared to be panning the clearing for activity, paying no mind to Jake who was nicely camouflaged by dense branches.

Jake reached for his rifle at a glacial pace. Thirty seconds later the butt of the rifle was secure on his shoulder and the crosshairs of the scope were fixed directly over the neck of his prey. Then it happened—eye contact. The beast's eyes were fixed directly on Jake.

Jake could see right into its eyes. He could see every bulging muscle of the animal's enormous neck and shoulders. The buck was clearly an elder, graying around the face and snout. *People hunt for years and never get a chance to shoot a deer this size. Stone will be green with envy,* Jake thought.

Jake slowly situated the crosshairs of his scope just below and behind the right shoulder blade of the animal, lining up a perfect heart shot. He quietly clicked the safety off and took a deep breath to steady his rifle. The mighty buck made no effort to break for the woods behind him.

By the time Jake found his way back to the fire lane, Stone was already sitting in the truck with the engine running. He was stripped down to his vest, with a beer in one hand and beef jerky in the other. He was yelling at the radio as he listened to the football game. Jake just shook his head as he opened the passenger door and loaded his gear into the truck.

"Any luck, Eric?" Jake asked.

"Nothin'. Too much damn snow. How about you, did you see anything?" Stone asked with enthusiasm.

"Not a damn thing," Jake said with a smile. "Let's go grab some lunch."

CHAPTER 11

SISTER SARAH

Unlike most Monday mornings, this morning found Jake unusually eager to spring out of bed and begin his week. His calendar was clear, Jonathan was home from Margaret's house, the storm had moved out, the roads were plowed, and he would pick up his sister at the airport in less than two hours.

Although Jake kept in touch with Sarah by telephone, he hadn't seen her in person for nearly three years. After completing medical school and a demanding residency, Sarah settled into a small family practice near San Diego. She married a real estate developer named Bud Wilcox, whom Jake secretly disliked from day one. No one was surprised when the two-year marriage disintegrated after Sarah caught Bud putting in some overtime with his twenty-six-year-old assistant in the back of his Escalade. The family *was* a bit dumbfounded, however, when Sarah moved in with a lesbian doctor from her practice, whom she introduced to Margaret the following Christmas as her partner, Denise. Margaret was devastated when Jake later explained to her that the title of *partner* did not mean that Sarah had advanced to partnership status at the clinic.

Tensions remained high between mother and daughter during the years that followed Sarah's Christmas outing.

They rarely spoke over the phone. Margaret was incapable of having a conversation with Sarah without asking, "So, have you met any nice men lately?" or "Do you know whose son I ran into the other day?"

Margaret disregarded Sarah's lifestyle as if it were a misguided choice, which was devastating to Sarah given how close they had been. Jake hoped the upcoming Thanksgiving would be a small step forward toward their reunion.

The majestic oaks at Jake's house were covered in snow like a winter wonderland. Another four inches had fallen since Stone plowed the driveway, and Jake resolved to shovel again after he and Jonathan returned from the airport. He opened the garage door and walked by the Riviera, gently patting his hand along its vinyl roof.

"Sorry, old girl. Looks like it's time to tuck you in for the winter. We'll get you covered up this weekend."

"Do you really think the Riviera can hear you, Dad?" Jonathan asked with skepticism.

"Probably not, pal. But I know Grandpa Henry is watching over his old car, and I've got to make sure he knows I'm treating her right."

Jonathan smiled and nodded, trying to decide how much credibility to lend to his father's explanation.

Next to the Riviera sat Jake's Jeep, a white CJ he'd cobbled together over the years.

Jake unclamped the charger he'd hooked up to the battery the night before, then wondered about the odds of firing up his winter chariot after its three-month nap. But the in-line six popped off on the second try and roared with anticipation as a blast of gray smoke purged from the tailpipe. "Purrs like a kitten," Jake proclaimed.

As he backed the Jeep out of the garage his cell phone rang. It was a call from Eric Stone.

"Hello, Detective. How are you this fine morning?"

"Well, aren't we in a good mood today? Finally hook up with that Cooper girl last night?"

"Boy are you way off base. Give it a rest already, Cupid."

"Alright, Counselor. I just wanted to let you know that I tried to call old Eisner this morning. I didn't get an answer. I'll stop by his place later today to ask him about his new tenants up at the cabin."

"Don't go out of your way, Kojak. I'm sure everything's legit. It's not worth a trip all the way up to Brinkley. Just give him a call later this week when you get a chance."

"You're probably right. I'm sure he's just dozed off in the easy chair and can't hear the phone. What are you up to this morning?"

"Jonathan and I are on our way to the airport to pick up Sarah."

"Oh, that's right. I forgot she was coming into town. Make sure to have her stop by to say hello. We can catch up."

"She's a lesbian now, you know. You can forget about firing up that motor again. In fact, she told me that it was a dissatisfying experience with an old high school boyfriend that shifted her over to the other team. Some guy by the name of Stone."

"Ah, funny man, Bishop. You'd better save a little of that wit for the courtroom."

"Dad, what's a lesbian?" Jonathan interjected from the passenger seat.

"I've got to run, Detective. I'll call you later."

"Good luck with that one, smart ass. Talk to you soon."

With Jonathan on his shoulders Jake scanned the crowd at the baggage terminal, looking for a tall blonde with a bright smile and a confident stride.

"There she is, Dad. Hi, Sarah, over here!" Jonathan yelled as he waved frantically.

Sarah's face lit up and her eyes filled with tears as she stopped in the crowd to admire them. Jonathan had grown quite a bit since the last time she saw him. They wouldn't recognize each other if it weren't for the photos they had been exchanging by e-mail.

Jake grinned with adoration as he walked slowly toward his only sibling.

"God it's great to see you, Sarah," he said as he lowered Jonathan down to his side.

"You too, Jacob. You look great," she replied, pulling the boys in for a family hug.

"Do you remember this young man?"

“I know this man. This is Jonathan the Great, heir to the Bishop throne.”

“Hi, Aunt Sarah. I’m glad you’re here to stay with us.”

“I’m glad too, Jonathan. I’ve really missed you boys. You’re so big I couldn’t tell you apart from your father.”

“He’s the big one,” Jonathan said in a serious tone.

“Let’s get your bags, Sarah. We’ll catch up on the way home,” Jake said as he put his arm around his sister and walked her toward the baggage carousel.

By some stroke of luck Sarah’s bags were among the first down the chute, and the Bishop family quickly departed the Dane County Regional Airport and found themselves motoring down Highway 12.

“Is the Lexus in the shop?” Sarah asked sarcastically as she glanced around the Jeep’s ragged interior.

“Nope. I just retired the Riviera for the winter and fired up the faithful steed.”

“Riviera? My God, Jake. You’re not still driving around in that old thing? I thought the Smithsonian would have called for it by now.”

“So, have you met any nice men lately?” Jake asked with a smile.

“Ah, touché, Jacob. Alright, no old car jokes. So how is Mom anyway?”

“Well, let’s see—she’s ornery, cantankerous, opinionated, stubborn, meddling, and feisty.”

“Hasn’t changed much, huh?”

“No, not much.”

"Are you sure you don't mind me staying with you boys for a week? I really don't want to impose."

"It's not an imposition, Sarah. We've been eager for you to arrive. We've got plenty of room. Feel free to stay as long as you want."

"Thanks, Jake. You know I love Mom, but I don't think I could handle her in a mega dose right now."

"I understand. Believe me, I understand."

The two siblings joyfully reminisced as they rattled down the highway, Jonathan in the backseat carefully listening to every word and curiously studying Sarah's profile.

"Can you come live with us forever, Aunt Sarah?" Jonathan interjected during a pause in the conversation.

"Nothing would please me more, Jonathan. But unfortunately I'll have to return to my work."

"To your doctor work?"

"Yes, to my doctor work."

"What do you do there?"

"I help sick people—or at least I try to help them."

"And sick kids?"

"Yes, I also help sick kids. Why, are you sick?"

"No, not today. But we have sick kids at our school all the time. You should probably move back to Maple Creek so you can help them," Jonathan said with a tone of finality.

"I would love that, Jonathan. But I'm not sure I could take all of this snow again," she said, pointing to the white landscape passing by outside. "Perhaps you and your father should move to California and live by the ocean with me."

"Can we, Dad? Can we move to California? We could bring Grandma Margaret, and I could go to school there!" Jonathan rattled off in one breath.

"No, pal. It's not that simple to move across the country. I have a law office to run, and I don't think you're going to convince Grandma Margaret to move to California."

"God I hope not," Sarah said under her breath through a smile.

Jonathan's enthusiasm to move closer to Sarah took Jake by surprise. The two had bonded over the phone, and Jonathan was always eager to receive the e-mails, pictures and presents Sarah would send along. But Jake suspected that Jonathan's relocation plans had less to do with California, and more to do with his desire to have someone like a mother in his life.

CHAPTER 12

THE HOLIDAY

Daylight filtered through the window of the second-story guest room where Sarah was sleeping. She opened her eyes slowly and tried to focus on the thick layer of frost bordering the window pane. She soon realized she was not waking up in San Diego.

At the foot of the bed she noticed a mahogany dresser from her childhood. It was covered with photographs Jake had collected over the years—photos of their family vacations, photos of Jake's athletic and academic accomplishments, and photos of his adventures in Peru.

The most touching photos were displayed in the middle of the dresser, an obvious memorial to Blanca—the unveiling of a beautiful bride, a newborn boy cradled in his mother's arms, and the soft image of two young lovers enjoying a Peruvian sunset.

Sarah wiped the moisture from her eyes and walked over to the bedroom window. She stretched her arms above her head as she gazed out on the winter morning. It was nice to be home.

She slipped on her bathrobe and headed for the shower. *No time to waste*, she thought. They would soon be leaving for Margaret's house, and she didn't want to keep the boys waiting.

Jonathan sat contently in the back of the Jeep with Major as Jake meandered through downtown giving Sarah a tour of Maple Creek. Jake wanted to show her how the town had changed since her last trip home. He showed her the new bank on the edge of town, a satellite branch that had strayed out from its large headquarters in Madison. He showed her the quaint new bistro, which he declared to have the best Reuben sandwich this side of Chicago, the vacant Mexican restaurant that had come and gone in six months, the new cell phone store, and, of course, the new green awnings their uncle had installed on the bank.

The town hadn't really changed much. Maple Creek was still far enough away from the mainstream, discouraging most entrepreneurs from venturing their capital there.

Jake's thirty-minute tour ended in Margaret's driveway where they unloaded the large shipment of groceries and Thanksgiving fixings that were packed tightly into the back of the Jeep.

As the three young Bishops carefully carried their supplies across the snow-packed driveway, the front door opened and Margaret appeared. She stood motionless with her hands cupped over her mouth and tears welling in her eyes. It had been three years since she'd seen her children together.

Jake smiled as he entered the home and heard Margaret's classical music playing softly on the old phonograph, competing with the sound of a football game she had randomly tuned to on the television.

They exchanged tearful hugs and kisses, and in short order the holiday was underway. Jonathan taped his paper turkey, *Henry*, proudly on the refrigerator, Jake started a fire in the fireplace, Sarah brewed the hot apple cider, and before he knew it Jake was multitasking between yelling at the television, basting the turkey, cleaning the fresh shrimp, arranging the hors d'oeuvres, pouring the wine, and stoking the fire.

As the smells of the meal wafted throughout the house, Jake paused to inhale a large dose of the heavenly aroma. He identified the smell of the butter and spices roasting with the savory turkey, the cinnamon from the pot of hot apple cider, the fresh apple pie baking in Margaret's backup oven, and the smoke drifting from the oak logs crackling in the fireplace. Something was missing, though, and after a few seconds of careful reflection, Jake identified the missing component: Henry's pipe.

Jake couldn't hear the doorbell over the football game, and before he realized she was there, Jonathan and Major had escorted Maggie into the kitchen with her fresh batch of pumpkin bars. As Maggie greeted Sarah and Margaret in the kitchen, Jake caught the commotion from the corner of his eye and quickly lost interest in the field position of Oklahoma State.

Maggie was stunning. *She's a natural beauty,* Jake thought. Her subtle makeup accentuated her delicate features and large brown eyes. Her thick, dark hair fell perfectly on her shoulders and bounced as she turned her head to follow the conversation. She wore a beautiful cashmere blouse that rested contently on her hips, a loosely woven vest buttoned just tightly enough to emphasize her small waist, and a brilliant sterling necklace that shimmered in the sunlight from the nearby window. Once again Jake wondered what he was getting himself into. He joined them in the kitchen and gave Maggie a hug and a quick peck on the cheek.

When the thermometer in the turkey finally hit its magic number, Jake declared the bird cooked to perfection. Sarah broke out Margaret's fine china and arranged the delicacies of the great feast on the table around an exquisite bouquet of flowers.

Jake carved the twenty-pound fowl and carefully placed it on the silver platter that Henry purchased for Margaret for their twenty-fifth anniversary. Margaret turned off the football game in the living room and adjusted the phonograph to provide the desired level of background music.

Since Henry's passing, Margaret had been the one to say grace at all of the holiday meals. Her prayer was brief, but earnest. There was a long silence at the end of the prayer before Margaret raised her head, which Jake knew was her silent plea to God to bless their wayward souls.

When Jake was certain that the blessing of the meal had concluded, he stood and raised his glass. "I'd like to offer a toast if I may."

His gracious audience readied their glasses and smiled with anticipation.

"Here's to another Thanksgiving with a wonderful mother; here's to a sister's homecoming, long overdue; here's to the best son a father could ask for; and here's to a very special friend who I'm thankful could share this day with us. Cheers, everyone!"

"Cheers!"

As the wine glasses worked their way about the table, clanking against one another with a melodic ringing, Jake's glass met Maggie's and they fixed their eyes on each other. It was as if they were having the exact same thought—as if their souls had connected. Jake finally broke the spell by taking a sip from his glass. It was becoming difficult for him to dismiss the chemistry developing between them.

Sarah lightened the moment with a joke about Jonathan's appetite, and soon the food was being passed around the table. The meal was delicious—the company, delightful. The holiday had turned out to be picture perfect.

As the night progressed, Sarah and Jake playfully quarreled over conflicting versions of their childhood antics. Maggie cautiously resurrected Jake's little-known history from high school, which made his family howl with laughter. And Jonathan giggled all night long as he soaked in the stories and slipped scraps of turkey to Major beneath the table.

For the first time since Blanca's death, Jake let his guard down enough to take in simple pleasures, and to enjoy the company of his family and a beautiful woman. As he sat at the table sipping on a cup of Maggie's freshly brewed coffee and savoring the last bite of his pumpkin bar, Jake tried to recall the last time he felt so happy, so content. *This day feels complete,* he thought. Sarah had blended in as if she had never left, Jonathan was happier than ever with new family, Margaret had gone nearly eight hours without criticizing him or Sarah, and Maggie seemed to be genuinely enjoying her Thanksgiving with the Bishops. It was almost too perfect.

The fire was on its final breath as Sarah dried the last dish and handed it to Jonathan to place in the cupboard. Margaret was already napping in her rocking chair, and Jake and Maggie made their way to the front porch to say goodnight.

"As usual, those were some delicious pumpkin bars, Ms. Cooper," Jake offered with a smile.

"I'm glad you liked them, Mr. Bishop. There's plenty more where those came from."

They stood face to face in the dim moonlight, fighting off the chill of the November air. Maggie's hands were occupied with the leftovers Margaret had packaged up for her, along with the nearly empty pan of pumpkin bars. Jake gently wrapped Maggie's scarf tighter around her neck and folded her collar up to block out the wind.

"Thank you for coming tonight, Maggie. Everyone

loved seeing you."

"What about you, Jake. Did you love seeing me?"

"Especially me. I'm really glad you came."

"I had a wonderful time, Jake. It's hard not having family nearby during the holidays."

"You always have a family here—you know that."

Maggie leaned slightly closer to Jake and looked up into his eyes. "Is that what we are, Jake, family?" she asked softly.

"I like you, Maggie, very much. But you know it's complicated with me."

"Does it have to be complicated?"

"I don't think I know another way. I know she's gone, but I just can't let her go. It still feels like it was just yesterday."

"She'll always be with you, Jake. You see her every time you look into Jonathan's eyes. But that doesn't have to mean you can't be happy."

"We'd have to move slow, Maggie, really slow. And that's not fair to you."

Maggie leaned in and kissed Jake gently on the lips. "Don't worry about me, Mr. Bishop. I'm a big girl. I'll see you tomorrow for your latte."

Jake watched from the porch as Maggie's taillights faded into the darkness. As he sat on the step, trying to revive himself from the large holiday feast, his cell phone rang. It was Addie Albright, Prof's wife. The news was not good.

CHAPTER 13

GOODBYE, PROFESSOR ALBRIGHT

Prof had left strict instructions with Addie about his funeral—no wake, no long service, no open casket. He despised the thought of the townspeople lining up to gawk at his lifeless body, shuffling past one by one to critique his appearance. He was also not fond of the idea of being eternally entombed inside of a wooden box and planted below the surface of the earth. Shortly before his death, Prof made Addie promise to honor his request to be cremated.

Prof was a spiritual man, but not particularly religious. Jonathan Albright questioned the foundation of organized religion and the roots of the ceremonial rituals and doctrine that fed it. He found greater intrigue in examining the ancient religions of the world.

Addie was determined to hold some form of memorial service for her beloved husband. Prof was a great man of many accomplishments, and one who had never neglected his roots in Maple Creek. And when his failing health forced him to retire from the large firm in the big city, Prof could think of nowhere else he would rather live out his last days.

Given his aversion to traditional funeral ceremonies, Addie decided to hold a brief memorial service somewhere close to town. Jake suggested they hold the gathering at the Majestic Manor, a rustic but impressive banquet hall a few miles outside of town. Holding it there was a bit unconventional, but then again, so was Prof.

Despite Prof's lack of religious affiliation, the gods gave him a beautiful, crisp December day to honor his memory. The sky was a brilliant blue and the clouds were scarce. Jake insisted on picking up Addie at the cabin and driving her to the gathering. He borrowed his aunt's shiny black Lincoln Towncar, dusted off his nicest black trial suit, and polished up his wingtips.

As he stood at the bathroom vanity adjusting his silk tie, Jake paused to look at the man staring back in the mirror. Loneliness suddenly overcame him. He couldn't ignore the finality of death—first his father, then Blanca, now Prof. Jake once believed in the afterlife, clinging to the hope that he would reunite with his loved ones. But now—now he just regretted that he hadn't taken one more opportunity to say goodbye to his dear friend.

Jake maneuvered the Towncar down the long gravel driveway that snaked through the woods to the Majestic Manor. He and Addie were astonished by the cars that lined both sides of the road and filled the two sizable parking lots in the woods nearby. Most of the license plates were from Illinois and Wisconsin, but some were from as far away as Michigan and Pennsylvania. Prof had a large circle of friends and colleagues, and word traveled quickly about his passing. There were half a dozen foreign luxury cars with Illinois plates, which Jake assumed belonged to the lawyers from the old firm.

Jake had been to the lodge for a wedding two years earlier, but he had forgotten just how beautiful it was inside. The great room comfortably held two hundred guests and was centered around an extraordinary fieldstone fireplace that towered clear to the top of the ceiling. The entire facility was an unlikely but pleasing combination of rustic charm and stately elegance.

Prof's niece, Amanda Albright, had made all of the arrangements for the memorial. As a young girl, Amanda had been very close to Prof and Addie. Her mother had battled mental illness for several years and ultimately took her own life when Amanda was only seven. Her father, Prof's brother, was a sales representative for a pharmaceutical company, and his travels frequently took him away from home. Amanda spent most of her youth living with Prof and Addie in Chicago.

Amanda was now an oral surgeon practicing in Milwaukee, and she spared no expense to honor the gentle man who had taken her in. The banquet tables were wrapped in soft white linen and adorned with fresh bouquets of flowers and silver platters.

A tribute table displayed the memorabilia that honored the accomplishments of the great Professor Albright—photos of him with politicians and celebrities, framed newspaper clippings of his noteworthy trials and charity work, letters of thanks and accommodation he had received, clippings of stories from the *Maple Creek Gazette* covering his many expeditions to Peru and other faraway places, and a few precious artifacts he had treasured over the years. Addie contemplated displaying the urn that housed her husband's ashes, but she knew he would not approve.

The most touching item on the table was a letter Prof had written just four weeks earlier, addressed to his friends, family, and colleagues, acknowledging the value and importance of their friendship. Jake made it halfway through the first paragraph before he lost his composure and decided to revisit the letter once everyone had left.

Hanging just above the memorial was a large projection screen showing a sequence of colorful images from Prof's life. Although the slide presentation was emotionally stirring, Jake was intrigued by many of the images. Amanda had a full compilation of photos chronicling Prof's life, each beautifully restored and converted into a crisp digital image. As the pictures cycled through the history of the Professor, from his simple beginnings as a young boy, to his impressive yet humble life as a grown man, one could not help but appreciate just how great his accomplishments had been. Jake was particularly touched by the images Amanda had included of Prof posing with him, Blanca, and Jonathan.

If it weren't for the slide presentation and the touching display of mementos, the gathering would have more closely resembled a formal cocktail party than a memorial. The guests mingled as they nibbled on the exquisite assortment of food and sipped from the fine wine Amanda had shipped in. A generous fire was dancing in the fireplace, and the old Bobby Darin song, "Beyond the Sea," was pulsing from the live band, also shipped in from Chicago.

As Jake worked his way through the crowd to greet the faces of his past, he heard friendly chatter as they compared their favorite Prof stories. Jake had heard most of the tales before, but never grew tired of revisiting them. He wondered if people would pay such heartfelt tribute to him when he passed—if they would come from distant places to exchange salutations and testimonials about what a generous and accomplished man he was. *Not likely,* he thought.

The crowd grew quickly, and it was becoming a sea of dark suits and black dresses. Jake settled in at the bar and panned the room in search of his family. Sarah planned to chauffeur Margaret and Jonathan, and had graciously invited Maggie.

Jake was having no success finding them, but he did catch Amanda Albright summoning him from across the room.

Amanda explained that although she had plenty to say, she would love to share the chance to honor her uncle. It would mean a lot to her if Jake could address the guests. After all, these were his people—the lawyers, judges, academics, philanthropists, entrepreneurs, and dignitaries whom he and Prof had cultivated in Chicago. Though it was hard to argue with her, Jake was less than enthused about the last-minute request.

His first inclination was to scurry off to a quiet place to prepare an acceptable draft of his speech. After all, the crowd was full of important people, and they would be expecting an impressive address. But then Jake thought about Prof, who most certainly would not approve of a long-winded flattering tribute, much less the fuss that had already been assembled in his honor. *Just wing it,* Jake thought.

The band wound down its first set, and the musicians began stirring to take their first break. Jake approached the lead singer about taking the stage, assuring him that he would be brief. The man handed Jake the microphone, appearing to have little concern about when he might get it back.

Jake took a deep breath and blew into the microphone a few times to make sure it was working.

"Can I have your attention, everyone?" The crowd focused on the head of the room.

"Thank you all for coming. My name is Jake Bishop; many of you know me from the firm in Chicago. Others know me as the local boy from Maple Creek. I've been asked to say a few words in honor of our dear friend, Prof."

As Jake addressed the crowd, he noticed Maggie and his family near the fireplace. She was gazing at him with her glistening eyes and gentle smile.

"First of all, I'd like to thank Amanda Albright, Prof's niece, for her generosity in arranging everything, for providing all of the food, spirits, and entertainment we're enjoying here today. Prof was like a surrogate father to Amanda as a child, and later to me when my own dad passed away. So we've not only lost a great friend, Amanda and I have lost a parent." The crowd fell silent.

"I won't take up a lot of your time. We all know how much Prof hated a fuss. Besides, it would be purely impossible to sum up a man like Prof in such a brief time.

"He touched each and every one of us in his own special way. That's the kind of man he was—generous with his time, generous with his love, generous with his knowledge. As I've mingled among the crowd, I've been listening to the stories many of you have been sharing. There's no doubt about it, Prof was quite a character. He was dynamic, he was powerful, he was charismatic, he was honorable, and at times he was quite a comedian. For better, or for worse, they broke the mold when they created the Professor.

"He loved his family, he loved the law, he loved the quest for knowledge, he loved diversity, he loved the ancients, he loved his scotch, and he loved each and every person in this room. Prof once told me that a wealthy man counted his fortune by the number of true friends he'd made, not the sum of money he managed to accumulate in the bank. By either standard, Prof was certainly a very wealthy man.

"Prof was blessed with so many true friends. He was able to relate to people at every level. He was not easily intimidated, and he never got caught up in politics. It didn't matter if he was dealing with a high-powered defense attorney, a foreign diplomat, a tribesman in a third-world country, or the girl behind the counter at the Kwiki-Mart. Prof treated everyone with the same degree of respect.

"When Prof learned of his illness, I never once heard him complain about getting short-changed on life. He never questioned why he was getting cheated out of the years he should have had with his wonderful wife Addie. He never complained about the things he would never get a chance to do. He spent most of his final days reminiscing about the wonderful people he had met, the places he had been, and the things he had seen."

As Jake paid tribute to his beloved mentor, the pictures from Amanda's slideshow rotated on the screen behind him, each one slowly fading away to make room for the next.

Jake raised his glass to the heavens to complete his eulogy. "Prof, wherever you are, we hope you can hear us. We consider ourselves far wealthier people for having known you. We'll never, ever forget how you touched our lives, and we'll miss you more than you'll ever know. Salute!"

"Salute!" came the ardent response from the crowd.

As Jake stepped down and the guests began speaking softly among themselves again, Addie Albright appeared in front of Jake with moist eyes and an approving smile.

"He was so proud of you, you know," she said.

"I can't believe he's gone, Addie," Jake said as he gently embraced her.

"It's hard to imagine the world without him, isn't it?"

"What will you do now?" Jake asked. "Will you go back to Chicago?"

"No, I think I'll stay at the cabin for awhile. It's peaceful there. I never thought I'd be much of a country girl, but it's growing on me."

"Why don't you come stay with Jonathan and me for a few days? You could spend some time with Sarah before she heads back to California."

"Thanks for the offer, Jake, but I could use some time alone to sort things out. I need to think about the next chapter in my life. I've always been an independent woman you know, but that man was everything to me. We logged a lot of miles together. I'm not sure where I go from here."

"I'd like to tell you that it gets easier, Addie, but I'm not sure I'd be telling you the truth. Not a day goes by that I don't think about Blanca. People like Prof and Blanca are extraordinary. They don't just come along every day."

"They were cut from the same cloth, you know," Addie replied. "He absolutely adored her. If there's an afterlife, I know they're chatting together right now, picking up right where they left off, catching up on their old scholarly debates about the ancients."

"I'm sure of it," Jake said softly, nodding in affirmation.

"Listen, Jake. Your Uncle Benjamin has offered to drive me home tonight. I need to mingle with some of these folks; they've come a long way and it's been quite a while since I've spoken with most of them. You go visit with your family and that cute little Cooper girl. I'll catch up with you later."

"Fair enough," Jake said as he kissed Addie on the cheek. "Just holler if you need anything, Addie."

"Oh, that reminds me, Jake. Can I stop by your office next week so we can go downstairs to Uncle Benjamin's bank and clean out Prof's safe-deposit box?"

"There's no rush, Addie. You can take some time to gather your thoughts before we start dealing with his estate."

"I know that. But I have to come into town anyway, and I'd like to make sure the Professor doesn't have any surprises locked away in that little bank box of his. He was always a bit mysterious about those trips to the bank, you know," Addie said in a light, yet dubious tone.

"Alright, we'll get together soon. Give Gertie a call before you come—she'll make sure my calendar is clear."

"Thanks, dear," Addie said as she turned toward the crowd to accept the condolences from her guests.

Jake detoured to the bar before resuming the search for his family. As the bartender refilled his glass, the band started into its next set with "I've Got the World On a String."

"Nice speech, Counselor," came a voice from behind.

"Thank you, Detective."

"I've got to tell you, this is the strangest damn memorial I've ever been to," Stone replied.

"Well, then it ought to be quite memorable for you—we'll call it a success."

As the two men leaned against the bar, quietly looking

out over the crowd, they both smiled. Some of the guests had actually begun dancing.

CHAPTER 14

EMPTYING THE BUCKET

Nearly a week had passed since Prof's memorial service. Most of the Thanksgiving leftovers had been consumed, and the good people of Maple Creek were already thinking about Christmas. While they went about their business planning for the holiday, shopping about town, congregating at church, and gathering for brunch, Katherine Kobs logged her time at the Rusty Bucket waiting tables, schlepping beer, warding off advances, and consoling disheartened patrons.

It was midnight, and the streets had turned cold and dark. After an arduous Sunday shift, Katherine was eager to close down the bar. Unbeknownst to her boss, this would be her last closing at the Bucket. The last few customers were slipping out the door, meandering home to their empty lives.

One customer, however, remained as Katherine quietly locked the front doors. Martin Vance, her new boyfriend, sat in a dark corner of the bar and sipped from his warm mug of beer as he watched Katherine perform her closing ritual. She turned off the overhead lights, then switched off the neon beer signs that had been glowing in the lingering cigarette smoke. She unplugged the jukebox and closed the mini-blinds covering the large bay windows facing the street. To the cars passing by, the Bucket appeared empty.

The dishwasher and the cook had both retired for the evening—the kitchen was clean, the garbage had been hauled to the alley dumpster, and the bathrooms had been sanitized. Katherine grabbed a broom and began sweeping the wood floors; everything had to appear normal.

Katherine finished cleaning at 1:30 a.m., when she and Marty spent the next 45 minutes trying out his new blend of weed and three new sexual positions in the large family booth in the corner.

By 2:15, Katherine decided the streets had sufficiently quieted and that it was time to set their plan in motion. As Marty stood watch near the front window, peeking through the mini-blinds for unwelcome headlights, Katherine emptied the contents of the register into her blue vinyl satchel. She left the checks and loose coins behind, but grabbed all the paper money.

Next was the floor safe, which was fatter with cash than usual. This was partly due to a prosperous weekend of beer-swilling football patrons, and partly due to Katherine "forgetting" to make the bank run the previous Friday.

Her hands shook as she clutched each wad of money, stuffing it by the handful into her travel bag. It was a new high for Katherine. Her heart was pounding like a drum, each beat echoing through her body. She had broken the law before—drug use, DWIs, vandalism, shoplifting, disorderly conduct. She had even gotten caught a few times. But this felt different. This felt like a crime.

Halfway through the contents of the safe, Katherine was visited by a brief moment of sanity. *It's not too late to turn back,* she thought. She could put the money back, close out the till, swear Marty to secrecy, head home for bed, and lock the doors behind her. Marty was so stoned he probably wouldn't remember anything the next day anyway.

Shit, this stunt could be the end of me. It could be the last brainless addition to her long criminal resume—the one that would finally seal her fate. She could end up incarcerated for the next decade or two.

But how could she get caught? The plan was foolproof. Get the cash, bust in the backdoor to stage the break-in, and dispose of the locking cover to the floor safe so the authorities wouldn't know if it had been cracked by a professional or opened by an employee with a key.

She wasn't scheduled to work until Tuesday. By the time the police even suspected her, she and Marty would have taken Sam far away. Far away from Maple Creek, far away from the townspeople who constantly judged her, and far away from Daniel Norby, the one-night stand who had been awarded custody and primary placement of her son.

Her car was packed and full of fuel, and she had placed several pieces of evidence around her apartment to give the appearance of a last-minute departure to Canada, a place she had no intention of visiting.

The only thing left to do was to call Sam's school the following morning to report him sick so the school secretary wouldn't contact Norby to inquire about his absence. Norby wouldn't learn of the abduction until Monday afternoon when he would arrive to pick up Sammy after school, following the scheduled weekend visit with his mother. By that time, Sam would be hundreds of miles away.

She stuffed the remaining cash into her bag. Despite the fact that the plan had been executed by a couple of stoners, it went off surprisingly smoothly.

The call came in to dispatch at 9:08 Monday morning, just after the day cook came in to prep for the lunch rush.

Officer Griffin was the first uniform to respond, and his initial impression was that the crime appeared to be an outside job. There was evidence of forced entry from the alley, the old register was busted up and had been emptied, the floor safe had been cleaned out, and according to the cook, a fair amount of the beer and snack food inventory was missing. Despite much prompting by police over the years, the owner had been too frugal to invest in any security cameras. Officer Griffin knew that without such hard physical evidence, solving the crime would prove to be difficult.

The crime scene was quickly secured and a text message was fired off to Detective Stone—standard protocol with any major crime. Serious offenses were fairly rare in Maple Creek, but the town did periodically fall victim to a burglary or violent crime. And when it did, the investigation always landed on Stone.

Stone and his officers would carefully scour the scene for forensic evidence, a very difficult undertaking for a crime committed in a public place. They would take dozens of photos and canvass the area for witnesses. There were a few old apartments above the downtown businesses; perhaps a night owl had heard some commotion or seen something suspicious.

It would be several hours before they got around to reaching out to employees for interviews, including the waitress who closed the establishment the night before. It would be two days before they would secure a warrant to search her apartment, nearly twenty-four hours after she failed to appear for work on Tuesday. Although Katherine Kobs would ultimately emerge as Stone's prime suspect, she had timed her exit to provide herself with an exceptional head start.

CHAPTER 15

THE BANK BOX

Addie Albright sat rocking in Prof's old chair, wrapped in his tattered red blanket, staring out at the leafless tree line from her front porch. The air was crisp, and the steam rose from her coffee as she warmed her hands on the thick ceramic mug.

Prof had been gone for over a week, but she could still sense his presence—the faint scent of his aftershave on the blanket, the creaking of his chair as it rocked against the wooden porch, last month's *National Geographic* tucked under the small wooden table next to his chair, the rings from his sweaty whiskey glass on the weathered table top, the old tin bowl half full of spent pistachio shells, and his favorite chimes gently blowing in the breeze just above her head.

"I miss you, Jonathan," she whispered into the void of the morning air.

As easy as it would be for Addie to withdraw deep into her soul, to retreat from the challenges she now faced without her beloved husband, she knew she had to forge ahead. *Stay busy, stay focused,* she thought. She picked up the phone and dialed Jake's number to arrange the meeting to inventory Prof's safe-deposit box.

Gertie's voice was firm. "Thank you for calling the Law Office of Jacob Bishop. Mr. Bishop will be out of the office today attending a legal seminar, and the office will be closed until tomorrow morning. Your call is important, so please leave a message and we'll return it as soon as possible. Thank you." The message was a little concerning to Addie as she had just spoken with Jake the night before and there was no mention of any plans to close the office.

Addie called Gertie's home number. She and Gertie had developed a close relationship over the years, and Addie knew the call would not be an imposition. Gertie answered on the second ring, explaining that Jake had departed early that morning for an estate planning seminar in Madison. With everything he'd had on his mind, he had probably forgotten about the seminar when he last spoke with Addie. It had been on the books for at least two months, as was the vacation day Gertie had scheduled to spend with her sister who was visiting from Milwaukee.

Addie informed Gertie that she would proceed to the bank without Jacob and drop off the contents of the box at their office the next time she was in town. Knowing that Jake would not want to risk the documents being lost or misplaced, Gertie graciously offered to meet Addie at the office at noon. Gertie also insisted that Addie join her and her sister for lunch. Addie eagerly accepted the invitation.

Addie Albright paid little mind to the squad cars that had congregated downtown. It wasn't unusual for officers to gather at the Creek Cafe for a mid-morning cup of coffee. Little did she know they were actually busy processing the crime scene next door.

The bank receptionist greeted the new widow in a consoling tone and politely escorted her back to the vault. Addie's name was listed on the depository declaration, so access to the box was not questioned. The receptionist quickly located box 238, then she and Addie each slid their key into its lock. She gently pulled the drawer out and placed it on the table beside her. She smiled and left the room to give Addie some privacy.

Addie sighed as she lifted the lid, unsure of what she might find inside. Though she and Prof had never deliberately kept secrets, each had been fairly independent when it came to business and financial matters.

There were more items inside than she expected: several official-looking legal documents printed on fine parchment, various insurance policies and financial certificates neatly folded and tucked into clear plastic sleeves, several savings bonds sorted and bound according to their designated beneficiary, and a sealed envelope marked "Mr. Jacob Bishop—Personal and Confidential."

As she reviewed the contents of the drawer, Addie wrote a brief description of each item on her notepad before transferring them into her brown leather briefcase.

1. Last Will and Testament.
2. Trust Document: Jonathan Albright Irrevocable Family Trust; beneficiary: Addie Albright.
3. Deed to Wisconsin Cabin.
4. Deed to Chicago condo.

5. (30) $100 series EE savings bonds, Jonathan Bishop.
6. (30) $100 series EE savings bonds, Jacob Bishop.
7. (30) $100 series EE savings bonds, Amanda Albright.
8. Certificates of Title to Lexus & Range Rover.
9. (4) Certificates of Deposit from First National Bank—$100,000; $50,000; $25,000; $25,000. Owner: The Jonathan Bishop Education Trust.
10. Trust document: Jonathan Bishop Education Trust.
11. Stock Certificate, 1,000 shares—First National Bank of Maple Creek.
12. Year-end statement for American Funds: IRAs, mutual funds, stocks & bonds; closing value $2.3M.
13. Land Contract for Florida property.
14. Certificates of Deposit: First National Bank $250,000; Chicago Sun Bank $200,000; Illinois Mutual $200,000; Badger State Credit Union $250,000; all POD to Addie Albright.
15. Life insurance policy—Centurion Life, $250,000, beneficiary: Jacob Bishop.
16. Sealed envelope—personal/confidential to Jake Bishop.

Addie removed the last item from the box and pulled it out from its clear plastic sleeve. She unfolded the certificate and reviewed its terms. Her heart pounded heavily as she stared at the document. She took a deep breath and tried to steady her hand as she recorded the final entry.

17. Life insurance policy—Fundamental Life, $3M, beneficiary: Jonathan & Addie Albright Irrevocable Family Trust.

In less than one hour Addie's life had changed forever. She had walked into the First National Bank of Maple Creek as a woman of very adequate means, but she would walk out as a multi-millionaire. It was an uneasy feeling, and she was suddenly overcome with emotion. Her knees began to shake and her lip quivered as she stood alone in the bank vault.

She missed him so much. He had been so good to her, so loving, so considerate. He always took care of her in life, and now in death. He had seen to it that all of his affairs were in order and that she would be financially set for life. She would never need to worry about her future, never fear growing old without adequate care. She could travel, volunteer, contribute to worthwhile charities. But Addie would gladly forfeit every penny if she could just have her Jonathan back.

Addie glanced at her watch and noticed that she had just two minutes to meet Gertie at Jake's office. She motioned for the receptionist to return to the vault, and the two women tucked Prof's box into its designated space and locked it together. Addie thanked the employee for her assistance, then made her way outside.

Gertie and her sister Genevieve were just pulling up in front of the bank as Addie stepped outside. Addie had never personally met Genevieve, but Gertie spoke of her often. Though Gertie was six years younger than her sister, the years had been kinder to Genevieve. A small, mousy woman, Genevieve was far less bold and confident than her more assertive sibling. She was dressed in a blue polyester leisure suit that hung neatly on her petite frame, and she sported a bouffant hairdo that looked like it stepped out of the 1960s. She said little, but offered a gentle smile.

Gertie gave Addie a generous and sympathetic bear hug, one Addie was not certain she'd survive without a broken rib.

After introductions and condolences, Gertie unlocked the office and invited her guests inside. She locked the door behind her and led the women upstairs. She situated her sister in the waiting room and brought Addie to a small library near the back of the office. There was no need to turn on any bright overhead lights that could give passersby the idea she was open for business.

Addie opened her briefcase and transferred its contents to the barren surface of the table. As Gertie scanned through the items, she took a mental note of the documents. Some she had seen before, as she had assisted

Jake when he drafted them on Prof's behalf. Many of the documents, however, she was seeing for the first time. She swallowed hard and tried to conceal her astonishment as she reviewed the benefits page of the life insurance policy.

Gertie was especially curious about the contents of the confidential envelope addressed to Jake. She placed the envelope in Jake's middle desk drawer with the rest of his important personal items.

She then gathered up the remaining items and placed them in a large file jacket, promising Addie they would be locked away in the safe until she could properly process them. Neither woman had any way of knowing that it would be several weeks before circumstances would call attention to Prof's confidential letter, nor did they know how important the letter would prove to be.

CHAPTER 16

AN UNEXCUSED ABSENCE

A young woman entered Evergreen Elementary School just after the children returned from lunch and settled comfortably back into their classrooms. She glanced at the notice posted on the front door instructing all visitors to sign in at the principal's office at the end of the hall.

Her stride was confident and her shapely body swayed under her overcoat as her black leather pumps clicked in perfect rhythm against the shiny linoleum floor.

Beneath the dark overcoat she wore a tailored business suit, charcoal gray with pinstripes, which contrasted perfectly against her crisp white shirt. Her complexion was dark, and her blonde hair was neatly pulled back over her black-rimmed eyeglasses. Over her shoulder hung a black leather business satchel, which she held securely beneath her left arm.

The principal's office was bustling with activity. Several teachers and students scurried in and out, while others had settled in for a longer stay. A young bully sat impatiently on the principal's office bench next to a little girl swinging her dangling feet. The school nurse escorted a sick student back to her office, and a young male teacher leaned against the filing cabinet, flirting with the office assistant.

The female visitor entered the principal's office and smiled at the head secretary who was engaged in a telephone conversation with a disgruntled parent. She approached the front desk and glanced at the visitor's sheet that was lying open in a three-ring binder on the countertop. She avoided the ink pen that was chained to the counter and pulled a black pen from her satchel. She posted the time in the requisite spot and signed her name in a swift and confident motion. The signature was impressive, but illegible. In the *print name* column she neatly wrote the name, *Sandra Jameson*.

The secretary held the phone to her ear with her shoulder as she typed furiously on her computer. With a scowl, she cleared her throat and motioned toward her assistant to tend to the visitor at the counter.

"May I help you, Ma'am?" the girl asked.

"Yes, my name is Sandra Jameson," she said, handing the assistant her business card. "I'm Attorney Bishop's Paralegal. His son Jonathan is a kindergartner here."

"Yeah, I know Jonathan. He's a sweetheart."

"Yes, I've heard a lot of great things about him. Unfortunately there's been a death in the family and Mr. Bishop has asked me to help out with Jonathan."

"Oh, that's too bad. Was it somebody close?"

"I understand that it was a great uncle who lived out on the East Coast; sounds like it was a very tragic car accident. Mr. Bishop is at a legal seminar in Madison today, but we'll be meeting up with him in Chicago. Jonathan and I have a flight out this afternoon."

"Do you know if Mr. Bishop made arrangements with our office?" the assistant asked as she studied the woman's business card.

"He mentioned that he would try to send you a fax from his hotel. Did you receive it?"

The young assistant glanced over at her mentor who was still on the phone debating with an irrational parent. "Let me see what I can find. I'll be right back with you," the girl replied.

The assistant shuffled through the daily activity basket, unable to locate the fax from Jonathan's father. She then delicately rummaged about the desk of the head secretary.

After a brief and fruitless search in the obvious places, the assistant peeked into the receiving tray of the fax machine. "Bingo," she declared. "It just hadn't been filed yet."

The document was in memo form, properly dated and signed, printed on the letterhead of Attorney Jacob P. Bishop. The assistant carefully reviewed the fax as she slowly walked back toward the counter. Her lips moved slightly as she softly read its contents.

To: Principal Dornfeld
From: Jake Bishop
Re: Jonathan Bishop

Dear Sir:
Please be advised that we've had a death in our family and that Jonathan will need a few days off

from school. Unfortunately, I'm out of town at a legal seminar today and cannot personally be there to meet him. I've asked my legal assistant, Sandra Jameson, to pick him up at school and escort him on a flight to Chicago. I will be meeting them there and we'll fly on to Philadelphia.

Please be advised that Ms. Jameson is relatively new with my firm, and therefore Jonathan has not yet had an opportunity to meet her. I would appreciate it if your staff could put him at ease and explain the situation when Ms. Jameson arrives.

Jonathan will likely be gone for approximately one week. If there is any homework that needs attention while he's gone, please ask Ms. Brown to e-mail the necessary information to my e-mail address shown below. Any other matters can be directed to my secretary, Gertie Liddle, when she returns to the office tomorrow.

Thank you for your attention to this matter.
Sincerely,
Jacob P. Bishop

The young assistant took a deep breath as she contemplated the fax. It certainly looked authentic. The fax header indicated that it had been sent from the Sheraton in Madison, and she recognized the telephone number as a Madison exchange. And the pleasant, sharply dressed woman on the other side of the counter definitely looked like a paralegal.

But the school policy, which was clearly posted on the Internet, required that a student was only allowed to leave with someone who was listed in their file as an authorized pick-up person. Any visitor who was not pre-authorized by the parent or guardian was strictly prohibited from leaving with a student.

The young assistant recalled the tongue-lashing she received from her surly mentor the last time she breached protocol, and she was not eager to invite an encore performance. "Ms. Jameson, do you have a photo I.D. that I could see?" she asked politely.

The visitor reached into her leather satchel and produced a Class D Wisconsin driver's license. The license was issued two years prior and appeared to be perfectly authentic. Several faint holographs of the state's official seal appeared across the face of the card, and it contained the right information—Sandra M. Jameson: Sex Female, Hair Blonde, Eyes Brown, Height 5'7", Weight 125. A Madison address was listed, and her date of birth revealed her age to be 25.

The assistant excused herself and proceeded to the filing cabinet to pull Jonathan's file. Only two individuals were listed on Jonathan's authorized pick-up sheet—his Grandmother Margaret, and his father's secretary, Gertrude Liddle. She then compared Jake's signature on the authorization sheet to the one inscribed on the bottom of his facsimile. They were a perfect match.

The assistant smiled at the woman and disappeared with Jonathan's file through a short hallway that let to the back offices. She gently knocked on Principal Dornfeld's door and stuck her head inside.

"Excuse me, sir. Can I have a minute?"

"Certainly, Amy. Come on in," the principal replied as he removed his reading glasses and took a swig from his diet soda.

"Sir, there's a woman outside who's here to pick up Jonathan Bishop; there's been a death in the family. She's not listed in his file as an authorized person, but she says she works for Mr. Bishop and she gave me this business card."

"Do we have any written authorization from Mr. Bishop?" the principal responded in a pleasant tone.

"This fax from Mr. Bishop came in this morning. It was sent from the Sheraton in Madison." She placed the memo on his desk. "The signature looks identical to the one in Jonathan's file."

Principal Dornfeld read the memo, and then studied the business card of Sandra Jameson, Paralegal, Law office of Jacob P. Bishop. "Is there anything suspicious about the woman?" he asked.

"No, nothing. She's very professional, and she seems perfectly legitimate."

"Did you try calling Mr. Bishop?"

"No, sir. I figured if he was at a seminar and all, he probably wouldn't answer."

"Well, I suppose it can't hurt to give him a call, can it?" he asked rhetorically as he picked up the phone.

Dornfeld's first call was to the cell number they had on file for Jake. It went directly to voice-mail. Without leaving a message he hung up and punched in Jake's office number, hoping to catch Gertie at her post. After three rings Principal Dornfeld was greeted by Gertie's recorded message—"Thank you for calling the Law Office of Jacob Bishop. Mr. Bishop will be out of the office today attending a legal seminar, and the office will be closed until tomorrow morning. Your call is important, so please leave a message and we'll return it as soon as possible. Thank you."

The principal hung up the phone without leaving a message. While it was his job to protect the students entrusted to his care, there didn't appear to be any reason to be suspicious of the circumstances, and he certainly didn't wish to interfere with the travel arrangements that had been made in preparation for a family funeral.

Principal Dornfeld eased up from his chair and escorted his assistant back to the front office. Halfway down the hall he caught a glimpse of his guest and slowed his pace to refasten the top button on his shirt and adjust his tie. Jerry Dornfeld was a large man with a barrel chest and a stocky build. He had the physical presence of a grizzly bear, but the temperament of a puppy. He lumbered up to the counter and introduced himself to the woman who was patiently waiting on the other side.

"Hello, Ms. Jameson. I'm Jerry Dornfeld, the principal here at Evergreen," he said as he extended his large hand in her direction.

"Nice to meet you, Principal Dornfeld. Please, call me Sandy."

"Well, Sandy, I understand you're here to pick up Jonathan Bishop?"

"Yes, sir, that's correct. Did you get a chance to review Mr. Bishop's fax?"

"Yes. Yes, I did. Everything appears to be in order. Why don't I escort you down to Ms. Brown's classroom and we'll gather up Jonathan's things," Jerry said as he made his way around the counter, rolling his shirtsleeves back down into their proper position. "Amy, why don't you call down to Ms. Brown's room and let her know we're on our way?"

The principal guided his lovely guest through the hallway of the elementary school, while making his best effort to appear charming. By the time they reached Ms. Brown's room, she had already packed Jonathan's knapsack and bundled him up in his winter jacket. Jonathan had a concerned look on his face as he watched Principal Dornfeld approach with the strange lady.

"Jonathan, this is Ms. Jameson. She's a friend of your father. He's asked her to pick you up today and bring you to Chicago to meet him," the principal explained.

"My dad's in Madison at school, and my grandma's on

a church trip. Dad said if he wasn't back in time, he'd have Gertie pick me up."

"I know, but he must have had to change his plans. I have a letter here that he faxed to me earlier today. It looks like you guys are going to be taking a trip to Philadelphia."

"Are we going to see Uncle Patrick?" Jonathan asked with enthusiasm.

The principal paused and swallowed hard as he contemplated his response.

"Jonathan, my name is Sandy," the strange lady said as she kneeled down to his level. "I'm afraid I have some sad news for you about your Great Uncle Patrick. He died early this morning in a car accident. Your father has asked me to bring you to meet him so you can be with him when he goes to Philadelphia. I'm very sorry about your uncle."

Jonathan's eyes filled with tears. He remained silent as Principal Dornfeld escorted him, along with his new guardian, to the front door.

Sandra Jameson thanked Dornfeld for his kindness and personal attention. The principal lingered in the vestibule and watched his departing guest as she made her way to the visitor parking area and buckled Jonathan into the backseat of her white sports utility. The principal drew in one last breath of the woman's lingering perfume, then confidently turned and headed back toward his office. *Always rewarding to comfort a student through a difficult time*, he thought.

CHAPTER 17

PAGING JONATHAN BISHOP

Gertie sat in her parked car and reminisced with her sister, as Elvis softly sang on the radio. They talked about their mother's love for the holidays. They talked about playing dress-up as little girls with their mother's clothing, and raiding her make-up cabinet while she was occupied with her housekeeping.

They talked about the crush Gertie had on Genevieve's much older boyfriend, and about growing up with two overprotective brothers. They talked about the grueling summer vacations when the four kids were all packed into the back of the family station wagon and hauled halfway across the country.

They talked about their alcoholic father, who they would hide from when he came home late at night, drunk and full of rage. They talked about the years passing them by, and how their children were somehow already grown and moved away.

Gertie's eyes scanned the parking lot as she chatted with Genevieve. She glanced at her watch, then checked the time against the digital clock in her dashboard. Most of the other cars had already picked up their cargo and departed, and the last of the school buses had pulled away.

"The little stinker should have been out here by now,"

Gertie said.

"Could he have gotten on the bus by mistake?" Genevieve asked.

"It's possible, but I kept a pretty close eye on the bus," Gertie replied, releasing a heavy sigh as she opened the car door. "I'm gonna go in and see if I can round him up. Why don't you sit here and keep warm?"

Gertie entered the school and walked toward the main office. She knew the route well, as both of her children had attended school there several years earlier.

As she walked past the empty classrooms and rows of tiny lockers, she glanced down each hallway in search of her tardy passenger. A scattering of children and parents lingered in the hallways, and a lonely janitor slowly swayed back and forth as he mopped the floor at the end of the east wing.

Gertie entered the principal's office and was greeted by the head secretary, the only office worker who had not yet departed for the evening.

"Well, hello, Gertie. What brings you by?" the secretary asked.

"Hey, Donna. I'm lookin' for Jonathan Bishop. His dad asked me to swing by and pick him up, but I haven't been able to locate him. I thought maybe you could round him up for me. Can you check with his teacher?"

"I would, but she left about ten minutes ago. Do you think Jonathan might have taken the bus home?"

"I don't think so. I've been watching the bus stop for

the last half hour. I didn't see him anywhere. I know he can be a bit of a dawdler, but he's got me more than a little worried."

"Don't worry, Gertie. We'll track him down. I'll try paging him on the intercom. I'll call the bus garage, too; they can radio his bus to see if he's on board."

"Thanks, Donna. I appreciate your help," Gertie said, anxiously glancing at her watch.

Two puffs of air purged through the network of intercom speakers, followed by a brief pause and the impending announcement: "Jonathan Bishop, please come to the principal's office. Ms. Liddle is waiting here to pick you up. Jonathan Bishop, please come to the principal's office right away. Thank you."

The announcement echoed throughout the school with little reaction. It echoed through the hallways, the vacant cafeteria, the dark kitchen, the empty gymnasium, and the silent chorus room.

One person, however, heard the announcement loud and clear. To him, the announcement brought pause, then panic. *Just a simple mix-up,* he thought. *There must have been a miscommunication. Some sort of oversight. Maybe Gertie was never notified about the arrangements.* The principal's mind raced as he replayed the day's events. *Just a simple mix-up*, he promised himself.

Jerry Dornfeld sprung up from his chair and walked briskly to the front office where Donna and Gertie were preparing to place a call to the bus garage.

"You ladies are looking for Jonathan?" he asked.

"Yes. Gertie was supposed to pick him up today, but we haven't been able to locate him. I was just calling the bus garage to see if he got on the bus," Donna replied.

"No, no he's not on the bus. Mr. Bishop's legal assistant picked him up after lunch today. She was bringing him to meet his father so they could go on to the funeral."

"Legal assistant? What legal assistant? And whose funeral? We *are* talking about Jonathan Bishop, right?" Gertie asked, completely perplexed.

"Yeah, Sandra Jameson—Mr. Bishop's new legal assistant. He faxed us instructions from his hotel in Madison. There was a death in the family—they had to fly out east to make arrangements," the principal replied as he fumbled through the filing cabinet in search of Jonathan's file.

"The only legal assistant Jake Bishop has is me, and I haven't heard anything about a death in the family! Where's Jonathan now?" Gertie demanded.

"Here, this is it. This is the fax we received from Madison." The paper shook in his hand as he removed it from the file and handed it to Gertie.

Gertie stared at the document in disbelief as she tried to digest its contents. Her expression was blank as she lifted her head from the document and looked at the principal. "My God, what have you done?" she asked softly.

"I don't understand. Everything was in order. It all checks out; the signatures match," the principal rambled.

Gertie's stomach turned to stone, and she began to tremble as she tried to block out the horrible images racing through her mind. She knew she had to stay calm—she had to focus.

"Mr. Dornfeld, nothing checks out. I've worked for Jake for the past three years. I'd know if there was another legal assistant working in my office! There's no Sandra Jameson, there's no funeral, and there's no flight to Philadelphia. I'm sure Jake is driving back from Madison as we speak. I suggest you call the police immediately."

As he picked up the receiver to dial 911, he desperately clung to the fading hope that Gertie was somehow mistaken—that Jonathan was safely en route to Chicago to meet his father.

But even he couldn't ignore the facts and haunting discrepancies as he began to replay the afternoon in his mind. What would he tell the police about the stranger he escorted out the front door with a parent's child? Would he tell them that she had a beautiful smile, a shapely figure, perky calves, a captivating stride? There were vague memories of her facial features and clothing, but like the scent of her perfume, they were quickly fading.

CHAPTER 18

NO GOOD NEWS

As the landscape blurred past his window, Jake attempted to process the knowledge that had been drummed into his head during the grueling eight-hour seminar. Credit shelter trusts, marital deduction formulas, family limited partnerships, grantor retained annuity trusts—the list went on and on. The tax laws were constantly changing, as was the complex arsenal of tools lawyers needed to preserve the financial estates of their wealthy clients.

The trip home from Madison was mostly highway—an easy drive Jake had made many times. But the sky had turned heavy and dull, and the late afternoon drizzle was beginning to freeze on the bridge decks. Jake was thankful he had opted to borrow his mother's Park Avenue, rather than braving the journey in his drafty Jeep.

As he approached the exit for Highway 12, he was startled by flashing lights in his rear-view mirror. Jake had been so engrossed rehashing the seminar materials that he hadn't noticed the state patrol car behind him. *He can't be after me*, Jake thought. *I'm practically crawling. Come on, pal. Go around me. Let's go, pass already.*

The trooper continued to trail as he carefully closed the gap between them. He was uncomfortably close, and it was obvious that the target of his pursuit was Margaret's Park

Avenue. *Shit. This is all I need. I suppose Mom forgot to put on her renewal stickers. And with my luck there's probably no registration in the glove box. Perfect.*

Jake tapped his turn signal and took the exit for Highway 12. Once up the ramp a safe distance, he carefully eased the Buick over to the edge of the roadway. To his dismay, the patrol car pulled in directly behind him.

He watched in his rear-view mirror as the trooper sat in his cruiser, apparently in no hurry to proceed with his business. He could tell from the shape and size of the silhouette that the officer was a man, and one of considerable size. The trooper appeared to be having a conversation over his radio, occasionally lifting the mic to his mouth, then back down again. The delay seemed unusually long and was beginning to make Jake nervous.

The trooper finally stepped out and positioned his large brimmed hat snugly on his head. He was well over six feet tall, and his thick build squarely filled his large winter patrol jacket.

"Is there a problem, officer? I'm quite certain I wasn't speeding."

"May I please see your driver's license, sir?" the trooper asked in an overly respectful tone.

Jake quickly produced his license. Although the trooper's pleasant demeanor put Jake a bit at ease, it was also making him suspicious.

The trooper studied the license and cautiously leaned in toward Jake's window.

"Sir, do you know a Detective Eric Stone?" again in a very courteous manner.

The question sent Jake's mind reeling. *Eric Stone? I'm in the middle of nowhere and this guy is pulling me over to ask me about Eric Stone? Is this some sort of joke? That damn Stone has gone too far this time.*

"Yes…yes, I know Eric Stone," Jake replied as if he had just exposed an episode of Candid Camera. "Did that sad sack put you up to this?"

"Sir, Mr. Stone has been trying to reach you on your cell phone. I'm told that it's urgent he speak with you immediately."

Jake could tell by the sober expression on the man's face that he was not joking. Stone had obviously pulled some strings to have the State Patrol track him down, and Jake quickly realized this was not a scenario that would end well.

"I've had my cell phone off; I forgot to charge the battery. My God, what's going on officer? Is everything okay?" Jake rattled.

"Sir, I'd like you to step back to my vehicle. I've got Detective Stone's number here. Let's try to reach him on my cell phone."

Jake's pulse began to race. His stomach felt like it had been filled in with concrete that was beginning to harden. He suspected that the officer knew more than he was letting on, but if there were more details, Jake wasn't sure if he was ready to hear them.

Inside the patrol car the trooper reduced the volume on his radio, quieting his dispatcher. He then flipped open his cell phone and punched Stone's number into the tiny keypad with his thick finger.

The phone rang four times; the delay seemed like an eternity to Jake.

"Detective Stone, this is Trooper Danielson with the Wisconsin State Patrol." Jake heard the words but was too numb to take them in. He stared out of the windshield, waiting for a bomb to drop.

"Sir, I'm sitting in my patrol car with Mr. Bishop. We're at the northeast quadrant of the I-94 and Highway 12 intersect," the trooper continued.

Jake began to take deep cleansing breaths, trying to calm his nerves for the conversation.

"I have Detective Stone for you, sir," the trooper said as he handed the phone to Jake.

"Eric, what the hell is going on?" Jake's voice was soft, but filled with fear.

"Jake, we may have a serious problem here. Do you know a woman named Sandra Jameson?"

"Sandra Jameson? I don't think so; it doesn't ring a bell. What's this all about?"

"Jake, did you send someone to the school to pick up Jonathan today?"

"Yeah, Gertie was supposed to pick him up after..." There was a brief pause as Jake realized where the conversation was headed. "Eric. My God, please tell me what's going on."

Stone took a deep breath and held it as he gathered his nerve. "Jake, there's no easy way to break this to you, and we don't have the time for me to ease into it. We believe someone has abducted Jonathan."

There was no response. Stone waited as Jake processed the news, but as the seconds ticked by he worried that the connection had dropped into dead air.

"Jake? Are you still with me?"

"Eric, who has my son?" Jake's voice was shaking now.

"A woman claiming to be Sandra Jameson came by the school today just after lunch. She claimed she was your new legal assistant. She had a business card, there was a fax from Madison on your letterhead authorizing the..."

"Eric, where in the hell is Jonathan?" Jake interrupted.

"She has him, Jake. We're not sure of her whereabouts, but I promise you I won't stop until I find her."

"*She*? Who is *she*? For Christ's sake, Eric. Tell me what's happening."

The trooper sat rigid in his seat, eyes closed, trying his best to fight back the tears that were beginning to well in his eyes.

"Jake, we don't know who the woman was. We have good reason to believe that it may have been Katherine Kobs. I'm working on pulling her driver's license photo so I can get a possible I.D. from the school staff."

"A possible I.D.? Don't they know her at the school?"

"No, her boy goes to school at Rocky Ridge. They're not familiar with her over at Evergreen."

Jake let out a long sigh as he shook his head in disgust. "I knew I should never have taken that case…Goddamn it!"

"The little Kobs boy never showed up for school today. Dan Norby reported him missing, and we can't find Katherine anywhere. We're pretty certain she's skipped town with him."

"What makes you think she skipped town? Maybe she just got her wires crossed on the exchange time for the kid. It happens all the time with split homes," Jake reasoned.

"Well, there's more. Someone cleaned out the till and the floor safe at the Bucket Sunday evening. At first glance it looked like an outside job, but under the circumstances I sure can't rule Katherine out as a suspect."

"Eric, I can't believe this is happening. What am I gonna do?" Jake sounded defeated. He had been clinging to the hope that this was all some sort of misunderstanding, but Jonathan was gone.

"Listen. It's best if we move quickly. I'm in the process of putting together an Amber Alert for Samuel Kobs. In my opinion there's reason to believe that Katherine has abducted Jonathan, as well. I'm going to add him to the alert and get him in the system. We'll need a recent photograph."

Jake drew in a deep breath and released it in halting whispers. "Have someone run by my house. Tell Sarah to look in the roll-top desk for the Thanksgiving photos. There's a good picture of him in there. On second thought, maybe you should go, Eric. I don't want someone else freaking her out."

"Alright, done. Now we need to get you back home as soon as possible. I'm going to have Trooper Danielson run you home. You're in no condition to drive, and he'll make much better time than you could. Leave Margaret's Buick in the Park & Ride lot on the north side of the highway there. We'll pick it up later."

"Eric, please find my boy. He's all I've got."

"Our boy, Jake. Our boy. I will."

Jake handed the phone back to the trooper, who listened carefully to Stone's instructions.

"Yes, sir. Yes, sir. Glad to be of assistance, sir. You're welcome, sir."

The trooper instructed Jake to drive his vehicle to the Park & Ride lot, which was visible from their location. There was no debate, no discussion. Jake knew that his fastest and safest way home was in the hands of the State Patrol.

He hastily drove to the parking lot and sped into the first available spot he saw, nearly sliding Margaret's Buick into the ditch ahead. He switched off the headlights, locked the doors, and nearly fell on a patch of ice as he jogged over to the patrol car.

It was nearly sixty miles to Maple Creek. Trooper Danielson wasted no time engaging his emergency lights and getting the cruiser up to speed. Even with the icy road conditions, he appeared calm as the speedometer approached eighty mph.

He remained silent as he drove—his large paws wrapped firmly around the wheel, his eyes frozen to the horizon ahead. The landscape looked cold and dull. What little was left of the sunset had been consumed by the low-lying clouds and the icy haze.

Jake was quiet as well. He stared blankly, as if his mind and spirit had left his body. It was all so surreal, like a very bad dream. His fear turned to anger, the anger to anxiety, the anxiety to despair. He tried to collect his thoughts—to collect even one thought. But they were all so obscure. The scattered images rattled through his mind—images of Jonathan, Blanca, Prof, even Henry.

Then it struck him. What would he tell Margaret… and Sarah? *Margaret may not be able to survive this*, he thought. *She's so frail. Much too frail to deal with the loss of her only grandchild.*

Jake slowly turned to Trooper Danielson whose eyes were still glued to the road ahead. "What are my odds, officer?"

"I'm sorry?" the trooper asked.

"Statistically, what are the odds of me getting my son back unharmed?"

There was a short pause as the officer carefully formulated his answer. "Sir, the odds are significantly improved when the abductor is a person you know… especially when there's a swift response by law enforcement as there was in this case."

The answer sounded as if it had come straight from the manual, and it did little to appease Jake's anxiety.

CHAPTER 19

TIME IS OF THE ESSENCE

Eric Stone had studied the investigative techniques used in child abduction cases, but he had little experience applying these techniques in the field. The few cases he'd actually investigated involved domestic disputes—abductions by noncustodial parents who had run off with their children in violation of a court custody order. All of those cases ended on a positive note with the exception of one: Taylor Vick.

Taylor was the three-year-old son of James and Cynthia Vick. Two months after Judge Montpetit awarded primary placement of Taylor to his mother, James Vick marched into his former home with a .38-caliber revolver, shot his ex-wife twice in the chest, and ran off with Taylor.

Stone had been hot on Vick's trail when police received a tip from a clerk at a rundown motel just off the interstate. The clerk reported a male guest traveling with a young child and acting jittery. The man paid cash in advance for the room and insisted on parking his car in the grassy clearing behind the motel, well out of view from the frontage road. Stone was sure he had his man.

Stone and his officers surrounded the small motel, established phone contact with Vick, and listened in horror as two shots rang out from the room. Not a day would pass when Stone wouldn't question his handling of the incident.

If only he had gotten there sooner. If only he would have said the right thing to Vick on the phone that day. If only he had called on the expertise of the FBI.

Stone was determined not to relive the horror of the Vick case. Jonathan was coming home, unharmed. Just minutes after meeting with Gertie and Principal Dornfeld, Stone's first phone call was to a coordinator at the FBI's Crimes Against Children Unit. He regretted not sharing this information with Jake, but felt it was best to only give his friend one overwhelming dose of information at a time.

The detective was astonished by the rapid response of the bureau. Since the case involved a young child who had been abducted by a stranger, it was given immediate priority. Within three hours of Stone's call, a four-member Child Abduction Rapid Deployment (CARD) Team from the FBI's North Central Region landed a twin-engine plane on the small runway at Brewster Field on the edge of town. Unbeknownst to the team, they had flown almost directly over Trooper Danielson and Jake, who were speeding along on the desolate highway far beneath the cloud deck.

By the time Danielson and Jake arrived in Maple Creek, all that remained of the storm was large fluffy snowflakes dancing in the glow of the streetlights. The streets and sidewalks were blanketed in fresh snow, and the blue flashing light of a lonely snowplow could be seen in the distance as its driver embarked upon a long night of work. Main Street looked nearly deserted, as if tucked in for a long sleep. The only movement was that of Danielson's patrol car quietly speeding into town, stirring up a flurry of snow in its wake.

Amid the deceptive peacefulness of the little town, the police station was brightly lit and bustling with activity. As the trooper rounded the corner and approached the station, Jake strained to see through the frost-covered windows of the old building. He could see the distorted shapes of several people moving about inside. He desperately hoped there was good news waiting for him. He envisioned Jonathan sitting safely on Stone's lap, the two of them happily playing a game of golf on Stone's computer. Jake drew in a long breath of reality, then released a loud sigh and exited the patrol car.

Danielson escorted Jake into the station, and the two men followed the sound of voices gathered in a large room at the end of the hallway. As they stepped through the doorway into the conference room, both men stopped abruptly. Even Danielson was surprised by the magnitude of the operation. The room had been transformed into a command post that looked worthy of the nation's largest manhunt.

The entire space was scattered with police officers—some uniformed, some casually dressed, some active duty, some retired. Jake recognized most of the faces, but a few were new to him. He noticed a computer technician who was busy toiling with a series of cables that appeared to be haphazardly feeding a large router nearby.

Everyone in the room seemed passionately immersed

in his or her task, too busy to even notice Jake standing in the doorway. They were busy setting up extra broadband and telephone connections, pinning up maps and aerial photos, discussing strategy and response plans.

Jake stood motionless in the doorway, doubtful that such commotion could really be all about Jonathan. He tried to gather his thoughts, but they were quickly drowned out by the sounds pulsing from the room—the chatter from the police radios and scanners, the mumbled tones of conversations in different corners of the room, the clicking of the computer keyboards, the beat of the copy machine as it spit out copy after copy of the most recent briefing, the ringing of different telephones all competing for attention, the belching of a large coffee percolator as its scalding water erupted over the fresh grounds.

As Jake scanned the room hoping to catch a glimpse of Stone, his eyes fell upon a chilling site. Posted on a bulletin board on the opposite side of the room was an enlarged photograph of his son. Jake recognized the photo as one he had taken on Thanksgiving. Jonathan's warm smile and innocent expression, captured as a precious family memory, were now painful.

There were other pictures displayed on the board as well. Jake recognized the school photo of Samuel Kobs, which was an enlarged duplicate of a wallet size version that had been given to him by Daniel Norby during the custody trial. Next to Sam were two blown-up driver's license photos—one of his mother Katherine and one of a scary-looking character with the name Martin Vance posted below it.

As Jake stared at the photographs, the harsh reality settled upon him like the weight of the world. Seeing Jonathan's picture somehow transformed the nightmare into reality. They took him. Those monsters took his little boy.

Just then, Jake felt a large hand resting on his shoulder. As he turned to see who was comforting him, he was greeted by the moist solemn eyes of his trusted friend. Stone offered Jake a sympathetic nod, then embraced him firmly. There were no words that could ease the pain.

The two men choked back tears and struggled to regain their composure. Stone extended his hand to Trooper Danielson who was standing quietly next to Jake. Danielson had a humble calmness about him.

"Thank you for getting my friend back safely, officer," Stone said as he shook Danielson's hand.

"It was my pleasure. We'll be doing all we can to help find your little boy, sir," Danielson said with a reassuring nod.

"I know you will, officer. Thank you for everything."

As the Trooper turned to leave, another figure appeared next to Stone. The man seemed to materialize out of thin air. He was a stranger to Jake, obviously not a local. Jake noticed the pistol holstered inside the man's gray tweed sports coat and assumed that he was a professional acquaintance of Stone.

The stranger was a distinguished-looking man with a dusting of gray throughout his hair and subtle wrinkles on his face. He was thin, perhaps the result of a stressful career, Jake thought.

"Jake, I'd like you to meet Agent David Fox. Agent Fox is with the FBI—he's an investigator with a special unit that handles child abduction cases."

"The FBI? Are you here about Jonathan?" Jake asked as he shook Fox's hand.

"I called them in, Jake," Stone interjected. "The Bureau has special expertise in these matters. They also have a lot more resources than we do."

"How did you guys get here so fast?"

"We strive for rapid deployment in these cases, sir. We've been working pretty hard to get set up here. Why don't we step into the interview room so we can talk privately?"

The three men entered the interview room and Stone closed the door behind them. Agent Fox rolled a large gray office chair away from the edge of the table and guided it toward Jake. "Please have a seat, Mr. Bishop."

Jake reluctantly sat in the chair, uncertain of the conversation they were about to have.

"Did somebody try to contact my mother?" Jake asked.

"We're working on that, Jake," Stone replied. "We've tracked down the hotel where her group is staying in Branson, but I haven't been able to reach her by phone yet. I've left a message for her to call me on my cell immediately."

"What about my sister? Did you talk with Sarah?"

"She's holding up pretty well. Two agents from Mr. Fox's team are with her at your house."

"Who took my boy, Eric? Was it her? Was it Katherine Kobs?"

"We're just not sure right now. The woman fits Katherine's general description, but neither Dornfeld nor his assistant could give us a positive I.D. from her old driver's license photo. We have a sketch artist coming up from Madison. She'll work with Principal Dornfeld and the school staff. Hopefully we'll get a better picture put together."

"It's got to be her. She vowed she'd get even with me. At the trial, she looked right at me with those crazy eyes and screamed that she would get even with me no matter how long it took."

"She certainly fits the profile. But based upon the information we've received from the school staff, this woman was extremely poised and professional. I'm just not sure Katherine could pull that off, but we have to pursue her strongly as a suspect. Either way she's wanted for the abduction of her own son, so we're working hard to track her down."

Jake looked almost despondent as he sat at the table listening to Stone. He'd never felt so hopeless, and the desperation was settling deep into his eyes. "What happens now, Eric?" Jake asked softly.

"Now we do our jobs, Jake. The Amber Alerts are already

being broadcast; we've got BOLO bulletins out to the local and regional law enforcement agencies; I've entered all of the information into the state enforcement system and the National Crime Information Center; Mr. Fox's team is using special mapping software to identify and locate any registered sex offenders in the area; we have a team putting together posters that they'll distribute to the airlines, bus stations, and transportation companies; I've got an officer searching through the recent traffic and parking citations, and reaching out to the neighborhood watch groups; we're also checking the neighboring jurisdictions to see if there have been any similar incidents in the region. We're hitting this hard, Jake. I promise I won't rest until we get to the bottom of this."

Jake's head sunk into his hands. "My God. I should never have left town. I should never have taken that damn case."

"Don't blame yourself, Mr. Bishop. There was absolutely nothing you could have done to prevent this," Agent Fox said in a consoling tone. "We know this is all overwhelming for you right now. We know you're in shock. But Jonathan needs you to be strong. Much of the information you can provide will be very useful to us."

Jake nodded as he drew in a deep breath.

Agent Fox slid some pamphlets and a booklet across the table toward Jake. "When you feel you're up to it, I'd like you to read over these materials. The information can be very beneficial to you and your family."

Jake gave another weighty nod.

"Now, Mr. Bishop. I want to apologize in advance if it seems like we're invading your privacy or overloading you with information. But time is of the essence here."

"I understand."

"You're going to be bombarded with questions. It can be overwhelming. Just remember that we're only trying to help. Information is key to our success. It's important that you be completely honest with us. And feel free to ask questions at any time."

Another silent nod from Jake.

"You're going to become a public figure overnight. The media will be in your face, and it will feel intrusive. The attention is usually a good thing. Always be honest with them or it will come back to haunt you."

"Alright, I understand."

"Your home has been secured, and so has the elementary school. We'll be conducting a complete forensic investigation. We'll need to take samples for DNA evidence and scent preservation for the bloodhounds."

"Bloodhounds? What bloodhounds?"

"Many abductors release or discard their victim within one mile of the abduction site. At least half of the victims are found within a thirty-mile radius."

"Discard?"

"There's good reason to be optimistic that your son is alive, Mr. Bishop, but our job is to consider all possible scenarios. We'll be canvassing the area and organizing search parties over the next few days. The weather is a factor. If the abductors released him in a remote area we need to work quickly."

"What about a ransom? Has there been any contact about a ransom?" Jake asked abruptly.

"No, nothing yet. Ransom and extortion attempts are fairly rare in cases involving young school-aged children, but we're setting up phone taps just in case. Does Jonathan have your home telephone number memorized?"

"Yes, our phone number and our address. I make him write them down all the time."

"Good. He may very well try to contact you if he gets a chance, or he may ask for someone else's assistance to do so. We'll need complete access to your home and your computer records. Will that be an issue for you, or will we need a warrant?"

"No warrants. You're welcome to full access to everything. I just want my son back."

"I've also got some release forms here for you to sign authorizing access to Jonathan's medical and dental records. Does Jonathan have any concerning medical problems or mental health issues?"

"Nothing I'm aware of."

"What about any unique birthmarks or scars?"

"No. Nothing like that," Jake replied.

"Is there anything atypical about his walk? Does he have any unusual mannerisms?"

"He's just a happy little boy," Jake said softly.

"What was your son wearing this morning, Mr. Bishop?"

"Um," another sigh, "let's see. We dressed in a hurry this morning…darker blue jeans, a blue sweatshirt with some white stripes on the sleeves, little tan hiking boots. Um, a blue and tan down coat, a blue stocking cap…and he was carrying a maroon knapsack."

"Good. Very good. That will be helpful to us. Detective Stone told us about the possible home invasion you had a few weeks ago. Have you noticed any unusual activity or any strangers around your home or office since then?"

"No. Nothing I can think of."

"Has Jonathan spoken of anything out of the ordinary, or has he been acting unusual in any way?"

"No, he's been fine. Agent Fox, I know you're just trying to do your job, but we know who took my boy. Shouldn't we be looking for Katherine Kobs?"

"We are, Mr. Bishop. Believe me, we are. But we have to explore all possibilities, and time is of the essence. You should go home and be with your sister. Stay close to the phone. Two of my team members will be there tonight; they'll give you instructions as to how to handle any incoming phone calls. They'll also have some more questions for you.

"Try to get some rest when you're able. You need to take care of yourself. Eat, sleep, and talk to someone about what you're going through. Your child needs you to be strong and healthy—physically and mentally. Tomorrow will be a busy day. We'll be organizing a search party and holding a press conference."

"A press conference? Already?"

"It's really the best way to generate leads from the public. You should choose a close friend or family member to serve as your spokesperson. Oh, and speaking of family, we'll need a list of your family members and close friends."

"My family? You can't possibly suspect anyone in my family?"

"Sometimes friends or family members can have information that you're not aware of. They may have seen someone or something out of place. They may be able to think of things that you may have overlooked."

"Alright, I'll put together a list tonight."

"It would also be helpful if you could provide us with a list of any disgruntled clients."

"I do divorce work, Agent Fox. That could be quite a list."

"Focus on any problem files, clients who might think they have a reason to hold a grudge. That should shorten it up a bit."

"I'll work with my secretary on that; she remembers everybody. Is there anything else I should be doing?"

"Just try to get some rest—any little bit will help," Fox said as he rose to his feet.

"Come on, Jake. I'll run you home," Stone said, patting Jake on the back.

Jake rolled his chair away from the table and slowly

rose to his feet. "Agent Fox, what are the odds of me getting my son back alive?"

"There's reason to be optimistic, Mr. Bishop. Don't get too caught up in the statistics; they're only numbers. Every case turns on its own facts."

"Mr. Fox, please don't feed me any more clichés. What are my odds?"

"Mr. Bishop, over 800,000 children are reported missing each year. That includes runaways and children who just wander off or get lost. Child abductions account for more than 200,000 of that number, and most of those are committed by family members. Over 50,000 are non-family abductions, and ninety-eight percent of those children are safely returned to their families."

Jake wasn't sure if the information made him feel better, or worse. What he was sure of was that tonight, on this cold and dark December evening, he was going home without his son.

CHAPTER 20

HOPE FADES

The tree limbs hung heavy with thick ice. It was a quiet morning, and the Sunday churchgoers had yet to make their pilgrimage. Jake sat alone at his desk in the den, staring blankly out the window. Although the sky was crisp and blue, the beauty of the landscape felt void to him this morning. The full cup of coffee he clutched between his hands had become tepid, and the toast Margaret had brought him nearly an hour ago was stale and cold.

More than two weeks had passed since Jonathan's disappearance. Jake rarely slept, with the exception of an occasional catnap when his body simply shut down from exhaustion. Despite the pleas from Stone and Agent Fox that he get some solid rest, Jake would not allow himself to lose consciousness for more than an hour or two at a time. He hadn't shaven for days, and his eyes had sunken behind dark circles. Life as he knew it was over, and any sense of normalcy felt like a distant luxury.

Early on in the search, each day seemed to bring new leads and fresh hope. But the hope was stripped away as the FBI proved each lead to be a dead end or a misguided hoax.

The most promising lead had been called in by the owner of a small diner in rural Illinois. The man reported a little boy fitting Jonathan's description struggling to escape from a woman dragging him into a car resembling the one described in the Amber Alert.

The FBI team investigated, and within twenty-four hours the woman in question was located through a partial license plate number. She was cleared after the agents learned that she had been traveling from Wisconsin to see relatives in Chicago and was simply trying to deal with her unruly five-year-old. Yet another false lead—another dead end. It was becoming nearly impossible for Jake to show even a facade of optimism. His hope had been replaced by doubt, and the doubt was eroding to despair.

Just as Agent Fox had predicted, Jake's life had taken a cruel turn. The media invasions, press conferences, false leads, bloodhounds, helicopters, fruitless searches, forensic teams—Jake's life felt like a miniseries, each development dramatically unveiled and marketed to the public. Jonathan's kidnapping started to capture national television coverage. Although Jake despised the thought of his family serving as bait for the media's feeding frenzy, he knew the coverage would keep the public interested in finding his son.

Jake gazed out the window, replaying the nightmare over and over in his mind. The past ten days were too much to digest.

As expected, Katherine Kobs had failed to show for work at the Rusty Bucket, and the search of her apartment yielded little information. Agent Fox wasn't buying into the appearance of her flight to Canada, but he gave the order to alert the border patrol nonetheless.

The forensic team had collected several pieces of evidence from Katherine's apartment with the hope of establishing that Jonathan had been held there, but they were still waiting for the lab to return the results.

The team also searched Jonathan's elementary school. Fingerprints, tire tracks, eyewitness interviews—the standard protocol. Since the crime occurred in such a high-traffic area, it would be some time before they could determine if any of the evidence was actually left by the blonde woman.

The school board was putting tremendous pressure on Principal Dornfeld to resign after walking a student out the front door with a perfect stranger. Dornfeld knew the district was looking for a scapegoat, and he wasn't going down without a fight. He worked tirelessly with the FBI's sketch artist to recreate the image of the mysterious woman who had charmed her way into his school. Despite the principal spending more time looking at the woman's figure than her face, the final rendition was far more accurate than he could have realized.

The likeness in the sketch was hauntingly familiar to Detective Stone. There was a faint resemblance to Katherine Kobs, but he was certain it wasn't her. He wasn't sure where, or when, but he was positive he had seen the woman in the sketch before.

Jake had no recollection of her, but at this point, he had little recollection of anything. The most difficult few days for Jake had been early in the search. As each day passed without a discovery, his hopes of finding his son alive dwindled. By day three, Jake was praying that the searchers would *not* find his boy, as he knew Jonathan couldn't possibly have survived the string of cold Wisconsin nights.

Sitting by the window, Jake sifted through the fragments of images that drifted through his mind, and his eyes welled with tears. He saw an image of Maggie—an angel of mercy in this dark time.

Maggie was instrumental in coordinating the search parties. In less than twenty-four hours she organized more than 350 people from three different counties. She called on every coffee shop contact she could think of. She enlisted customers who were members of the Rotary, the Elks Club, the Masonic Lodge, 4-H, the local churches—even her close friend who organized the cancer walks every year. The public support was overwhelming, and Maggie thanked each volunteer personally, providing a hot cup of coffee and a free coupon to her shop.

The search dragged on for five days. Shift after shift, wave after wave, the volunteers scoured every snowy field, every patch of woods, every thicket, every ditch, every creek bed.

Each time a piece of evidence was discovered, a local law enforcement or FBI team member was called over. A knit hat, a torn mitten, an old boot, some weathered school papers, a shell casing, an unrecognizable animal carcass—nothing was overlooked. And as each report filtered back to base camp, Jake's heart tightened.

Jake was most fearful of what had been found during the FBI's sweep of his home. They had discovered listening devices on both of his landline phones, and computer forensics revealed that his computer's hard drive had been accessed at the same time of his home invasion weeks earlier. Not only did the intruders gain access to his schedule and personal data, they had installed a spyware program they could access remotely—someone had been anticipating Jake's every move, tracking every keystroke.

Stone was devastated. Jonathan's abduction could have been prevented, and he felt responsible. For days he had tried to work up the nerve to articulate his apology to Jake, but he simply couldn't find the words.

Finally, the evening Sarah left for California, Stone joined his intoxicated friend on the cold, dark porch for a consoling glass of scotch. Four drinks later, sufficiently tranquilized, Stone had offered his gut-wrenching apology.

"Jake, I know there's nothing I can say to make this right. I've been trying to find the courage to apologize. I just haven't been man enough."

"Apologize? Apologize for what?" Jake asked.

"My god, Jake. I've failed you in every way. I didn't send your computer into the lab the night your home was hit. I didn't check your phone lines; I missed the spyware; I treated the whole thing like a juvenile break-in. It was right under my nose the whole time!" Stone's voice was trembling.

Jake couldn't believe his ears. "No, Eric. You're not taking the blame for this. There was no reason to think someone had planted bugs and spyware in my house. You couldn't have known."

"You don't understand, Jake. It's my job to know. It's my job to investigate. I should have torn that damn house apart until I was satisfied that you and your family were safe. I failed you, and..." Stone broke down as he finished his sentence, "I failed Jonathan."

Jake shook his head and placed his arm around his friend. "You haven't failed us, Eric. You've always been there for us, as far back as I can remember. And you're here for us now. You're not responsible. If anyone's to blame, it's me. You told me to get the computer analyzed. I didn't listen. I thought the break-in was nothing more that some punks looking for electronics and a liquor cabinet. This one's on me. All the signs were there. I should never have taken that case. I shouldn't have let Katherine Kobs into our lives. Don't carry this on your shoulders, Eric. Stay strong. You're our best hope. Find Katherine Kobs, and we'll find Jonathan."

Despite Jake's reassurances that night, Stone still carried a guilty conscience. He also still had his doubts about Katherine Kobs, and he didn't want Jake disappointed by yet another unproductive lead. The job was just too sophisticated for the likes of Katherine and her stoner boyfriend. Marty Vance did have a military background, but no special ops training, and certainly nothing that would give him the know-how to install the surveillance equipment in Jake's home. Vance had been dishonorably discharged from the service after spending time in military confinement for larceny and distribution of a controlled substance. Not exactly a Navy Seal, Stone concluded.

But there was one thing that deeply troubled Stone. Martin Vance's name had popped up on the national sex offender registry. Marty had a history of collecting a variety of pornography, and was once convicted of sexually assaulting a ten-year-old boy, the son of a stripper he was screwing back in Texas.

If Marty was involved with Jonathan's abduction, the odds were not good. Stone had reluctantly shared the statistics. Strangers who abduct children with the intention of fulfilling a sexual desire often murder their victims within the first three hours. To make matters worse, Vance was traveling with a woman who had a history of impulsive behavior, substance abuse, and psychiatric instability. She and Vance were a dangerous combination, and Stone was determined to find them if for no other reason than to eliminate them as suspects.

He was certain Marty and Katherine were headed west. Before leaving Maple Creek, Marty had apparently stolen his mother's credit card. The master criminals had been leaving a trail of credit card activity from one Podunk gas station or café to the next. Probably an attempt to preserve the stolen cash from the Rusty Bucket, Stone presumed. Fox and Stone decided not to alert Mrs. Vance that her card was missing, fearing the old woman might contact the credit card company and they would deactivate the account.

They were sure that if they kept the trail fresh, they'd get lucky and stumble across a decent image from a surveillance camera. Perhaps one of those images would offer proof that Jonathan was still alive. But so far, their net had come up empty. Either Katherine had a propensity to only visit the rundown shitholes throughout the heartland, or she was intentionally choosing them for their lack of modern surveillance equipment. Either way, the two were proving elusive.

There had also been no cell phone activity by Marty or Katherine, and Stone was sure they had discarded their old phones, possibly picking up a burner phone along the way. But Stone assured Jake that the duo would slip up. A payphone call to Katherine's mother, a speeding ticket, a traffic violation, a brief pass by a security camera, a hit on the Amber Alert. It was just a matter of time.

Jake's house seemed so quiet without Jonathan. His life was empty. He couldn't help but wonder what Jonathan was doing each moment, if he were still alive. What kind of dark, damp basement did they have him locked in? What dumpy little hotel were they held up at? Was he running happily along the edge of a pond, playing with little Sammy Kobs? Or was he bound up in Katherine's trunk? His thoughts provided very little comfort.

CHAPTER 21

A CALL FROM AN OLD FRIEND

The phone rang, piercing the morning silence. The screen on the surveillance monitor read "CELLULAR PHONE: 312-555-4812." Jake fixated on two chickadees fluttering around the birdfeeder outside. One ring, two rings, three rings. Jake stared blankly out his den window.

Margaret picked up the phone in the dining room where the FBI had set up their makeshift surveillance center.

"Hello, Bishop residence," she answered in her inviting tone. Margaret had become accustomed to the telephone calls—offers of condolence, media inquiries, well-intentioned tipsters, and of course, the occasional hoax.

There was a brief pause before the caller finally spoke. The voice sounded altered, almost mechanical.

"There is little time. Please ask Mr. Bishop to join us." The voice was calm.

"I'm sorry? Who is this?" Margaret was caught off guard by the sound of the caller's voice.

"You're wasting valuable time, Mrs. Bishop. I suggest you put your son on the phone if you ever want to see Jonathan again."

Margaret's heart began to race. *Could this be the call we've been waiting for?* It wasn't the first caller claiming to have information about her grandson. But this was different. This man had personal information. He was direct, professional, bold—he clearly had an agenda.

Stay calm, be polite, responsive. Keep the caller engaged, Margaret thought as she remembered Agent Fox's instructions. "I'll be happy to get Jake for you, sir," Margaret said calmly as she motioned to Abigail Foster, the young FBI agent who Fox had assigned to phone duty that day. "I would greatly appreciate if you could tell me if Jonathan is alright," Margaret said respectfully.

Agent Foster sprang to life as she used one hand to adjust the earpiece on her headset and the other to engage the surveillance software.

"You seem like a lovely woman, Mrs. Bishop. As much as I would enjoy conversing with you, our time today is limited and I have business with your son. I must caution you that it would be in everyone's best interest for you to put him on the phone."

"Please don't hang up. I'll get him for you right away." Margaret walked as briskly as she could to Jake's den. She stopped at the doorway, searching carefully for the words.

Jake detected a frail silhouette bathing in the bright morning sun spilling in from the dining room windows. He was unable to see the bewildered shock on Margaret's face.

"Jake, there's a man on the phone. He says he has information about Jonathan."

"Can't Agent Foster take the information?" Jake asked

calmly, his vacant eyes turning back to the playful birds outside.

"Jake, you need to take this one…this may be the call." Margaret's tone was grave.

Jake slowly rose from his chair, his eyes suddenly filled with fearful curiosity. He moved closer to see the expression on his mother's face and realized the caller waiting on the other end of the line was about to change his life.

"Hello, this is Jacob Bishop."

"Mr. Bishop. Listen, do not speak. We have your son. I won't be taking questions today; you should listen very carefully to the instructions I'm about to give you."

"Where do you have my son? Is he alive?" The adrenaline was already racing through Jake's body.

"Mr. Bishop, every syllable you speak is a waste of valuable time." The caller's mechanical voice was void of emotion.

"Please, you have to let me talk to Jonathan. I'll do anything you want."

The ten silent seconds that followed seemed like an eternity. Agent Foster's eyes were closed as she hung her head and released a sigh of desperation. Her screen read "CALL TERMINATED."

"Hello! Hello! Please talk to me! Please. Hello, are you still there?" Jake's heart was slamming against his chest. He had lost his son all over again. "My God. What have I done?" Jake asked desperately.

"It's okay, Jake. He'll call back. And we have a

number—it's a start," Agent Foster said confidently as she sprang back to work, tapping on her keyboard.

"A number? You got a trace?"

"Not a trace, just the number. But with that we can track his cell site information."

"What if he doesn't call back? What then?" Jake already sounded defeated.

"This is a business transaction, Mr. Bishop. He'll call back. He's just letting you know who's in charge. But even if he doesn't call again, we may be able to track his location through his cell phone."

"What do you mean we *may* be able to track his location?"

"Well, as long as he keeps his phone on, it registers its location with the closest tower every several seconds. Each time he moves, the phone searches for the nearest tower. With a court order, the phone carrier will provide us with that data."

"How close can you pinpoint him?" Jake asked, a bit more optimistic.

"It depends," Foster replied, still typing. "If he's using a newer model phone and hasn't deactivated his GPS chip, we can pinpoint him to within about fifty feet with a good signal. Otherwise, we'll have to try to triangulate the signal from the cell towers. Our success with that all depends upon the number of towers around him."

"You said you got a number. Do we know who the number belongs to?"

"I'm working on that right now." Agent Foster's voice sounded tentative, her eyes still glued to her computer screen.

The silence hung in the air as Jake and Margaret waited for Agent Foster's screen to refresh. Then it appeared in black and white—a name. Jason Kingsley, 6013 Washington Avenue, Chicago. "We have a hit," Foster declared. "Jason Kingsley. Wasn't he one of the names on your problem client list?" Foster asked as she typed Kingsley's name into the search field of the FBI's database.

"Kingsley. I'll never forget him. He was my first felony criminal defense case when I worked for the firm back in Chicago," Jake said.

"Why did you consider him for your suspect list?"

"He was a very dissatisfied client—generally just an angry son of a bitch."

"What do you remember about him?"

"He was a mid-level drug dealer, originally from Milwaukee. When he became successful, he moved his game to Chicago. He eventually got busted purchasing felony weight from an undercover narcotics officer. Criminal law wasn't really my field back then, but it was a relatively low-profile case for the firm, and the partners wanted me to cut my teeth on it."

"I take it you didn't get the acquittal?" Foster asked.

"Not even close. It was an impossible case to win, but no matter how hard I tried, I couldn't get the asshole to take the plea. I should have tried him on insanity—that would have been a better fit."

"Our caller didn't sound very insane."

"No. He didn't sound very angry either," Jake said, his mind traveling back to his days at the firm. "If Kingsley is part of this, there's no way he isn't getting help. An elaborate kidnapping plot just doesn't fit his skill set."

"You don't sound optimistic about this guy, Mr. Bishop." Foster replied.

"I'm just puzzled. The Jason Kingsley I knew was a fairly successful businessman, but only because nobody dared cross him. The guy is practically a thug. Most dealers are smart enough not to use their own product. This guy not only moved a lot of product, he used a lot as well. And the cocaine took its toll. Describing this guy as angry would be a gross understatement. If he really wanted revenge, he would have put a bullet in the back of my head by now."

"You seem pretty confident."

"I just keep thinking back to the last thing Kingsley whispered in my ear after the verdict was read," Jake said in a worried tone as he turned to Foster.

"What was that?"

"He said, 'You rookie suit, I ought to put a fuckin' bullet in the back of your skull.'"

CHAPTER 22

MEET MR. KINGSLEY

Agent Fox silently navigated the halls of the affluent Chicago condominium with his team. He brushed his thumb across the safety of the 9mm Beretta that was loosely resting in its holster.

Twenty-four hours had passed since Kingsley's call. Given the high media profile of the case, Fox had little difficulty convincing a district court judge to issue an order for the wireless service provider to furnish information for Kingsley's phone. His Honor readily agreed that probable cause existed that would yield evidence of a crime, and within hours Fox and his team had confirmation that the phone was exchanging signals with the towers surrounding a three-mile radius of the drug dealer's lavish home.

As Fox crept down the gaudy hallway, gently placing one foot after the other on the plush burgundy carpeting, a sense of uncertainty lingered in his mind. *Why hasn't there been another call from this asshole? What is he waiting for?* Fox thought. *Did something spook him? Is he playing mind games with us? Or is this whole thing just another hoax?* Fox stopped short in mid-prowl and drew in a deep breath. It was time to get perspective, time to clear his head so he could think straight. Then suddenly the clarity returned. Regardless of the outcome, Fox decided not to labor over violating the civil liberties of a drug wholesaler.

As he approached the entrance to Kingsley's suite, Agent Fox captured his team's attention and motioned his eyes to the small security camera perched in the corner above the doorway. If his highness was at home, he knew he had guests.

Fox stepped clear of the door and pressed the doorbell buried deep within the inlay of mahogany trim. An elegant series of chimes rang out a stately melody, and Fox rolled his eyes toward his colleague.

As the agents listened closely, they could hear footsteps coming from deep inside. The muffled steps grew louder as they approached the front door, sounding clumsy with an aimless stride. The heavy wooden door creaked open, revealing their kidnapper.

Their host opened the door wide, seemingly with nothing to hide. His black silk robe hung sloppily over his large dumpy build, showing his thick carpet of black chest hair and striped boxer shorts. He stood in the doorway in the presence of the four agents, two with their hands on their holsters, and two with guns in hand.

"Relax, folks, I'm unarmed," Kingsley announced with a grin as he casually spread his arms open, revealing even more beneath his robe.

"Are you Jason Kingsley?" Fox asked.

"Yeah, that's me. What can I do for ya?" Kingsley enunciated his syllables like a Mafioso misfit who had been orphaned from his criminal family.

"Mr. Kingsley, my name is Agent Fox. My team and I are with the FBI, and we need to ask you a few questions. Do you mind if we step inside?"

"You guys bring a search warrant?" Kinsley inquired, his arms still raised half-mast, a cup of coffee in one hand and a section of newspaper in the other.

"We've got one on the way. Do we need it?" Fox replied.

"I suppose not. I got nothin' to hide from you fine federal employees. Come on inside and have a bagel." Kingsley slowly lowered his arms and motioned the agents inside.

Fox signaled the two younger agents to hang back in the hallway as he and his senior agent, David Stockton, entered the residence. "Is there anyone else home with you today, Mr. Kingsley"? Stockton asked as they followed their host into the dining room.

"Nope, it's just me today, boys. My lady friend is all pissed off; haven't had a sighting of her for awhile."

"How did you happen to get on her bad side?" Fox inquired.

"Oh, you know how it is. Left the toilet seat up, forgot her birthday, insulted her mother, who the hell knows?" Kingsley replied as he closed his robe and sat down at the dining room table. Fox and Stockton were both comforted by their ability to see through the glass-top table to detect that no weapons were visible below. They were also relieved Kingsley had closed production on his silk underwear display.

"So, what line of work are you in, Mr. Kingsley?" Fox asked.

"Well, I imagine you boys have a pretty good idea of my vocation," Kingsley replied as he offered a basket of bagels.

"You mean your distribution of narcotics, money laundering, and racketeering?" Stockton responded as he waived off the bagels.

"Nah, you boys have me all wrong. That's all in the past. I've done my time—been rehabilitated. It's all legit nowadays. I even gave up the drugs, that shit'll kill ya. I'm into investments, real estate mostly. Got a couple clubs downtown, some apartment buildings, even a strip mall out in the burbs."

"Sounds like the makings of another Donald Trump," Fox offered sarcastically.

"Well, it is what it is, guys. A man's gotta make a living. Now I know you didn't come all the way over here today for a social visit. What's got you sniffin' around?"

"We'll get right to the point, Mr. Kingsley. We're investigating the disappearance of a little five-year-old boy, and our investigation led us straight to you through your cell phone activity," Fox stated bluntly as he watched Kingsley's reaction.

"You guys are lookin' into that Bishop kid, aren't you? I saw Mr. Bishop on the tube a few times. He was my old attorney, you know?"

"We have information to that effect," Fox replied casually. "We also know that you threatened to harm Mr.

Bishop when he wasn't able to get you kicked at your criminal trial a few years back."

"Oh, man, that was a long time ago, guys. Just some trash talk by a desperate man, that's all that was. I've got no beef with Mr. Bishop. You boys have wasted a trip out here today."

"I've got just one problem with that, Mr. Kingsley. Mr. Bishop received a call from your cell phone yesterday. The caller claimed to be holding Jonathan Bishop. So, it appears that we have something to discuss."

Kingsley raised his eyebrows to display his best quizzical expression. Suddenly, they all heard the muffled sound of a distressed voice.

"Excuse me, gentlemen, I need to check on something," Kingsley said as he sprang up to respond to the commotion.

"Sit your ass down and put your hands flat on the table," Stockton barked. He pulled his weapon and leveled it directly at Kingsley's head."

"Easy, boys! It's not what you think. I got nothing to do with that kid. I'm telling you the truth," Kingsley cried out as he complied with Stockton's instructions.

"Who's here with you?" Fox snapped, pulling his small walkie from his inside pocket.

"Nobody...just a lady friend. Look, guys. I don't wanna get jammed up with my old lady. There's nothing here you'd be interested in."

Another muted call came from further inside the condo. "Danby, Sturgis, step in here and help me clear the premises," Fox instructed through the walkie. The two agents swiftly entered, almost before Fox had time to release the button on his transmitter.

As Fox quickly briefed his agents, Stockton stood watch over his prey. Stockton's firearm was freakishly steady as it extended out from his husky forearm. Kingsley thought about the half-eaten bagel just inches away from his right hand, but opted against reaching for another helping after glancing into his captor's eyes.

Fox and his agents went from room to room, carefully searching every shady nook. As he navigated through the maze of over-decorated rooms, Fox was assaulted by bulky Victorian furniture, pretentious artwork, and ornamental knickknacks. *Real estate investor my ass*, he thought to himself.

By the time Fox and his agents reached the end of the long hallway they had cleared every room but one—the master suite. As Fox reached for the doorknob, they heard another stifled moan from the other side of the door. He knew what his agents were thinking; he was thinking it, too. The headlines flashed through Fox's head: *FBI FOILS KIDNAPPER!...LOCAL AGENT CREDITED WITH SAFE RETURN OF BISHOP BOY.*

The agents positioned themselves on either side of the doorway as Fox prepared to breach the room. After a deep cleansing breath, Fox burst through the door, scanning the room down the barrel of his weapon. The room was dim, lit by a single lamp, and he saw a naked body, totally immobilized, sprawled out like a snow angel across the large canopied bed. He quickly surveyed the room for others. The clear view into the large master bath revealed no one, and the perimeter of the room was occupied by French provincial furniture that offered no cover for unwelcomed guests.

The only person in the room with Fox was straddled across the bed, screaming through a mouthful of silk handkerchief, staring at him with a desperate look of terror.

Fox turned on another lamp nearby to get a better look at the figure on the bed; it was a young female. She was tied to the four corners of the bed by her wrists and ankles. Judging by her physical size and the development of her body, Fox guessed the woman to be between eighteen and twenty-one years of age.

"Clear that closet over there," Fox shouted to the younger agent who was standing next to him, gawking at the woman.

"It's okay, ma'am. I'm an FBI agent. We're here to help you," Fox said as he lowered his weapon and secured it in its holster. He carefully approached her and pulled a sheet over her exposed body. He then gently removed the wad of cloth from her mouth, which was packed much tighter than he expected.

She gasped for air, struggling to cough up a string of vulgar declarations.

"Where is that fat-ass, needle-dick, son of a bitch? That mother fucker has a lot of nerve tying me up and leaving me in here to rot!"

"Calm down, ma'am. You're safe now," Fox assured her. "I'm going to untie you now. Why don't you tell me what happened?"

"Ah, shit! I suppose you assholes are going to arrest me. I just got out last week. Don't you cocksuckers have better things to do than harass us working girls?"

"You're a prostitute," Fox declared softly as he released a sigh of defeat.

"Yeah, that's right. What the hell did you think I was doing in here all tied up? I was doing alright until that fat prick decided to play gag the play date."

"You a regular of Mr. Kingsley?"

"I've been up here a few times. He pays well, so I don't mind putting up with his shit. But today he jambs that damn rag down my throat and goes off to make breakfast. I've been tied up for almost an hour while that lard ass is out there cooking up bacon and eggs!"

"Have you ever seen Kingsley with any young children, or heard him talk inappropriately about young children?"

"No, he ain't into the child porn; not that I know of anyway. He likes the ladies." She rubbed the stiffness out of her wrists.

Fox untied the last of the restraints, tossed the woman's clothes onto the bed, and glanced over at his other junior agent. "Get her dressed, get her information, and get her the hell out of here."

As Fox left the bedroom, his cell phone rang. "Fox."

"Sir, it's Rafferty. I've been going over Kingsley's cell phone records. I think we have a problem."

"I'm listening."

"There's no activity showing for the time that the call came into the Bishop residence."

"What do you mean no activity? His number came up on the system."

"It was his number, but not his phone. We think the caller ran the call through a spoof card service. He just borrowed Kingsley's number to throw us off his trail."

"Can we track the origin of the call?"

"It could take awhile. There are a number of spoof card providers, and they're not always cooperative without a court order."

"Keep me apprised. I'll check in with you later." Fox hung up and cursed the technology invading his life. "I'm getting too old for this shit," he mumbled.

Fox gave Stockton the all clear to holster his weapon. He then assembled his team and motioned them toward the exit.

"Have a nice day, Mr. Kingsley."

"That's it? You guys aren't running us in on the prostitution charge?"

"Not our department. Besides, you'd both be out before lunch. Good luck with your real estate investments."

Stockton was the last out the door, giving Kingsley a wink and a shooting gesture with his index finger and thumb.

Fox and his men marched down the hallway without saying a word. None of the other agents knew the nature of the phone call Fox had received or why they were leaving without Kingsley, but they could tell by Fox's stern expression that it was not the time to ask questions.

CHAPTER 23

DEAR MR. BISHOP

The letter came in a plain white envelope addressed to Mr. Jacob Bishop. Jake's name and address had been hammered on by an old manual typewriter. Margaret noticed the absence of a return address, but this failed to arouse her suspicion. In the weeks following Jonathan's disappearance, Jake had received hundreds of letters from all around the country, many without a return address. Some were monetary pledges, others simply offers to help, but most were notes of sympathy and support.

What Margaret failed to notice was the absence of a postmark on the envelope. This letter had not been delivered by the postman. She tucked the letter into the pile with the rest of the day's mail and shuffled into the house to escape the chilly morning air.

"Good morning, Jacob. How did you sleep?"

"Mother, I asked you to use the side entrance. You're going to fall on those icy steps one of these days." Jake sat at the kitchen table trying to choke down another bite of his toast.

"Why don't you let me whip you up a real breakfast?" Margaret asked.

"No, thank you. This will do."

Margaret set the pile of mail on the breakfast table

and poured herself a cup of coffee. "Jacob, you need to start taking better care of yourself. You need to start getting your life back on track. You're no good to anyone like this."

Jake took another bite of dry toast and poked through the mail with his free hand, showing little interest in his mother's lecture.

One piece of mail stood out from the pile of bills and marketing flyers. Jake noticed his name and address sharply imprinted onto the crisp white envelope.

"Who uses a manual typewriter anymore?" Jake asked rhetorically, reaching for a clean butter knife to open the letter.

"Oh, there's still a few of us old-timers who keep them around," Margaret replied.

Jake removed a thick white piece of paper from the envelope and squinted to focus on the typed message. From where she was sitting, Margaret could tell that the author's message filled the page and spilled onto the back of the paper.

"Who is it from, dear?"

Jake sat motionless as he read in disbelief.

"Jacob, what is it? Who is the letter from?" No longer able to take the suspense, Margaret set her coffee cup down on the counter and positioned herself behind Jake where she could get a clear view of the letter.

Dear Mr. Bishop,

It was unfortunate that you were unable to follow my instructions during our brief telephone conversation this past week. Your unnecessary delay proved to be as fruitless as your pursuit of Mr. Kingsley. Our business surely could have been concluded by now.

Your son is a very nice little boy. We have enjoyed his company. It would be a shame if anything were to happen to him due to your inability to maintain your focus.

If you have any doubts about the legitimacy of this letter, or as to whether we are truly your son's captors, allow me to share a few interesting observations about young Jonathan.

We have been amused by his love for Dean Martin music, his stories about Uncle Prof and his Grandfather Henry, and his aversion to peanut butter. We also couldn't help noticing the small birthmark on his left thigh, and the unusual necklace he wears around his neck. Some sort of artifact replica is it? It seems to have great significance to him.

You would be well advised to take this matter seriously. This will be the only proof we will offer of our authenticity. It is not our practice to provide physical evidence to the FBI.

We couldn't help noticing that you and your mother enjoy a comfortable net worth. By our calculations, your liquid resources combined exceed $1.5 million. However, there is no need for us to be greedy now, is there? Grandma Margaret deserves a comfortable retirement. With that bad knee of hers, she'll probably need money for the nursing home someday.

Our business can be concluded for the sum of $1 million. Follow our instructions and Jonathan will be released unharmed. Cash is not acceptable. An order has been placed with a private diamond broker in Chicago. The broker's name is Niles Westerby. You may contact him by e-mail: niles@westerbygems.com. He will expect contact from my assistant buyer, Jacob Bishop, who has business in Chicago this Wednesday. He will fill the order with loose cut diamonds, no laser inscriptions, no trademarks.

Mr. Westerby will provide you with the necessary routing information to wire your funds to his business account. Once he confirms receipt of the money, Westerby will release the diamonds to you. You will travel to Chicago to pick them up. You will take your mother's Buick. Nobody will accompany you on your trip to Chicago, or on your return trip home. There will be no surveillance of your vehicle, and no tracking devices of any sort. No law enforcement or FBI will contact Mr. Westerby, nor will they be involved in the acquisition of the product.

You will receive further instructions upon your return to Maple Creek with the merchandise.

Failure to follow these instructions precisely will result in disastrous consequences.

Sincerely,
Friends of Jonathan

Jake and Margaret stared at the letter, both paralyzed with fear. Each wanting to speak, but neither knowing what to say. The same thoughts played in their minds: *How could they possibly have such detailed information? None of it was released to the media. They have Jonathan. He's still alive.*

"Jacob, you can have my savings…all of it. Just get him back," Margaret said in earnest, breaking the silence.

Jake's mind raced miles ahead of his mother's voice. He could not notify Stone or the FBI—involving law enforcement would cost Jonathan his life. He could have the money together by noon. Most of their accounts were tied up in money markets and certificates of deposit, easily liquidated. Margaret would need to sell some stocks, but that was just a phone call to the investment broker downtown. The wire to the Chicago diamond broker would be done from his uncle's bank to ensure privacy.

He couldn't use his phones or even his computer. The

FBI had traces on everything. He would e-mail the broker from the computer at Maggie's coffee shop, and pick up a pre-paid cell phone at the Wal-Mart in the next town.

If Stone or Fox inquired about his absence, Margaret would tell them he was meeting a wealthy client in Chicago who was on his deathbed and needed to complete his estate plan.

He would gas up Margaret's Buick, pack a light suitcase, and fill the extra clips for his 9mm Beretta. No risk was too great now. It was time to get his son back. The FBI had gone long enough without results. Jake was in the diamond business.

CHAPTER 24

BANKING BUSINESS

Detective Stone was scarcely visible behind the files stacked around his desk. The workload had become so overwhelming it was spilling onto the conference table he had commandeered from the break room.

Working with the FBI, Stone was logging double shifts to sift through the thousands of leads that had poured in on the Bishop case. The media frenzy had proven to be a double-edged sword—it had generated public interest, but then again, it had generated public interest. Stone and the FBI simply didn't have the resources to keep pace.

Stone pushed aside the donut box on his desk and looked beneath the pile of sandwich wrappers and loose papers, hoping to locate his phone before the fifth ring.

"Stone here."

"Eric, its Benjamin Bishop."

"Ben, what a surprise. I'm not late on my mortgage again am I?"

"God, I hope not. We don't need any more foreclosures on the books. What a mess."

"Yeah, I imagine you bankers are having to earn your money these days. Have you spoken with Jake lately?" Stone inquired.

"Well, to tell you the truth, Jake is the reason I'm

calling," Benjamin replied hesitantly.

"Is everything alright, Ben?"

"Well, I'm not really sure I should be calling you… especially with the privacy laws and everything. It's probably nothing, but…."

"Ben, what is it? Whatever it is, I'll keep it off the radar if I can."

"I don't think you're keeping this one off the radar, Eric."

"Is Jake in danger?"

Benjamin Bishop drew in a deep breath and released a long sigh. "When I returned from my afternoon coffee break, I overheard one of my chatty tellers mentioning that Jake and Margaret had stopped by the bank to do some business earlier today."

"That doesn't sound so concerning," Stone replied.

"They cashed out four CDs and a money market account—took a penalty on two of them."

"Maybe they had a good reason. Did they reinvest the funds or did they withdraw them?"

"They consolidated everything into Jake's non-interest-bearing checking account—over $650,000.00."

"That *is* strange. Maybe they're reinvesting them with another bank or investor. Has everything been okay between you and Jake?"

"Hell yes, everything's fine. Listen, Eric, the story doesn't stop there. After the tellers changed shifts for lunch, Jake came back in to check on an incoming wire transfer from a brokerage account. Then he requested an outgoing wire transfer, reminded the teller to keep the whole thing on the Q.T. Little did he know he picked the wrong teller; Janell can be a bit of a gossip. I checked the records. He routed the money to some account at a bank in Chicago—all one million dollars of it."

"Chicago?" Stone replied. "Who does the account belong to?"

"Some outfit called Westerby & Associates, LLC—routed to First American Bank in Chicago. Look, Eric, something stinks here. There's no way my sister-in-law and her son would ship that kind of money out of this bank without speaking with me first. This is my family. I've been involved in every major financial decision they've ever made. I'm telling you, I think that boy's in some trouble."

"Have you told anyone else about this, Ben?"

"Just you, and I damn sure had some reservations about that."

"You did the right thing. Listen, don't mention this to anyone else. I'll have a little chat with Jake and Margaret. I'll try to keep you out of it for now."

"Thanks, Eric. I know you'll handle it the best you can. Keep me posted."

Stone hung up, grabbed his half-eaten pastrami sandwich with one hand, his black wool overcoat with the other, and rushed out of the station without a word to his colleagues. Not an unusual occurrence at the Maple Creek Police Station.

Stone was reluctant to involve the FBI until he had more facts. If Jake was moving that kind of money around without calling him, there had to be a good reason. But he hoped it had nothing to do with Jonathan.

Since Jake's phones were still being monitored, Stone dismissed the thought of making contact by telephone. This development required a face-to-face visit. Jake had been putting very little time in at the office since Jonathan's abduction, and Stone knew the most likely place to locate him would be at home, tucked away in the dark seclusion of his den.

As Stone wound through the streets of Maple Creek, his mind drifted out on the snowy landscape. Memories of his childhood arose at each curve in the road. He passed Pendergrass Pond where he and Jake played hockey when they were kids; he drove down Dead Man's Pass, the steep hill that served as their sledding run in the winter and their soapbox derby hill in the summer; and in the distance he could see Partridge Bluff, where Jake accidentally shot him in the ass with his BB gun during one of their big game hunts.

He drove past the street where Jake's childhood home was located. As his cruiser rolled through the intersection, Stone glanced down Vine Street to catch a glimpse of Margaret's house, a habit carried over from his high school days on the prowl.

Noticing Jake's white Jeep parked in Margaret's driveway, Stone checked his rearview mirror for traffic then slid the car to a stop on the snow-packed road. "Perfect, two Bishops for the price of one," he said to himself as he threw the cruiser in reverse.

As he waited on Margaret's porch for her to answer, Stone began to question whether anyone was home. Jake's Jeep was in the driveway, but Margaret's Buick was absent from the garage. The kitchen was dimly lit, but the rest of the house appeared dark, blending into the dismal December haze.

"Margaret, are you home, dear?" Stone yelled out, knocking loudly on the front door. "Hello…Margaret?"

"Who's making all the racket out here?" Margaret swung open the squeaky maple door.

"Sorry, Margaret. I didn't think anyone was at home."

"Well, hello, Eric. What brings you out today, son?"

"I saw Jake's Jeep in the driveway. I thought he might be around."

"No, he borrowed my car again. I swear, I don't know why that boy doesn't just get rid of that old Jeep and that relic Riviera and buy himself something with a good heater."

"It must be the nostalgia."

"I suppose. His father was the same way, you know."

"Yes, I remember Henry could be a bit sentimental. So where did Jake run off to with your Buick?" Stone asked casually.

"He had to drive down to Chicago to meet a client. Some big estate plan…I guess some poor man is on his deathbed."

"Well, I'm sorry to hear that. I wonder how Jake picked up a client from Chicago."

"Someone from his days at the firm there I suppose. Should I tell him you stopped by?" Margaret asked, seeming anxious.

"I would appreciate that, ma'am. It's urgent that I speak with him, and he's not answering his cell phone." Stone could almost see the gears spinning in Margaret's head. He had clearly triggered her curiosity.

"Is there a new development in the case? Something I should know about?"

"Well, I can't go into the details, but I am a little concerned for Jake's safety."

"Eric, you're scaring me now. Is Jake in danger? What's happened?"

"I'm sorry, Margaret; I don't mean to worry you unnecessarily. I probably shouldn't have mentioned anything at all. You know I'm not really allowed to discuss the details of the case. The FBI has me sworn to secrecy on the progress of the investigation. I'm sure Jake will be fine. I'll have him check in with you as soon as I'm able to locate him," Stone replied, adding more bait to the hook.

"Eric Stone, who do you think you're talking to?" Margaret scolded. "I took you over my knee more than once when you were a snot-nosed delinquent, and you can be damn sure I'm not afraid to get down to business right now. If my son is in trouble, you had better give me every detail right this instant."

It was everything Stone could do not to crack a smile. *There's the old Margaret I remember*, he thought. "Margaret, as part of the investigation we have been monitoring Jake's bank accounts," Stone lied. "There's been some very unusual activity, and it's got me plenty concerned."

"I don't understand," Margaret replied, clearly feigning her confusion.

"Jake made a transfer of funds to a bank in Chicago today; a very *large* transfer."

"Really?" Margaret tried to express her most credible look of intrigue.

Stone studied Margaret's face carefully as he threw his next pitch. "It was such a large transfer of funds that it almost smells like a ransom reply." He paused briefly as he waited for Margaret's response, but there was none. He could tell she was conflicted.

Stone increased the heat. "If Jake is caught up in the middle of a ransom drop, he could be in grave danger." Still no response. "Any number of things could go wrong…The statistics aren't on our side, Margaret…We could end up losing them both."

Margaret Bishop stood quietly in the doorway with a blank stare, appearing as if her thoughts were a million miles away. "Oh my," she whispered.

"Well, I'm so sorry to trouble you, Margaret. We may be worrying for nothing. I'll be in touch very soon." Stone patted Margaret's shoulder, then turned and walked down the sidewalk toward his vehicle. He felt as if he was abandoning Margaret on the porch like a piece of collateral damage.

My God, I hope I'm right about this, he thought. *I hope she really knows something. If not, I've just needlessly tortured my best friend's mother.*

Stone kept a steady pace down the sidewalk, waiting for Margaret's response, but heard only the rustle of the crisp oak leaves blowing in the wind. As he reached to open the car door, he heard the call.

"Eric, wait!" Margaret cried out, reluctantly pulling the ransom letter from her apron pocket.

CHAPTER 25

THE BLACK JACK MOTEL

The squad car rolled slowly through the motel parking lot, destined for the diner at the end of the roadway. It had been a slow shift for the deputy, nothing but a few domestic disputes, a disorderly conduct citation, and three drunk driving arrests. As always, he was looking forward to ending his shift with a light breakfast, a cup of decaf coffee, and some flirtatious banter with the married waitress who worked at the diner. Just another morning on the dusty outskirts of Las Vegas, Nevada.

As he drove, Deputy Brink instinctively glanced at the license plates on the cars lined up in front of the motel rooms. He noticed a few out-of-state plates, but locals mostly—regional salesmen, construction workers, young lovers, and of course, the married unfaithful.

The last license plate caught the deputy's eye, and his cruiser rolled to a stop. It was a Nevada plate, but the sticker had expired last month. *Shit, an expired plate. Hardly worth screwing up my breakfast,* he thought. But knowing his sense of duty would ultimately prevail, Brink glanced at his watch and let out a sigh. *I suppose it can't hurt to run it through the system.*

"The plate is registered to a Linda Lightfoot, 923 Rodeo Drive, Las Vegas. 2001 Toyota sedan, blue, no wants…no warrants," the dispatcher's voice crackled through the radio.

"10-4," Brink responded, realizing that his breakfast had just been put on hold. "Sandy, we've got an illegal tag here. The plate is affixed to an Oldsmobile Cutlass, white, late-nineties model. I should probably have some backup on this. I'm over in the parking lot of the Blackjack Motel, in front of room twelve. Is Dodge still on duty?"

"Roger that, Bill," Dodge jumped in. "I'm just up the road. ETA four minutes. Hang tight."

Brink eased his patrol car down the parking lot and backed into a space that offered a good view of the Oldsmobile and the door to room twelve.

Inside, a little boy lay belly-down on the bed, giggling while he watched *SpongeBob SquarePants*. The cartoon carried his young mind far away from the real world. He was no longer missing his comfortable bedroom or his toys. He wasn't thinking about how desperately he missed his father, nor was he wondering why he was sitting alone in a dimly lit hotel room in a strange town, miles away from anything familiar.

Then, there was a loud pounding on the door. The voice that followed sounded loud and mean, sending a chill up the boy's spine.

"Police. Open the door. We have some questions."

His heart pounded like a broken drum. The boy wasn't expecting visitors. The only time the door was ever opened was quietly, with the key. He had strict instructions. *Don't open the door for ANYONE. Even if they claim to be your friend or the police.*

More pounding on the door. “This is the police. Open the door immediately!” The voice was louder, angrier.

The boy was frozen on the bed, unable to think. He tried to remind himself to breathe, but he was too scared. Then, he heard the familiar sound of a key sliding into the lock. He waited for the door to slowly swing open, then watched two men in police uniforms cautiously peer inside. In that instant, the boy knew he was going home.

CHAPTER 26

THE REVELATION

Stone gazed out the window of the FBI helicopter, admiring the reflection of the afternoon sun bouncing off the icy Illinois landscape. He knew that, somewhere below, Jake was traveling back to Wisconsin in Margaret's Buick, accompanied by a one million dollar cargo of diamonds. Agent Fox convinced him that it would be best to let Jake follow through with the acquisition of the precious stones.

Fox's reasoning was sound—Jake had already left for Chicago and the purchase was already in play. Surveilling him from a safe distance allowed them to monitor the situation while still allowing Jake to believe he was independently running the show. Stone and Fox agreed that the kidnapper would likely attempt to intercept Jake on his way back from Chicago, so they had to be prepared to move in quickly.

Stone's eyes drifted shut as he listened to the thumping of the chopper blades overhead. He had been working nearly round the clock, trudging through hundreds of leads. He was relieved to learn that the Vegas Police had apprehended Katherine Kobs and Marty Vance, and that young Samuel Kobs had been safely returned to his father, Daniel Norby. Although he was disappointed Jonathan was not among the individuals recovered in Vegas, he was not particularly surprised. He had always reserved his doubts about Katherine's involvement in Jonathan's abduction. Nevertheless, he knew they would need to interrogate Kobs and Vance if the latest ransom escapade proved fruitless. He suspected a trip to Nevada was in his future.

Just as Stone was beginning to nod off, Agent Fox nudged him and motioned to three deer below, running from one patch of woods to the next. Stone saw a sizeable rack on one of the deer, even from their elevation in the chopper. The detective thought back to his last deer hunting trip with Jake, just before Jonathan's abduction. Although it had only been a few months, it seemed like an eternity.

A slight smile appeared on the detective's face as he thought about their past hunting trips. He recalled sipping blackberry brandy from Jake's thermos as the old pickup bounced along the snow-covered logging trail. He remembered reminiscing about the stories Henry would spin around the dinner table after a long day of hunting. He thought about Eisner's old cabin and the good times they enjoyed there—drinking Irish coffee by a roaring fire, a cigar in one hand and a bad hand of poker in the other. It was the one place that a guy could truly get away from the real world. Escape into the wilderness, far away from the demands of a complicated life. *Nobody could find you there,* he thought.

Then, in an instant of clarity, it hit Agent Stone like a bolt of lightning. *It was her. The woman…the dark-haired woman at Eisner's cabin. It was her. My God,* he thought, *she was the same woman from the police artist sketch. The sketch from the witness accounts of the blonde woman at Jonathan's school. She had to be wearing a wig—or maybe dyed her hair. How the hell could I have missed it? I had her at the cabin that day! I could have prevented this whole thing. It's my fault…my God, it's all my fault.*

Stone immediately saw the bloody image of Taylor Vick. The thought of the lifeless boy weaved with the innocent pictures of Jonathan in his mind. *I can't let it happen again,* he thought. *It can't end like this…he's got to be alive. Think, damn it. I can fix this. I've got to fix this.*

He wasn't sure exactly what to do with his new revelation, but there was no doubt in his mind that the woman from Eisner's cabin was somehow implicated in Jonathan's disappearance.

It was all beginning to make sense. The woman's suspicious behavior, her comfortable handling of the Winchester rifle, the satellite phone, and the white SUV Principal Dornfeld reported had to be the same white Ford Explorer they had seen at the cabin that day.

As Stone sorted through the images in his mind like pieces of a jigsaw puzzle, he kept coming back to the white SUV. Something about the vehicle had haunted him—had been right in front of his nose the whole time. *Of course! The break-in at Jake's house,* he thought. The payphone call on Jake's caller I.D. The waitress at the diner remembered a light-colored SUV parked at the outside payphone just before the break-in, at the same time the call was placed to the Bishop home. She recalled a black-haired man on the phone, and she remembered a female passenger.

This was no random kidnapping; no amateur caper. The surveillance, the planning, the precision, it was becoming obvious to Detective Stone—whoever was behind this was intelligent, experienced, motivated, and very well-funded.

But all of that effort, all of that risk, for a million in stones? The math still didn't add up.

CHAPTER 27

A DIAMOND IN THE HAND

Jake was exhausted. The meeting with the diamond broker in Chicago had been successful, and surprisingly easy. Mr. Westerby seemed to harbor no suspicions—the receipt of the wire transfer was confirmed, and the product was delivered.

Jake was convinced Westerby had no knowledge of the kidnapping, or the true identity of Jake's fictitious employer. Westerby's casual demeanor made it seem as though the transaction was just another routine exchange brokered with an out-of-town buyer.

Jake was surprised just how few diamonds scattered out on the black velvet tray when Westerby offered them up for inspection. He wished he had taken the time to research the precious stones before taking delivery on his million-dollar purchase. "I'm sure those will do fine," Jake had responded with an air of pretention.

"Mr. Bishop, don't you wish to give the stones a closer inspection?"

"It is not my satisfaction that should concern you, Mr. Westerby. My employer is a most powerful man; I trust these stones will meet *his* satisfaction?" Even Jake was beginning to buy his own bullshit.

"I'm quite certain they will, sir," Westerby replied respectfully.

Westerby's confidence in his product seemed genuine, and Jake was content with his purchase. When he left the Chicago high-rise with his gems locked safely in his black leather briefcase, Jake was overcome by a sense of optimism. It was the first time since Jonathan's disappearance that he actually thought he might see his son alive. But now, as he traveled alone down a secluded county highway, Jake was having second thoughts.

He thought back to the instructions in the kidnapper's letter and the strict warning at the end. *Failure to follow these instructions precisely will result in disastrous consequences.*

Jake slid his hand beneath the leather coat that was folded neatly on the passenger seat beside him. He could feel the cold grip of his Beretta as he repositioned the weapon and let out a sigh. He suspected he might confront the kidnapper before reaching his destination, and he was beginning to question the wisdom of flying solo.

As the sun set, Jake noticed the brilliant colors painted across the western horizon. Under other circumstances, he would have been taken in by the beauty, but the vastness of the landscape offered him nothing but loneliness. Jake was unaware of the cavalry hovering several hundred feet above his head. He was also unaware of the transponder secured to the frame of Margaret's car, which had been sending his precise location to the kidnapper for the past two days. Jake had no idea how complicated things had already become.

Just as he switched on the headlights, Jake was startled by an unfamiliar cell phone ring. It was muffled, as if coming from somewhere beneath the dash of the car.

Trying to keep his eyes on the road, Jake leaned closer to the passenger side to pinpoint the source of the ringing. With every muffled ring, he tuned in closer. As he lifted up the corner of the carpeted floor mat, Jake discovered the brightly illuminated display of a foreign cell phone, ringing louder now that it was uncovered.

Jake picked up the phone and examined the display, "UNKNOWN CALLER." His first thought was that the phone had slipped out of the purse of one of Margaret's lady friends. He decided the least he could do was answer and learn the identity of its owner.

"Hello, can I help you?" he answered pleasantly.

"Mr. Bishop, it's nice to hear your voice again."

"Who is this?"

"I believe you have a delivery for me."

Jake's heart raced. He quickly checked his rearview mirror, then panned the darkening landscape around him. He was unable to detect any other headlights nearby.

"Is my son alive?"

"Of course—he wouldn't be much good to me any other way, would he?"

Jake didn't recognize the deep throaty voice of the caller. It was no longer altered like the last call from the kidnapper, but it did sound as if the caller was disguising his true voice.

"Please tell me where he is. I'm begging you."

"All in good time, Mr. Bishop. You're close to the end of

your journey. Don't mess this up again by failing to follow my instructions."

"What do you want me to do?"

"There's a diner coming up on your right in less than four miles, Abbey's Family Diner. Terminate this call, call no one, talk to no one, alert no one. Pull into the diner parking lot, turn off your engine, wait for further instructions."

"Will my son be there?…Hello?…Hello?"

The caller was gone.

Jake pressed the red button on his new cell phone to ensure that the connection had been terminated and then he slid it into the pocket of his black fleece vest. As he increased his speed to close the gap on the diner, he fought the urge to dig out his own cell phone and call Detective Stone. *I can't screw this up. Stay cool. Follow the instructions. It's almost over.* Without thinking, Jake slid his hand back onto his Beretta, his thumb resting anxiously on the safety.

Jake could see a dim grouping of lights on the horizon. As he approached he could make out the glowing canopy of a service station. Just past the gas station was a small diner nestled snugly into a few acres of woods.

As Jake pulled into the parking lot, he noticed the large illuminated sign braced across the roof: *ABBEY'S FAMILY DI ER.*

"Great," Jake mumbled. "Of all the letters to be burned out—not a good sign."

Jake was comforted by the cars and the two tractor-trailers resting along the outskirts of the parking lot. *Safety in numbers*, he reasoned. He positioned Margaret's Buick centrally in the lot, in clear view of the patrons he saw dining inside. As instructed, he turned off the engine and waited for his next call.

Jake set his new cell phone on the dash and waited patiently. Five minutes passed, then ten, then fifteen. No call. It didn't take long for the temperature inside the Buick to drop, and his warm breath soon steamed up the windows. He folded his scarf into a square, wiped the moisture from the inside of the glass, then cracked open the driver's window to let in some fresh air.

As he sat alone, lit by the glow from Abbey's sign, Jake's eyes carefully scouted the dark edges of the parking lot. *The kidnapper could be anywhere,* he thought. He could be inside the diner enjoying a meatloaf sandwich, tormenting him by making him wait out the next call. He could be hunched down in one of these cold cars, waiting for just the right moment. Or he could be lurking beyond the parking lot, just inside the shadows of the tree line, assessing whether Jake had come alone as instructed.

Jake held up his arm and tried to position his watch to catch enough light to read the time. Twenty minutes had passed since his arrival, and there had been little activity at the remote roadside diner—at least none that looked promising. Jake watched one of the truckers exit the diner and stroll back to his rig, and then throttle loudly through the gears as he made his way back to the main road. A few minutes later, an elderly couple slowly shuffled back to their pickup truck, the old man gently holding his wife's arm as they walked carefully across the icy lot. *Probably not the kidnapper,* Jake deduced.

He also watched a half-dozen snowmobiles come and go while he waited, appearing and disappearing by way of a nearby trail that led into the woods just behind the diner. There were several miles of groomed trails throughout the region, and Abbey's was a popular stop for snowmobilers looking to take in a warm meal and top off their gas tanks for the next leg of their journey.

What Jake had not noticed was the helicopter periodically hovering over his head for the last hour, which was now set down in a nearby field to conserve fuel. He also failed to detect the two FBI agents surveilling his vehicle from the black sedan in the shadows of the service road a few hundred yards away. And as he sat silently in the darkness, fighting off the cold, he was surrounded by friends, yet overwhelmed with loneliness.

CHAPTER 28

SEVERED EXPECTATIONS

The ring nearly made Jake jump from his skin. He took a deep breath and checked the display on the cell phone, "UNKNOWN CALLER."

"Hello." Jake's tone was tired—tentative.

"Mr. Bishop, listen carefully. Place the sack of diamonds in your coat pocket and enter the diner. Sit at the counter, order a cup of coffee, then wait for your next call."

Jake couldn't resist the question. "Please, when can I see my son?" But once again, the caller was gone.

Jake checked the safety on his pistol, then tucked it into the waistband of his pants to conceal it beneath his vest. He removed the black velvet pouch from his briefcase and secured it deep in the pocket of his leather jacket. Next he slipped the cell phone into his other pocket and tucked his car keys under the driver's side floor mat. He took an inventory: *Car keys, wallet, cell phones, gun, diamonds. My God, what have I gotten myself into?*

As Jake entered the diner, he surveyed its customers. There were three men sitting contently at the counter, each working on his meal and minding his own business. *All locals,* Jake thought. A long row of vinyl booths ran the length of the front wall, each offering a clear view of the parking lot.

None of the guests sitting at the booths looked particularly suspicious to Jake. An older couple sat quietly pecking at their meal. A middle-aged businessman wearing a disheveled blue suit and amply loosened tie, stared out the window, neglecting the half-eaten turkey dinner and the spreadsheets scattered on his table.

The remaining booths seemed equally innocuous. A young couple dining with their two small children; four snowmobilers warming their hands on their coffee cups while enjoying a piece of homemade cherry pie; an old farmer wearing heavy bib-overalls, pushing his empty plate away to make room to open his daily newspaper; and two high school boys in letter jackets devouring their greasy double-decker cheeseburgers while laughing at each other's crude jokes. If there were a kidnapper among the group, Jake was unable to pick him out.

Jake took a seat on one of the stools and ordered a cup of black coffee from Darcy, the heavyset waitress working the counter. He set the phone on the shiny Formica surface then checked whether his Beretta was still concealed.

An uneasy feeling settled in as Jake sat alone at the counter with his eyes fixed forward and his back to the world. He felt vulnerable. He realized he had no way to monitor the traffic behind him, and he wondered how long his mysterious caller would make him wait for his next set of instructions.

The coffee was hot and surprisingly good. The warm cup felt comforting between Jake's chilled hands. He tried to relax and act composed as he passed the time scanning the menu board and glancing at the two-day-old sports section that was sitting nearby. Occasionally Jake took an incidental glace over his shoulder to see if there was any change in the scenery.

Then, halfway through his coffee, Jake received his next call. He answered the phone on the first ring, to avoid drawing attention.

"Hello."

"You have thirty seconds. Walk immediately to the men's restroom. Unlatch the window and tilt it open. Drop the sack of diamonds out the window. Return to your stool and finish your coffee. Wait ten minutes, then drive west ten miles to the roadside rest stop. If the product is genuine, you will find your son there, alive and well. It was nice doing business with you, Mr. Bishop."

"I'll do what you say; just let me talk to my son," Jake said softly. But again, the kidnapper was gone.

Jake stuffed the phone back into his pocket, threw a five-dollar bill on the counter, and briskly proceeded to the restroom. It was dark and empty, and Jake was able to locate the light switch just to the left of the door frame. When he switched on the light he stood still in his tracks, carefully listening for any signs of life outside the bathroom wall. The only sound he could detect was water dripping from the leaky bathroom faucet, slapping the sink in perfect tempo.

Jake twisted the window latch counter-clockwise

and felt the window loosen in its frame. Somehow, he could sense someone waiting just on the other side of the window. There wasn't much time. Jake knew he had to make a decision. Either drop a million dollars worth of diamonds out of a bathroom window in the middle of Nowhereville, Illinois, or race outside and attempt to apprehend his son's kidnapper. This was his life savings… his mother's life savings. This would clean them out. What if it was all a hoax?…But, what if it wasn't?

Jake removed the black velvet bag from his pocket and slowly tilted the window open. As he held the bag up to the window opening, his heart pounded violently and he was suddenly hit by a wave of nausea. Jake emptied his mind, took a cleansing breath, and without wavering, he released the bag. He heard the pouch hit the soft snow outside.

Jake switched off the bathroom light, then opened and closed the door to simulate his exit. He then stood motionless in the dark men's room, listening for something on the outside.

Within seconds, he heard footsteps just outside the window. Then, the brief grinding of an electronic starter that quickly sparked the roar of an engine. Jake knew that sound; it was a snowmobile.

The customers all watched Jake as he ran past them in full stride and burst out the front door. It was a short sprint to the outside corner of the building where the restroom window was located, and Jake struggled to maintain his balance as he slid to a stop with his gun in hand.

The snowmobile engine wailed as Jake watched the taillight disappear into the wooded trail. He leveled his Beretta directly at the bouncing red light, switched off the safety, and drew in a deep breath. He had a fifteen-shot magazine, surely he could hit at least once. But after a short pause, Jake exhaled and lowered his weapon. *I can't take a chance on killing this guy. I've got to get to the rest stop to find Jonathan.*

Jake turned to walk back to his car and was suddenly greeted by the headlights of an approaching sedan. He concealed his gun inside his coat, and then raised his hand to shield his eyes from the bright lights. The driver's side window lowered as the sedan pulled up alongside him.

"Mr. Bishop. Agent Jax, FBI." The driver held his credentials up where Jake could see them.

"What in the hell are you guys doing here?"

"We have a helicopter nearby, Mr. Bishop. We need you to come with us. But first, hand me that gun you just tucked inside your pants."

Jake recognized the female agent on the passenger side of the vehicle, and she already had her weapon out of its holster. He slowly pulled out his Beretta and handed it, barrel-down, to Agent Jax.

"Hop in back." Jax motioned to the backseat with his head as he unlocked the backdoors.

"Don't you want to check me for other weapons?" Jake asked.

"Do you have any other weapons?" Jax responded calmly.

"No."

"Then buckle up."

As they pulled away, Jake looked out the back window of the cruiser and caught a glimpse of the customers gathered in the front window of the diner watching the excitement.

"We have to go to the rest stop, just up the road ten miles west," Jake insisted. "They said my son will be there… they said he's still alive."

The two agents briefly glanced at each other with absent expressions. "We'll drive up there and check it out for you, Mr. Bishop," Jax said in a respectful tone.

"We have Mr. Bishop," Jax announced into his handheld radio. "We're in route to a rest stop located ten miles west of our last location. The suspect claims Mr. Bishop's son is there."

"Roger that," came the voice from the other end of the radio. "I'll notify the State Patrol. Tune your mobile unit to that frequency and leave your handheld on this channel."

"Is that Agent Fox?" Jake asked.

"Yes, sir. He and Detective Stone are in pursuit of your snowmobile suspect."

"That *suspect* has a million dollars of my diamonds on him!"

"We know that, sir."

Jake sat quietly in the backseat and tried to piece together the evening. He wasn't sure how the FBI knew about his location, or how they were able to respond so quickly. But he was relieved. He was also terrified about what they might find at the rest stop. Deep down, he knew the truth. The chances of his son being found alive were remote. But he was desperate to believe there was hope.

The radio below the dash suddenly cracked again with the familiar voice. "This is Fox. We've got the suspect lit up with the flood lights. He's approximately two miles southeast of the diner. He appears to be following a major trail running east along the edge of a small lake."

"Roger that, sir. This is Trooper Compton. I'm familiar with that trail. In about five miles that should bring him out near the intersection of Highway 10 and County Road D. We'll attempt an intercept."

"It might not take him long. I think we've spooked him, and he's moving at a pretty high speed."

"Roger that."

The spotlight spilling onto the snow around the snowmobile was clearly terrifying its driver. He weaved along the trail, trying to shake the airborne bloodhound and slip into the darkness. For a brief time, the snowmobile's headlight switched off, but it soon reappeared. Fox knew that at such a high speed the driver must have realized he couldn't navigate a dark trail.

As the sled shot out from a thick canopy of trees, the trail opened into a spacious field. The clouds were clearing and the moon reflected off the crystalline snow. With the benefit of the open territory and the improved visibility, Fox motioned the pilot to close in.

As they descended, Detective Stone furrowed his brow. A seasoned snowmobiler, Stone knew the sled below was traveling much too quickly for the terrain and night conditions. He feared that an offensive move on their part would cause more harm than they were after. If this really was their kidnapper, he may be their only hope of finding Jonathan alive. Stone considered challenging Fox's game plan, but quickly reconsidered. After all, he was merely a guest of the FBI tonight, and it wasn't his place to interfere.

"This is Fox. Be advised that our suspect deviated from the trail. He's traveling across open farm fields…heading due south…he's moving at a pretty good clip. I think he's desperate for cover." The chopper was trailing so close that Stone saw the flurry of snow being stirred up by the blades.

"Agent Fox…Trooper Compton. Are there any structures or landmarks near your location?"

Jake was at the edge of his seat in the cruiser, just a mile from the rest stop, listening eagerly to the radio chatter and waiting for news from Fox and Stone.

"Not much for landmarks," Fox replied. "Just small groups of lights dotting the landscape…farms I suppose. There appears to be a small town lit up about ten miles to the southwest of us. I can see a large depression just ahead, maybe a mining area. There's tree cover just beyond that. Our suspect seems to be headed straight for the woods."

"That's a retired gravel pit—a big one. If your suspect

doesn't know where he's going, he could launch himself right over the edge."

"Roger that, Trooper Compton. We'll try to set down and intercept. Stand by."

The two minutes of radio silence that followed seemed like an eternity. Jake and his escorts parked just inside the entrance of the rest stop and turned off their headlights. There was a small public building with restrooms and an unmanned tourist booth, which Agent Jax refused to explore without a command from Fox.

Jake's nerves were unraveling with every second. He stared at the radio, trying to will it to speak. His eyes shifted to the small building in the distance, then back to the radio, then back to the building. His son could be just inside. Jake fought the urge to storm toward the building. He regretted surrendering his weapon.

Then it came—word from Agent Fox. "This is Fox. We're on the ground. We have the suspect…he had an accident."

"Agent Fox, Trooper Compton. Can you give me your coordinates? I can arrange for airborne medical transport."

"That won't be necessary…he met up with a barbwire fence. He's gone."

Stone stood in the field next to Agent Fox, looking in disbelief at the headless body in the beam of Fox's flashlight. Not far away was a bloody helmet in the white snow, its contents still intact. It was almost too gruesome for Stone.

For those seeking answers in the isolation of the cold Illinois countryside, the evening would prove a complete failure. An empty rest stop would yield no child, no kidnappers, and no evidence of foul play. A decapitated snowmobiler with a detective's badge in one pocket and a pouch full of diamonds in the other would later be identified as Earl Murphy, a special investigator from a neighboring agency who had worked closely with Stone at the beginning of the Bishop investigation. And an empty Dodge Ram pickup truck with a tall topper and a custom snowmobile ramp would be found parked in a field not far from the main snowmobile trail, positioned for a quick getaway.

Once again, at the end of another long and trying day, Jake was left with more questions than answers.

CHAPTER 29

HOME AWAY FROM HOME

The morning sun spilled over the crest of the foothills, bathing the valley in a comforting glow. The light filtered through the dense canopy of trees and dappled across the golden skin of the woman sitting on the patio below.

It was a peaceful morning, with the exception of an occasional celebratory squawk from one of the large birds perched in the nearby trees. There was also an unfamiliar sound—a sound that pleased the woman very much. It was a young boy playing in the courtyard, giggling as he danced between two dogs that were trying to grab the stick he was waiving high above his head.

This was the happiest the woman had seen the boy since his arrival at the compound. For weeks the boy had been sullen, withdrawn from his new surroundings. It was understandable. He had traveled far from home and was surrounded by strangers who all gave him an unusual amount of attention.

From the moment he arrived, the woman had taken a special interest in the boy. She was determined to make him as comfortable as possible. She shared her meals with him, took long walks with him, bathed him in the evening, helped him dress in the morning, and comforted him whenever he was frightened. Although the boy still harbored reservations about the gentle woman who had embraced him as her surrogate son, it was difficult to deny the affections.

As she watched the boy playing in the courtyard with the two German Shepherds, she lowered her newspaper just enough to reveal her dark eyes and compassionate smile. She had a content expression, but it was also conflicted. A part of her was fulfilled by the presence of the boy—the part that longed to nurture a child, to share her life with the innocence of youth. But deep down, she knew the boy did not belong with her.

A cloud of dust lingered in the wake of the cargo truck as it bounced down the unpaved road toward the compound. The woman called the boy to come in from the yard, first in Spanish, but quickly shifting to English. The boy ran back to the patio with the dogs at his heels, still laughing as he reached the chair next to his beautiful hostess.

"It is nice to see you smile, little one," the woman said softly as she poured fresh orange juice into a crystal glass.

"The dogs are fun today," he responded.

"You may play with them again later. They have to work now," she said, looking up at the truck entering through the gates.

The boy had seen the truck, or one like it, several times before. The truck, the guards, the dogs—it had become routine. Each time a truck pulled up to the large brick storage building with the shiny steel roof, the guard dogs would dutifully take their positions on each side of the entrance. The boy knew that within seconds, two men would exit the guesthouse, dressed in camouflage and armed with guns strapped over their shoulders. Two other men would appear from the back of the truck and off-load their cargo with military efficiency.

The boy had no idea what was in the crates. He once asked the woman what was in the boxes the men carried into the forbidden building, but she answered dismissively, revealing nothing.

She showed little interest as the men unloaded their cargo. Her focus was on the little one. She wanted to hear his stories about his family back home.

As they sat at the table together, a man exited the main house and approached the patio. Well built, with a dark complexion, the middle-aged man carried himself with an air of pretension. He was wearing the same uniform he wore most days—a tight, black, short-sleeved shirt, gray cargo pants, and black work boots. His clothing was clean and well kept, rarely soiled by his profession.

"Good morning, my dear. I trust you slept well?" The man caressed the woman's hair as he joined them at the table.

"I slept fine," she responded, twitching under his advance.

"How about you, little one? How did you sleep?"

"He slept fine, as well," she interjected.

"I'll need you in the field later today. We'll leave in an

hour. You may bring the boy if you wish."

The woman offered a submissive nod, acknowledging that she understood the day's assignment. There was little eye contact between the man and the woman; even the boy could sense the tension. But the man seemed content as a king, sitting at the patio table reading his morning paper. A small Latina woman wearing a crisp white apron served him a large breakfast.

The boy was too young to comprehend their life of luxury. The servants, housekeepers, and drivers all seemed like part of the family. It was a different kind of family, though. Most of them spoke Spanish, and they all treated the dark-haired man with great respect—the kind of respect commanded by a strict father. The boy was not yet certain just where he fit into the family. The only thing he knew for sure was that the pretty lady spoke English well, and she always treated him with a gentle hand. For now, he would not venture far from his new friend.

CHAPTER 30

WHAT HAPPENS IN VEGAS

The ice trembled in Jake's whiskey glass as the 727 hit another wave of turbulence. The flight from Las Vegas to Chicago had been rough, but Jake's nerves were dulled by four miniature whiskey bottles during the first two hours in the air.

The trip to Vegas had been productive, but not in the way Stone had hoped. After several hours of questioning, and a thorough polygraph, Katherine Kobs had all but been cleared as a suspect in Jonathan's disappearance. The news release would continue to identify her as a person of interest, along with Marty Vance. But Stone was convinced, now more than ever, that the two knew less about Jonathan's whereabouts than he did.

The lengthy interrogation had tortured Jake as he watched from behind the one-way glass of the surveillance room. Hour after hour, question after question, he listened desperately for clues. At the start of the interview, he was convinced Katherine was the woman who marched into Evergreen Elementary School and escorted his son out the front door. But as the interview dragged on, as Katherine's responses were carefully studied and logged by the polygrapher, Jake's hopes were stripped away. In the end, even Jake had to accept that Katherine was not his son's abductor.

The plane shuddered again and Jake politely waved his empty glass in the air to capture the attention of a nearby flight attendant. Stone released a sigh of disapproval, but failed to summon the courage to confront Jake's fifth drink. He was tempted to join his companion in the attempt to drain the drink cart.

For Stone, the last several weeks had been one blunder after another. Or at least *he* thought so. There had been so many signs, so many obvious details, so many suspicious circumstances, all in plain view, but he had failed to recognize them. Nothing punished him more than missed opportunities and false leads, and there had been plenty of both since the start of the investigation.

There was the botched extortion scam by Earl Murphy. It was the perfect crime of opportunity. Murphy had inside information, everything he needed to know about the Bishop family. He had direct knowledge about Jake's balance sheet and details about the investigation. Murphy's embarrassing episode, executed right under Stone's nose, had proven to be a colossal waste of time and resources, and an embarrassment for him, his team, and the FBI.

And then there was Katherine Kobs. Stone and his men had chased down countless leads tracking that bitch halfway across the country, only to find her sitting in a Vegas holding cell with a bad dye job and seven dollars left to her name. The safe return of the Norby boy to his father was a small victory, but one that offered little consolation. Jonathan was still missing.

But what had defeated Stone entirely was meeting the blonde woman at Eisner's cabin. Her haunting image was etched into Stone's memory. And he knew that, for now, the memory of her was all he had. The trail was cold.

Just before leaving for Vegas, Stone had visited the cabin with his junior detective, looking for any evidence that may have been left behind. But they found nothing. The cabin had been wiped clean. No prints, no DNA, no weapons, no satellite phone, no white SUV. It was clearly a professional job.

Stone drove up to the nursing home to visit with old Eisner about the guests who had been staying at his cabin. Even in his state of failing health, battling dementia, in a moment of lucidity Eisner made it adamantly clear that he had no nephew in Chicago, and he was certain he hadn't granted permission to anyone other than Stone to use his cabin. Stone had no leads on his blonde fugitive, if she was even a real blonde. She had been handed to him on a silver platter and he had let her slip away.

After nearly three months, thousands of leads, thousands of tax dollars, and countless nights of missed sleep, they would return to Wisconsin to pick up the investigation from the beginning.

As the plane descended through the clouds, Jake gazed through the little oval window, studying the landscape below to estimate their position. No discernable landmarks availed themselves, at least not to the drunken attorney. It all looked the same to Jake, vast cropland separated by pockets of timber and broken terrain.

Much of the snow had yielded to a late-January thaw. The thought of moving into a new season without his son brought tears to his eyes. He pictured the Christmas presents still sitting beneath the tree, waiting for Jonathan. Sadly, a new season meant change, and change meant abandoning the past. He realized his son might be gone forever.

Stone thought about the last time he and Jake had sat side-by-side on a return flight from Vegas. It was just two years earlier, shortly after Jake had pulled out of the long depression following Blanca's death. They ate like kings, drank like fish, caught Jay Leno's stand-up act, and broke even playing blackjack—or at least so they told everyone back home. *Those were the good old days,* Stone thought.

For the last hour of the flight both men sat quietly, swimming in self-pity, each blaming himself for Jonathan's absence. There was nothing about this trip that resembled the good old days.

CHAPTER 31

THE GHOST WRITER

Jake sat alone in his office staring at the mound of files Gertrude had piled neatly on his desk. Most files were covered with sticky notes, each presenting a question or set of instructions.

For months, Jake had been nearly absent from the office, but Gertie had managed to keep the operation running fairly smoothly. She could handle a probate with her eyes closed and with one rather large and intimidating hand behind her back. And as far as the estate planning and family law intake, that was a matter of practicing law without a license, something Gertrude Liddle had been doing for several years. About the only thing she couldn't get away with was showing up to court on Jake's behalf.

Jake had been sitting at his desk for twenty minutes and he still hadn't touched his first file. He stared at the pile, his hands wrapped around Maggie's lukewarm latte in the thin paper cup.

Only three months earlier, he and the coffee shop girl had stood on the porch on a crisp Thanksgiving night, her soft lips pressed against his for that goodnight kiss. It had been the start of something—something great. But those feelings had vanished, replaced by the dull ache of losing his son.

Jake's melancholy was interrupted by Gertie's voice crackling over the intercom.

"How we comin' on those files, Counselor?"

After a long delay, his reply journeyed through the intercom. "We're making some real progress in here. I'll keep you posted, dear."

Gertie smirked and chuckled to herself.

Jake released a deep sigh and opened his desk drawer in search of his favorite pen. After Gertie's verbal warning, he knew it would just be a matter of time before she came lumbering through his door to take inventory of his progress. It was time to get to work.

As Jake rummaged through the drawer, something caught his attention. It was an envelope—a sealed white envelope.

Jake studied it, puzzled by its presence in his desk. The typed words were perfectly centered—*Mr. Jacob Bishop, Personal and Confidential.* He knew he'd been away from the office for several weeks, but he had no recollection of the envelope.

Jake held it up to the light to see if he could decipher the contents. He could detect the faint outline of handwritten lines that appeared to be penned in a very neat script. But the words on the paper, folded over upon themselves within the confines of the sealed envelope, were indecipherable.

He retrieved his letter opener and sliced with slow precision, taking extra care to preserve the envelope and its contents. There was something about the handwriting that looked familiar to him, even through the envelope.

He removed the letter and unfolded several pages of fine parchment. Jake recognized the handwriting instantly as that of his surrogate father, Professor Albright. His heart skipped as he wondered what message his dear mentor could possibly be sending him from the grave.

My Dearest Jake,

I hope this correspondence finds you and Jonathan well. My apologies for the post-mortem communication, it was certainly not my intention to cause you any discomfort or pain.

By now you must have successfully slept off the hangover from my memorial. Yes, I knew you all too well, my friend. Despite my specific instructions, I knew you could not resist a proper sendoff. It was a hell of a party, Jake. Thank you.

There are so many things I could say to you, but I feel we've already said them in so many ways over the years. I hope you know how fulfilling you and Jonathan made my life. I left this world with no regrets, no wants, and no sorrows. Thanks to you and my family, I was the luckiest son-of-a-bitch who ever lived.

My dear friend, I will get directly to the purpose of my message. You know that during my life I kept very few secrets. To you, Addie, my friends and family, my life was an open book. But sadly, I regret that there was one secret I have kept from you—a secret that I simply could not take with me. So many times I wanted to share this information with you, but I just couldn't bring myself to do so.

As you know, in my last years I took a few trips back to Peru to visit the ancients. I so treasured my experiences there. Peru is a beautiful land—a land of immense intrigue, mystery, and treasure.

There is treasure there for everyone, Jake. Your Blanca taught me that. And I found my treasure every time I journeyed back. In the people, their culture, their mystique, and in the tombs and ancient ruins that bless the hidden recesses of their landscape.

My last trip to Peru was a mix of business and pleasure. My passion for the ancients led to an indiscretion on my part, one for which I may never be forgiven. I had been contacted by an acquaintance in the art world, a collector of antiquities who specializes in Peruvian artifacts. He had been contacted by a broker, a black marketer, who was a master of smuggling artifacts to investors beyond the borders of Peru.

A recent archaeological expedition had led to an unprecedented discovery, unveiling a wealth of artifacts with no known links to any other civilization. This discovery was significant, and completely off the grid. It wasn't reported to the government or to academia, and has been kept far away from the wire service and the media. My artifact, my small piece of history, was among the pieces unearthed at the site.

I was told that the project's leader planned to leak information about the discovery to the archaeological community once the most valuable pieces had been successfully extracted and the site had been sealed.

A piece of this find, even a small piece, would pay unimaginable dividends to its holder. I simply couldn't resist. The piece that I purchased, the piece that I could afford to purchase, is now sitting in an undisclosed safe-deposit box at your uncle's bank. The key is taped to the bottom of Addie's sock drawer. Jake, the artifact belongs to the people of Peru. Please arrange to have it returned, and offer my apologies to their government. This should be done discreetly and anonymously to avoid the obvious complications.

Unfortunately, the secret I must reveal to you is not my illegal purchase of antiquities. It is what happened in Peru on the day I acquired my treasure. Jake, for what I am about to tell you, please forgive me.

Upon arriving in Lima I chartered a small plane to fly me north to the city of Trujillo. Arrangements had been made for me to meet my contact there. This contact drove me inland to the town of Cajamarca where I would meet the broker. Alone, unarmed, and without a plan, I found myself absolutely terrified.

I met the broker at a crowded outdoor café near the center of town. Not far from our table stood two very large men with weapons under their clothes, each looking out of place, and each following the movements of the broker attentively. The location was bustling with activity, all of the locals celebrating the festival of Fiestas Patrias, Peru's Independence Day. The presence of the crowd put my mind at ease a bit; although, in hindsight the broker could probably have killed me in cold blood and returned to his hacienda to count my money before my body was cold.

We enjoyed a cold drink, and he briefed me on how I would remove the artifact from his country. I was also sternly warned about the consequences of disclosing to anyone the means by which I acquired my antiquity.

Although he never took off his sunglasses, the broker looked familiar to me, Jake. But I was unable to place where I might have seen him before. At that point my primary objectives were to make the exchange, secure transportation back to Trujillo, and get myself and my illegal artifact out of the country as soon as possible.

The exchange took place without incident. The broker didn't even bother to count my money. Hell, he didn't even open the satchel! He did, however, assure me that I would not make it out of Cajamarca alive unless all of the funds were present. He then congratulated me on my acquisition, reminded me of my obligations of secrecy, and ended our meeting.

I watched him weave through the crowd and disappear into the back of a black sedan parked right next to the SUV that had delivered me to the village. As his driver held the door open for him, I saw a woman lean forward to look outside, the sunlight catching the side of her face. She was a woman of great beauty, with the delicate cast of an angel. Jake, she looked like your angel! She could have been Blanca's identical twin.

Our eyes met, and I could tell that she too felt a connection. I rose to my feet, about to rush across the square, but the doors closed and the vehicles disappeared into the crowd. The woman's face was burned into my memory, and it has tormented me every day since.

I returned home on a commercial airliner, having arranged to ship my freight back to the States by a separate carrier. It was on my flight home that I was struck by a revelation. The man at the exchange, the broker, I remembered where I had seen him before. He looked just like the man at Blanca's funeral. Jake, I'm almost certain that my antiquities broker was Arturo Lopez.

Since that day, I've struggled with the thought of disclosing this information to you. When you lost Blanca you suffered through such pain. The alcohol, the depression, I just couldn't bear to see you suffer through it all over again. I was terrified to resurrect the ghost of your precious Blanca. But now, in contemplation of my imminent death, I know I must reveal these things.

Jake, if I am wrong about any of this, please forgive me. And if I am right, please forgive me as well. But I believe your angel may be alive. Go to Peru, Jake—sometimes you find treasure where you least expect it.

Missing you for eternity,
Prof Albright

CHAPTER 32

Déjà vu Peru

Jake was awakened by the flight attendant politely requesting that he tilt his seat forward and prepare for landing. With a blurry glance at his watch and some scarcely conscious math, he realized that he had been sleeping for just over three hours. The on-board movies had been a mild distraction during the first couple hours of the flight, but he drifted off soon after they switched to Spanish dialog with English subtitles. Though Jake's Spanish was good, his focus was poor. His mind was still occupied with thoughts of Blanca, which had even filtered into his dreams during the flight.

A glance across the full-bodied woman sitting to his right provided Jake with a partial view of the coast. Peru was as beautiful as he remembered. He had always been fascinated by the region, truly a land of extremes—extreme climate, extreme geography, and an extreme clash of cultures.

The last time Jake flew into the Jorge Chavez International Airport he was returning to arrange Blanca's funeral. On that day he had barely been able to see the City of Kings below, which for several months of the year is smothered by a blanket of pollution and coastal fog. But not today; today the fog had burned away, the sun was glistening off the water, and he could see the sprawling city of Lima in all its glory. *Blanca would have loved the view,* he thought.

From the narrow desert running down the western coast, the dense Amazon rainforest situated to the east, and the majestic Andean mountain range sandwiched tightly in between, Jake had visited every region with Blanca. He remembered the scorching heat of the world's driest coastal desert, the oppressive humidity of the rainforest, and the freezing haze that covered the highest peaks of the Andean mountains. One glimpse out through the small window of the 757, and the memories flooded back.

His short life with Blanca had been an adventure. She was proud of her country and eager to share it with the love of her life. Her people's adaptation to the harsh climate and landscape over thousands of years had cultivated a variety of cultures, cuisines, art, and folklore. Most tourists come to Peru to gawk at the remnants of Machu Picchu and other ancient sites. But, according to Blanca, most of them leave both mystified and illuminated by the unexpected treasures they've found within the eclectic geography and soul of the people.

With Blanca as his tour guide, Jake's first expedition of Peru overloaded his senses. The great mountain city of Machu Picchu; the mysterious Nazca lines etched into the desert landscape; the vast ancient city of Chan Chan, burial site of the Lord of Sipan; and the sacred Lake Titicaca, the world's highest navigable body of water—all a far cry from the prosaic world he had left behind in Maple Creek.

As the plane descended, Jake laid his head back on the headrest, closed his eyes, and continued to sift through the images of his past. He pictured Blanca mingling with the people living in the village high in the Andean Mountains, their harsh lives remaining nearly static for hundreds of years. He recalled the indigenous people living deep in the Amazon, long forgotten by their government—a people whom, Blanca would explain, had battled many enemies throughout their history including the Spaniards, the rubber trappers, the land developers, and more recently, the oil and gas barons.

He remembered the diversity of wildlife—a rare encounter with a puma in the Andes, a giant python coiled on a tree limb, a flock of colorful macaws playing along a vine-covered cliff in the jungle.

He hadn't thought about such things in a very long time. The hardship of losing Blanca, and now Jonathan, had overshadowed anything positive in his life. But now, as he once again prepared to touch down in Lima, to return to Blanca's homeland, he remembered how blessed his life had once been.

It always amazed Jake that a small-town boy from Wisconsin could end up married to an exotic beauty from a distant land. What were the odds that such entirely different people, from such entirely different lands, could find one another on such an enormous planet? The thought of it brought a smile to his face.

When they first began dating, Jake and Blanca would sit for hours questioning each other about their lives. They would exchange stories about their family, their childhood, their hopes and dreams. Jake was captivated by Blanca's charm and humble demeanor, and loved listening to her talk about her life as a young girl. Her life had been so different from his.

A rollercoaster of uncertainty and political turmoil, life in Peru was a challenge for Blanca's generation. As a young girl, she lived with her family under the military rule of General Juan Velasco, a man with tight political ties to the Soviet Union. This meant that Western culture was effectively banned, including the Western music and clothing she and her friends desired.

Peru returned to civilian rule in 1980, but by then, there was great frustration among Blanca's people. After a dozen years of military leadership, the guerrilla group Sendero Luminoso, translated as the Shining Path, had gained great power, and the government grossly underestimated the group's following. It wasn't long before the strong campaign against the insurgence resulted in the return to military rule over much of the country. Strikes, protests, marches, and human rights violations were common, and thousands were killed.

By 1989, Blanca and her people were disillusioned with the failing economy and the usual politicians. They were eager for change, which came with the election of their new president, Alberto Fujimori. Fujimori, an engineer of Japanese descent, promised the country a return to prosperity. Less than twelve years after he took office, however, Fujimori fled the country amid a scandal of bribery, corruption, and illegal drug dealings. By then Blanca had left the country, but she watched the brief report on the news from her apartment in Chicago.

She also witnessed the election of Alejandro Toledo in 2001, the young man educated at Harvard and Stanford who had ambitions of restoring the country's political and economic landscape. Blanca was intrigued by the promise of change and assured her family that there was hope for the future. And, for the most part, President Toledo did deliver positive change and economic growth to the people of Peru.

Jake's stomach sank as the plane seemed to freefall its last few hundred feet. The landing, however, was surprisingly smooth, and within seconds the large ship came to a gentle roll. As brakes engaged, Jake felt every ripple and bump of the runway, and reality settled in—he was back.

CHAPTER 33

BROTHER FROM ANOTHER MOTHER

Amid the sea of hurried travelers appeared a familiar and welcome face. Armando Vasquez was a dashing man with an enduring smile. He wore his father's broad shoulders and was blessed with his mother's arresting eyes and wavy black hair. His finely tailored sports coat, crisp white shirt, gabardine slacks, and designer shoes all fit perfectly. The young pilot always dressed well beyond his means. *He hasn't changed a bit*, Jake thought as he picked Armando out of the crowd.

Armando was Blanca's older brother, and the family resemblance took Jake off guard. He thought he'd prepared himself for the reunion, but he stood frozen in his tracks in the middle of the terminal, staring at Armando. Jake's ghosts were suddenly haunting him.

The two men hugged like brothers returning from separate wars. Neither knew quite how to begin the conversation. So much had happened since they last met.

"My brother, I have missed you in a great way. How was your flight?" Armando asked in a thick Spanish accent, choking back his emotion.

"Very long. I had forgotten what a journey it is to visit your great land."

"You are so thin; do they not feed you in North America?"

"Ah, my appetite has failed me for some time now," Jake replied. "Too many distractions I guess."

"I understand," Armando said, realizing the implication. "You look fine, my friend. Come, let's talk as we walk." Armando swept up Jake's satchel and shuffled through the crowd.

"It feels strange to be back," Jake said loudly as he tried to keep pace.

"Much has changed; much is the same. We'll take a little drive of the city before returning to the family. It's early yet; traffic is still moving…a little."

"Are you still flying?"

"Yes, it is in my blood. I'm a lucky man to love my work."

"What about your love life? Is there a Mrs. Armando Vasquez yet?" Jake asked in jest, already knowing the answer.

"You didn't receive a wedding invitation did you?"

"No, I guess I didn't," Jake replied with a chuckle.

"You know, my friend, women are like the fine wine," Armando explained. "Once you commit to the bottle, all of the other grapes are spoiled for you."

Armando's unusual analogies had always amused Jake. He never quite understood their meaning; perhaps too profound for his taste, or perhaps they were simply nonsensical. But Armando had a passion for life and sought analogy in unusual places.

"How is the family?" Jake asked.

"They are well," Armando replied with some hesitation. "Father's engineering firm has a few large contracts that keep him quite busy. Mother is still teaching the students at the primary school."

"How are their spirits?" Jake asked, reading between the lines of Armando's ambiguity.

Armando's gait slowed as he processed Jake's question. "Not so good. They have both been very quiet ever since. . . ." Armando quickly regretted the sentence he had started.

"Ever since Jonathan?" Jake asked.

"Yes, ever since Jonathan," Armando replied, stopping in his tracks as travelers parted to flow around them. "They have been sad; they feel so...how do you say... helpless. I am sorry for the things life has taken from you, my brother."

Jake could see the tears welling in Armando's eyes. "There have been great losses for us all, Armando." Jake patted his brother-in-law on the back. "We'll get through them together."

Armando nodded and resumed his stride at a slower pace. "What brings you to Peru? You were not so clear on the phone," Armando asked, happy to change the subject.

"A journey of sorts, I guess." Jake paused as he considered how much to share with Armando in the middle of the airport. "Perhaps some ghosts I need to release. We'll talk more over drinks."

Armando looked intrigued by Jake's comment, but what dwelled beneath it would have to wait. He kept the conversation light as he led the way to the parking lot, an obvious attempt to avoid any topical landmines.

Armando's shiny red Volkswagen Golf was parked on the far end of the lot. Jake knew the drill. Armando kept his vehicles in pristine condition, no small feat in a city where a bumper tap was a comfortable substitute for a toot of the horn.

"Nice car. Is it new?"

"Last year. She really moves. Would you like to drive?" Armando asked as he gestured a toss of the keys in Jake's direction.

"No, thanks. I'd rather we arrive in one piece."

"Where is your sense of adventure, Mr. Bishop?" Armando joked as he loaded Jake's bag into the hatch.

"I believe I left that somewhere in the Andes the last time your sister trekked me into the highlands."

Armando smiled as he recalled a very risky climb the three of them had once taken. Mountain climbing, paragliding, hiking into the Amazon, or digging for undiscovered archaeological gems—Blanca was a fearless explorer.

The same spirit apparently coursed through Armando's veins, and his driving was just as Jake remembered. The mid-morning rush hour was thick, but the little red Golf negotiated the lanes, weaving through every opening, no matter how narrow the passage. Soon it seemed as if they were traveling nearly twice the speed of the rest of traffic, and for the third time in as many miles, Jake discreetly gave his seatbelt a safety tug.

But before long, Armando exited the freeway opting for a more scenic route down the coast. Soon Jake was lying back with his head on the headrest and a cool breeze ruffling his hair, admiring the late-morning sunlight edging over the mountains.

New visitors to Lima are often overwhelmed with mixed feelings about their initial impressions. The city pulses with conflicting images—from the slums and shanty towns lining its highways, to its stately mansions and gated communities; from its chaotic traffic and heavy smog, to its tranquil neighborhoods and lazy beaches; from its seedy bars and dark alleys, to its fine art galleries and quaint bistros—the mix of wealth and poverty was astonishing to Jake.

As Armando navigated the outskirts of the city, he steered clear of the historic downtown district, which was often overrun with tourists. A rookie's first visit to Lima wouldn't be complete without discovering the treasure trove of Spanish colonial buildings mapped out in every guidebook—the Plaza Mayor (Main Square), Palacio de Gobierno (Government Palace), and the Covento de San Francisco (Church and Convent of San Francisco).

Jake, however, had taken in these sites on more than one occasion in the past, and today he was perfectly content cruising along the Circuito de Playas in a little red car, enjoying the view of the ocean along the sandy cliffs of Miraflores.

Past the string of fine beach resorts, tennis clubs, and restaurants, the road swept its way along the scenic beaches of the Pacific. The two men said little as they took in the sights, sounds, and smells of the coast.

A familiar landmark appeared in the distance, and Jake instantly recognized the Victorian-style restaurant on the pier, jutting out from the beaches of Costa Verde. Appearing almost mystified, he nudged Armando and pointed toward it, "Remind me…what's the name of that restaurant?"

"La Rosa Nautica," Armando replied, reducing his speed a bit as they approached.

"La Rosa Nautica," Jake mumbled as his mind drifted back to his first anniversary dinner with Blanca. It was a perfect evening. A beautiful companion, a magical conversation, a superb meal in a fine restaurant, a blazing sunset melting into the ocean, a romantic walk along the surf, a bottle of red wine, and a late night of passion on a beach blanket. It felt surreal to be back.

"Are you hungry, my friend?" Armando asked, interrupting Jake's daydream.

"I could eat a little. In fact, I could really go for a beer, but it's a little early," Jake replied, glancing down at his watch.

Armando grinned as he dropped the stick-shift down into third gear and pressed swiftly on the accelerator pedal. "It's never too early for a beer. I know a place."

Jake glanced in the side mirror and watched La Rosa

Nautica fade away with the memory of his anniversary. Neither one of them noticed the black Mercedes with darkened windows that had been tailing them since the airport.

CHAPTER 34

BLACK MARKET MUMMIES

The late morning sun warmed the woman's shoulders and gradually illuminated the shadows of the terraces etched into the hillside above. She took great care studying the markings on an ancient water vessel, the latest artifact that had been delicately extracted from the ruins.

Piece by piece, she and her team had been recovering their treasure from the chambers concealed deep within the terrain. The maze of these chambers was part of a pyramid-like structure buried beneath several tons of mud, likely swept down centuries ago from a highland lake during one of Peru's merciless earthquakes. The site excavation had been exhausting, and the project was now well into its third year. But hers was a labor of love, and aside from the anger she harbored toward her employer and his methods, their findings had been fruitful well beyond their expectations.

Despite her experience and wealth of knowledge, what she had discovered in the past several months had all but annihilated her conventional wisdom about early civilization in the Americas. Nothing about the site was textbook. Situated in a remote northern region, it was miles away from any territory traditionally associated with the civilizations of that time period. Far from the coastal river valleys and irrigation canals that fed the once fertile agricultural settlements—far from the ruins of burial sites that once secretly guarded royalty and warrior priests.

The site was so remote that the expedition attracted little attention from neighboring villages. The group's changes to the landscape were so subtle that no orbiting satellite would find cause to give the project a second look.

They worked in small teams, with minimal equipment, and their labor was performed in gradual stages—one imperceptible step at a time. They transported their cargo at dusk under heavy guard, and no more than two vehicles were allowed to travel together so they could avoid attention. These safeguards had prolonged the project far beyond schedule, but the rewards were astonishing.

As the woman gently whisked away hundreds of years of fine dust particles from the artifact, she smiled in bewilderment. The piece had many of the same unusual markings found on the treasures they had already extracted, markings that, prior to this project, the woman had never encountered.

There were also traditional markings on the piece, with which the woman was well acquainted. Head portraits, demonic beings, combat and hunting scenes, all comparable to artwork adorning pieces she had discovered at previous sites. And like those previously discovered treasures, she strongly suspected the piece was the work of the Moche civilization. But the predominant markings on her newly acquired artifacts were nothing like those she had seen on any Moche piece, or on any other artifact for that matter.

She knew the Moche well, despite them having vanished over thirteen hundred years before her time. She had published several articles, and even books, on their history and had participated in dozens of high-profile explorations of their sites. She was intrigued by the sophisticated skills and vast accomplishments of the Moche, a people who flourished between 200 BC and 700 AD. Their settlements stretched 250 miles along the hot, arid coast of northern Peru. They were skilled architects with a legacy of monumental temples, pyramids, and palaces. They constructed irrigation canals and aqueducts to transport water between neighboring valleys to hydrate their crops of maize, squash, avocados, and beans. Experienced farmers, warriors, fishermen, and hunters, the Moche were an accomplished people.

The discovery of an unadulterated Moche site was like hitting the mother lode—often replete with elaborate murals and ceramics, skillfully crafted pottery and erotic vessels, artful depictions of sacrificial ceremonies and daily life, and an array of precious metals crafted into priceless treasures. The Moche were masterful metallurgists with gold and silver, and they had perfected an electrochemical plating technique used to bathe their prized possessions in brilliant copper.

But she knew that despite their many accomplishments, despite their undisputed sophistication, the one thing the Moche had never been credited with was the existence of a written record. Their story, their message, their life, was known only through the vivid images artfully memorialized on their possessions…until now that is.

These newly discovered markings clearly suggested some form of an alphabet. A series of unique symbols, sixty-three discovered to date, complex in design and neatly painted or inscribed in various combinations on almost every piece the team had unearthed. The significance of the find was beyond comprehension, and from the moment the first artifact was extracted, she knew their discovery would have global significance.

She'd since had many heated debates with her employer, pleading for him to adopt a universal consciousness. These precious treasures deserved to be carefully preserved, studied, and freely shared with the world's archaeological community, she argued.

The discoveries were inexplicable, far beyond the reaches of conventional history. A subterranean cemetery of treasures situated deep in the bowels of an ancient pyramid, discovered far from any logical location, filled with artifacts that were inscribed with an unrecognizable and mysterious nomenclature. Their discovery itself was as eerie as it was exciting.

As she continued to bring the vessel back to life, she paused to gaze out over the valley. Once again, she tried to imagine the people who once thrived there. It had become a daily ritual for her. Clearly, whoever occupied this valley several centuries ago were an exclusive and powerful people who went to great lengths to conceal their existence from outsiders, both present and future.

Not since the discovery of the Lord of Sipan had there been such significant revelations. And as astonishing as the Sipan treasures were, they now paled in comparison.

Their most significant find had occurred just three months into their exploration of the hidden pyramid. She would never forget the image—twelve mummies, each carefully wrapped in hundreds of feet of cotton linens, all buried together deep within one chamber. The mysterious dozen had been resting eerily in the dark silence for hundreds of years—undisturbed. Resting alongside them, meticulously placed in an adorning display, was an unimaginable wealth of priceless artifacts.

Of the twelve, the two mummies situated in the middle of the grouping were clearly individuals of greater significance than the ten decorated warriors resting on either side of them. One was male, one female, each extremely tall, measuring well over six feet. They were undoubtedly a royal couple among their people.

Carefully positioned on the mummified royalty were a massive gold headdress, a burial mask, and an exquisite collection of necklaces, bracelets, rings, and other unique ornamentation. Most of the jewelry was inlayed with lustrous red stones. Appearing almost glassy, yet extremely dense and seemingly indestructible, the fiery red gems were like nothing the team had ever encountered—not in the field, not in their studies, not in any realm of earthly science.

The ten soldiers guarding the royal couple were also highly decorated, laid to rest with fine weapons. Their copper clubs, gold-plated spears, and shields were all positioned neatly around their bodies in an obvious display of respect.

Each warrior was also adorned with a brilliant gold necklace of impressive size and weight. Fastened to each necklace, resting just over the sternum of each soldier, was a gold ring with a large gem protruding from an elaborate setting. The gems, fiery red, matched those on the royalty. The ring, she had speculated, likely had an honorary significance, worn on the hand of each warrior during his lifetime, then removed and laid to rest on his chest.

Even more perplexing was the similarity of the gems found in the ten rings. The team had yet to detect any distinguishing features among the stones. They appeared to be identical in size, shape, density, and substance. It was almost as if they had been mass produced from some high-tech, ultra-durable material, then smuggled into the sealed tomb as part of some elaborate hoax. Although she did not subscribe to this theory, it was as good as any other she could offer her colleagues.

But perhaps the most disturbing aspect of their discovery was when they carefully unveiled the tattered wrappings of one of the twelve mummified inhabitants. It took some doing, but she had persuaded her employer to resurrect just one. Studying the preserved remains could provide invaluable information about this mysterious culture. Information, she explained to her employer, that would make the remaining eleven mummies all the more valuable to his international bidders.

One digital camera had been permitted during the procedure, with non-negotiable instructions that none of the team members be captured in any image. Step by step, cut by cut, they painstakingly memorialized the process. Her employer was present for the procedure, but more out of morbid curiosity than scientific interest.

An expert in her field, she had witnessed similar unveilings and had thought she was mentally prepared to see the preserved being within.

Like a skillful surgeon, she worked slowly to lift away the fragile layers of ancient cloth as delicately as possible. Though appearing calm, her mind raced with anticipation, imagining the vast significance of their discovery and the penalty they would face if caught extricating one of Peru's most important treasures. But she had calculated the risk, and she knew this would be her only opportunity to properly study and photograph one of the mummies before they were shipped beyond her grasp.

Even before the final layer was lifted away, she sensed something unusual about the person beneath the fabric. The texture, the coloration, and the composition of the body emerging from beneath the final wrapping were all wrong. But as her employer stared curiously at the partially exposed body, he thought little of its unusual condition. While he had sufficient expertise in the valuation of

Peruvian antiquities, this was his first mummy unveiling, and the cadaver simply looked morbid to his untrained eye.

But she knew differently. She had realized instantly that the body was deformed, appearing mutated beyond human form. All appendages and digits were accounted for, but their size, configuration, and attitude were all slightly off. The cranium was unusually large and misshapen, and the plating of the skull appeared much thicker than any cadaver she had studied.

The skin, while appearing preserved by the mummification process, was extraordinarily thick and seemed to have undergone an unusual transformation. Scorched, hardened, and deeply damaged, the hide looked nothing like that of a human. *Perhaps sudden and intense heat, or an unusually high dose of radiation,* she thought. But this was only conjecture.

The only thing she knew for sure was that she was proud of herself for persuading her employer to unwrap one of their mystery cadavers. Her black-market boss had no understanding of their significance; their scientific value was beyond words.

With hopes of preserving the precious specimens, she finally talked him into purchasing the outrageously expensive chambers necessary to properly sustain them. Their unusual characteristics were sure to raise international interest, which meant unprecedented value in the marketplace, she explained.

She just needed to find a way to get their precious find

into the right hands, and do so without jeopardizing her own life or the life of the boy. It wouldn't be long before their twelve mummies would be secretly auctioned off, along with the rest of the treasures they had recovered.

As their expedition was nearing its end, they unearthed fewer and fewer artifacts each week, and those that were discovered were far less valuable. Soon her employer would shut down the project, cover his tracks, and abandon the site for good.

A few of the smaller pieces had already been strategically tested in the marketplace, and rumors were already spreading. The profits would be unimaginable. Once the bulk of the unusual pieces hit the market, her employer would be miles away from any evidence that could link him to the site, or link the site to the treasures.

As a man of great power and wealth, he had little desire for scientific notoriety. He saw no reason to call attention to himself. The pieces would be disseminated on the international black market, quickly and cautiously.

She knew her employer was extremely good at his job. Any attempt to circumvent the process would be a great risk. For the time being, she was content to know her twelve subjects, whatever species they may be, were comfortably resting in their individually sealed chambers in a dark, secluded, and well-guarded warehouse.

As she covered the water vessel with packing materials and gently placed it in its protective container, she took a deep breath and looked out over the valley. *Who were these people? If they even were people. Who laid them to rest?* Perhaps there would never be answers to her questions. They found no other remains anywhere near the pyramid. There was no village or settlement, no other structures or dwellings, nothing to link these beings to other beings. They were, indeed, the mysterious twelve—perhaps extraterrestrial, perhaps aberrations of nature, but for the moment, inexplicable.

CHAPTER 35

A BEER ON THE BEACH

Jake and Armando visited the isolated beach of La Herradura for their late morning beer and breakfast. It was tourist season in Peru, and by noon the beach would be a flurry of activity.

Armando knew the owner of a small outdoor café overlooking the surf, and with a wink, a wave, and a rapid exchange of friendly Spanish, he and Jake were served fresh ceviche and cold beers. Ceviche was one of Jake's favorite Peruvian treats. It was a simple dish, fresh whitefish marinated in onions, peppers, and lemon juice, which Jake preferred to complement with a cold Arequipena.

Jake sipped his beer and chuckled to himself as he thought back to the first time he ever laid eyes on a plate of ceviche. It was the night Blanca and Armando introduced him to their parents. Their mother enjoyed watching him squirm as she dished the raw fish onto his plate. He made his best effort to eat around the delicacy, politely returning for extra servings of the more palatable side dishes. But each time he added an extra helping of corn or sweet potatoes, Francesca would slide another piece of fish onto his plate.

To not offend his future mother-in-law, Jake eventually dove in. He finished the entire meal before realizing that Francesca was only exploiting his civility for her own amusement. That night Jake learned what a playful sense of humor Francesca Vasquez possessed. Oddly enough, before it came time for the young man from Wisconsin to return to North America, he had actually acquired a taste for the dish.

Armando offered up his beer for a toast. "Here is to the journey of life and the ghosts we seek. It is good to have you home, my brother."

"It feels good to be back," Jake replied. Their bottles met with a clank, and Jake took a long swig from his beer. He closed his eyes and laid his head back in the chair, slowly letting the cold brew bathe the back of his throat. He savored the warm breeze as it washed over his face. A thin smile appeared as he listened to the waves dissolve on the beach and the gulls squawking and bouncing playfully in the wind. It *was* good to be back.

Jake drew in a deep breath of fresh salty air mixed with the delightful scent of marinated fish. There were simply too many pleasures competing for his senses. He opened his eyes to find Armando intently watching him with an approving grin.

"You are well deserving of a rest," Armando said, offering a nod of validation.

"Maybe well deserved, but not so well timed."

"What things compete for your time these days?"

"What brings me down here? Is that what you meant to ask?" Jake's tone was light, but direct.

"I'm glad to see you, no matter what the reason. But I can't say I'm not curious as to the purpose of your visit."

Jake took another drink of his beer and fixed his eyes on two young boys playing in the sand near the surf. The older boy was just about Jonathan's age. Jake's grin started to fade.

He reached into the inside pocket of his sports coat and pulled out an envelope. On the front of the envelope were the typed words, "Mr. Jacob Bishop—Personal and Confidential." Without taking his eyes off the boys on the beach, he slid the envelope across the table toward Armando.

"You're the first person I've shown this to."

"What is it?" Armando asked.

"It's complicated…It's about Blanca. I'm not sure that I should burden you with this, but I didn't know who else to turn to." Jake nodded toward the envelope, inviting Armando to pick it up.

As Armando began the letter, he showed little expression. Prof's trip to Peru, his love of antiquities, the meeting with the broker; while it was all very intriguing, it was not terribly surprising. Armando knew Prof well, and knew of his infatuation with the ancients. It would not have been entirely out of character for him to dabble in the black market.

But as Armando continued, Jake watched him stare vacantly at the letter—his eyes no longer moving with the words, but fixed in the void as he tried to digest its contents. Just as Jake had done, he knew Armando was piecing together the memories of Blanca's funeral and her former connections to Lopez.

Jake took another swig of his Arequipena and wondered whether he had done the right thing by sharing Prof's letter with Armando.

A strong gust of wind rolled down the beach and folded back the letter in Armando's hands, startling a small bird that was scavenging for crumbs on the tabletop.

Armando looked up at Jake. "Do you think my sister is alive?"

"I honestly don't know what to think, Armando. I don't think Prof knew what to think. He never spoke of this to me when he was alive."

"You saw her body, Jake. And we saw her car. It was destroyed."

"Yes, I saw *a* body. But she was…it was unrecognizable."

"Did you check into her dental records?"

"There didn't seem to be a need. The car was rented in her name, she was found alone at the scene, and her belongings were scattered all over the bottom of the canyon. Nothing appeared suspicious at the time…aside from the *cause* of the accident."

"I saw him, you know…Lopez. During Blanca's funeral, I saw him hanging back in the crowd. I remembered him from the days Blanca worked for him. He is an evil bastard, Jake. *El Diablo*."

"Do you think he could have had something to do with the accident?"

"There's nothing that would surprise me with him.

He is a powerful man, from a very wealthy family. He has always been beyond the reach of our authorities."

"Blanca used to talk of him being involved in the black market. She suspected that he had some pretty shady business practices in the antiquities trade."

"Yes. She told me the same things, many times. It is why she severed relations with him."

"Perhaps I should pay Mr. Lopez a visit," Jake said in a very matter-of-fact manner.

"He is not the sort of man you simply visit, Jake. He is very…how do you say…elusive, and very protected. But I know a man who you should talk to. He is very knowledgeable in the matters of the ancients. He's also well connected."

"Who is he?"

"A professor at the university, a former colleague of Blanca—his name is Elijah Rios."

"Rios, yes. I remember meeting him the first time I visited the university with Blanca. He's somewhat of an archaeological superhero in these parts, isn't he?"

"Very much so. If there's a person who would know of the whereabouts and dealings of Arturo Lopez, it would be Elijah."

Jake nodded slowly, contemplating his next move. The pause in the conversation grew, and the sounds of the coast once again filled the void. There was so much left to say, yet neither Armando nor Jake knew where to start. Both men knew that a visit to the university was inevitable, but neither knew what the purpose of the visit would be. Neither knew exactly what to make of Prof's letter, or how Lopez fit into the picture, if at all.

And neither man knew exactly how to react to the possibility, however remote, that Blanca might still be alive.

CHAPTER 36

BACK TO SCHOOL

Pontificia Universidad Catolica del Peru. Déjà vu settled in as Jake scouted the grounds for Professor Elijah Rios' office. Jake recalled a similar visit several years earlier, when a young Blanca returned home with her fiancé to show him off around campus and introduce him to her colleagues. He beamed with pride that day—proud of his beautiful fiancée, proud of his accomplishments, and most of all he was proud that Blanca, the love of his life, was so proud of him.

The campus hadn't changed much, but Jake's recollection of it was foggy. He didn't mind, though. It was another beautiful day in Lima. The air was unseasonably crisp, the sky uncommonly clear, and the trees were full and green.

Jake's attention constantly shifted between Armando's hand-drawn map and the small groups of oncoming scholars parting around him. He had hoped to persuade Armando to tag along and serve as his tour guide, but there were two flights up the coast that day in need of a pilot, and a pilot in need of the money. Armando would meet up with Jake later that evening for drinks and dinner.

As he contemplated the need for a change in course, Jake slowed his pace to a stop and focused on Armando's scribble of directions. Frozen in his tracks in the middle of campus, he realized Armando spoke English much better than he wrote it.

Before he could figure out which way to go, he was startled by the ringing of his cell phone. *No doubt it's Armando,* he thought.

"These are some directions you gave me, Columbus. I should have left a trail of breadcrumbs."

"What the hell are you talking about, Bishop? Have you been out in the jungle too long?"

"Stone? Is that you?"

"In the flesh; how's it going down there in Inca land? Are you having a nice break?"

"I am actually. I had a great day with Armando yesterday, ate dinner with the in-laws. It was nice to see everyone. Is everything okay back home?"

"Things are fine here. I ran into Maggie at the coffee shop this morning. She asked me to say 'hi,' and to tell you that she's hot for your body."

"You're even a smart ass when you're burning up my international minutes."

"I'm worth every penny, pal."

Jake chuckled and rotated Armando's map in hopes of a revelation. "You wouldn't possibly be able to give me directions to Professor Rios's office, would you?"

"Rios? Who's he? What are you up to, Counselor?"

"Never mind—just visiting some old friends. Anything new on the case?"

"Well, that's partly why I'm calling."

Jake lowered Armando's map, wondering if he should brace himself. "Is it bad news?"

"No, nothing like that. I debated whether to even call you until I had a chance to follow up on things."

"Follow up on what things, Eric?"

"Well, I don't want you to get your hopes up prematurely, but we may have a pretty good lead."

There was no reply from Jake, and the silence began to make Stone uncomfortable. "It was the damnest thing, Jake. Agent Fox got a call from a sheriff out in some Podunk county in New Mexico. Some gal there reported that she was in Walmart and saw a woman with a young boy who matched the description of a child she saw on one of those missing children posters. I'm telling you, Jake, nobody looks at those damn posters, but this gal did. Her nephew was abducted ten years ago, and she got in the habit of scanning the bulletins."

"Eric, I think my heart has already seized up. Could you please get to the point?"

"Sorry. So anyway, we've pulled the surveillance footage from the store. It's definitely not conclusive. She had a hat on the kid and the camera angles aren't the best, but the resemblance is there. And, it was clear that the woman was acting very guarded. She was jittery, and she made a real effort to keep the boy on a short leash. It's a promising lead, Jake."

"Have they tracked her down?"

"Not yet. She paid with cash. The cameras in the parking lot picked up a good picture of her car, but not the plates. They've got all of the law enforcement agencies on alert out there. Fox and a few of his people are already on their way to check things out."

"I'll see if I can get a flight out today. What part of New Mexico are they in? I'll try to get a connection."

"Jake, I know you want to be here if anything develops, but I really do think it's premature. We've had hundreds of false leads. This could be just one more goose chase. I'll keep you posted, I promise. There's no need to rush home."

"I don't know. What if it is him? What if you find Jonathan? He's going to be terrified. I want to be the first person he sees."

"I know you do. But listen, I think you're putting the cart way ahead of the horse again, and that's understandable. But this is why I hesitated calling you. It's early yet. Let us check it out. There's no way for us to know if the boy in the video is Jonathan. I promise I'll stay on top of this. I'll call you with any news."

"Can you send me a feed of the video?"

"I'll talk to Fox and see what I can do."

"Alright, I'll give it a couple days. But if anything breaks I want a call, day or night."

"Done."

"One more thing. Can you stop by and look in on Margaret?"

"Sure, I'll swing by tonight."

"Try not to get her hopes up. She's been through a lot."

"I suggest we hold off altogether on sharing this one with your mother, Jake. Wait until we know more."

"I suppose. But I'd better call my sister. She's been following the case pretty closely through Fox. I don't want her learning about this from another source and then leaking it to Mom. I'd never get out of that doghouse."

"Very wise," Stone said. "Listen, Jake. I'll be in touch soon. Whatever it is that you're doing down there…please be careful."

"Not to worry. Thanks for the call, Eric."

Jake closed his phone and took a seat on a bench nearby. He wasn't sure what to think. There had been so many fruitless leads, and the case had all but gone cold.

As Jake sat, alone and unsettled, the campus suddenly seemed lifeless. Most of the students had shuffled off to their next class, and he felt detached from the world. Everything familiar was suddenly a million miles away—Stone, Maggie, his mother, Maple Creek, and most of all, Jonathan.

He was tempted to get his hopes up for yet another round of blind optimism. *I should be back in the States,* he thought. *Hell, I should be in New Mexico scouring through evidence with Agent Fox. This could be the big break.* What if the case broke and he wasn't there?

But there was something about sitting on that bench, something about being back on Blanca's old campus, back in her homeland—it felt right, almost obligatory. Jake couldn't explain it, not even to himself. But he could feel it deep down in his gut. He had business there.

CHAPTER 37

THE MEDALLION

He studied the piece, handling it with great respect. He would never have anticipated the day would take such an unusual turn. What were the odds that this unexpected visitor, this apparition from the past, would walk through his office door carrying such a rare artifact? He had seen markings like this only once before. His colleagues had also spoken about similar pieces surfacing from underground, but he had thought they were just rumors.

Professor Elijah Rios was respected by his peers. He was native to Peru, but had traveled the world in search of answers. The origin of the universe, the existence of a great deity, the inexplicable marvels left behind by the ancients, the countless mysteries of civilizations that had once occupied the far reaches of the globe.

The years had been kind to the professor. He had celebrated his sixty-third birthday just four days earlier, but most would guess him closer to fifty. He was trim and relatively fit for a man who had never exercised a day in his life. He had never married, rarely finding time for anything that might distract him from the passions of his profession.

Rios looked the role of the scholar—from his distinguished salt-and-pepper beard, corduroy blazer, wrinkled shirt, crooked bow tie and round eyeglasses, right down to the worn-out soles of his tasseled cordovan loafers.

"Where did you say you obtained this artifact, Jacob?" Rios asked without looking up from his magnifying glass.

"Actually, Professor, I didn't say. I'm not at liberty to disclose that information. But I've taken a great risk bringing this piece back to its homeland. I was hoping that you could tell me where it may have originated."

Rios removed a handkerchief from his inside blazer pocket, laying it on his desk, placing the ancient bronze medallion upon it. Reluctantly shifting his focus away from the artifact, the Professor raised his head, and with a warm smile and raised eyebrows he looked directly at his guest.

"Jacob Bishop. I still can't believe it's you. I haven't seen you since…."

"Blanca's funeral," Jake nodded as he finished the Professor's dwindling sentence. "Yes, it's been awhile," Jake added. "I'm sorry I haven't kept in touch. My life has become…complicated."

"So I've heard. I was very sorry to hear about your son. Has there been any progress with the investigation?"

"It depends on the day, I guess. We've had several leads, but nothing productive yet. I never give up hope, though. He's always on my mind."

"I'm certain that he is. We'll keep you in our thoughts, Jacob."

"Thank you, Professor."

"So what brings you to Peru, aside from this intriguing piece?" Rios inquired, gesturing toward the medallion.

"Oh, I was long overdue for a visit. I hadn't seen Blanca's family for some time. But I was also hoping you could help me locate someone." Jake tried to sound casual.

"I'll certainly help if I can, Jacob. Who is it you're looking for?"

"I'm trying to make contact with a man Blanca once worked for, a man by the name of Lopez—Arturo Lopez." Jake knew that the name would rouse interest in the professor, and he was right. Rios could barely conceal his grin as his eyes shifted back toward the artifact resting upon his desk.

"Jacob, may I ask what interest you have in Mr. Lopez after all of these years?"

"Well, it's complicated, Professor. And I'm desperately hoping that you'll keep this conversation strictly between us."

Rios offered an affirming nod.

"I apologize for the secrecy," Jake continued, "but I'm really just playing a hunch at this point. That seems to be what my life has come down to…a series of flimsy hunches." Jake's attention drifted out through the window, as if the answers to his questions were waiting just beyond the panes of glass. He imagined Blanca drifting across campus on the way to her next class, her arms folded around her books, her long, beautiful dark hair dancing in the wind behind her.

"Well, Jacob, it's very interesting that you come to me with this particular artifact, and that you're inquiring of

Mr. Lopez," the professor replied.

"Why is that?"

"The markings, they're very unusual. There have been rumors of pieces with similar markings surfacing in the market over the past several months. This is only the second one I've actually seen up close."

"The second? Where did you come across the first?"

"It's really quite spectacular, Jacob," the professor replied, obviously ignoring Jake's question as he leaned back over the medallion with his eye to the magnifying glass. "How do you believe it's connected to Mr. Lopez?" the professor asked, clearly fishing now.

"I don't know that it is. Are you aware of a connection, Professor?" Jake was intrigued by the professor's question.

The professor hesitated as he looked back down at the artifact. "I, too, have secrets, Jacob—secrets that I have never spoken of. But under the circumstances, I think it may be prudent to disclose a few."

Noticing that the door to his office was still slightly ajar, Rios walked over and pushed it closed. He turned the lock until he heard the click of the bolt. As he returned to his desk he wrung his hands together, appearing hopelessly lost in his thoughts. He lowered himself into his chair, and with his eyes fixed on the artifact, he released a deep sigh.

"Some time ago I received a telephone call from an acquaintance overseas," Rios began. "He's a very wealthy man, known to partake in the acquisition of illegal antiquities. He knows that I disapprove of such practices, but he's been a strong private financial supporter of our university, and he has great respect for the work we do."

"What does he have to do with Lopez?"

"He told me he was considering an investment—a very large investment. He had been contacted by a broker claiming access to a very rare collection. The collection was reportedly unearthed in South America, along with a covey of very well-preserved mummies. The broker was offering only a select number of pieces for sale, apparently an attempt to raise capital and stimulate the interest of future buyers. My colleague was presented with a catalog of sorts; it contained the images of ten extraordinary pieces. One of the pieces was an ancient headdress, the one my friend ultimately acquired."

"Let me guess, did the pieces in the collection look anything like the piece sitting on your desk?"

"You might say that, Jacob. In fact, one of the pictures in the catalog…it *was* your piece."

Unable to speak, Jake turned his attention away from Rios and back to the medallion. Questions about Professor Albright suddenly raced through his mind. Jake hadn't understood just how dangerous the business Prof had been dabbling in was. And he doubted Prof himself had fully appreciated the danger.

"I had the opportunity to inspect the headdress during a recent visit with my colleague in Germany," Rios continued. "It possessed markings nearly identical to those on your medallion, and it appeared to be authentic—as does your piece. And the man my colleague met with to acquire his artifact, a man who claimed to be an employee of the broker, closely fit the description of Carmello Diaz. Diaz is a well-dressed thug with a scar running down the right side of his face. He's known to be a close personal associate of your friend Arturo Lopez.

"It all adds up, Jacob. This is exactly the sort of illicit project Lopez would have a hand in. And during the past couple years, he has totally dropped out of his social circles. There's been speculation about where he's run off to. His affairs have probably been consumed with this latest archaeological undertaking."

"You mentioned some mummies. Have you seen pictures of those as well?"

"No," the professor said with regret. "But my colleague mentioned that a very select group of prospective purchasers will receive an invitation for a viewing. He may have already received his, but I haven't spoken with him for some time."

"What type of capital would a buyer need for such a purchase?"

"I have no idea. There isn't much precedent for black market mummies with extraterrestrial features."

"Extraterrestrial features?" Jake's brows were instantly elevated.

"The broker is presenting them as having some sort of mutations—a species of human never before discovered. Apparently the owner believes them to be of extraordinary value. He's been keeping them sealed in hermetic chambers."

"Sounds like the start of an elaborate hoax to me." Jake offered a pessimistic smirk.

"You could be right. But these artifacts, these markings, they are inexplicable. We've never seen anything like them. They are complex, and they are remarkable. If this proves to be a hoax," Rios said gesturing to the medallion, "it may prove to be the most elaborate one we've ever seen."

Jake sat silent for a minute, staring curiously at the medallion and gently tapping his finger on the professor's desk. As an attorney, he had been trained as a student of logic, a scholar of analytical reason. These tales of mutated mummies, alien alphabets, and a powerful underground broker selling illegal antiquities from a colored catalog were difficult to accept. But Jake also couldn't ignore the obvious. If two knowledgeable and trusted academics like Albright and Rios could find credibility in the tale, there may be something to it.

"Professor, I appreciate your candor in sharing this information. You've always been a good friend to Blanca and me. Since you've been so trusting to share your story, I'd like to share one of mine."

Once again on his feet, staring out the window, Jake told the story of how he came to possess the medallion. It was a story about a secret archaeological expedition, one from which a limited number of extraordinary pieces were offered on the black market by a mysterious broker.

It was a story about an American's journey to Peru, his private flight to Trujillo, and his trip inland to Cajamarca to meet with a broker who very much resembled Arturo Lopez—a meeting which took place in the middle of a busy festival, under the watchful eyes of two armed bodyguards.

But most of all it was a story about a woman, an angelic figure who the American saw tucked away in the back of the broker's car.

CHAPTER 38

PLAYING WITH PIGEONS

It was an unusually cool morning in Lima, but not too cool for Jake to sit alone at the outdoor café, warming his hands on a cup of thick, muddy coffee. The café was just around the corner from the hotel where Jake had rented a small room on a week-to-week basis. It wasn't in the best part of town, but it certainly wasn't in the worst. The neighborhood was quiet, reasonably safe, and there was decent food and drink around almost every corner.

Jake took another slurp of java and saw a little boy on the steps across the street, desperately trying to bait a curious pigeon with a morsel of stale bread. It reminded him of how much Jonathan enjoyed feeding the mallards at Pendergrass Pond, which reminded him of home. So many things reminded him of home. Once again he found himself missing his past, and questioning his present.

Nearly three weeks had passed since Jake's visit to the university, his recent days having been consumed by his search for the elusive Arturo Lopez. With every break in Armando's schedule, he would fly Jake from town to town, hopping up the coast to visit all of the spots Professor Rios suggested Lopez had been known to frequent.

They hit the galleries and the gem dealers, the finer restaurants and hotels, the cafés and bars, a few villages, and a fresh archaeological site that would certainly be of interest to someone like Lopez.

They had even visited Lopez's palatial *hacienda* nestled in the highlands, but were unable to gain access to the well-guarded fortress. From the air, they were able to scout the grounds of the property through Armando's high-powered binoculars. But they discovered little activity stirring at the Lopez estate beyond the cyclopean guard pacing back and forth at the gate. He appeared to have the equivalent of a small bazooka strapped over his shoulder. Armando couldn't help but comment that the weapon seemed awfully large for the job of guarding some llamas and a small herd of sheep.

During the past three weeks the men had casually questioned the local villagers, merchants, gem dealers, and museum curators—anyone who might have knowledge of Arturo's whereabouts. There had been no sightings for months. It was unusual. Lopez was almost a legend to the locals in the region. He was admired for his many contributions to archaeology, and he had spent time in the small villages during his many expeditions.

A benefactor to his ancestors' vast mining fortune, Lopez was notorious for living the life of pleasure and luxury, and for generously spreading his wealth among the local dining and drinking establishments. Most everyone knew him to be a professional playboy, and more importantly, a very generous tipper.

There were also rumors of a dark side. He was known

to travel with heavily armed guards, and was an increasingly powerful player in the cocaine trade. His colleagues in the archaeological community suspected him of being involved in several black market transactions, based on reports leaked from inside the small circle of his trusted entourage. This growing speculation had greatly discredited Lopez's standing in the archaeological community in recent years.

Jake knew Arturo Lopez couldn't have simply dropped off the radar. He had to believe that if he just kept turning over stones, the snake would eventually rear its ugly head.

And while Jake scoured the Peruvian countryside, Gertrude was back home manning the office, and she was running out of time, money, and patience. While her loyalty to Jake was strong, it was not limitless. The only thing keeping the ship afloat was private aid from an anonymous donor. Unbeknownst to Jake, his mother had been funneling money into the firm for a month, while swearing Gertie to secrecy with each contribution. The small infusions were enough to keep the lights on and cover Gertie's payroll, but Gertie knew Jake would not approve of the slow depletion of Margaret's savings. Gertie took every opportunity during their telephone calls to tell Jake he best "get his ass home" before she had to "close the damn doors and wind down this dog and pony show." Jake promised her that he would soon return.

Stone's report revealed that the abduction in New Mexico had been legitimate, but the little boy the FBI recovered was named Brendon Michaels. A delusional librarian had mistaken him for the son she had lost to a drunk driver thirteen months earlier. For Brendon's mother, his safe return was nothing short of divine intervention. For Jake, it was just one more disappointment in a series of many.

Jake tipped back another wash of thick black elixir from his coffee mug, and his cell phone suddenly jumped to life, vibrating across the table.

"Hello, brother. I trust you slept well?"

"Well, good morning, Armando. I wasn't expecting to hear from you this morning. I thought you were flying down to Arequipa?"

"No, change of plans today. They grounded me with a bad fuel pump. Our mechanic is working on it. He'll have me in the air soon."

"Where are you off to this afternoon?"

"I have no charters for the rest of the day. They already gave my afternoon flights to the new guy. I thought you and I might cover some new ground today. Why don't I pick you up around noon and we'll get some food before we take off?"

"Your flying is hard enough to take on an *empty* stomach!"

"Ah, but the price is right!" Armando volleyed back.

"Indeed it is, brother. I'll be ready at noon, and lunch will be on me."

"I'll pick you up in front of your palace, *Mi Presidente*."

"I'll watch for the limo."

Jake closed his cell phone and turned his attention back to the little boy sitting on the steps across the street. If only his life were that simple.

Today would bring another flight up the coast—another day pounding the dust and questioning villagers and merchants. Jake treasured his time with Armando, and appreciated his generosity. But Peru was starting to seem like another fruitless journey. Maybe it was time to return home. Maybe it was time to give up the search, for whatever it was he was searching. Yes, it was time to get back to his life—or whatever was left of it. He decided today would be his last journey with Armando. He was going home.

CHAPTER 39

THE MERCHANDISE

Fritz VonKlecker was no stranger to danger. He was a German man of means, a millionaire many times over. He had flown stunt planes, run with the bulls, killed African game, and trekked through the most dangerous regions of the Amazon. But as he sat blindfolded in the back of his host's black sedan, under the watchful eyes of an armed guard, the silence of the two-hour car ride was making him uneasy.

VonKlecker understood the magnitude of the transaction at hand, and he understood the broker's desire for secrecy. But the safeguards seemed superfluous. In twenty-four hours he had changed planes twice, changed vehicles three times, and he figured he'd traveled through at least five towns or cities.

He silently told himself he had no reason to worry. It was just a business deal. It wasn't as if he had the money on him—it would be wired at a later date if the merchandise proved genuine. Nevertheless, there was a sense of peril, but it comforted him to know the goon who patted him down at the start of the treasure hunt had failed to detect the GPS chip planted securely in the heel of his shoe. He, too, had people—people who were tracking his every movement. And his people were a force the broker's people would not want to encounter.

The light shining through the edges of VonKlecker's blindfold was diminishing, and he knew the sun must be low. It was nearly dusk as they drove through the gates of the property, followed by the Range Rover that had escorted them for the last leg of the journey. A quick nod to the heavily armed guard at the gate, and the small convoy was waved through.

The sound of the vehicles pulling into the courtyard caught the little boy's attention as he sat in his bedroom playing with the small dump truck and bulldozer he'd received as a gift the day before. He slowly approached his second-story window and peeked through a gap in the curtains.

He watched the vehicles pull up to the brick outbuilding and waited for the guard dogs and armed camouflaged men to exit the guesthouse to take their positions. But the guesthouse was dark, and no dogs were stirring. This visit was different. There were no large trucks or vans, no offloading of crates and boxes.

Two men exited the first vehicle, then two from the second. The boy recognized them, even in the fading light of the evening sunset. Two were guards he knew from the guesthouse, but tonight they were dressed in nice clothing and had no guns strapped over their shoulders.

One of the remaining men was the boss who lived down the hall, and the other man was someone the boy had seen sitting at the patio during lunch meetings with the boss.

The guards opened the back door of the sedan and assisted a fifth man from the vehicle, carefully guiding his head to clear the opening. This man was different from the others. Light-skinned, blond-haired, bearded, and blindfolded! At first the sight of a blindfolded man being escorted by the two guards was unsettling to the boy. But as he watched how respectfully the man's handlers directed him toward the building, the boy sensed that the stranger would be safe.

VonKlecker was guided over the raised threshold of a doorway, and he felt himself stepping onto a hard, level surface. Once inside, his tour guides stopped him in his tracks, and he heard a heavy door close firmly behind him. The noise echoed through what sounded to be a very spacious building.

"Señor VonKlecker, we have reached our destination. I thank you for indulging us with our security measures. I would like to remove your blindfold now, but I ask that you direct your attention forward. Please walk straight toward the light at the end of the corridor. Do not turn around; do not touch anything you pass along the way. I will remain behind you at all times. Agreed?"

"Agreed."

VonKlecker was gently spun forward and his blindfold was removed. He blinked several times trying to adjust to the new environment. The lighting inside the building was scarce; just enough illumination was cast from above for him to discern a walkway between a long series of shelves on either side, which reached several feet toward a distant ceiling.

The shelving was full of crates, each marked in Spanish codes and numbers he didn't understand. At the far end of the path, he saw a dark cavernous opening that was broken up by several narrow beams of light from above.

As VonKlecker walked toward the light at the end of the corridor he began to sense the magnitude of the warehouse. Through the narrow openings between the crates on either side of him, he detected several adjacent rows of shelving, each containing a series of neatly organized crates extending upwards far into the darkness. He had underestimated the magnitude of the broker's operation.

As VonKlecker reached the end of the corridor, he came to a large opening in the warehouse. He had arrived at the columns of light—twelve beams, each perfectly positioned to illuminate its corresponding sealed chamber below.

He was suddenly exhilarated. He had waited so long; he had traveled so far. If the bodies of the ancient beings resting within the chambers were authentic, their value would be immeasurable. He would possess the most unique, most well-preserved trove of mummies in the world. It would be the perfect addition to his collection—a collection that would someday, after his death, be shared with the scientific community. It would be his legacy.

As the German awaited instruction, he heard the

broker's voice echo from the darkness behind him. "You may approach the product, Señor VonKlecker. But I ask that you not open the chambers. The woman in the chamber directly in front of you is the one we've already unveiled. We believe she was their queen."

VonKlecker approached the middle chamber with tentative steps, as if he was approaching the Holy Grail. She was illuminated under the museum lighting and could be seen clearly through the window of the chamber. With one glimpse, VonKlecker's knees weakened.

The texture of her skin, the unusual coloration, the composition of the body—it was just like the photograph. VonKlecker would require genetic confirmation, but he knew there would be no need. He was already convinced the specimen was genuine, and it was extraordinary.

The strange configuration of the limbs and digits, the large misshapen cranium, the thick discolored and hardened skin—the product was just as promised.

"How can I be sure the merchandise is authentic?" the German spoke loudly into the darkness.

"If you look on her shoulder you will see a very small triangular section of skin that has been removed. The skin has been preserved, along with a section of the linen that she was wrapped in. I assure you that the sample specimens will withstand any scientific testing."

"And the other eleven?"

"Those you take as is. They have not been disturbed, so there is no reason to believe they differ from their matriarch. We will unveil them if you wish, but only after payment has been made in full."

"No, that won't be necessary. They're worth more to me as they are."

"You're correct, señor. They are more valuable in their present state."

"May I take the sample pieces back to Germany with me for testing?"

"They will accompany you when we return you to your country."

"Very well," the German replied with a smile. "I look forward to doing business with you."

Chapter 40

THE LAST FLIGHT

There was no better view of the Peruvian sunset than from the passenger window of Armando's Cessna. As Jake admired the soft glow spilling into the curves of the highlands, he thought about how small the planet truly was. He thought about how the entire world relied on the same glowing ball to light and warm its inhabitants. But if the world really was so small, he thought, why was he not able to find any answers within it?

Jake had departed Lima earlier that day with a renewed sense of optimism. During his trip to Chiclayo the day before, Armando had crossed paths with a retired pilot friend who once flew for the Lopez family. Although the old pilot knew nothing about the present whereabouts of his former employer, he did recall flying over some activity a few months earlier in the remote area just south of Bambamarca, which could easily have passed as an archaeological site. In fact, he remembered thinking that one of the pricey utility vehicles he saw at the site resembled one belonging to Lopez himself.

No doubt Lopez had been off the grid for so long, because he was occupied with his secret project in a secluded region of the Andes, far from the comforts of his social circles. Today they would find the elusive Arturo

Lopez. It was the day they would find answers—answers about Blanca's accident, answers about the mysterious alien artifacts, answers about the woman in the back of the black sedan.

But so far, the day had been a bust. They made one stop in Trujillo to top the tank off with fuel, then spent the afternoon flying throughout the region between Cajamarca and Bambamarca looking for any signs of archaeological activity. But if someone had been digging around in the countryside, there was no longer any evidence of it that was detectible from the air.

Armando gave Jake a nudge of the elbow. "We should head back. Our visibility will soon be gone, and I'm running low on fuel."

Jake nodded, offered Armando an affirming smile, and returned his attention to the sunset. He felt fortunate to have such a great friend and regretted never bringing Jonathan down to visit Blanca's family after her funeral. Blanca made a number of trips back to Peru with Jonathan when he was quite young, but despite Jake's good intentions, he failed to carry on the tradition. Life always seemed to get in the way. But as Jake looked out the window of Armando's plane, taken in by the amber glow of the setting sun, he vowed to himself that the family would be reunited if Jonathan was ever safely returned to him.

Armando banked the plane sharply to the left to close out his last circle of the region. He thought it best to work his way back to the coast to salvage what remained of the evening light, knowing that once the sun dipped below the horizon, darkness would fill every crevasse of the mountains.

The first sputter of the engine was almost undetectable, and Armando responded casually by checking his gauges to make sure everything was in order. *Probably just a little debris in the fuel line,* he thought. But as he leveled out his turn, the sputter that followed was not so subtle, and even Jake took notice.

"What the hell was that? Are we out of fuel?" Jake asked.

"We shouldn't be. I'm still getting a decent reading on the gauge," Armando replied calmly, tapping on the instrument panel.

After a slight adjustment of the throttle, they breathed a sigh of relief as the engine continued to purr.

"Just a little misfire. Everything seems fine now," Armando said reassuringly. "We must have picked up some bad fuel today."

But Armando wasn't thinking about bad fuel. He was thinking about a fuel pump that had been repaired earlier that morning by a new mechanic who seemed less than competent to do the job—the same mechanic who just the day before had been slinking around the passenger window of a strange black sedan with tinted windows.

There was certainly no reason to alarm Jake, but a night flight all the way back to Lima would be too risky. He would reduce his elevation and set his bearings for Trijullo.

They would eat a nice meal, get a good night's sleep, and have the plane checked out in the morning.

Armando adjusted his course and prepared to contact the tower at Trijullo. But as he reached for the radio transmitter, there was another noticeable cough from the engine. In an instant, the plane became eerily quiet. There was no longer a hum of the engine, no sputter from the exhaust, no vibration in the fuselage—nothing but the sound of the wind drifting over the wings.

Jake watched in horror as the propeller stopped, and he waited for his heart to seize along with it. Just like the moments before a car accident, time slowed. Jake wanted to speak but was unable to form the words.

In a flash, he was consumed by a feeling of finality. This would be the end of his journey. He could feel it in his gut. He had lost his wife, then his son. And now, in the dark isolated highlands of Peru, he and his brother-in-law would crash into a fiery ball. It was almost as if Jake was expecting his life's story to end exactly in this way, and he was ready.

But as Jake watched his life pass before his eyes, Armando gave a quick mayday call, adjusted the flaps, slid the throttle, and pushed the engine button. Neither man said a word as the engine reignited and the propeller sprang to life.

The power was back, but the velocity was failing. Armando's hopes hung on every revolution of the propeller, but he could tell by the pulsing of the engine that their time in the air was limited.

"Strap yourself in tight, Jacob. We need to find a landing strip."

"Out here? What did you have in mind, a pile of rocks?"

"Look for something level—a road, a field, a clearing... anything flat."

They surveyed the landscape. The countryside was scarcely visible in the waning sunset—nothing but shadowy slopes, dark rocky canyons, and obscure pockets of tree cover. Armando needed a closer look, but he didn't dare to descend much lower into the valley in fear that he wouldn't be able to climb back out if the topography changed.

As the plane scarcely cleared the crest of a massive hill, a faint light became visible in the distance. Armando nodded with approval and pointed. "There! At two o'clock. A road. Do you see it?"

Jake squinted hard and peered into the distance, his heart slamming against his chest. "I'll take your word for it," he replied, his voice devoured by his nerves.

Armando adjusted his flaps and reduced his air speed to get down for a closer look. But as he tapered down the throttle, he felt a surge of unexpected power and then the deadening sensation of a non-responsive aircraft. Once again, a silence fell upon the cockpit.

Jake panicked as he watched Armando finesse the yoke and the flaps, reposition the throttle, hit the engine button, curse in Spanish, and shout a hurried mayday call over the radio. But the aircraft was quickly losing altitude.

"I think I can make it to the clearing, Jake. I'll try to hit that road down there if I can." The instant the words left his mouth Armando knew he had chosen them poorly.

"What do you mean *hit* the road?" Jake bellowed in alarm.

"Make sure your safety belt is secure. I'll set this bitch down in one piece if it kills me!" Armando mumbled under his breath in Spanish as he reprimanded himself for another poor choice of words.

Armando abandoned his attempt to restart the engine. As gravity pulled the small craft from the sky, the earth below swiftly invaded their airspace.

Jake braced for impact, clenching both hands firmly into the dash of the cockpit. He frantically peered out through the windshield hoping to see a feasible landing site, or whatever fate might be waiting in its place.

Suddenly, Jake could see the light Armando had detected. He watched the light get closer, larger, brighter. As the aircraft continued to descend, the landscape faintly revealed itself through the atmosphere. A scant crimson hue from the setting sun was desperately clinging to the edge of the horizon.

Fighting off the panic, Jake shifted his focus back and forth between his desperate pilot and the obscure vision barely detectable through the window.

Then, with one blink, his eyes adjusted to the shapes below. A clearing in the distance, a canopy of trees, some sort of rock formation, it all jumped into focus. Before his mind could process the image, the aircraft met the earth.

CHAPTER 41

IN THE LIGHT OF DAY

Nights in the Andes can be cold, even during Peru's summer season. Jake had no idea how long he had been unconscious, nor did he know where he was or how he got there. There was silence, the void of the darkness, the sharp smell of fuel, the numbness in his legs.

As he bobbed in and out of consciousness, he pieced together the mystery. He had been flying…with Armando; the engine failed; they were trying to land; there was a crash.

Jake slowly turned his head to the left and strained to bring the cockpit into focus. He ran his bloody hand across the empty seat where Armando had been. Instantly, a panic overcame what limited consciousness he could gather. Where was his pilot? Had he been thrown out? Dragged off? Crushed? Was he lying out in the cold, dark wilderness of the Andes? Jake fell out of consciousness once again.

In his next wave of clarity, Jake felt the piercing light of the morning sun streaming through the window. It warmed his face as if it were trying to coax him back to life. He was barely able to focus as he opened his eyes. He questioned whether the whole thing had been nothing but a bad dream, but his pounding head and the pain radiating down his leg told him otherwise.

As he lay in bed scanning the perimeter of an unfamiliar room, he was suddenly startled by the presence of a small figure sitting nearby. The boy in the chair looked no older than twelve or thirteen, and he was staring curiously at Jake as if he was trying to read his mind.

"¿Está usted bien, señor?" the boy asked. *Are you alright, sir?*

"¿Cómo te llamas, hijo?" *What is your name, son?*

"Roberto."

Jake struggled to prop himself up on his elbow to get a better view out the window. "Bueno en conocerte, Roberto. ¿Me puedes decir dónde estoy?" *Nice to meet you, Roberto. Can you tell me where I am?*

"Usted está en nuestra casa. Su avión se cayó del cielo. Usted ha estado durmiendo." *You are in our home. Your plane fell from the sky. You have been asleep.*

"¿Cómo llegué aquí, Roberto?" *How did I get here, Roberto?*

"Mi papa y el otro hombre lo trajeron—en el camión." *My father and the other man brought you—in the truck.*

"¿El otro hombre? ¿Cuál otro hombre?" *The other man? What other man?*

"El hombre del avión, Sr. Vasquez." *The man from the plane, Mr. Vasquez.*

"¡Sr. Vasquez! ¿Dónde está? ¿Él está bien?" *Mr. Vasquez! Where is he? Is he alright?*

"Si, si. Él está afuera con mi papa. Ya se lo llamo," Roberto replied. *Yes, yes. He is outside with my father. I will get him for you.* The boy bolted from the room, excited to bring the good news of Jake's recovery to the men outside.

Still foggy and fighting the pain, Jake pulled himself upright and sat on the edge of the bed. He clutched a small table to steady himself as the room spun around him.

As things came into focus, Jake saw three blurry figures appear through the open door. Armando was grinning from ear to ear as he entered the room. He was moving slowly, limping, and his face was camouflaged with bruises and scrapes.

"You look like hell," Jake said with a smile.

"You should see the other guy."

"I think I *am* the other guy. Do I look as bad as you?"

"You could only hope to look this good. Do you think you can walk? Your leg was pinned pretty badly."

"I think I can manage with some help. How bad is the plane?"

"We're not flying it home if that's what you're thinking," Armando responded as he offered a shoulder to help Jake to his feet.

Jake chuckled and grimaced at the same time as he rose from the edge of the bed. "How far are we from civilization?" he asked.

"It's a haul. Our friends here have an old truck. Roberto's father has offered to transport us."

"How soon can we leave?" Jake asked.

"Soon. But I think we should let you rest a little more before we make the trip. And before we go, Roberto has something you should see—let's take a walk into the other room."

Jake's curiosity was piqued as he hobbled next to Armando, following his lead into the next room of the modest home.

"Roberto, por favor enséñale a Jacob la pieza que me enseñaste esta mañana," Armando said. *Please show Jacob the piece that you showed me this morning.*

Roberto ran ahead to the main room and pulled a small chest out from beneath an old wooden bench. The boy opened the chest, lifted out a bundle of linen, and set it on the table. He unwrapped the ragged towel.

Jake approached the table and carefully lifted the artifact to look at it more closely. It appeared to be the partial remains of an ancient bowl, well preserved except for a missing portion along half of the rim. It was clearly an old piece. Jake studied the various hand-scribed markings adorning the surface of the bowl. They were hauntingly familiar.

"Roberto. ¿Dónde encontraste esta pieza?" Jake asked. *Where did you get this piece?*

"En las cuevas. En las cuevas donde la gente estaba excavando," the boy replied. *It came from the caves. The caves where the people were digging.*

"¿Tú viste gente excavando? ¿Sabes quienes eran?" *You saw people digging? Do you know who they were?*

"Los científicos que excavan por el tesoro," Roberto replied. *The scientists who dig for the treasure.*

"Roberto, ¿Había una mujer excavando por el tesoro

en las cuevas?" *Was there a woman digging for treasure at the caves?*

"Si, muchas veces habían dos mujeres allá," Roberto said. *Yes, there were two women there, many times.*

Jake struggled to pull the wallet from his back pocket, his body still too sore to comply. He pulled out a faded old photograph. "¿Es ésta una de las mujeres que viste en las cuevas?" he asked, holding the photo up to Roberto's face. *Is this one of the women you saw at the caves?*

The boy studied the photo, the furrow in his brow revealing his careful contemplation.

"Puede ser ella," the boy said tentatively. *It could be her.* "Puede ser la mujer más alta—la jefa. Sí, yo creo que es ella, pero no estoy seguro. Nunca me llegué muy cerca de esa gente cuando estaban trabajando allá. Yo me quedaba lejos, detrás de las rocas. Pero cuando ellos se fueron yo me colé en la cueva por una entrada de atrás." *It could be the taller woman—the boss lady. Yes, I think it is her, but I can't be positive. I never got too close to the people when they were working there. I stayed in the distance, behind the rocks. But when they left I snuck into the cave through a back entrance.*

"¿Una entrada de atrás?" Armando perked up. "¿Nos puedes llevar a esa entrada?" *A back entrance. Can you take us to this back entrance?*

"Si, la conozco muy bien," Roberto declared proudly. *Yes, I know it very well.*

"Roberto. ¿Qué viste en la cueva?" Jake asked. *What did you see in the cave?*

"Muchas cosas. Habían muchos cuartos pequeños, excavaban mucho en la tierra. Los científicos se llevaban muchos tesoros con ellos en los camiones cada noche." *Many things. There were many small rooms, much digging in the earth. The scientists took many treasures with them in the trucks each night.*

"¿Tú viste si ellos removieron algo que parecía como ataúdes?" *Did you see them remove anything that looked like coffins?*

"Si." Roberto replied. "Ellos metieron doce cajas grandes, y luego esa noche sacaron doce cajas grandes. Las cajas eran largas como ataúdes." *Yes. They carried twelve big boxes in, and later that night they carried twelve big boxes out. The boxes were long, like coffins.*

"¿Tomaste algunas otras piezas del sitio?" Jake inquired. *Did you take any other pieces from the site?*

"No. Esta fue la única pieza que ellos dejaron. Ellos ponían todo en cajas cada día y lo ponían en sus camiones en la noche." *No. This was the only piece they left behind. They boxed everything up each day and put it on their trucks at night.*

As the boy's story continued, his father listened curiously. It was obvious from the expression on the man's face that this was the first time the boy had shared this information.

He knew his son had been absent from the homestead more than usual and had been neglecting his chores and studies. But he had no idea that Roberto had been wandering off more than an hour's hike up the valley to play explorer. Roberto suspected there would be consequences for his secrecy.

To Jake and Armando, the boy's story was the best news they'd heard in weeks. The secret expedition, the female scientist, the night hauls of treasure, the twelve long boxes. Had they stumbled on their link to Lopez? They knew a trip to the caves was inevitable, and Armando reluctantly agreed that Jake was fit enough to travel. They would leave for the caves just after lunch.

CHAPTER 42

BROKER BETRAYAL

The German was nestled into the soft leather of his Mercedes limousine, on his way to a meeting with the board of directors to debate his overseas acquisition. VonKlecker was all about the power, and the power was all about the money. And the money was what gratified Herr Fritz VonKlecker.

He set his cognac down to free up a hand, then took a long drag on his cigar as he examined the screen on his ringing phone. There was no identifying information. VonKlecker exhaled the costly smoke and barked his greeting.

"VonKlecker."

"Mr. VonKlecker, this is your friend in South America; I am calling to personally thank you for the first half of your wire transfer."

VonKlecker smiled, amused by the naivety of his caller. The broker had no clue his anonymity had been breached. The German not only knew the broker's identity, but thanks to his GPS and his intelligence team, VonKlecker knew the exact location of his hacienda, as well as the fine details of his financial holdings. The playing field had been leveled.

"Yes, my anonymous friend. You have your installment.

I assume you are calling with confirmation of shipment."

"I'm afraid there's been a complication. We need to reopen the negotiations," the broker replied casually, as if telling the German that his dry cleaning was delayed.

There was a thick pause. "For your sake, I hope you're calling to propose a reduction in the price of your product."

"You are a man of business, Mr. VonKlecker. I'm sure you understand the consequence of supply and demand."

"Yes. Yes I do. And as a man of business yourself, I'm sure you understand the consequence of revoking a commitment. And I must warn you…" the German pulled another drag from his cigar, "the consequences in this case would be fatal."

"There is no need to make such threats, señor. They do not work on me. I'm simply calling to inform you that there has been renewed interest in the product. However, for an additional twenty percent I can ship the items on Friday."

"Listen to me…*señor*," VonKlecker replied, "I have paid you handsomely for your product. The first half of the money has been transferred to the account as requested. We have an agreement on the shipping arrangements. There will be no further negotiations."

"Well, as I see it, you are not in the best position to be making such an assessment. The product is in my possession, and so is your fifteen million. The price has been increased by twenty percent. The product has already been prepared and secured on the transport. It will be in the air on Friday at noon. I must receive confirmation of the second wire transfer by 12:30 p.m. that day. If that happens, the plane will land at the location we've agreed upon."

"You can't really believe that I would trust you with the second installment prior to my receipt of the merchandise," VonKlecker replied, almost amused by the broker's instructions. But there was no reply. The line was dead.

VonKlecker washed down a heavy gulp of cognac, then pulled another drag from his cigar. He slowly exhaled the smoke as he stared out the window of the limousine. After a brief deliberation with his thoughts he opened his briefcase, retrieved a different cell phone, and pressed one key.

„Ich bin's. Stellt das Team zusammen. Wir machen einen Ausflug." *It's me. Assemble the team. We are taking a trip.*

CHAPTER 43

A SACRED SITE

The rear entrance to the cave was just where Roberto said it would be. But things had changed since his last visit. The narrow opening in the earth he had shimmied through before was now blocked by a large stone slab. It was obvious that the previous visitors had placed the obstruction there as the final seal on the tomb.

Exhausted by defeat, Jake and Armando sat on the rocks next to Roberto and his father. They knew the old truck was no match for the large rock, and there wasn't a suitable piece of equipment for miles around with enough muscle to dislodge it. But before they could discuss their next move, Roberto sprang to his feet and scampered down the hillside leaving the dust stirring behind him.

"Roberto!" his father yelled. "¿A dónde vas? ¡Regresa inmediatamente!" *Where are you going? Come back here at once!*

The men walked to the edge of the steep hill and watched the young boy slide and skid down to the bottom. "Ese niño terco. Nunca obedece. Igual que su madre," the father mumbled. *That stubborn child. He never listens. He is his mother's son.*

Jake forced a painful smile, stretching the cuts and bruises on his face, still fresh from the crash the day before.

He could see Roberto at the bottom of the hill, jumping up and down with excitement, waving the men down to join him.

"Él sabe dónde está la entrada principal. Seguramente él vió a los trabajadores usarla durante meses," Jake said, quite proud of his new little friend. *He knows where the main entrance is. He probably watched the crew use it for months.*

Roberto's father wasted no time navigating the rickety truck down the hill. By the time the men joined the boy, he was already using his hands to shovel the dirt and debris away from a small area of the hillside that appeared depressed from the surrounding soil.

"Era aquí," Roberto declared. "La entrada a las cuevas—por aquí fue donde ellos sacaron el tesoro." *It was right here. The door to the caves—this is where they took the treasure out.*

Jake circled the area where Roberto was kneeling and studied the terrain. Whoever had sealed the entrance had camouflaged it to match the surrounding landscape. The plugs of native grass and brush had begun to fill in, but he could see the shallow depression where the soil had settled.

The men eagerly grabbed two shovels and some old gardening tools from the back of the truck and joined Roberto's digging. The dirt was shallow, no more than ten inches deep, and as the earth was removed they started to see a wooden surface.

They said very little as they worked—Jake and Armando both grimacing in pain, but each anxious to discover what might be waiting behind Door Number One. In a short time, they had removed enough soil to expose the entrance.

The thick double door measured nearly eight feet across and contained no visible locking device. The panels were made of heavy timber slabs, each door fitting perfectly over its ancient stony frame.

Roberto watched with excitement as the men slid the first panel open. But the natural light spilling into the passage was scarcely sufficient to illuminate the cavity. Nothing was revealed but a dark, dusty cavernous void.

It was decided that Jake and Armando would proceed alone. Being a native Peruvian, Roberto's father harbored a genuine respect for the tombs and had no desire to rummage around in an ancient burial site. He and Roberto would guard the entrance and wait for the safe return of their colleagues.

The two explorers lit their lanterns and stepped into the shadows. They moved cautiously as they found their way into the subterranean cave. But they quickly discovered that it wasn't a cave at all, but rather an intricate maze of well-engineered chambers, seemingly part of an ancient structure—a structure that had somehow been covered by earth and buried in time.

Even in the dim glow of the lanterns, Jake could see that the sanctuary they were exploring was exceptional. Blanca had taught him much about her work during their time together, and he had visited many ancient sites—but nothing like this one. The engineering and craftsmanship were remarkable. The stonework was intricately fitted, and the walls were precise and flush.

Jake's heart doubled its beat as he led the way through the perplexing maze of ancient corridors and chambers. One hallway led into the next, and each room seemed to open into another. There was little evidence remaining of the people who once inhabited the dwellings, the contents likely having been looted at the hands of Lopez and his crew.

As the men ventured deeper into the complex, Armando finally broke the silence.

"My God, Jacob. What is this place?"

"I was just about to ask you the same thing," Jake replied, holding his lantern up to light the way into the next chamber. "This is no mud hut; whoever built this thing was centuries ahead of their time."

"It's like we've stepped inside the mother ship," Armando replied. "I think we should have left a trail of bread crumbs so we can find our way out of here."

"It's too late for that now, brother; we'll have to rely on our sharp memory and keen sense of…." Jake stopped as the light from his lantern spilled onto the doorway suddenly in front of him. They had reached the end of the path. Jake waved his lantern across the face of the door, studying the markings on its surface.

"These are the same symbols—same as the ones on Prof's piece, same as Roberto's piece, same as the ones from the catalog."

"What do you think they mean?" Armando asked.

"I have no idea," Jake replied, running his fingers along the surface of the door. "Maybe it's some sort of alphabet—one damn old alphabet."

"I didn't think these ancient civilizations had a written language," Armando said, noticeably awestruck by the markings adorning the portal. "Blanca used to show me photographs of the drawings and artwork she discovered, but none of it was this sophisticated."

"Well, this whole damn place looks like something straight out of a science fiction novel," Jake mumbled, exploring the doorframe in search of a latch or handle. "I'd like to know where this wood came from; this is pretty advanced craftsmanship for its time—whatever time that was."

Armando nudged Jake and pointed up toward the ceiling. "Look at the way the rock is recessed above the doorway. I think this thing opens upward."

Jake set his lantern on the floor, crouched down to gain some leverage, then let out a groan as he threw his best effort into lifting the door. It raised nearly a foot before slamming back to the ground, narrowly missing Jake's toes.

"How about some help here, Hercules?" Jake asked, motioning to Armando.

They hunched down and positioned themselves for the next lift. On Jake's count of three, they heaved the door upward. It rose at a snail's pace, reluctant to give in to the intruders.

As the door reached shoulder level, they suddenly felt a release of the deadweight. The door surrendered and disappeared into the ceiling, making a loud crashing sound as it locked into place. Jake and Armando tucked their heads into their arms, sheltering their eyes from the falling dust and debris.

As they stepped across the threshold, the light from their lanterns spilled into the new chamber. It was noticeably different from the rooms they had passed through on the way. The chamber was much larger, rectangular in shape, and about six hundred square feet. The walls were coated with a gold pigment and adorned with murals and symbols.

As the men explored the chamber they moved their lanterns around themselves to light the shadows. Twelve stone platforms lined the edge of the far wall, each one perfectly spaced apart from the next. Above each platform was a lengthy script containing various characters of the mysterious ancient alphabet.

"Twelve slabs—this is where the mummies were. And check out the paint job in here; this was obviously some elaborate shrine," Jake said.

"They've stripped this place clean," Armando replied, venturing away from Jake to examine another area of the chamber. "It must have taken years for Lopez to clean everything out of here without anyone noticing."

An unnatural silence settled in as they continued to explore the dark corners of the chamber, and an eerie feeling came over them. Each of them tried to envision the beings who once inhabited the dwelling, and what ancient rituals had taken place there.

Armando walked slowly around the twelve platforms throughout the chamber, studying the craftsmanship of the stonework, amazed by how precise each block fit snugly together with the next. He could see a discoloration on the surface of each platform that resembled the shape of a mummified body. A chill ran up his spine as he assessed the dimensions of the outlines. It was obvious that the ancient cadavers once entombed there were much taller than the average human.

Just as Armando rounded the corner of the last platform, the reflection from a small object lying on the floor caught his eye. He crouched down to examine it, brushing away the sand and pebbles. It was small, black, shiny, and plastic—clearly not an ancient artifact. He picked it up and held it closer to his lantern. "Jake, come take a look at this!"

Jake had been examining a large mural in the middle of the headwall and joined his partner in the far corner of the chamber.

"Is that what I think it is?" Jake asked.

"If you think it's a camera, I think you may be right."

The camera was very small, obviously digital. Jake watched with excitement as Armando fiddled with the tiny buttons to turn it on. This had to be the break they were hoping for. The answers to all of their questions had to be in the digital recesses of this small black box. But despite their best efforts, the battery seemed to be spent. The truths embedded in the camera's memory card would have to wait.

CHAPTER 44

THE GREAT ESCAPE

It was the perfect night to execute their escape. The woman knew she would never get a better chance. Her employer was not due back from Lima until late the next day, and the guards were intoxicated from their unauthorized party, which had begun just after two o'clock that afternoon.

She packed light, one bag for her, one bag for the boy. It would be at least a three-mile walk to the woods. She offered a short prayer, praying that her friend's brother had hidden the old car as promised, and asking God to bless the battery so that the car would still start.

She wasn't allowed to have friends, aside from a few of the staff members who worked for her employer. But she had become particularly close to one of the housekeepers on the estate. Rosario, a long-time employee and trusted servant, was one of the few staff members with privileges to visit family in the city. And against her better judgment, Rosario was eventually persuaded to enlist her brother to aid with her friend's escape.

A mechanic in the city, her brother had ensured her that he could secure a car for her friend. The car would be old, but reliable. Most importantly, it would be untraceable to either of them. He agreed to hide the car behind the abandoned shed just down the main road from the compound.

Rosario knew her assistance was offered at great risk, but she felt it was necessary. Her friend had been enslaved, under constant watch, unable to establish contact with the outside world. And now there was the boy. The boy was the last straw. It wasn't fair that he, too, was confined to the compound, unable to return to his true home.

The woman woke the boy, carefully rubbing his chest without startling him. She instructed him in English that it was time to take the secret journey they had talked about.

A peek between the slats of wooden blinds from the second-story window revealed a quiet courtyard; none of the sentinels were visible. As of Rosario's last meal delivery to the guardhouse, the men were out of commission. Three were passed out on the furniture, and four were still nursing their tequila at the poker table, their heads bobbing into their cards.

The guard shack at the entrance gate was also unmanned; its watchman, having abandoned his post, was now comatose at the poker game. It was unprecedented for the guards to be so relaxed in their duties. But it had been unusually quiet at the compound the past week. Their boss had been away on business; there were no blindfolded visitors, no deliveries, no shipments.

The woman secured her bags and nervously glanced at the clock. It was nearly 3:00 a.m. Their departure had to be now or never. The sun would be up soon, the guards would be stumbling into the daylight, and servants would be entering the main house to prepare breakfast for the crew.

She and the boy were both dressed in dark clothing, hoping to blend into the darkness. With a small duffel bag strapped over her shoulder and a satchel in her hand, she quietly led the boy down the stairwell to the main entrance of the house. She gripped his tiny hand as they slinked down one creaky step at a time.

The front door was risky—it led directly into the open courtyard, which was well lit. The back door led to a much darker patio, nicely sheltered by shrubs, but it was just paces away from the guards' quarters where the poker game was dwindling to its intoxicated finale.

She slowly opened the front door and peeked outside, scanning across the open compound. All was quiet. She and the boy stepped onto the porch and quickly slipped into a shadow just beyond the reach of the porch light. They edged their way toward a set of stairs, clinging to the house to avoid the light.

The two escapees made their way down the porch steps and scurried to the edge of the botanical gardens nearby. They wove their way through the garden and took cover in a sparse grove of trees not far from the stone wall that surrounded the compound.

She led the boy from tree to tree, scampering through the shadows, masked from the moonlight above. They settled into a thick section of foliage where she could better surveil the courtyard. There were still no signs of movement. The guardhouse was dimly lit, and she could detect the faint silhouettes of drunken poker players through the window. The main house was also dark, with the exception of a glow from the lamp in Rosario's bedroom. Just to the west, she saw the corner window of the guard shack at the main gate—it, too, was dark. She was beginning to think their escape might be a success.

Across the compound to the east she could see the main storage building. If only she had access, she thought, she would fill her bag with enough evidence to imprison her employer for life. She could show the world a sample of the amazing treasures they had discovered. She could reveal the mysterious twelve and their extraordinary ancient alphabet. The thought of the treasures being auctioned off to the highest black market bidders sickened her to her core.

There was a sudden stirring in the bushes nearby. She covered the boy's mouth and motioned him to be silent as they watched a man shuffle toward them. He stumbled slightly, caught his balance, then continued along the garden path. He was quite large, nearly blocking the half-moon behind him.

As the giant approached, the woman's heart pounded wildly, and she could feel the boy trembling in her arms. She tightened her grip over his mouth and kissed him on the top of his head. The man stumbled to a stop just a few feet from their blanket of bushes. As he turned, the moonlight caught the side of his face. She knew this giant—it was Manuel, the guard who was assigned to the shack at the gate. He had regained consciousness and was working his way back to his post.

Manuel stood in the moonlight, his body swaying to and fro, facing the fugitives as if looking directly into the whites of their eyes. Then, without warning, he let out a loud belch as he lowered his zipper and began relieving himself on a nearby tree.

As the guard drained his tequila, her mind raced to determine her next move. The gate was only paces away, and once he returned to his post their escape would be compromised.

She leaned into the boy's ear and whispered softly, "be very, very quiet my little one—you cannot make a sound." She removed her hand from his mouth and felt the ground around them. There had to be something she could use as a weapon, she thought—a large stick, a rock, anything heavy enough to knock Manuel back into his coma. But the only thing she could find in the perfectly manicured garden was a harmless rock, scarcely bigger than her hand.

Manuel stood firm in his tracks, still swaying as he fumbled to zip and secure his pants. He released a sigh of frustration struggling to guide his belt latch into its designated hole. Realizing he was too drunk for the task, Manuel aborted the belt refastening, released another belch, and resumed his shuffle toward the guard shack.

Just as he turned away, she rose to her feet and launched the rock as far as she could in the opposite direction of the front gate. She heard the rock rustle through a thicket of leaves and branches before meeting the wooden toolshed with a thud.

Manuel nearly lost his balance turning toward the noise. He pulled his pistol from its holster and lumbered down the garden path toward the tool shed. As he disappeared into the shadows, she took the boy's hand and they scurried quietly to the gate.

A dim lamp was on in the guard shack, and for the first time in years, it was unmanned. On the counter sat a pint of whiskey, a thermos, a half-eaten sandwich, a neatly folded sports section, and a nudie magazine—all signs that the boss had been away.

As she slunk through the gate, something in the guard shack caught her eye. There was movement on the surveillance monitor. She stopped briefly to take a closer look through the window. She could see several images on the monitor, each pane revealing a different view of the compound. The images changed as the surveillance software cycled through dozens of cameras placed strategically about the grounds. She saw a panoramic view of the guard shack, with her and the boy peering through the window. Certainly not helping her conceal the details of their escape, she thought.

As her eyes panned across the monitor, there were two other images that concerned her. One was the footage of Manuel holstering his gun and working his way back toward his post; the other was a pair of disheveled guards slowly stumbling out on the porch of the main guardhouse. The poker game was apparently over, and there would be little time before the morning revealed their absence.

She secured her bags, grabbed the boy's hand, stepped through the gates of the compound, and disappeared into the darkness.

CHAPTER 45

A HAUNTING IMAGE

Jacob Bishop sat on the edge of the bed after waking from his twelve-hour hibernation. It was the best sleep he had enjoyed since arriving in Peru. There were few words that could describe his past few days. "Inconceivable" probably fit better than any other. The plane crash, the village boy, the artifact, the secret chambers—Jake shook his head in disbelief.

The room was dark, but the door was ajar and he smelled breakfast drifting in from the kitchen. It smelled like a good-old American breakfast—coffee, bacon, eggs, potatoes, and something with blueberries, pancakes perhaps. *Maybe it had been a dream,* he thought. Maybe he was back home, in his own bedroom, waking up to one of Margaret's surprise Sunday morning breakfasts.

But as he sat there, collecting his thoughts, he felt the pain radiate across his back and down both of his legs. *The plane crash,* he thought, *was no dream.*

Jake rose to his feet and walked slowly toward the delightful smells. With each step he shifted his weight, contorting his body to lessen the pain that had settled deep into his muscles.

He opened the bedroom door and peeked into the world. Armando's apartment was small by American standards, but very livable for a Peruvian dwelling. It was a typical bachelor pad—lots of black leather, a large flat-screen television, and nothing frilly in sight. Standing in the kitchen with a skillet in one hand and a spatula in the other, Armando greeted his guest with an inviting smile.

"*Buenos dias*, brother. I was beginning to think you would never wake."

"Nobody could sleep through all these smells. This food looks fantastic. You shouldn't have gone to so much trouble."

"It was no trouble. I cook breakfast for all of my overnighters," Armando replied with a grin, still focused on the eggs in his pan. "Pour yourself a cup of coffee."

Jake poured the thick black java into his cup and searched the kitchen for some sugar. At the end of the counter next to Armando's notebook computer sat the camera they had found in the caves. A green light was blinking from the apparatus as it soaked up the charge from its new power cord.

"You found a cord! Where the hell did you find one to fit that thing?"

"Ciro, the kid downstairs. He's an engineer—works for some electronics outfit. He had a big box of cords and cables down there. It took him about ten minutes to rig it up for us."

"Are there any pictures on it?"

"I haven't checked yet. It's been charging for awhile. Why don't you take a look? Ciro said that once the camera was charged we could plug it into the laptop with that other cable there," Armando explained while lifting the corner of his eggs from the pan to see if they were cooked to his satisfaction.

Jake pressed the power button on the camera, and the small screen instantly came to life. He plugged the USB cord into Armando's computer, fiddled with the menu that appeared on the screen, downloaded the images, and within a few minutes stumbled into his first picture. It was a close-up shot of a wide-eyed llama flaunting a silly grin. *Cute,* he thought, *but not at all helpful.*

He scrolled through the images, one by one, searching for anything that might reveal the secrets from within the caves, or the people who last occupied them. But each photo in the lineup was benign. They could have been taken by any common tourist. There were pictures of local villagers, small farm animals, mountain landscapes and beautiful sunsets—nothing useful.

As Jake scrolled deeper into the collection of images he came across a candid photo of a Caucasian woman in her late twenties, wearing khaki pants and a field jacket. The woman was in the city and appeared to be admiring a fountain in the background. She was clearly unaware that she was being photographed. *Probably a member of the archaeological crew,* Jake thought.

Soon Jake found photos of other individuals as well—various combinations of the same small group of people taken at different locations. Some were taken in a bar or restaurant, some outside in the city, others somewhere in the country. It was obvious that none of the people had been posed, each photograph a candid image of a spontaneous moment. The photographer was either fond of candid photography, or it was important to her that the subjects not know they were being photographed.

Jake studied each photo. He was hoping to uncover the elusive mummies, or perhaps the mysterious artifacts that were entombed with them. But there was nothing but people and places. Some of the places looked vaguely familiar, but the people were all perfect strangers. That is, until he scrolled onto image number fifty-seven.

He stared at the photograph in disbelief. It was a picture of three people having a meal at an outdoor café. It was taken from a distance, but not so far away that he couldn't make out their faces. There were two men and one woman, all three finely dressed. The man clothed entirely in black was speaking, his two guests hanging intently on his every word. They seemed very interested in what the man had to say. Jake, too, was interested in the man in black; he had been looking for him since arriving in Peru. There was no doubt in his mind that it was Arturo Lopez.

The site of Lopez in the photo brought a satisfying grin to Jake's face. It instantly validated his suspicions about Lopez's connection to the site and the mysterious artifacts. He could feel that he was one step closer to something; he just wasn't sure what that something might be.

"What are you smiling about over there, brother?"

Armando asked as he poured his latest Bloody Mary concoction into two tall glasses.

"Oh, just looking at an old friend," Jake mumbled, too captivated to reveal his findings.

As he stared deeper into the photo, Jake looked at the woman sitting at the table with Lopez. She was attractive, probably mid-twenties. She appeared Caucasian but was nicely tanned. Her dark brown hair was thick and full, just long enough to brush the top of her shoulders. Her eyes were dark, almost black in the photo, and her smile—artificially white. Jake knew he had seen her somewhere before. He carefully examined her features, searching his mind for a match. He just couldn't place where he knew her from.

Jake moved on to examine the remaining photos, intrigued by what he might find next. There were more photos of the various members of the group, even a few more of Lopez. There was a photo of him taking a drag from his cigar, another of him raising a glass of dark red wine for a toast. Somewhere in the background of almost every photo of Lopez was one or more of his guerillas, each displaying his most intimidating expression.

It was the last photo to flash on the screen that made Jake's heart skip. It was a picture of a Spanish woman walking the edge of the surf, seemingly laughing at something, or someone, just outside of the camera's eye. She was strikingly gorgeous. The shutter had captured her long black hair dancing in the wind; her captivating smile and delicate features could be discerned even through the glare of the sun that had reflected off the camera's lens.

If only he could see her eyes, Jake thought. Her sunglasses were just dark enough to conceal them. But even with the dark glasses and the glare from the sun, the resemblance was remarkable. Her smile, the shape of her face, the lines of her body—it could definitely be her. Or, perhaps she was just an uncanny Blanca look-alike—the mysterious stranger Prof once caught a fleeting glimpse of in the back of a black sedan.

Jake sat at the counter motionless, neglecting the plate of breakfast Armando had served him. Armando could tell that his friend had drifted off to another place.

"What are you staring at for so long over there, Jacob?"

Jake took a deep breath, then turned the laptop in Armando's direction. He watched Armando's eyes widen in disbelief. He was soon lost in the photograph, just as Jake had been.

"Remind you of anyone?" Jake asked rhetorically.

"My God, Jacob. Do you think it's really her?"

"I don't know how it could be."

"But just look at her; how could it not be her?" Armando replied. "This woman is my sister."

"I want to believe it's her, Armando. I really do. But I've been searching for Jonathan a long time now, and I've learned something important. I've learned not to build up false hope. Believe me, fate doesn't always take the turn you'd like it to."

"I suppose you're right," Armando replied. "They say everyone has a twin somewhere in the world; perhaps this woman is Blanca's twin," he added, not believing his own words. "But I'm telling you, Jacob, I have a strong feeling about this."

Jake slowly began to peck at his cold omelet. He had no idea how to process the image. He still wasn't quite sure who, or what, he was chasing in Peru. But somewhere, buried deep beyond the realm of all things reasonable or explicable, he, too, had a feeling it might be her.

CHAPTER 46

FRIENDS IN HIGH PLACES

It had been so long since she'd been in the city without her employer and his thugs. It was liberating. Even for a woman who was on the run, cloaked in a second-hand raincoat, shrouded under a dark scarf, she felt like a free person.

The boy was disguised as well. Generic street clothes, a new haircut, kiddy sunglasses, and a baseball cap. For him, the last two days had been like a secret adventure—new places, new people, new sights and sounds. He was fascinated by the city. It was full of life and energy—busy with important people doing important things, all bustling around him.

Hand-in-hand the two fugitives crossed the street, weaving their way through the afternoon traffic. They stopped at the entrance to a building, and she took a deep breath as she gazed at the sign above the doorway. Comisaria Policia Nacional del Peru—Lima.

The plan was simple. They would enter the police station; the woman would explain how she had been held against her will by the son of a powerful mining mogul. She would explain that the man had been involved in the illegal exploration and exhumation of a treasure trove of national antiquities. She would tell them how he pilfered the precious artifacts so that he could sell them on the black market. She would tell them how the man's operatives abducted the little boy, and how he had been raising the child as his own. Surely they would help her escape the wrath of such an evil man. They would help her put things back to the way they were supposed to be.

She looked down at her young companion who was watching a small dog tugging furiously at the end of its leash, apparently trying to hasten the pace of its owner.

"Shall we go inside, little one?" she asked the boy. He offered a generous nod and stepped into the building eagerly. The receptionist behind the counter was typing fiercely on her keyboard. Without looking up from her work, the woman politely asked them to have a seat, promising that someone would be with them shortly.

As they sat together in the waiting area, they listened to the sounds of the office—a symphony of tapping keyboards, ticking clocks, ringing phones, squeaky chairs, mumbling detectives, and a bubbling water cooler that was leaking its contents onto the dingy tile floor. The inside of the station was old and tired, most of its furniture and equipment aged years beyond the people using it.

After twenty minutes, they were greeted by a young detective who escorted them to a conference room. He situated them at the table and offered them a beverage. She politely declined and wasted no time getting down to business. She was noticeably shaken and nervous, but still managed to retain her composure. She had a story to tell, and she had waited a long time to tell it. The words flowed as if she was narrating a novel.

The detective was sympathetic, and he listened intently. He scratched in his tablet, and periodically extended a smile to the boy whenever he was mentioned in the dialog. He asked questions, but few were necessary. The woman's account was clear, concise, and very thorough.

After nearly two hours, she finished her amazing story, a chronicle of heroism and courage. She was relieved to finally share it with someone who cared, someone who could help.

The case certainly had appeal—a powerful mining family, abuse of money and power, theft of extraordinary national artifacts, black marketeering, and kidnapping. She knew her case didn't fit the crimes that typically crossed the detective's desk, but she could tell from his caring demeanor that he genuinely wanted to help her.

The detective looked down at his notepad with thoughtful contemplation and slowly nodded. He assured her that he could help—she had come to the right place. He would call his colleague in a special crimes unit downtown who specialized in kidnappings and had the necessary connections at the embassy. He excused himself, and the room soon fell silent with the exception of the bothersome ticking of the wall clock.

Five minutes passed, then ten, then twenty. Just as the boy was getting restless, the receptionist entered with a tray of cold soft drinks, stale cookies, and a few bags of mixed nuts. As the next hour dragged by, the boy sat contently at the table eating his cookies, slurping his soda and sketching on the notebook the detective had left behind.

The woman's eyes filled with tears as she watched the boy draw, and the hint of a smile settled on her face. In his drawing there was a family feeding ducks at the edge of a pond. There was a mom, a dad, and a small boy with a large smile. There were rolling hills, and the sky was lined with fluffy clouds. A large dog stood faithfully by the family with what appeared to be a stick in its mouth, and there was a fish jumping out of the pond as if frolicking in the sun. The scene was comforting, inviting. It reminded her of home, and that made her feel both happy and sad at the same time.

As the clock consumed the day, she began to worry. They had been waiting for more than two hours. Perhaps she should leave the room and search for the detective. Or perhaps this was all a mistake and they should just quietly slip out the back door—if there even was a back door. But just as she slid her chair away from the table, the door opened. It was the detective, now accompanied by another man.

The stranger was thin and well over six feet. He was a ruggedly handsome man with a dark complexion and a five-o-clock shadow. He had thick, wavy black hair and a well-trimmed mustache, and wore a long black coat over his black suit.

"Ma'am, my name is Dimitri Castillo," he said with

a deep, coarse voice and an extended hand. "I'm told you speak very fluent English."

"I get by, I guess," she responded, shaking his hand and sizing up her new acquaintance.

"You and your companion have been through quite an ordeal," he said, smiling at the boy. "It's truly a miracle that you were able to escape your captor. We are very grateful for your safe return."

"Thank you. We, too, are grateful. We're both anxious to return to where we belong," she replied.

"Well, let's see what we can do about that. I have a car just outside. I would like to bring you downtown to our headquarters. We're much better equipped to assist you there."

"I suppose that would be alright," she replied in a guarded tone. "But it's getting late. Can't we meet with you in the morning?" she asked.

"I don't think that would be wise. You've run away from a very powerful man. He's most certainly looking for you. Your lives are in danger; you should remain in my care until we can sort this all out. I promise that you will be in good hands," he assured her, gesturing toward the door.

She sat on the edge of her chair, gazing at the boy, contemplating her options. The man seemed genuinely sincere. And Lopez was not a forgiving man. She knew his guerillas would already be searching for them. They may not have worked their way down to Lima yet, but it wouldn't be long.

"Shall we go for a ride?" she asked the boy.

"Can I bring my picture?"

"Yes, I'm sure that would be alright," she replied, looking to their detective friend for his nod of approval.

"Why don't you take the whole tablet? You might want to draw some more pictures," the detective said as he approached the boy and extended his hand. "It was very nice to meet you. You're going to go with Mr. Castillo now. He'll take very good care of you. Maybe someday you can come back and visit me."

Castillo escorted them through a back entrance and into the alley where his vehicle was waiting. He seated them in the back of the SUV, politely asked them to fasten their seatbelts, and then took his place in the front passenger seat next to his driver.

The afternoon rush hour was beginning to dwindle, and the driver navigated through traffic with ease. The driver was a small, quiet man who looked more like an accountant than a special agent. He drove without saying a word.

Castillo, on the other hand, had plenty to say. He filled the silence with idle chatter, mostly about the city and its history. While she appreciated her host's attempt to make them comfortable, she was very familiar with the city and was hardly in need of a history lesson.

But whether she needed it or not the narrative continued, and before she realized how far they had traveled, the driver was turning into a long private drive, miles from the heart of the city.

"I thought your headquarters were downtown. What are we doing here?" she asked, trying not to appear concerned.

"Please don't be alarmed," he replied. "My partner needs to pick up a package from another agency up north. This is our meeting place—we were on our way here when we got the call to meet with you. It will only take a minute, I promise you." Castillo's words were gentle and assuring, as was his smile. Within seconds, a dark sedan pulled up behind Castillo's SUV. There was little left of the daylight, especially under the thick trees that lined the driveway. She looked out the back window, but she could see nothing but the bright headlights.

She heard the slamming of car doors, then watched two silhouettes approach, one on each side of their vehicle. The silhouette on the passenger side tapped on the boy's window, and the sound of the automatic locks releasing sent fear down the woman's spine. Before she knew what was happening, the boy's door flew open and a large black glove grabbed him by the collar and extracted him from the vehicle.

She scrambled out of the SUV, hopelessly trying to reach the boy. The wind left her lungs as she fell hard onto the ground. She tried to rise to her feet, but was paralyzed by a large shoe firmly on her chest.

As she lay flat on her back, struggling to recover her breath, her teary eyes focused and in an instant she was terrified. She recognized both men—the man restraining her, and the man holding the boy with a gun to his head.

"Señor Lopez is waiting for you in the car. I trust that you will not keep him waiting," the guerilla said as he removed his foot from her chest.

She slowly rose to her feet, gasping for breath, searching for another way of escape. But one wrong move would cost the boy his life. She knew Lopez was an animal who would go to any length to exact his revenge. She reluctantly followed the bodyguards back to Lopez. The interior of the car was thick with smoke, Lopez still puffing passionately on his cigar. They sat in silence as one of the guards walked back to Castillo's car. He approached the driver's window, exchanged a few words with Castillo's driver, then handed a thick envelope through the window. The deal was done.

Tears flooded her eyes. She felt like a fool. She knew Lopez was powerful, but she had no idea of the breadth of his command. She should never have trusted the authorities. She should have found another way—smuggled the boy out of the country, back to the United States where he belonged. She had failed him.

On the ride back to the compound, Lopez sat comfortably, dragging on his cigars and sipping his well-aged scotch. It was as though nothing had changed. For miles the woman said nothing; she just stared blankly out the window, stroking the boy's hair, unable to face Lopez. The boy was also silent, too young to understand what was happening, and too frightened to ask.

Twenty minutes into the journey, Lopez broke the

silence as he freshened up his drink.

"You are a difficult woman to please," he said with no emotion.

She offered no response.

"I've gone to great lengths to make you happy here. I have let you work on our team. You have seen unimaginable treasures. I have even been patient with you in bed," Lopez said smugly, raising his eyebrows. The woman's lips shook as she bit down on her tongue, trying not to show her contempt.

"We were meant to be together, my dear—ever since the day we first met. It was meant to be."

"I've helped you collect your treasures. You have your mummies and your gold. Why don't you let me and the boy go now?"

"Oh no, my love. I cannot break up our little family. It was a very difficult task bringing the boy here. I brought him here for you—he deserves to be with his mother."

She began to weep softly. She feared the conversation they'd had so many times before, knowing how the topic angered him. "Arturo," she said gently, "I've tried to tell you—I cannot be the woman you want me to be. That is not who I am. And the boy…he does not belong here. He should be home with his family."

"Silence! Don't speak to me of your crazy ideas. I've told you, you are not well. You must learn not to challenge my authority."

Lopez took an angry slosh of scotch, looked out into

the darkness, and then closed his eyes tightly. She could tell from the pressured sigh that followed that he was trying to cool his blood, not a typical reaction from the hot-tempered madman.

After nearly a minute, Lopez opened his eyes and took another drink. He turned toward the woman who was nestled snugly with the boy, trying to avoid eye contact.

"You must trust me," he said calmly. "Some day you will remember the way things were. You'll be happy again—be patient, my love."

CHAPTER 47

TWO FOR DINNER

The guard sprang to life as he noticed the little red car approaching. They didn't get many unexpected visitors at the compound, aside from the occasional misplaced tourist straying in from the main road. The locals never visited; they knew enough to stay away from the Lopez compound.

The car rolled to a stop as a cloud of dust drifted past the guard. He stood squarely in front of the iron gate brandishing his automatic rifle.

Looking at the guard's firepower, Armando suddenly regretted his decision to pack his pistol under the seat of his car.

The guard approached and leveled his AK-47 straight at Armando's head.

"What is your business here?" he barked.

"We were hoping to meet with Mr. Lopez. Would that be possible?" Armando asked respectfully.

"Señor Lopez is not expecting visitors. You two look familiar. Haven't I chased you out of here once before?" the guard asked, leaning into the car for a closer look.

"No. I'm sure you're mistaken. This is our first visit to the area," Armando replied.

"Turn around and go back the way you came."

Jake leaned forward in the passenger seat and slowly

lifted his hands as a sign of submission. "Please, señor. It's very important that we speak with Mr. Lopez. We are old acquaintances—my wife worked for him many years ago. Would you please tell him Jacob Bishop and Armando Vasquez are here to see him?"

The guard glared inquisitively at the two men, his rifle swaying back and forth between them. He slowly stepped backward to his post, lifted the receiver of the phone in the guard shack, and dialed his boss's extension.

Armando and Jake squirmed in their seats as the guard exchanged words with his employer, his AK-47 still pointed at the cab of the Volkswagen. They weren't sure if the guard was receiving his orders to invite them in for dinner, or to kill them right there at the gate. Armando quietly shifted the car into reverse, preparing for a quick exit if necessary.

After a lengthy exchange the guard hung up the phone and returned to his guests. "Mr. Lopez has agreed to see you. You will leave your car here for now. Park in that space over there and exit the vehicle. Another guard is coming out to search you."

Armando and Jake turned toward each other, suddenly overcome with a wave of fear.

"Are you sure about this, brother?" Armando asked.

There was a brief pause as Jake sorted through his options. They had come too far to turn back now, he thought. If there were answers to be found here, this was the time to find them. He turned back to Armando with a smile and replied, "Leave the gun. Take the cannoli."

Armando backed the car into its space as instructed, then tucked his 9mm further under his driver's seat. He and Jake cautiously walked to the guard shack where they were greeted by a second guard who was even larger than the first. They were given an invasive pat down, then escorted through a small pedestrian gate that opened directly into the compound. They entered with the armed ape trailing just behind them, his automatic rifle swinging casually back and forth with his clumsy stride.

Jake and Armando were astonished by the size and beauty of the estate. Off to the left was a stately two-story mansion with a wraparound porch, surrounded by a plush, green, meticulously manicured courtyard. There was a network of stone walking paths meandering through the gardens, all shaded by groves of mature, indigenous trees.

A few smaller homes were sprinkled about the compound, each one nestled in a canopy of beautiful vegetation. *Probably servants' quarters,* Jake thought.

"What's in that building over there?" Armando asked, pointing toward a large brick structure that resembled a warehouse.

There was no response from their escort.

Jake and Armando couldn't help but notice the heavily armed guards stationed at the entrance to the building, and the two military-style cargo trucks parked just outside.

As they approached the south end of the courtyard, the guard instructed them to walk toward the building with the red door. Jake could see the structure just paces from the mansion. Equipped with vine-covered lattice, flourishing flower boxes, a red brick sidewalk, and a series of lanterns lining the walkway, the little stone cottage resembled something in a fairytale.

But as the men approached the building, it became obvious that it was not a fairytale cottage at all. It was more like a small fortress. The steel-framed windows were set deep into the stone wall, defended by hefty decorative steel bars. The heavy red door was hung on massive iron hinges, latched securely by an industrial looking lock-set. Motion sensors and surveillance cameras were perched in plain sight to see all, and for all to see. Lopez's black SUV was parked in the drive, sitting proudly next to the notorious black sedan.

Armando was the first man through the mysterious red door. It was as heavy as it appeared, and opened slowly like the door of a bank vault. He and Jake felt as if they were entering someplace forbidden—a place from which there would be no return.

The door led to a small waiting room lined with ornate chairs, four on each side, and four large pieces of pretentious artwork on the walls. The small room appeared to be enclosed, with no other visible entrances or exits. With the guard standing in the only doorway directly behind them, the men questioned the wisdom of their visit.

"Please wait here," the guard instructed. "Mr. Lopez will be with you momentarily."

The red door closed firmly behind the guard as he left,

and they heard the distinct sound of the lock engaging securely in place.

The men looked up at the camera in the corner of the room and made their best effort to appear casual for whoever was screening their arrival.

"What the hell is this place?" Jake whispered to Armando.

"I'm not sure. It's too plush for a prison cell," Armando whispered back. "Whatever it is, I don't like the feel of it."

The two men continued to look about the room, trying not to appear concerned by their captivity. They paced about, eyeing the artwork, checking their watches, and thinking about their options—which they realized were very limited at the moment.

Just as Jake was about to park himself on one of the fancy chairs, a voice crackled through an overhead speaker.

"Welcome, gentlemen. Won't you please join me?"

The voice was followed by a mechanical buzzing sound, and the paneled wall at the far end of the waiting room instantly slid open.

The large room on the other side was a masterpiece—beautifully decorated, exquisitely furnished, abounding with precious artwork and antiquities. The room consumed the remaining footprint of the stone structure and satisfied the requisites of an office, library, den, and game parlor. It was the ultimate man cave.

At the opposite end of the room, sitting behind his mahogany desk, surrounded by a backdrop of literature and priceless antiquities, and wallowing in a cloud of cigar smoke, was the man himself—Arturo Lopez.

. "Good evening, gentlemen. Please join me," Lopez said pleasantly as he waved his cigar toward the chairs on the opposite side of his desk.

"We don't get many visitors here—what brings you to our small part of the world?"

"Well, Mr. Lopez," Jake replied as he and Armando settled comfortably into the soft leather chairs. "I don't know if you remember me, but…."

"Oh, I remember you very well, Mr. Bishop. Your wife was a lovely woman. I still think about her to this day. She was a priceless treasure—and one of the best archaeologists I've ever worked with."

"Thank you. We miss her as well," Jake replied, not exactly sure what to make of Lopez's comment. "The reason we're here is that we have reason to believe my wife may still be alive."

Jake and Armando carefully watched Lopez's reaction, hoping it would reveal something. But Lopez's face was almost expressionless, like a high stakes poker player sitting on a royal flush.

After a brief pause, he took a slow drink from his crystal tumbler and offered a casual reply. "That comes as quite a surprise, Mr. Bishop. It was my understanding that your wife perished in a tragic car accident in the mountains. I attended her funeral, you know."

"Yes, well, her body was not identifiable."

"But there was a body discovered, was there not?"

"Yes. There was a body, and it *was* her rental car," Jake replied.

Lopez took another drag from his cigar, then patiently watched the smoke drift away as he exhaled.

"May I ask what makes you believe your wife is still alive?"

"Let's just say that a very reliable source has confirmed a sighting here in Peru."

"A sighting of a dead woman—that would have to be a very reliable source indeed."

"We also have photographs," Armando chimed in, feeling the need to counter Lopez's sarcasm.

Lopez leaned forward in his chair, suddenly intrigued. "Photographs? What sort of photographs?"

"We've seen photos," Jake quickly interjected. "Photos of a woman resembling Blanca. Nothing definitive, but they piqued our curiosity." Jake wished Armando hadn't tipped his hand about the photos. He would rather avoid explaining the camera they found at the site of Lopez's last illegal grave robbery.

"Did you bring these photos with you? I would very much like to see them."

"No...no. We've been looking for my wife for a long time. A man in Cajamarca showed us the pictures. He had some group photos of an archaeological team that was working out near the Amazon. He thought one of the women resembled the photo of Blanca that we showed him—we thought so too." Jake impressed himself by how quickly he was able to spin his story.

"Mr. Bishop, forgive me for saying so, but it sounds as if you are…how do you say? Chasing the wild goose."

"Yes, I'm sure it appears as if we're on a wild goose chase," Jake replied. "But I trusted my colleague very much. If he believed he saw my wife here in Peru, then I believe it too. If Blanca is still alive I have to find her."

"If your wife were still alive, what would she be doing here? Why wouldn't she be back in the States with you?"

"I don't know, Mr. Lopez. Perhaps she has amnesia. Perhaps she's being held against her will. I have no viable explanation. But I just have this feeling that she's alive, here in Peru."

Lopez leaned back in his chair. "Well then, I wish you the best of luck in your search. But what brings you to my home? Surely you don't believe your wife is here?"

"Armando and I remembered that you were an instrumental figure in the archaeological community. We figured that if Blanca were still alive, she might be working in the field. We were hoping you might have some information about any active sites where she could be working."

"It's true," Lopez replied, "Archaeology is my mistress. But I haven't had the pleasure of working any projects for some time. The precious stone market has kept me very busy—the travel is quite taxing."

"I can imagine," Jake replied.

"Tell you what, Mr. Bishop. I'll place some phone calls to my colleagues. If you have a photo of your wife, I will circulate that as well. Perhaps someone has seen her, or her look-alike as the case may be."

"That's very generous. We appreciate any help you can give us."

"It's getting late—too dark to travel. You will be my guests tonight."

"We don't want to intrude," Armando offered, his voice cracking.

"It's no intrusion. I insist. A good meal, some fine brandy, a game of billiards, and a good night's sleep. You'll enjoy your stay. I'll have my man show you to your quarters," Lopez said as he pushed one of the buttons on the gold control panel embedded in his desk.

Within seconds the paneled wall slid open and the armed guard who had brought them to the cottage was once again standing in the doorway.

"Alonso, show these men to the guest quarters. They'll be staying with us for the night. Gentlemen, please make yourselves comfortable. My staff will get you anything you need, and we'll call on you for dinner."

CHAPTER 48

A ROOM AT THE RAMADA

The holding cell was small, barely ten-by-ten. There was no fine brandy, no game of billiards, no good night's sleep, and the meal that had slid through the thick steel door the night before…tasteless. The only amenities were a rust-stained toilet in the corner of the room and a single water spigot protruding from the wall, which dripped rhythmically into the drain beneath it. It was no room at the Ramada.

As Jake sat on the edge of the stiff military cot, staring hopelessly at the concrete floor, he wondered how he could have been so foolish. How could he have allowed himself to trust a man like Arturo Lopez? How could he hope to find answers buried in a fortress deep in the Peruvian countryside?

Both men considered their captivity to be a bitter-sweet development. The fact that they had been escorted to the holding cell the night before meant they had struck a nerve. Lopez was threatened by their presence, and he clearly had something to hide. But on the other hand, whatever secret Lopez was hiding would probably never leave the compound.

As Jake brooded over their predicament, Armando paced back and forth along the back wall of the cell, stopping periodically to glance out through a small, barred window. The morning sun was rising and streamed in to provide the cell's first source of light.

"Armando, I'm sorry I got you into this mess. I don't know what I was thinking," Jake mumbled.

"Don't be so hard on yourself, Jacob. We came here to see if Lopez was hiding something—I think we have our answer."

"Do you think she's here? The woman in the picture?" Jake asked.

"I know she's here," Armando replied as he peered through the window. "Come look at this."

Jake sprang to his feet and joined Armando at the window. They stood on their tiptoes, straining to see between the bars through the hazy glass window just above their heads. They were suddenly hypnotized by a figure strolling across the compound. The woman was tall and shapely with long, flowing dark hair. She walked like an angel, floating across the courtyard. They couldn't see her face, but they both knew it was her—the woman captured on the digital camera from the tombs.

Jake watched her stroll leisurely through the gardens, making her way to the estate house. He remembered how Blanca swayed when she walked—uninhibited, captivating. *It could be her,* he thought. *It could be Blanca. But why would she be here in Peru with a monster like Lopez?*

The thought that she could leave a perfect marriage and a child she adored was impossible to fathom.

Jake and Armando watched her saunter up the

back stairway of the estate house and disappear through the backdoor. She vanished just as quickly as she had materialized.

The men took turns monitoring the back door of the home, hoping to catch another sighting of her. But after two hours with no results, they decided to stand down.

The remains of the morning proved to be slow and uneventful. There was little left to say. Armando returned to his pacing, Jake to his moping. Both men processing the same thoughts of the mystery woman, thoughts of escape, thoughts of their impending fate.

With the exception of an occasional drip from the faucet, the cell was hauntingly quiet. So quiet that Jake could hear the ticking of the second hand on his watch. The seconds soon ticked into minutes, the minutes into hours. Just after 1:00 p.m., the guard stomped down the stairwell and slid another plate of food through the slot in the cell door—rice, beans, flatbread, and fresh fruit.

Having survived breakfast without incident, the men wasted little time inspecting their lunch before devouring it. But lunch was soon interrupted by the sound of vehicles pulling into the compound, and Jake and Armando were once again perched at the window on the balls of their feet.

There were two vehicles. The first was a black sedan, identical to the one parked in Lopez's driveway. It rolled into the compound and stopped abruptly at the entrance of the large brick storage building. The second vehicle, a dark gray Range Rover, pulled in directly behind it.

Two armed guards exited the Range Rover and approached the back of the sedan. The larger guard opened the back door and assisted a passenger out of the vehicle. The passenger, a man with silver hair, was dressed in an expensive but wrinkled designer suit. He was blindfolded but not restrained, and the guards handled him with respect.

The visitor was guided in through the entrance of the brick building, and the guards disappeared inside directly behind him. Jake and Armando remained fixated on the entrance, waiting for the mystery man to return. After nearly an hour, the door finally opened and the guards escorted their blindfolded visitor back to the sedan. The visitor was smiling slightly, apparently pleased with what he had seen inside.

There was a final figure to emerge from the building; Jake and Armando immediately recognized Lopez's swagger. Lopez slid some sort of card through an electronic fixture next to the door, apparently securing the door behind him. He nodded to the guard who was standing watch at the entrance, then walked over to the sedan where his blindfolded guest was waiting with his armed escorts.

Lopez conversed briefly with his guest, then shook the man's hand and assisted him back into the rear of the sedan, gently guiding his head under the rooftop. He lit up a cigar as he watched the cars disappear through the gates of the compound, smiling with satisfaction as he watched the front gates close behind the cloud of dust. Jake and

Armando watched their host swagger back to the estate house. The afternoon's business had apparently been a success.

The compound remained quiet for the rest of the day. There were no more black sedans, no further sightings of Lopez or the dark-haired woman. Jake and Armando passed the time speculating about the mysterious blindfolded man and the contents of the brick building. And as the sun set, the light in the cell withdrew back through the window. One last meal was slid through the door, and before long, the men were once again sitting in the darkness.

CHAPTER 49

THE MOTHER SHIP

The guard at the gate never saw it coming. It was a quick and painless death—a silent bullet delivered just below the base of the skull.

The team was well-financed, well-trained, and well-prepared. Satellite maps, night vision goggles, a detailed layout of the compound, and enough firepower to take down a wealthy dictator.

Dressed in black, under the cloak of a cloudy night sky, the mercenaries rappelled down the walls of the compound without detection. Each of them had a mission—one to secure the estate house, one to secure the warehouse, two to secure the guardhouse, and one to locate and detain Lopez.

Although Lopez's men were trained to confront an invasion, they had become too careless to detect the intruders that had quietly slipped into their domain.

One at a time, Lopez's men dropped—a silent bullet to the head, a strategically placed knife blade, a sudden twist of the neck. In less than ten minutes, eight men lay dead—slumped over at their posts, lifeless in their beds.

Jake and Armando were unaware of what was happening outside of their window. They stared into the darkness, waiting for the morning sun. They hadn't slept the night before, either, and the uncertainty of their fate was looming over them.

As a cricket chirped somewhere in the cell and the water dripped from the faucet, Jake thought about riding in the Riviera as a young boy, listening to Dean Martin on the 8-track, and watching Henry puff on his pipe. He thought about Margaret and wondered how she would survive without her only son. He thought about Thanksgiving with Maggie Cooper, convinced that he would never get the chance to steal another kiss on the front porch.

As his eyelids became heavy and his thoughts turned to dreams, he heard a muffled pulsing sound in the distance. The pulsing became louder and grew into a thunderous clapping orchestra hovering directly over the compound.

Jake and Armando strained to look out through their cell window, but all they could see was a dust storm churning into the lights that were floating above their heads like a UFO.

As the lights got closer, they saw the shapes of two vessels drifting toward the earth, descending in unison just above the rooftops. Suddenly, Jake and Armando were blinded by another panel of lights activated from the bellies of the ships. They illuminated the compound as the first ship touched down amid a flurry of dust and debris. Within seconds another ship landed just yards away.

As the noise abated and the dust began to settle, two large helicopters emerged from the haze. They were military-grade, heavy transport birds.

As the rotors spun to a slow whirl, figures scurried out

from the compound and joined a second group who were exiting the two helicopters. They conducted a brief meeting near the aircraft, then quickly dispersed into the darkness of the compound.

For the next few hours, Jake and Armando watched them move back and forth across the grounds, their flashlights dancing about in the darkness. The lights flickered between the helicopters and the estate house, the estate house and the guardhouse, the guardhouse and the warehouse. The compound was bustling with activity.

With the passage of the early morning hours, the activity gradually shifted to the warehouse, and by dawn all of the flashlights had disappeared inside. The morning sun lit the helicopters that sat like ships in a harbor.

Jake and Armando hadn't slept for two days. Their legs were shaky, their heads foggy with exhaustion. They hadn't spoken for over an hour. There just wasn't anything left to say. There were no more theories about the people invading the compound, no more conjecture about the purpose of their attack, and no more discussion about what it meant for their own fate.

Suddenly, the door to the warehouse opened and a small group of people in black clothing stepped into the daylight. They were all men, all very muscular, and all heavily armed. Behind them came the cargo. They carried out long, coffin-shaped wooden crates two at a time. Jake counted them as they were carried to the helicopters. Two, four, six, eight, ten…and twelve. It had to be the mummies.

Once the cargo was safely secured inside the helicopters, four of the men in black walked to the estate house and entered through the main door. They returned just minutes later with a male hostage in silk pajamas. The man's hands were bound behind his back. As they escorted him into the courtyard, taking turns pushing him with the barrels of their rifles, his bare feet stirred the dust. When they reached the middle of the courtyard, they ordered the hostage down on his knees, and prompted him with the swift blow of a rifle butt to the back of his neck.

Jake didn't recognize the hostage at first. The man was meek and scared, and complied without a hint of resistance. But as the man looked up at his captors, Jake couldn't believe his eyes. Arturo Lopez had been reduced to a prisoner in his own castle.

As Lopez knelt on the gravel, the barrel of a rifle just inches from his head, the entry gates swung open. A black Mercedes entered the grounds, its occupants concealed behind tinted windows. It rolled to a stop not far from the helicopters, and a large, elderly man was assisted out of the back seat by one of the men in black.

He placed a gray Fedora on his head, fastened the top button of his suit coat, and casually sauntered to his prisoner. There was a brief conversation between them, and Jake could tell from Lopez's desperate gestures that he was pleading for mercy.

The stranger held his hand out to one of the men who promptly gave him a pistol, still equipped with a silencer from the evening raid. He leveled it directly at Lopez's head, and Jake watched it recoil in the man's hand. The powerful Arturo Lopez buckled to the ground. His business with the man in the fedora had concluded.

CHAPTER 50

A GIFT FROM AN ANGEL

The footsteps echoing down the stairwell sounded different than they had in the past. They were lighter and quicker than those of the bullish guard who had delivered their meals. Jake and Armando rose from their bunks and stood anxiously in their cell, waiting to see what fresh hell was about to visit them.

When the footsteps stopped, they heard a key sliding into the lock of the cell door, then the lock tumbling open. Jake's heart pounded wildly. The door opened and fresh air poured into the cell as if breaking the seal to a 2,000-year-old crypt. Jake and Armando were speechless. Their visitor wasn't a mercenary, or an assassin in a fedora. It was her, their angel—the woman from the photographs. She stood in the doorway like a holy figure, the light from the hallway softly illuminating her.

Jake approached her slowly, cautiously, staring at her as if looking into an apparition. He tentatively reached out his hand and brushed the hair away from the side of her face. Staring into her eyes, a flood of emotions churned inside of him. He had last seen Blanca when he dropped her off at O'Hare Airport for her last trip back to Peru more than three years ago. And now, she stood before him, resurrected from the dead.

"My God, is it really you?" he asked.

"Do I know you?" the woman replied.

"Blanca? It's me, Jake. Don't you remember?"

The woman closed her eyes and slowly bowed her head, releasing a long, discouraging sigh. "You are Mr. Bishop," she said as she looked up, her inflection posing more of a statement than a question.

"Yes, that's right. Bishop…Jacob Bishop. And this is Armando Vasquez, your brother. Don't you remember us?"

"I'm so sorry, Mr. Bishop; I'm not who you think I am." She paused. "My name is Maria Cruz. I never met your wife, but I've been told that I bear a remarkable resemblance to her."

Jake reached out and gently took the woman's right hand. He turned her palm upward and softly caressed her forearm. As he inspected her delicate golden skin Jake offered an affirming nod of defeat. "No birthmark," he whispered. "You're telling the truth aren't you?"

"Yes, I'm afraid that I am. I am sorry to disappoint you."

"May we ask why you are here?" Armando inquired.

"I'm an archaeologist from Colombia. I met Señor Lopez at a symposium in Lima more than a year ago. He invited me to this place to examine his collection of artifacts, and he's been holding me here against my will ever since. He is convinced…*was* convinced, that I am the woman you call Blanca."

"The resemblance *is* remarkable," Armando interjected.

"In fact, it's the reason we're here. But couldn't you prove your true identity to Lopez?"

"I tried many times. He wouldn't listen to the truth when it was standing before him. The man was insane."

Jake looked over at Armando, his expression unable to mask his defeat. "I'm sorry, Armando. It looks like I've dragged you into this mess for nothing. We need to get you home. Is there a safe way out of this place?" he asked, turning to the woman.

"Mr. Bishop, you have not wasted your time coming here. There's something I need to show you before you leave," Maria replied. "Follow me. We must hurry. We need to go before the Germans are done exploring the inventory in the warehouse."

"Germans?" Armando asked.

"I'll explain later. Please, come with me."

Jake and Armando followed Maria up the stairwell, into the courtyard, and through the gardens that led to the estate house. The grounds were quiet. They passed two of Lopez's guards on the way, stepping over their bodies that were blocking the path.

Maria led them into the back entrance of the estate house, then up a hidden stairway to the second floor. They followed her into Lopez's private quarters, passing by the body of yet another guard.

Jake and Armando watched curiously as Maria examined the hundreds of books lining the shelves of an immense bookcase that spanned the full length of the study. She counted down the rows of books to the tenth shelf, then ran her fingers across the bindings, counting as she progressed down the row. "Treinta y uno" *Thirty-One,* she declared as she located the book.

Jake recognized the publication immediately. *Marvels of Archaeology,* by Blanca Bishop. The book debuted six months to the day from Blanca's untimely demise—another bittersweet reminder of the treasure he had lost.

Maria slid the book away from the shelf a few inches, and it came to an abrupt stop, audibly locking in place. The midsection of the massive bookcase jarred open, revealing a visible crack of light from the other side. Maria pushed on the edge of the wall of books until it pivoted open, just enough for passage to the other side.

"Please, follow me," she said as she disappeared through the wall.

The passage fed into a short hallway that led to yet another closed door. Maria quietly opened the door and stepped inside, her companions following closely behind. The chamber resembled a small studio apartment, containing everything necessary to harbor Lopez and a select few for a month or two if necessary. The room was lit only by the flickering television that had been left on.

In the glow of the television was a bundle of blankets piled on a couch. Maria approached the couch, stopping to switch on a nearby lamp. She gently rubbed her hand along the top of the blankets and they began to move.

"It's time to get up now, little one," she whispered.

A groggy boy emerged from the blankets, rubbing his eyes from a long hibernation.

"There's someone here to see you," Maria said softly.

As the boy stood and turned toward the doorway, Jake's heart raced and tears welled in his eyes. He was afraid to speak. Afraid to spoil the moment. Afraid that what he was witnessing was just another illusion—another cruel gift of false hope.

The boy stared inquisitively at the men, his eyes slowly coming into focus. A faint smile appeared, then an uncontrollable grin. Suddenly, his eyes were open wide and bright.

"Dad!" he yelled.

As Jonathan ran toward him, Jake dropped to his knees with his arms open wide. Jonathan spilled into his father's arms and they locked in an intense embrace. Jake began sobbing uncontrollably, gripping Jonathan so firmly that the boy could barely take a breath.

He'd been searching for so long. He had all but given up hope. Yet against all odds here was his son, in the middle of Peru, alive in his arms. Jake didn't know how Jonathan got there or why he was taken, but he knew that he could never let him go—never again.

"I've been waiting for you. I knew you would find me!" Jonathan said as he gasped for a breath.

Jake loosened his grip and began laughing between his sobs. "We've been looking for you everywhere," he replied. "Everywhere except here. How in the world did you come to be here in Peru?"

"I came on the airplane," Jonathan replied rationally.

"Mr. Bishop," Maria interjected with a smile, "I believe that I can answer all of your questions. But we really must go now. We have very little time."

"Brother, I'm not anxious to meet up with those Germans. I say we listen to Maria," Armando added as he wiped his eyes.

Jake swept Jonathan up into his arms as he rose to his feet, his knees still weak with emotion. Maria led the way back through the secret passage, down the stairwell, and across the back porch to the courtyard. Armando trailed in the back of the pack, and as he stepped over the cold body of one of Lopez's guards, he lifted a 9mm handgun from its holster. He tucked the piece into the back of his pants, concealing it beneath his shirt.

They followed Maria through the gardens of the courtyard until they reached Lopez's cottage. They hid behind a clump of thick bushes and quietly surveyed the open compound. The helicopters sat unattended, accompanied only by the Mercedes that had delivered the man in the fedora. There was no sign of the Germans, who were still rummaging through the artifacts in the warehouse.

Maria hunched down and scurried over to Lopez's car, quietly opening the passenger door for a peak inside. *No keys.* She left the door open and snuck back to the bushes to join the others. She held her index finger to her mouth and whispered to them, "Please wait here quietly. I need to find some keys for the car."

"Car?" Armando asked softly. "Why don't we fire up one of those helicopters and I'll fly us out of here?"

"Too risky," Jake replied. "They'd gun us down before you could even warm it up."

"The car is the only way out," Maria whispered harshly. "Now please, wait here. I'll only be a moment."

"I'm coming with you," Armando replied as he fell in behind Maria, who was already well in motion down the garden path.

Maria moved swiftly, weaving her way along the pathways. They soon came upon the guards' quarters and she stopped firmly in her tracks.

"The guards should have an extra set of keys to Lopez's car," she said softly, sounding a bit short of wind from her sprint through the gardens. "I think I know where we can find them."

Armando nodded and pulled the pistol from beneath the back of his shirt, taking the lead up the path to the guardhouse. Maria was surprised by the presence of the gun, but relieved to see it just the same.

Armando opened the door slowly, cautiously, quietly. Neither he nor Maria knew what they might find on the other side. The inside was silent. As they carefully explored the interior rooms they discovered the bodies of three more fallen guards.

In the rear sleeping quarters, Maria found the body of the guard they all called El Toro. Once the commander of

Lopez's prestigious security unit, El Toro had been reduced to a corpse, his neck twisted morbidly beyond its natural limits.

Maria knew from her trips to the city that he was the only guard with access to the extra car keys. She rummaged through his bureau until she found two sets of car keys in a small upper drawer—one set to the sedan, the other to the Range Rover.

With the keys firmly in hand, Maria and Armando fled the guardhouse and made their way back to Jake and Jonathan outside the cottage.

"Anything happening out here?" Armando whispered.

"Two of the men have been back and forth to the cargo truck. They've been loading some crates on board," Jake replied.

"Where are they now?" asked Maria.

"They're back in the warehouse. The coast is clear for the time being."

"We have to go now," said Maria. "We might not get another chance."

Armando held his hand out toward Maria and smiled with a boyish grin. "I'll drive," he said.

Maria handed him the keys, and they shuffled to their getaway car, keeping their heads low.

Jake tucked Jonathan safely in the backseat with Maria, then took the front passenger seat next to Armando. Armando slid the key into the ignition, mumbled a brief prayer under his breath and started the engine. He slipped the car into drive and set his sights for the front gate.

The gate was still open, and they could see their freedom on the other side. Armando gradually picked up speed, trying to close the gap without alarming the Germans.

They were less than one hundred yards from the exit. In seconds they would pass through the gate and Jake would be on his way home, back to the United States with his son in his arms, back to a life he never thought he would have again. But as they approached, the iron gates slowly began to close. Armando picked up his speed, hoping to clear the gauntlet before it was too late.

Suddenly, a man stepped out from the guard booth and stood in the center of the closing gates, raising his machine gun.

For a split second, Armando contemplated running the gate and taking the guard down with it. But as they closed in on the guard, Armando heard a shower of large-caliber bullets striking the front grill of the car.

"Everyone down!" he yelled as he slammed on the brakes, skidding the car sideways in the loose rocks. As the car came to a stop, the gunfire stopped as well. They sat in a cloud of dust, the car's engine steaming from a pool of leaking fluids, its front end collapsed on two flat tires.

As the dust and the steam dissolved, the crew could see the man approaching, the sights of his weapon fixed squarely on them. Jake glanced at the entrance to the compound and watched their freedom disappear between the narrowing gap of the closing gates.

CHAPTER 51

IT'S A SMALL WORLD

The soldier paced the room, tossing a cold stare to his prisoners each time he turned. He wasn't a particularly large man, but he was intimidating just the same. His compact physique was well-defined under his black military clothing, and his face was covered in dark camouflage war paint.

Jonathan sat on his father's lap, nestled firmly in his arms. The presence of the guard's gun terrified him, especially after witnessing the gunfire in the courtyard. His young mind was frozen with fear.

As the guard turned away briefly to look at the clock, Jake glanced at Armando and Maria, who were sitting on the adjacent sofa. Jake knew from the expression on Armando's face that his mind was racing for an escape plan. What he didn't know was that Armando still had the pistol tucked into the back of his pants, and he was working up the courage to use it.

The guard seemed dissatisfied by the clock, as if a strict schedule had been compromised by the latest turn of events. He looked out the window toward the warehouse, then pulled the two-way radio from his ammunition belt and softly mumbled something German.

As the guard waited for his reply and neglected his

prisoners, Armando carefully reached behind his back and slipped his hand around the grip of the pistol. The guard was wearing Kevlar, which meant that a head shot would be his only opportunity for a clean kill. There was no room for error; injuring the man would only result in another spray of ammunition from his machine gun.

Armando focused intensely as he pictured the shot in his mind's eye. He knew he could make it. It was now or never. His hand still behind his back, he took a deep cleansing breath and slid the safety off to ready his weapon as quietly as possible. Suddenly, the large wooden doors swung open and the guard turned around. Armando slid the safety back on and returned his hand to plain sight.

The elderly man in the fedora walked into the study and sat confidently behind the large desk as if he owned the place. Jake and Armando hadn't seen him since he executed Lopez that morning.

The German inquisitively studied the group, as if trying to decide what to do with them. After several seconds, he pulled a gold pocket watch from inside his suit coat, flipped it open, then closed the cover and returned it to his pocket.

"Well, I'm not sure what to make of this group," he said in very clean English. "You look like an American," he added, looking directly at Jake. "Do you speak English?"

"Yes," Jake replied.

"Good. Because I don't speak much Spanish," he said as he opened the humidor on Lopez's desk.

The German took his time choosing his cigar. He

opened the middle drawer of Lopez's desk and found a cigar cutter and a silver lighter. He trimmed the cigar to his liking and drew in deeply as he lit it. He then threw the cutter back in the drawer and dropped the lighter into his pocket.

"It will be dusk soon—time for us to leave this place. I suppose I could lock you in the basement with the other servants. But of course, they cannot identify me—can they? You on the other hand, you have knowledge of the events that have transpired here."

"We have absolutely no concern for your affairs," Armando assured the German. "We're just here for the woman and the boy. You have our word that you can release us and we'll never speak of this place."

"Your word?" the German said with a chuckle. "Just who are you that your word should mean something to me? Tell me, American, what is your name?"

Jake thought for a moment about giving a ficticious name, but quickly remembered that he had a wallet in his back pocket full of identification. "Bishop. Jacob Bishop."

"What brings you to this place, Mr. Bishop?"

"Well, that's a very long story."

"I'll understand if you give me the condensed version," the German said.

"We came to rescue my wife and child," Jake replied hastily. "Lopez has been holding them here as hostages."

"So this is a family reunion then?"

"Yes, I guess you could say that," Jake replied, looking

over to Maria in an effort to solicit her collaboration.

"Lopez was a monster," Maria proclaimed. "You did us all a favor by eliminating him. You are a hero."

"Well, I'm glad we could be of assistance to you. Tell me, Mr. Bishop. What led you to believe that you would find your family here?"

"A former colleague of mine in the States told me. He was convinced that he had seen her here during a business meeting with Lopez."

"A business meeting? What sort of business did your colleague have with the late, great Mr. Lopez?"

"He was an admirer of antiquities. Enamored with the ancients. He came here to acquire a small piece of history."

"Interesting," the German replied. "Has your colleague been negotiating with Mr. Lopez concerning any larger pieces of history?"

"No. I'm afraid not. He died a few months ago after a long bout with cancer."

The German stopped short halfway through the long drag on his cigar, then leaned forward in his chair with a curious expression. "Your colleague, what was his name?"

"Jonathan Albright. Professor Jonathan Albright," Jake replied, not certain as to what interest the German could possibly have in his friend.

"Prof Albright!" the German said, his tone suddenly jubilant. "This is the same Professor Albright who was a partner at a large law firm in the States?"

"Yes, that's right," Jake answered, perplexed by the

German's knowledge.

"Tell me, Mr. Bishop. In what city was Prof's law firm located?

"Chicago. Why do you ask?"

"Chicago. Yes, Professor Jonathan Albright from Chicago, Illinois. That's right."

The German took another long, contemplative draw from Lopez's cigar, then grinned as he exhaled, watching the smoke disperse into the room.

"How well did you know Professor Albright?" he inquired.

"My father and Prof were like brothers. He was a very close family friend. I was pretty young when my father died. Prof stepped in as my surrogate parent. He helped me through college, got me into law school, offered me a position at the firm. He even introduced me to my wife. He was a good man. I miss him dearly."

"As do I, Mr. Bishop."

"You knew Professor Albright?" Jake asked, dumbfounded.

"Jonathan Albright and I go way back, Mr. Bishop. Back to his days as a young international law attorney, back to his days as a member on the board of the museum. I've sought his counsel on many occasions over the years. He has been a good friend and a generous advisor. I was very sorry to learn of his passing."

The German leaned back in his chair and gazed at the ceiling. He grinned and exhaled the costly vapor and mumbled to his guests, "You might say I owe him dearly. In fact, this might just be your lucky day," he declared, leaning forward in his chair and looking directly at Jake.

"Mr. Bishop, my name is Fritz VonKlecker. I tell you this because of what I am about to tell you. Mine is a name that you and your friends should soon forget. The things you have seen at this place must never be spoken of. I have a small fortune invested in my acquisitions, and I've gone to great lengths to protect that investment."

"We understand, Mr. VonKlecker," Jake replied.

I'm a powerful man with many resources," VonKlecker continued. "My anonymity means a great deal to me. As you've witnessed, I will kill to safeguard that anonymity when I think it's in jeopardy," he said looking in Jonathan's direction.

"There's no reason to threaten my family. We have no interest in your affairs."

"I need to be sure that we understand one another, Mr. Bishop."

"It's been a long journey for me, Mr. VonKlecker. I've been halfway around the world, desperately searching for my family. I was convinced I would never see them again. Then I came to this place, and I found them in the hands of a monster—a monster who imprisoned me and my brother with every intention of killing us. I have no interest in your treasure; I've found my own. You've killed the monster, Mr. VonKlecker. It's time for both of us to bring our treasure home. Trust me, we understand one another."

VonKlecker stared at each of them, assessing their credibility. He was faced with a dilemma. Leave no witnesses—that was the rule. But this was Prof's family. VonKlecker knew he'd never forgive himself if he slaughtered them like the others. He didn't like the idea of freeing them, but he had no choice.

"Yes indeed, Mr. Bishop. Let's bring our treasures home," VonKlecker proclaimed with a smile.

CHAPTER 52

INTO THE EVENING SKY

The choppers lifted off at dusk. They were flying heavy, packed with precious antiquities, mysterious crates, and armed Germans. What didn't fit into the choppers was packed into two of Lopez's cargo trucks. The treasures would be delivered to a landing strip 200 miles up the coast, where it would be offloaded onto a large cargo plane destined for a secret location in Germany.

Maria watched the priceless cargo rise into the evening sky. She was saddened by the loss. They were treasures that were meant to be shared with the world. Twelve priceless mummies, each an aberration of nature, entombed with a bounty of inexplicable symbology.

The scientific community would have marveled at the sight of such artifacts. But the sacrifice was one that Maria was willing to make. Jacob Bishop had saved her life. He and a man she had never met—a man by the name of Professor Jonathan Albright—had unexpectedly happened into her life to set her free. Surely the German would have killed her had Jake not fabricated a story about finding his long-lost wife captive in the hands of Lopez the monster. He would have slaughtered her and left her to rot alongside Lopez and his bodyguards. The loss of the treasure was a small sacrifice in exchange for her life.

She had committed blatant crimes against the archaeological community and the Government of Peru, having been forced to loot the most remarkable tombs ever unearthed. Her freedom had come at an unconscionable cost, both professionally and personally. She had been sexually abused by her captor, forced to perform unthinkable acts at the hands of his demons. Each day had been a psychological balancing act to pacify the ego of a madman. It was time to go home.

As the helicopters vanished, Maria and her new family watched the cargo trucks depart through the gates of the compound, followed by VonKlecker's Mercedes. The Germans vacated the Lopez estate as quickly as they had arrived, leaving no evidence that could link them to the brutalities that had occurred there. No evidence, that is, except the four family members of Professor Jonathan Albright.

With the Germans gone, they were eager to flee the compound before any more danger came to visit. Maria hurried to the estate house basement and freed the five servants who VonKlecker's masked mercenaries had imprisoned there. She then ran upstairs to pack a few things—a light load for a quick departure. The crew loaded their things into Armando's red Volkswagen and prepared for their trip back to Lima. But before they left, Maria couldn't resist the opportunity to take one last walk through the warehouse.

Jake, Armando, and Jonathan accompanied Maria on

her tour through the building. Just as she remembered, the sheer magnitude of the priceless inventory was immense. Row after row, crate upon crate, the volume of artifacts was beyond comprehension. There was much that the Germans had left behind, being limited by the cargo holds of their two helicopters and Lopez's trucks. But as she suspected, the most priceless treasures were gone. The twelve hermetic chambers and their mysterious inhabitants were all missing, along with the extraordinary artifacts that had been discovered with them. Every single piece containing the inexplicable alien alphabet had vanished.

Maria's plan was to make an anonymous call to the Lima authorities to report the artifacts remaining in the warehouse. But she knew that the scientific world would suffer immensely without ever having the opportunity to study the treasures that had become extinct with VonKlecker's exodus.

Maria said goodbye to her fellow servants and took a fleeting look at the compound, then she and her new companions left through the gates of the Lopez Estate. The time passed quickly during their road trip back to the city. Jake and Jonathan caught up on all they had experienced over the past several months apart, and Maria revealed the amazing things she and Jonathan had seen on their expeditions. It was an unusual family reunion.

As they approached the city, Maria asked to be dropped off at the Jorge Chavez International Airport. With her passport in one pocket and a bundle of cash in the other, all procured from the desk in Lopez's study, she was ready to return to her family in Colombia. They would be shocked to see her after all this time.

She embraced the young boy she was leaving behind. She looked Jonathan in the eyes with her tender gaze and promised she would come visit him in the States one day. And then, with a warm smile and a gentle kiss on the boy's cheek, she was gone.

Jake knew his travel plans would prove to be more of a challenge. Jonathan was in the country without a passport. He considered trying to smuggle his son home by private jet, which wasn't entirely out of the question given Armando's connections as a pilot. But there was a risk of getting caught, and the penalties were severe. And even if they did make it back to the States, the FBI would be looking closely at Jonathan's reappearance. They would have to tell the truth. Or at least as much of the truth that could be revealed without identifying VonKlecker.

It took the better part of two weeks working with the embassy and the authorities before they were cleared to leave the country. His story was a hard sell—the search for his long-lost wife based on the tip of a deceased colleague, his extensive pursuit of Arturo Lopez, his two-day imprisonment in Lopez's secret holding cell, his reunion with his son, and an airborne invasion by unidentifiable assailants who seemingly flew into the compound for the sole purpose of assassinating Lopez.

But as bizarre as Jake's story was, it was hard to refute.

The details matched the gruesome pieces of the puzzle that were discovered at the Lopez Estate, as well as the accounts offered by the five servants who survived the attack. And aside from Lopez's father, there were few people who were sorry to learn of his untimely demise. There were dozens, if not hundreds, of people who wanted to see him dead, and ultimately there was little incentive for the authorities to spend valuable time and resources tracking down a team of mysterious airborne assassins. Sure Lopez was a wealthy and powerful man, one who was generous when the occasion demanded. But once the money was gone, the man was soon forgotten.

Jake and Armando were cleared as persons of interest in the Lopez murders, and exactly six weeks after his arrival in Peru, Jake was returning to the United States with his new traveling companion. He and Jonathan said a tearful goodbye to Armando and Jonathan's grandparents, then they eagerly boarded the plane and watched Lima vanish beneath the clouds.

CHAPTER 53

UNEXPECTED TREASURES

He gazed at the little boy sleeping in the seat beside him as the plane descended into O'Hare International Airport. It had been three weeks since their reunion, and Jake still couldn't believe his eyes. He never thought he would see his son again. He was convinced that he had lost everything dear to him. Yet there he was, his precious Jonathan, sleeping comfortably by his side.

It was as if their life could resume where it had left off—as if Jonathan had never been taken from him. They would land in Chicago where Stone would be waiting for them, then drive back to Maple Creek to meet up with family and friends. Of course there would be the mandatory debriefing by Agent Fox and his FBI colleagues, during which Jake would disclose only select details of their adventures in Peru. The following day Jake and family would celebrate the homecoming with food and festivities. And inevitably, once the celebrations ended, the boys would settle back into their ordinary day-to-day lives. Jake would return to Gertrude and his practice, Jonathan to his friends and school. The thought of returning to an unremarkable, uneventful routine brought a smile to Jake's face.

Jonathan began to wake up as Jake stroked his hair.

"Hey, buddy. Time to get up. We're almost home."

Jonathan rubbed the sleep from his eyes, then slid the window screen open to the brilliant sun glistening off the cool surface of Lake Michigan.

"Is that Chicago?" he asked with groggy enthusiasm.

"That's Chicago. Did you sleep well?"

"I think so. I was dreaming about Maria. Do you think she'll come visit us?"

"Maybe someday. Would you like that?"

"Yeah. She was really nice. I think I'll miss her."

"I'm sure you will. She was a good friend, wasn't she?"

"Yep. She was really nice," Jonathan repeated as he looked out the window. "Dad, do you think I'll ever have a mom again?"

Jake paused to think. Perhaps he had underestimated how close Jonathan had grown to Maria during their time together. Perhaps he had underestimated how much the boy missed having a mother in his life. After all, every little boy needs a mom—someone to nurture him, to love him, to console him when he's sad, to nurse him when he's sick. Margaret was a wonderful grandmother, but it just wasn't the same. Every boy should have a father, *and* a mother, he thought.

"Would you like to have a new mom?"

"Yeah. I think I would," Jonathan replied softly.

"Well then, we'll just have to see what we can do about that. But it might take a little time, buddy. Picking a mom is pretty important business, don't you think?"

Jonathan grinned. "Yes. Very important business," he declared.

Jake chuckled at Jonathan's response as the wheels of the jet hit the runway. He listened to the sweet sound of the blacktop rumbling beneath the landing gear. They were home—back on American soil, far from harm's way. Far from the Lopez compound, far from VonKlecker and his hired assassins, far from the Peruvian authorities.

The boys swiftly made their way through the terminal and down the escalator to the baggage claim. They stood at the carousel and waited for pieces of luggage to begin sliding down the conveyor belt. Jake looked around for Stone, then flipped open his cell phone and punched two keys on his speed dial. The call rolled straight to Stone's voicemail.

After twenty minutes, the bags began to fall through the chute. It seemed as if the handlers were taking a coffee break between each piece they offloaded. While all of the weary travelers grumbled, Jake and Jonathan remained patient. After everything they had been through, waiting for luggage hardly seemed worthy of a reaction.

The Bishop bags were among the last down the chute, but they were both intact. Jake hit the speed dial on his phone again, but he was sent to Stone's voicemail for a second time.

"Well, buddy. It looks like your Uncle Eric is running a little late. Let's find a place to sit down and have a snack," Jake said as he grabbed the luggage. Jake turned around to see Jonathan running full speed in the opposite direction. His heart pounded with panic. But then he saw her standing in the distance, holding up a large sign that read "BISHOP."

"Maggie!" Jonathan yelled as he spilled into her arms.

Jake walked toward them, his eyes filled with tears and his smile stretched from ear to ear.

"Did someone call for a limo?" she asked, holding the sign up with one hand while she embraced Jonathan with the other.

"Are you ever a sight for sore eyes," Jake said. "What did you do with Stone?"

"Oh, he's fine. I sent him off on a goose chase."

"Is Uncle Eric really chasing a goose, Maggie?"

"No, sweetheart," she laughed. "That's just an expression. I just explained to Uncle Eric that the only person who should be picking my boys up is me!"

"Great!" Jonathan replied. "Can we go to Navy Pier now?"

"Navy Pier?" Jake asked. "How did you come up with that idea?"

"You took me there last time we came to Chicago! Can we please go, Dad? Please?"

Maggie looked at Jake with her warm eyes and sympathetic smile, her head tilted and one eyebrow raised for effect. "*Please,* Dad," she said.

"Well, I guess Maple Creek can wait awhile longer. Navy Pier it is."

Jonathan grabbed Maggie's hand and pulled her into the crowd, eager to leave the airport. As the three made their way out to the parking ramps, Jake watched Maggie and Jonathan walk hand in hand, exchanging questions and answers, laughing like old friends.

She hadn't changed a bit. She was still the same doe-eyed girl he had dated back in high school—her thick chestnut hair kissing the neckline of her sweater, contrasting beautifully against her alabaster skin, her gorgeous lips, her petite figure springing with energy as she walked. Jake's mind was suddenly drifting back to Margaret's front porch—back to that kiss.

They made their way through the sea of cars in the parking garage, talking and laughing as they walked, Maggie taking the lead to search for her parking space. Jake scouted casually across the rows, expecting to catch a sighting of Maggie's little yellow Beetle. Maggie didn't break her stride as she led them past row after row of parked cars, and after pounding the pavement for several minutes, Jake was beginning to wonder if she remembered where she parked. And suddenly, there it was—sitting alone at the far end of the parking garage, far from harm's way, resting safely—Henry's Riviera.

"You drove the oldie car!" Jonathan shouted.

"Maggie Cooper. You drove my old Buick all the way from Maple Creek?"

"That I did. And you owe me big time, mister. Driving that thing was like navigating a cruise ship!" she said as she handed Jake his car keys.

Jake reached over and gave Maggie a gentle hug. "Thank you," he whispered softly. "Now I feel like we're really home."

Jake fired up the Riviera and slid her into drive, and they were on their way. It took Jonathan just seconds to plug in Henry's 8-track tape, and they were soon listening to the warped sound of Dean Martin singing "Memories are Made of This."

The trio had a magical day. They enjoyed deep-dish pizza at Giordano's, hot chocolate and scones at a little coffee house downtown, and then a brisk walk along the lake. It was off-season for Navy Pier, too early for most tourists, so the lines were shorter than usual. After a ride on the Ferris wheel with Maggie, Jonathan dragged them to almost every ride on the pier. Jake couldn't remember a time when he had seen his son so happy.

As Jonathan took his last ride of the day, Jake and Maggie sat on a bench by the carousel, hot coffees in hand.

"I'm really happy you're home, Jake," she said. "Both of you."

"Thanks, Maggie. It feels good to be back. It still doesn't seem real though. It's like it was all a dream…a very bizarre dream," Jake said. "I never thought I'd see him again, Maggie. I never dreamed that I would be here with you, sipping a latte at Navy Pier, watching my son ride around in circles on a carousel. And it's all because of Prof. I would never have gone to Peru if he hadn't seen a ghost there."

"I'm sorry you didn't find everything you were looking for," she replied softly.

"Oh, but I did," he said, looking deep into her eyes. "I found my son…I found my life. I knew Blanca was gone. I knew she died that day when her car slid off the side of that mountain. I just never said goodbye. I think I had to go to Peru to say goodbye. And in the most unexpected place, at the most unexpected time, I found my son. You know, a very smart man once told me that we find treasure where we least expect it. I found my treasure in Peru."

"I'm so happy for you, Jake. I'm so happy you have your son back."

"What about you?" he asked. "Have you found your treasure?"

"My treasure is right here in front of me," she replied as she leaned in and kissed him softly. "And you're right. It was where I least expected it—right under my nose the entire time."

The three silhouettes walked hand-in-hand in the glow of the setting sun, back to the old Riviera to start their long drive home. For the first time in a long time, Jake was at peace.

The package arrived in Colombia just days after Jake's departure from Lima. It was a small but sturdy box, wrapped in plain brown paper with no return address.

Maria opened it slowly, cautiously, curious as to who might have sent her the parcel. She gently reached her hand into the box and fished around the mound of foam peanuts. She discovered a flat solid object inside and removed it from the packaging. It was a medallion. She recognized the piece from their excavation of the tombs, but remembered that it had later disappeared from the inventory in the warehouse.

She smiled as she recalled Jake telling her about the medallion Prof had purchased from Lopez. She carefully dumped the packaging material out on the kitchen counter, and along with it came a small piece of paper folded perfectly in half. It was a typed note that simply read: *They will never be forgotten. Don't ever give up your search. P.S. We'll miss you.*

Maria studied the medallion. She, too, had found her treasure where she least expected—packed carefully into a small cardboard box that drifted in with the afternoon mail. While the loss of the mummies and their treasure was devastating, she was grateful she and the boy were free from Lopez. She knew that she couldn't reveal VonKlecker's identity or the events at the compound that day. But she also knew that the amazing discoveries they had made at the tombs were too complex and inexplicable to be an isolated find. Somewhere, buried deep in the earth, there had to be similar treasures. Jake was right, the ancients would not be forgotten.

ABOUT THE AUTHOR

Stephen Kosa is an attorney who resides in the quaint river town of Hudson, Wisconsin, with his lovely wife, Diane. They are the best of friends, and share a passion for traveling and exploring new cities. In his spare time, Steve enjoys writing and a love of photography, an obsession he shares with his son, Gabe. *Vanishing Trail* represents a compilation of Steve's interests, experiences, visions, and dreams. It was a challenging story to tell, and he's grateful for the opportunity to share it with others.